ELLA GUNNING

FOR CLARA

ELLA GUNNING

A Novel

by Mary Deasy

An Atlantic Monthly Press Book

Little, Brown and Company · Boston

The persons, organizations, and events in
this novel are fictitious, and are not intended to portray any actual persons, organizations, or events.

ATLANTIC-LITTLE, BROWN BOOKS
ARE PUBLISHED BY
LITTLE, BROWN AND COMPANY
IN ASSOCIATION WITH
THE ATLANTIC MONTHLY PRESS

PRINTED IN THE UNITED STATES OF AMERICA

Prologue

THE sidewalks on Cobb Street were made of red brick, and the bricks, which were old and pressed deeply into the earth, were set in slantwise, like pigeon tracks. Along each side a row of narrower bricks had been laid in lengthwise to form a border.

When she was three years old she walked up the street with Lillie Wessen, carefully placing each foot in a single brick, and her feet made pigeon tracks all the way to the corner. She wore a blue-and-white striped dress, and she knew a song with German words:

> *Vom Himmel hoch da komm' ich her,*
> *Ich bring' euch gute neue Mär'* . . . .

Old Mrs. Wessen clapped her hands and threw back her small neat white head as she laughed.

She lived with her mother in the Wessens' house on Cobb Street, in Bard City. She learned that: it was so early when she learned it that afterwards she could never remember the time when she had not known it. She learned that the character she was playing on the world's stage was named Ella Gunning, and that she was one of approximately half a million citizens of Bard City, in the valley of the Ohio, where she had been born, on the fourteenth of April, 1917, to an Irish-American attorney and his wife. Perhaps she would have liked it better if she had been able to play another character, who had another name and lived in another house in another town; but it happened that that had all been taken care of beforehand by a great many other people, some of whom she had never even seen.

There was her father, Stephen Gunning, for example, the hand-

[1   ]

some lawyer with the red mustache and the fine tenor voice, who had earned his first dollar, when he ran away to Bard City from his Indiana home for two weeks the year he was sixteen, singing "Open Thy Lattice, Love" with a blackface minstrel troupe, and who, even after parental insistence had forced him into the law, could always win more applause singing *M'appari* to a convivial circle than he ever won making a speech to a jury. There was Anne Gunning, her mother, who came out of a country parsonage in the northern part of the state to marry a man no more suited to her clear, sober, brusque nature than fire is suited to cold spring water. There were the Wessens, mother, son, and daughter, who had found themselves, in 1917, with a new tenant whose husband had paid a month's rent and then disappeared, leaving her, with a child coming and two hundred dollars, in a city where she had never been before. Whatever Stephen Gunning had hoped for from his sudden move to the big, leisurely, music-loving city on the river to which he had run away as a boy twenty years before, his dream had not materialized there, and perhaps in a last defiance of his wife's prudence and of the responsibility of fatherhood which she was about to fasten upon him, he had walked out of the sober little house that she had found for them and was never heard of in Bard City again. So, with a gesture, he added to the things which he had already bequeathed to his daughter — his name, his quick Irish emotions, his oddly passionate feeling for music — the final touch in the legend of the errant father that he left behind him.

Into the character of Ella Gunning that these people and a great many others had combined, in one way or another, to create, the real Ella Gunning — the one who had no more, intrinsically, to do with this character than she had to do with the clothes she wore — had the problem of somehow fitting herself. It was not a new problem; it might even be called the universal one; but in Ella Gunning's case it was complicated by the fact that she was a musician — not the kind that is made by education, but the kind that is born with music inside and no way to get free of it, as other people are born with eyes of a certain color and faces of a certain shape. She grew up with a piano in the house, because it was one of the things that Stephen Gunning had left behind him; but that had very little, really, to do with it. Neither did the fact that her father's brother, who was a mining engineer, managed, between his own improvidence and the demands of a childless, egocentric wife, to see that she had lessons, intermittently, with the neighborhood piano teacher until he died, the year that she was ten.

After that she was on her own, as far as music was concerned, and from the time when, at thirteen, she spent the ten dollars she won as a prize at her graduation from grammar school on singing lessons from the same neighborhood *maestra* who had taught her to play the piano, music was even something of which almost everyone she knew actively disapproved. That was in 1930; Lillie Wessen, in spite of the Depression, was making fifty dollars a week as secretary to the president of the Bard City Telephone Company, and everybody on Cobb Street had decided that Ella, who was a bright girl, quick and clever, could do nothing better than take a commercial course in high school and follow in Lillie's footsteps. Even Anne Gunning, who, left to make her own way in the world, had turned the front room of one side of the Wessens' old-fashioned, one-story double house into a dressmaking shop, with a never quite adequate succession of dowdy, eccentric, or economy-minded customers, agreed that that seemed the best thing to do. She had the blood of three generations of Congregational ministers behind her, and she would have gone hungry before she would have seen her daughter deprived of an education; but what she did not understand was that there was another kind of education which was of infinitely more importance to Ella, as it had been to her father years before.

So Ella Gunning went to high school, and took the commercial course, and studied typing and shorthand and business English. She had firsthand experience of the sacrifices her mother made to keep her there: both of them wore made-over dresses and became acquainted with the most economical forms of nourishment, and on Saturday nights, when Ella's schoolmates went in chattering flocks to the movies or donned new dresses to experiment with love-making on their first dates, she and her mother sat in the little dark parlor behind the fitting room and tried to figure out where the money was coming from for the next week's rent and food.

Those were the kinds of things that were happening to Ella Gunning up to the time that she was seventeen. They were the logical things to happen to a girl who lived on Cobb Street, who might or might not have had a father living somewhere, and whose mother made dresses that always looked, in spite of her best efforts, as if they had been made in a great hurry and with the greatest determination. Unfortunately they were not the logical things to happen to the real Ella Gunning, the one inside, the artist with the dark voice ripening in the narrow throat, the passionate dreamer of a single dream. You pass a girl on the street in an Ohio Valley town: a thin girl in a cheap dress, with straight dark hair and a slender, rather handsome face noticeable chiefly for a look of latent determination and a pair of well-cut greenish eyes. Let her carry a stenographer's notebook and a textbook of shorthand, and the chances are a million to one against your thinking that where that girl belongs is on the stage of the Metropolitan, that she has Delilah in her, somewhere behind the cheap dress and the greenish eyes, and Amneris, and Orpheus, and Klytemnestra and Kundry. Even if you hear her speak, it won't occur to you that this is a voice that has rightly to do with Schubert and Gluck and Mozart, and not with American colloquialisms and business reports. She won't even know that yet, herself; all she will know is that there is something inside her that she has to fight for as a mother fights for her child — the ruthless, tender egotism of the artist, who can never separate himself from his gift, and so seems to do battle for himself when he is really battling for that *Doppelgänger* that he carries around inside him.

But how she must fight, what wars she must seek out, what battles there are before her to win — those are things too that she will not know now, as she sits on the front steps of the house on Cobb Street, watching the last light leave the sky over the row of little brick houses opposite. The spring that she had her seventeenth birthday she sat on those steps almost every evening, trying to figure

[4]

those things out, trying to see some road, to pick some possible path out of the darkness before her. After the sun went down it grew cooler quickly, and the dusk came, and a little later the street lights went on with a sudden and beautiful finality. The street was different for her at night from the way it was during the day. After sundown the air had the cool dampness of an Ohio Valley spring, and there was sometimes a mist that made the street lights even better. In the dark the whole street was like a stage set, and the voices of the people going by, and the lights that fell from the windows of the houses opposite on the cool green mist of the solitary maples, were like things that had been deliberately planned by someone to produce a particular effect. In the dark, sitting there alone, it was possible to believe that this was so. There were many things that it was possible to believe in the dark, and sitting there on the steps of the Wessens' house that spring Ella Gunning believed them all.

Chapter One

SHE graduated from high school two months after her seventeenth birthday, and the following day Lillie Wessen took her out to the E. J. Finn Furniture Company, where she herself had worked until the time that she had gone with the telephone company, to see about an opening that she had heard of there. Ella wore a blue crepe dress that her mother had made; it was a little too large for her, so that it made her look almost younger than her actual age, but in spite of that, and in spite of the fact that she had hardly a word to say for herself during the interview, Lillie's recommendation was worth enough with Mr. Finn to get the job for her. Her salary was to be fifteen dollars a week, and there was a good deal of excitement in the house on Cobb Street when she and Lillie came home with the news. They all sat out on the back porch together, listening to Lillie telling about what had happened.

"She's a pretty lucky kid to be starting out in a place where she has a chance to get ahead if she does the right thing," Lillie said. She spoke in a positive tone; she was used to having her opinions count for something on Cobb Street. "Because I can tell you, jobs like that aren't growing on trees nowadays—"

She was pleased with herself because she had succeeded in getting the job for Ella; sitting in one of the wicker chairs crowded on the small back porch, she let her prominent, intent light-brown eyes pass slowly from one to the other of them, demanding their admiration and appreciation.

"Well," Anne Gunning said quietly, "she owes that to you, Lillie. That's your doing."

"And fifteen dollars a week to start," old Mrs. Wessen exclaimed. "Isn't that fine! Our little Elly—"

She glanced proudly at Ella, who stood leaning against the railing of the porch, looking out over the small yard, which a single willow tree and a tiny grass plot shared with the little vegetable garden. She had been sitting on the steps beside Ray Wessen, but there was a kind of cold restlessness in her now, after the excitement of the afternoon. She did not quite know what was going on inside her; it had all happened too quickly, the rush of school ending, her graduation, the interview that afternoon in Mr. Finn's office, during which she had been conscious only of her own confusion, like an actual physical ache within her. She had shrunk almost physically from exposing herself in that interview. The rather superb self-confidence that she had inherited from her father was there inside her when she was alone, but it had been violated too often in her seventeen years of living for her to be able to rely on it in her dealings with others. So, although she found little to admire in Lillie Wessen, really — in her hard, unimaginative practicality that reduced all of life to the level of her own motives and desires — she would have given a great deal to have been like her that afternoon. She had envied her smart brown silk dress, her air of assurance, even her tall, rawboned figure, which she used with such brisk efficiency.

"*You* don't seem very excited about it," Ray Wessen said suddenly, to Ella.

He turned to look up at her from his seat on the steps — a tall, sandy-haired man of forty, with something oddly complex and lost in his eyes and in the sharp clear lines of his rufous face. In this house where thrift and industry were held in such regard, he was the anomaly, the spendthrift and the drifter, who had never in his life kept a job for more than six months. But there was a certain bond between him and Ella. In spite of his lack of purpose, his bitterness against a world in which he was not at home, he had a fumbling, cynical appreciation of the things she was groping after that often set them together against the others.

Old Mrs. Wessen looked at him a little nervously. There was a persistent, rather ugly friction between him and Lillie, so that the mother was alert, through long experience, to the first signs of a disagreement.

"Now, Ray," she said, quickly and placatively, "of course she's excited."

"Why not let her say so herself, then?" he asked. He turned to Ella again. "Come on, Ell, how about that?" he said. "Do you like the idea or don't you?"

"What are you trying to do — start something?" Lillie demanded. She turned about in her chair to look coldly at him, but he returned her gaze with a prepared composure.

"No, I'm not trying to start anything," he said. "All I'm trying to do is to find out whether Ell's been taken in by all this talk about how glad she ought to be to get a job in an office at fifteen dollars a week. Fifteen dollars a week! She'll get rich on that in a hurry, all right."

There was a short silence. Lillie stared at her brother with a rising color on her face.

"She'll get rich a good deal faster on fifteen dollars a week than she will on nothing at all; you ought to know about that," she said.

"Ray — Lillie!" old Mrs. Wessen said, in an entreating voice.

Lillie got up abruptly. "Never mind, Mama, I'm going in anyway," she said. "I'm not going to waste my breath talking to him."

She walked across the porch to the screen door and went inside, slamming the door behind her. The others did not say anything till she had disappeared.

"You oughtn't to quarrel with her, Ray," old Mrs. Wessen said then, shaking her head.

He shrugged his shoulders. "What did I say? She gets on that high horse of hers — All I want to find out is whether Ell is satisfied now, because E. J. Finn's going to pay her fifteen dollars for pounding a typewriter all week." He came up the steps and stood near Ella, leaning on the railing. "Just tell me this — is that what you want to do with yourself?" he asked her, putting out his hand, which was covered with freckles and sandy hair, and turning her around so that she was facing him.

[8]

"You leave Elly alone, Ray," said old Mrs. Wessen. "She doesn't want to listen to any of your crazy ideas."

"How do you know what she wants to listen to?" he demanded. "She might as well listen to me as to the rest of you, that aren't thinking about anything but how much cash she's going to bring home next Saturday."

"People have to live, Ray," Anne Gunning said. She looked straight at him with her clear, moderate gaze. "We're doing the best we can for Ella."

Ella wished that they would not talk about it. She knew what Ray wanted to say, she knew what was making him angry; but she knew also that it would not help to talk about it. It only made matters worse to bring it out into the open, because there was nothing that he or anyone else could do about it.

"A kid with all the talent she's got, stuck in an office for the rest of her life, like Lillie, or till she meets some thirty-dollar-a-week clerk who'll marry her — is that what you want for her?" Ray was saying, to Anne Gunning.

Ella looked at her mother. She sat there quietly, refusing to be drawn into an argument.

"It's not always what we want in this world; it's what we can have," she said. "Ella will have to work out her own life, just as the rest of us are doing."

Ella saw her long, plain face with its firmly closed mouth that seemed to accept, without asking favors, whatever life had in store for her. Her mother never battled with existence; she merely endured it, the best and the worst that it brought to her. It made the blood flame with impatience in Ella's veins often to see her so. Still she knew that she had that same sort of unyielding endurance in herself, too; something strong and durable inside her that nothing would ever be able to break.

She did not want to listen to them talking any longer. She went inside, through the house to the little dim parlor behind the fitting room. At the window she stopped and stood looking out. The lace curtains at the windows of the house next door were looped back, and she could look straight into the living room and see Mrs. Ledru giving a piano lesson to a thin blonde little girl about eleven years old. The little girl was playing a piece and Mrs. Ledru was beating time. She was a big woman of about fifty, with heavy black hair that she wore piled up on the top of her head.

Ella stood at the window, listening as the lesson progressed. It reminded her of the time, years ago, when she had been taking piano lessons from Mrs. Ledru. She remembered how it had begun, one evening when her uncle, on one of his visits to town, had heard her picking out on the piano the pieces that she had listened to Mrs. Ledru's pupils playing next door. The money that he used to leave after that with Mrs. Ledru for her lessons was never quite enough to cover the period until he came again, so that there was always a time, every three or four months, when Mrs. Ledru, instead of bringing her in when she came for her lesson, stood in the doorway with her arms folded and said that she positively could not give her one more lesson till she had paid for those she had already had. And after her uncle had died, of course there had been no way of paying her at all, and Anne Gunning had had to do some sewing for her to make up for the money that was owing for the lessons.

Still Ella had gone back to her with her graduation prize money when she was thirteen, because by that time the voice had begun to come, and Mrs. Ledru, who said she had studied singing with an Italian professor in Chicago, was the only person she knew who could tell her what to do about it. Mrs. Ledru had brought out some old songs that had her maiden name, Marie Grasselli, written on them, and had given them to Ella, along with a book of vocalises. She was very enthusiastic about Ella's voice, and she said it would be a pity if it was not trained, but when the money ran out she lost interest and told her that an alto voice was no good anyway for a career; people wanted to hear sopranos, the higher the better.

Ella, watching now from the window, saw that the little girl's lesson had come to an end; she was getting up from the piano and gathering her music together, preparing to leave the house. Ella turned away from the window and went over and sat down at her own piano. She touched a few keys with the fingers of her right hand, very gently, one at a time. The piano was badly out of tune. The sharp tones sounded queer, coming disconnectedly into the dim hot room.

She wanted very much to feel like singing, but she didn't feel like singing in the least. She felt like crying. Her mind kept going over everything that had happened that day in quick, secret leaps, and when she tried to settle it down to something it only jumped away from her the faster. She could feel her heart jumping inside her too, under her dress. And all the while she knew it was stupid, because it was only a job. It was only a job that she could quit any time. She thought about E. J. Finn and about the office, and she felt more than ever like crying, but the tears did not come.

She laid her arms on the piano and put her head down on them and closed her eyes. It was good thinking about the music inside the piano, even if it was out of tune. After a little she began to make up music in her head and herself singing — slow, gentle music with violins reaching and straining up for purer, sweeter tones, and after that something harsher and grander, and her voice bursting out, she almost feeling it now in her throat, her chest filling and tightening with deep lungfuls of air, and the flexible swoop of the sound parting from her lips. She knew it would come some day because she needed it and willed it, because she had the sharp appetency of it in her, and the hard determination, and the feel of it down to the inmost fiber of her body. It made her feel better to be sure of that, and after a little she began to cry. She did not cry much, only a little, but it made her feel much better almost at once.

On Sunday night it rained, and in the morning, when she left the house to walk up to Jefferson Street for her bus, the red brick of the sidewalks on Cobb Street had a scoured damp look, as fresh as if it had been newly scrubbed and the dampness still undried behind the scrubber. The leaves of the maple trees hung out green against the red-and-white fronts of the little houses.

It was all strange to her, a queer summer's dream. But she felt the responsibility of the new life closing about her. Something had fitted her into a new place, a new way of living, and she had to make out now as best she could. She thought of the dark brick building on Callendar Street where she had gone with Lillie, the bare-looking rooms that seemed to have something depressing and important about them, with the sun falling inappropriately through the windows on the desks and the typewriters and the dark-green file cases against the walls. She could not believe that that was to be her world, her reality. All the way out on the bus, as the streets fell behind her one by one, she felt like an exile, leaving her native country behind her forever.

She got off with a group of others on Callendar Street, at the Finn Company. A young man in a light gray suit and a blue tie, coming up the steps before the entrance at the same time that she did, held the door for her, examining her with an air of quick interest as she entered the corridor. She felt a moment's self-consciousness, glancing at him from under her lids. She had seen him before, coming out of E. J. Finn's private office with a sheaf of papers in his hand, the afternoon that Lillie had brought her there. He was thin and dark, a little above middle height, with smooth black hair and a prompt, composed, attractive manner. He went on down the corridor and after her into the general office.

The bookkeeper, Barstow, a thin tall middle-aged man with a thatch of savagely red hair, put her under the care of Miss Dillard, Rita Dillard, who had a desk near the door, on the edge of the lax Monday-morning busyness of arrival, beginning clack of typewriters, mingled with low-voiced rehearsals of Sundays spent dancing, or on a picnic, in cars threading a way through traffic to a park, another town, anywhere removed from the week's six dull days. Ella heard one of the girls talking to the young man who had held the door for her.

"I saw you out at Sherwood Park last night." She called him Eddie. "You *did* have company for yourself, didn't you?"

She was a thin blonde with a long, colorless face masquerading attractiveness under a judicious brightness of make-up. Barstow called over to her companion: "Bernet. Mr. J. T. wants you in his office."

He passed by Ella on his way out, not pausing while he said something in a low voice to Rita Dillard. Rita looked up and after him, smiling at him, but a little absently. She was a year or two older than he was, twenty-five or -six, tall and well-built, with a cool, sweet, decided-looking face. Ella noticed that she did not join the others in their Monday-morning gossip: there was something about her that was different from them, and that she seemed, though not emphasizing, to make them remember. Only one of the girls, the thin, fair-haired one who had been talking to Eddie Bernet, seemed to share her confidence. Ella noticed that she had a way of imitating Rita's cool, hardly inflected voice, even the expressions that she used; obviously she admired her, and made a great deal of her friendship with her. She was Inez Shoup, Rita said; her husband was a student in the University law school.

While Ella listened to Rita's explanations, the room — a square jumbled with desks, telephones, typewriters, the morning sun sifting over it in a fine dusty haze — swung into the clattering daily routine about her: voices impinging in fragments of sentences on her consciousness, the movement of people going in and out, or stopping by the desk and Rita Dillard saying to them: "This is Miss Gunning." They spoke to her politely, their eyes going over her curiously. She wore a dark-blue dress that her mother had made; beneath its unshaped lines her thin, deep-breasted figure scarcely asserted itself.

Rita Dillard gave her some reports to type, and she spent the morning on them, feeling herself an island of strangeness in the midst of the friendly, businesslike banter of the others. There was that curious, intimate, gossipy atmosphere in the general office that comes when a group of people have worked together for some time under a rather lenient authority. The salesmen went in and out, exchanging jokes with the stenographers; the girls put their heads together for a few minutes as they passed one another's desks to comment on the work they were doing or on their own private affairs. She had always imagined that an office would be something as orderly and as strictly disciplined as a classroom. Now she felt pleased and at the same time a little lost; everyone seemed so much more experienced than she was, even those girls who could not have been more than a few years past her own age.

At noontime she went across the street with Rita and Inez Shoup to the drugstore where most of the Finn Company office workers ate. It was a small, dark room with a lunch counter, and at the back a few marble-topped tables with the kind of spidery wire chairs that used to be found in ice-cream parlors. It was beginning to fill up when they came in, and they stood at the door, looking for a table.

"This filthy place," Rita Dillard said.

A group of girls got up from the front table, and she and Inez and Ella sat down. Ella sat listening to them talk about Rita's new job; she was going across the hall to be Mr. James T. Finn's secretary when his present secretary left at the end of the week. While Ella listened, she let her eyes move about the room, watching the people coming in and out, or laughing and talking with each other as they sat at the lunch counter over their sandwiches and coffee. She saw Eddie Bernet come in the door alone. He had to pass their table, and paused behind Rita Dillard's chair, putting his right hand on her shoulder. Rita turned her head.

"Oh — Eddie," she said.

"Darling, don't sound so happy," he said. He had a quick, expressive voice, a good light baritone, rather effective. "Who did you think it was?" he asked. "Your new boss?"

"It had better not be," Rita said. She spoke with emphasis, looking up at him with her cool wholesome smile. She said to him: "Did you meet Ella Gunning this morning? This is Eddie Bernet. He's our rising young man."

His eyes went over Ella again as they had that morning when he had paused to hold the door open for her, quickly, with brief, flattering interest.

"Am I not," he said. "I'm riding a balloon these days."

"I'm waiting for them to name you Acting Vice-President," Rita said. "The next time J. T. doesn't show up in the morning."

He smiled his slight, prompt, self-composed smile. "Actually, I'm not expecting that just yet," he said.

[14]

Rita laughed. "Oh, Eddie, really," she said.

He looked at her, raising his brows almost a little sulkily, as if it irritated him to be dismissed so lightly, and after a moment went on down the room to another table. Inez Shoup looked after him with narrowing eyes of interest.

"I think he's crazy about you, Rita," she said. "Honestly I do." She watched him threading his way back through the tables, his rather narrow shoulders in his neat gray summer suit. "Haven't you noticed the way he looks at you?"

"No," said Rita. She stirred sugar into her cup of coffee. "You've got a vivid imagination, Shoup."

"And he always finds some excuse to stop by your desk and talk to you," Inez said. "Everybody's noticed it. Tottie Dunlop would give a month's salary if he'd pay that much attention to her."

"I wish he would," Rita said.

"He's good-looking too; don't you think he's good-looking?" Inez asked, leaning on her elbows, gazing after him.

"Eddie? Oh, he's all right, I suppose."

"Don't you think he's good-looking?" Inez said to Ella.

Ella hesitated, darting a glance at Rita. "Well, yes," she said.

"The way his eyebrows go," Inez said. "I like those queerish eyebrows on a man."

"You'd better not tell that to Tommy," Rita said.

"Oh, Tommy," said Inez.

She smiled consciously, moving her thin shoulders inside her dress.

Afterwards, when Rita had gone over to talk to someone at another table, Inez, sitting with Ella, lit an after-lunch cigarette and began to talk to her about Rita.

"She comes from a very good family," she said; "Tommy's — my husband's — folks used to know them. Her father was a judge; Rita used to have everything before he died. He lost his money in the crash." She spoke in a detached voice, pausing between sentences while she unhurriedly drew on her cigarette. "Rita isn't high-hat at all, but I think you can tell, the way she feels about people, that she used to have money," she said. "Eddie, for instance. I think she's awfully foolish, the way she treats him. Of course maybe she thinks, because he's only a clerk now — But that boy's going to get someplace some day. He's terribly ambitious."

Ella looked down the room at Eddie Bernet, who was sitting at a table now with another young man, and then at Rita, barely out of earshot at the next table. It made her feel uncomfortable to sit there and listen to Inez discuss them so calmly; there seemed to be a kind of disloyalty about it. But the other went on talking in her thin, monotonously inflected voice.

"Nobody'd be taking a chance tying up with Eddie," she said. "He's got the nicest manners, hasn't he? He knows exactly how to get around E. J. And there's nothing wild about him. I mean, I don't think Rita would be making a mistake. He likes music, things like that; he takes vocal lessons over at the Institute—"

She went on talking about Rita, but Ella did not hear what she was saying; she sat looking tensely, not at Inez but sidewise down at the table, her eyes widening blackly in her face. She was at an age when coincidence seemed fraught with meaning, the inscrutable "Fate" of romance taking a sudden hand in her destiny. She wanted to look across the room at Eddie Bernet again, but she hardly dared; she only sat quite tense, clutching her hands nervously together in her lap.

"Rita's twenty-five. She ought to be thinking about getting married," Inez's voice went calmly on. "I try to tell her sometimes. She could have lots of men; she's very attractive. But Eddie's really her best chance, is what I think; only he *can* be awfully exasperating sometimes, as if he was about five, and I think that puts her off. He wants his own way, you know; I suppose people have spoiled him a bit, but with an attractive boy like that, what else can you expect? Isn't that what you think?"

"Oh — yes," said Ella vaguely, seeing that Inez had paused for her answer.

She sat listening to hear more about Eddie Bernet. But Rita came over to join them again; it was time for them to go back to the office. They went outside together, crossing the street in the bright early afternoon glare to the dark brick bulk of the Finn Company opposite.

The corridor smelt dark and resinous when they went inside, the dry, resinous odor of new wood that on a hot day was as inescapable in the building as spilled perfume. And it seemed to Ella that that odor was already familiar to her, in the way that new things which one knows will be experienced day after day quickly and almost instantly become familiar. It made her feel as if the place had taken hold of her already in a swift, ruthless, businesslike way, and that she was now only a part of its routine. But at the same time she was beginning to see the job as something more than an abstract fact lying coldly across her life. She began to like the feeling of being with new people who had nothing to do with her outside the work, and with whom she might build up her own relationships as an individual. It seemed to open an opportunity to her, one that she had never known before.

Chapter Two

AT dawn of the mid-July morning the rolling black clouds began to cover the sky; a warm, wet south wind blew up from the river, and the city breakfasted to the first wild dash of the storm against its windows. The bus that Ella took to work, sliding through the wet streets with its augmenting freight of umbrella'd or damply steaming passengers, was late: it was ten minutes past the half-hour when she got off at the Finn Company building on Callendar Street.

She went inside, hurrying, entering the general office with quick, silent movements. Rita Dillard was standing beside her desk.

"Ella," she said.

Ella came over. "My bus was late," she said, standing before Rita, breathing a little fast. She was wearing a new dress penciled with red and blue stripes, which she had bought that week in a Jefferson Street shop.

"Yes," said Rita. But there was a preoccupied expression on her face; she had hardly listened to what Ella had said. "I came over to ask you if you'd finished that Anderson report yet," she said. "J. T.'s going to want it the first thing this morning."

Ella shook her head. "No. But it won't take me more than half an hour to finish it. I'll do it right away. I didn't know there was any hurry."

She sat down quickly at her desk. As she ran the first sheet of paper into her typewriter she glanced across for a moment at Eddie Bernet, who was standing at the other side of the room talking to Barstow, leaning on his hands which were outspread flat upon the desk. In the weeks that she had worked at the Finn Company, she had scarcely exchanged a word with him; he seemed conscious of her existence only in a civil, offhand way. But she had not lost the feeling of a romantic destiny attendant upon them; she waited for what was to come with a conviction that was the stronger because she had never involved herself before in such an expectation. Watching him, she saw him go out of the room and cross the hall to Mr. James T. Finn's private office.

When she went across there herself half an hour later with the completed report, Rita was in the outer office, sitting at her desk and talking to someone over the telephone. She put the receiver down sharply in a moment and looked up at Ella.

"J. T.'s not in yet," she said, "and the old man's *baying* for that report. Have you finished it?"

Ella nodded.

"Then let Eddie have a look at it, there's a good girl, and if he O. K.'s it, take it over to E. J. right away. Will you do that?" She nodded toward the door of the inner office. "He's in there. I don't know what J. T. *would* do if he didn't have Eddie around to do his work."

Ordinarily Ella rather resented Rita's brusque, pleasant way of talking to her, which seemed to put her in the position of a child or of an upper servant, but now she scarcely noticed it; she was looking toward the door of the inner office, which was standing slightly ajar. After a moment she walked across quickly, pushed it farther open, and went inside. Eddie Bernet was standing beside the desk, scribbling something on an open note pad. He looked up as she came in.

"I've brought the Anderson report," she said.

He took it from her and began to read through it, leaning against the desk with his back to the light. She stood watching him, twisting a pencil nervously in her fingers.

"Yes," he said after a little, still reading. "This is all right."

He turned around and bent over the desk while he made a notation in pencil on the last page. Then, as he handed the report to her, she saw him looking at her — at the dark hair brushed straight and falling with scarcely the hint of a curl to her shoulders, the lips that met firmly at the center and then thinned along in their enigmatic, winglike curve, the new dress that fitted sleekly to her narrow figure.

"I do like that dress," he said after a little, speaking deliberately, not hurrying the words, as if he wanted her to have the full value of them.

She glanced up at him sidewise, her heart beginning to pound in slow regular thuds.

"Do you?"

"Yes. It makes you look exciting — like something meant to go off on the Fourth of July."

His eyes went over her face exploringly. She smiled almost in defense, an odd, placative smile, feeling his eyes on her face. In the silence she could hear Rita moving about in the outer office.

He did not say anything more to her, and after a moment, because she did not know what to do, she said, "I have to get this report back—" and turned away from him toward the door. It was still ajar, as she had left it when she had come into the room; but he moved past her and with his shoulder, without looking behind him, pushed it to so that the catch was touching the door frame. He stood there looking at her out of his dark eyes, which were as definite and unreadable now as a child's.

"You can't be in such a hurry as that, can you?" he said. And then, after a moment, in an analytical voice: "You're an odd kind of girl," he suddenly added.

"Am I? How do you mean—?"

She gave him a confused glance, trying to laugh. She did not know at all what was going to happen now.

"I've been noticing you," he said. "You wouldn't believe how much time I've spent at it already. And I always come out with the feeling that there's more inside you than you let anyone see."

"Oh — do you?"

She felt still more confused, and stammered, but it was a thrilling confusion. No one had ever tried to analyze her before. It made her feel consoled and important that he saw something in her that interested and puzzled him. But she was afraid of disappointing him. She knew that she had something in her that no one else seemed to see, but she did not know what it was, how to put it into words for him.

"You don't talk about yourself," he said. "Here you've been working here for almost a month now, and I don't know the first thing about you."

"There isn't very much to know," she said. She drew in on herself, in fear of her own insufficiency. "I mean, nothing's really ever happened to me," she explained. "It's not very interesting—"

"I might like to find out about that myself," he said. He tilted his head back a little, in a sudden movement. "For example — just what are you doing with yourself tonight?" he asked.

She stared at him soundlessly for a moment, her pupils widening so that her eyes looked almost black in her slender brown face.

"Nothing," she said. "I'm not doing anything."

"Then what about coming out someplace with me? There must be a good picture somewhere in town—"

The pulse began to throb in the hollow of her throat, above the red-and-blue dress.

"Yes," she said. "Yes, I'd like to, very much."

"About eight? Where do you live? I'll pick you up."

She gave him the address, repeating it carefully for him.

"All right," he said. "At eight, then. See that you're ready, now—"

"Oh, I will be!"

She watched him go out of the office. He seemed to take it all for granted, as if it were something only natural that had just happened between them. Only to her it was a confusion. She tried to estimate what it had meant to him. But she could get no further than his definite, guileless eyes, which seemed to interpose a calculated wall of self-confidence between himself and the rest of the world.

The morning passed in a blur of suspense. She had to force her attention on her work; she was glad that it was only a half-day, a Saturday. When she went out at noon, the weather had cleared; there was a hot clear mid-July day about her, with puffs of white cloud fixed motionless overhead, and the red brick buildings on Callendar Street looking in the bright sunlight as if they had been enameled against the flat blue background of the sky.

On the way home, her week's salary in her purse arming her for the decision, she stopped in at a dress shop on Jefferson Street; when she came out again, she had in a box a slim black jersey dress, very plain, with sleeves that barely fell over the shoulder. Coming into the house on Cobb Street, she saw her mother looking at the box, and she said quickly, to forestall questioning: "Oh, I *had* to get it; I'm going out tonight; it's terribly important—"

"I should think it must be, to need all this," Anne Gunning said. She lifted the dress out of the box, looking with only half-approval at the sheath of dark soft stuff that she held in her hands. "There's your new blue crepe you've hardly worn—"

"But he's seen that one; I wanted to be wearing something new," Ella said. She looked excited and pleading, her eyes glittering with nervous urgency.

"He, is it?"

"It's Eddie Bernet. He works at the office; he's asked me to go to a movie with him tonight—"

"He must be a very particular young man if he can't look at a girl twice in the same dress," Anne Gunning said.

She sat down, a little dry, but not unprepared to be sympathetic. There was perhaps a touch of wounded pride in her attitude because Ella had indicated for the second time that she was no longer satisfied with her mother's skill as a dressmaker; but she was not the sort to measure a situation by her own pride. Ella, however, was reticent. Her mother's habit of reserve had bred an equal reserve in her; each lived in an intense single world of feeling of her own, which went out to meet the other's only in moments of sudden emotion, and even then seldom in direct words.

"He's awfully clever; everyone at the office says so," she began, "and awfully nice—"

It was all that she could say; she could not tell her mother what it was that she saw in Eddie and felt about him — the first person she had ever met who opened doors in her imagination to the kind of future that she wanted for herself.

"He studies voice at the Institute," she said at last; and Anne Gunning looked at her shrewdly, saying: "I wonder if he'd charm you so much if he didn't."

She did not know herself how much that had to do with it; something, she thought; but she could not analyze her excitement, the feeling that something important was about to happen in her life.

That evening, a little after eight, sitting in the fitting room all ready to leave in a white hat and the new black jersey dress, she heard a horn sound outside and, looking out from between the curtains, saw a gray coupé drawn up before the curb in the long July twilight. She snatched up her purse and ran out of the house, pausing to pull the door shut behind her, then turning and going quickly down the steps to the walk.

Eddie came round the car to open the door for her.

"Hullo," he said. "You're on time, you are really. Get in."

She smiled a little uncertainly and bent her head, stepping inside the car. He went round again and got in beside her; as he started the car she glanced over at him quickly. He caught the glance, his eyes going over her in appraisal.

"Very nice," he said.

"What?"

"You. That dress."

"Oh." She smiled again, still doubtfully. "Thank you."

"Don't thank me. I'm the one who ought to be doing the thanking." He brought the car to a stop at the corner, then started it forward again smoothly, watching the Saturday-night traffic while he talked to her. "I'm the one who's going to have to look at you all evening," he said.

"Yes. Well. You didn't have to, did you?" She looked down half-uncomfortably.

"No, I didn't have to. But I did want to." He glanced across at her again. "You lovely women," he said. "You spend half your time fixing yourselves up, and then act innocent when anybody looks at you."

There was a kind of satisfaction for her in his odd, confident abruptness; it seemed to set them together at once on a plane of intimacy where there was no need for a false courtesy between them. Only she did not know how to take his tone; she sat beside him silently, watching the darkening streets wheel slowly by.

"Where do you want to go?" he asked. "There's a Grace Moore picture at the Strand."

"Yes," she said. "I'd like to see that."

"Do you like music?" he asked. "I mean good music, opera. If you don't, we'd better go somewhere else; we don't want to bore you on our first evening."

She shook her head quickly. "No, I like music. Let's go there."

She could not say anything more to him about it; she felt imprisoned and silenced by her own timidity. The thick early evening heat seemed to press in on her, weighing her down, from the blur of streets and buildings and lights that they passed outside.

They drove into town, and he brought the car into a parking lot. The theater was just around the corner, the long rectangles of light on the marquee dashing brightly against the dark-blue summer sky. When they went inside, the picture was on; they could see the tiers of heads ranged before them in almost unbroken rows as they followed the usher down the darkened aisle.

They had a pair of seats together near the middle of the theater. She sat holding her arms in her lap, rather self-conscious, pretending to be watching the screen. After a little he reached over and took her hand. She looked across at him, smiling confusedly, still holding herself tense.

"Be easy, there's a good girl," he whispered to her. "Nobody's looking at you—"

She nodded without speaking, fixing her eyes on the screen again, feeling his fingers warm and firm about her own.

Then the music began, and she felt herself turning in on herself, the music plaintive and compelling insinuating itself slowly into her consciousness, into the darkness there, till at last she might have forgotten that she was not sitting there listening to it alone if it had not been for the steady pressure of fingers about her hand. One part of her, nervous and almost irritably sensitive, seemed to be all concentrated in that hand, as if it were somehow the center of her existence and were sending out impulses and sensations in all directions, like a brain; and another part of her was listening to the music, greedily drinking it in, the violin sweetness, the practiced emotion of the voice, the reedy mournfulness of the wood winds. It was as if she were two people at once, and two people who resented and fought against the presence of the other.

She felt Eddie's fingers tighten about her hand.

"Do you like it?" he whispered.

"Oh, yes. Yes, I do."

She looked at him in the peopled semidarkness, smiling, the dialogue falling against her ears without meaning, the figures on the screen reduced to mere shadows which flickered purposelessly, seen from the corner of her eyes. He turned back to watch the screen again, but she felt his fingers in the darkness slowly exploring her own, moving blindly over the narrow joints, discovering the contours of the palm. The music was beginning again, and she tried to focus her attention on it, but the feel of his fingers moving steadily over hers made everything else seem thin and unreal. She found herself giving up the pretense of following the action of the picture; she only heard the music, which flowed through her mind like an incongruous background to her emotions.

When the lights went up at the intermission, he took his hand away and sat talking to her in an unconcerned manner, as if there had been no contact between them, as if she were someone whom he had just sat next to accidentally in the theater. She could not adjust herself; it disconcerted her. He talked to her about things he had done, places where he had been, which she had never seen. His experience, rather narrow in itself, seemed infinitely wider to her than her own. She was ashamed to have him find out how little she knew about anything beyond her home and the schools she had attended; she felt nervous and humble and defensive with him. It was not at all the way she had expected to feel.

The lights went out again; the first scenes of the newsreel flashed on the screen. Eddie did not take her hand again. She thought that he might be bored, or contemptuous of her. She sat miserably in the dark, trying to see the expression on his face. He seemed to be watching the screen. She tried to fix her attention on it too, but there was a film of nervousness over her eyes; the figures on the screen were distorted and blurred.

When the picture came around again to the part that they had already seen, Eddie looked over at her and they got up. They walked up the aisle together; then they were outside on the sidewalk again, in the hot thick darkness that was lit whitely by the electric glare of the marquee lights. They could smell the summer Saturday night of the city: traffic fumes, flowers on an open stand, the river smell coming up cool from the landing, blocks away.

"Do you want to go someplace and get something to eat?" Eddie asked.

She stood uncertainly, watching the people passing by.

"I don't care," she said.

He looked at her, smiling faintly, with his composed, equable manner.

"Look, you really must make up your mind," he said; "do you or don't you?"

"Well, I *don't* care."

"Would you rather take a drive?"

She did not want to hesitate again. "All right," she said.

They went back to the parking lot to get the car. She watched him as he turned it into the stream of traffic; he drove as she had seen him work at the office, quickly and nervously, with a kind of self-confident expertness.

He drove out from the city toward the northern suburbs. The cooler air, smelling dark, came into the car as they began to pass

[26]

the big, shadowy houses and lawns. This was an old part of the town, still very well kept up; it was rather unfamiliar to her. After a time Sherwood Park loomed up on their right.

"Isn't it nice here?" she asked, pleased.

He drove more slowly. "Would you like to get out and walk around for a while?"

"Shall we?"

He stopped the car beside the curb. She got out and stood looking about. It was dark and quiet; all the Saturday-night holiday-seekers were over on the other side of the park, where the picnic tables were, and the boats.

"Isn't the Musical Institute somewhere near here?" she asked him suddenly, a little nervous to be bringing this up.

"It's not far — down that way." He gestured east.

"Could we walk past?"

He looked at her, raising his eyebrows. "What on earth for? It's a perfectly ordinary-looking place." He put his hand on her arm, drawing her forward. "It'll be much nicer in the park."

"All right," she yielded.

But she was disappointed; something fell in slight bitterness in her mind. She walked with him in silence along a curving path that led up a slope under the trees.

"Why *did* you want to go over there?" he asked her, as if half-exasperated, after a little.

"Oh, I—" She spoke reluctantly, afraid that he would dismiss her words again. "I'd like to study there some day. I like to sing."

"Have you got a voice?"

"I don't know. I suppose I think so." She could not look at him; she kept her eyes on the path before her. "Inez says you have a wonderful voice," she said after a moment, turning to him suddenly.

"It's fair." She wondered at the way he could speak of it, as unconcernedly as if he were passing judgment on someone else. "I don't expect to do anything with it."

"I'd like to hear you sometime." She walked along beside him

[27]

mechanically, hardly noticing where she was going. "You take lessons over at the Institute, don't you?" she asked.

They turned into another path.

"Yes," he said. "I studied with Hobart Tharp last year. He's one of the big names over there; you've probably heard of him—"

"I've seen his name in the newspapers." She looked over at him seriously; it seemed almost incredible to her that she should know someone who was familiar with Hobart Tharp. "Tell me about him —what's he like?" she asked.

"Tharp? Oh, about sixty-five — tall, dresses well, has a rather cosmopolitan outlook on life. He's really an interesting person to know; he studied in London and Berlin; then he lived in England for a good many years, sang in opera and oratorio there. He's very well-known—"

"Yes," she said, in a tense, abstracted tone. She was trying to make up her mind to something; she walked along slowly, twisting the handle of her bag. "How much does it cost to take lessons from him?" she asked all at once, in a quick, determined voice.

"Five dollars a half-hour lesson."

She drew in her breath. "So much!"

"Yes, I thought it was worth while, as long as I intended to study, to go to someone really good," he said, in the same equable tone. He was walking alongside of her with his straight, nervous stride, walking free of her, without touching her. "I studied for a while, a few years ago, with a woman who has a studio out here in Auburn," he said, "and when I went to Tharp I found out I had to forget everything she'd taught me, from breathing on up, before I could begin learning anything from him. They all have their own methods, and some of them won't do anything more for you than ruin your voice quicker than you could ruin it alone."

"Yes, I suppose so." She spoke in a low tone, her head bent, her eyes fixed anxiously on the ground. "I've been thinking about taking lessons, now that I'm working," she said. "But I didn't know who to go to. I didn't know—"

[28]

"Take my advice and go to somebody good if you're going to study," he said. "Have you ever had any lessons before?"

"Yes, I — A few," she said, in the same low voice. "Mrs. Ledru — she lives next door to us."

"Oh," he said. "Well—"

He took her arm as they walked slowly along; she could feel his fingers about her arm just at the elbow. He sounded as if he were losing interest in talking about the singing.

"But I couldn't afford five dollars a lesson," she said, still looking down at the ground, scarcely noticing his hand on her arm. "Do you know anybody good who wouldn't charge that much?"

"Well, I might find out for you," he said. He drew her a little closer to him, walking more slowly. "Let's forget about singing," he said. "It's too nice a night."

"Why, don't you like to talk about it?" She glanced over at him, surprised.

"Yes, but not now. Now I'd rather talk about you."

He looked at her insistently. But she did not respond; there was a serious, determined look on her face. She walked on a little faster, so that he had to accelerate his pace to keep up with her. He was suddenly annoyed, almost a little sulky.

"Where are you going in such a hurry?" he asked.

She stopped, turning toward him, surprised by the question. He put both arms about her then and kissed her quickly on the mouth. She did not move; she stood there on the path. He kissed her again, longer, and then she moved away a little, and he put one arm around her waist behind her back, and they began to walk along the path once more.

She could feel his arm around her waist as they walked along, the steady pressure of it circling her body. And she could feel on her face where he had kissed her, but inside she did not seem to feel anything at all except a kind of dim surprise.

"You're a sweet kid," Eddie said. His voice sounded different, relaxed and possessive. "Do you know something? The first time I saw you I thought, there's something about her, something different;

I'm going to get to know her better. Do you remember that first day? I came out of E. J.'s office."

"Yes," she said.

It was not the way she had expected to feel. She was a little uncomfortable now. Eddie seemed different. She had to tell herself to walk slowly.

"A girl like, well, a girl like Rita Dillard thinks too much about what you have, not what you are," he said. He was talking rather quickly now, as if something had begun ticking out inside him all at once, like a clock set in motion by a sudden jar. "Some people may not have been born with a silver spoon, but that doesn't mean they're not going to go just as far, maybe farther, than people who have. It may take them a little longer, that's all it is. Now a girl like you — you're the kind that appreciates that. You've got ambition yourself, and you appreciate it when you see it in somebody else."

"Yes," Ella said.

Something began coming alive inside her too at the words; a strong bond of mutual determination suddenly seemed to unite her with him in a way that their physical closeness a few moments before had not been able to do. She understood then in a moment, with an odd feeling of surprise, that his background was probably much the same as hers, and that he was facing the same problems that were confronting her.

"Yes," she said again. "I know what you mean. But you — don't have to worry; you're going to get ahead; everybody says so," she continued, turning her head and looking up at him. "Everybody says so," she repeated.

"Well, they don't know the half of it," he said. He sounded certain of it, but when they came out into the open from under the trees she could see something in his face that looked worried and angry and uncertain, the way she felt often inside herself. "I know what I want," he said, "and I'm going after it. That's the advantage I've got over most people. Even if they know what they want, most of them are afraid to go after it. They sit around and talk about it, and then, in a little while, they're too old to start—"

His arm slipped down and he took her hand instead, and they walked along that way. There was nobody around, and they felt as if they were all alone in someplace big and dark and open, bounded only by the sweep of the dark-blue sky with its stars.

"Yes," Ella said. "I know how you feel." When she looked up he could see her profile, with the chin jutted forward as if defiantly, and the straight fall of her hair cutting off her pale face like a piece of black paper. "I'm going to be somebody some day too. I'm going to be a singer. That's what I've always wanted to be."

"Too many people think, because you have to start out in life on a small scale, you're never going to get any farther," Eddie went on. "That's not the way I feel about it. The way I feel, it's people like us, you and me, who're the kind that really get to the top. Take a lot of rich men's sons — J. T., for example — they never get an inch farther than their old man got; they take it easy, don't even try to get ahead, because they figure they've got enough to begin with. Now, anybody that's had to work to get where they are isn't going to stop halfway. Oh Lord, if I had what J. T. had at my age, I wouldn't be sitting around an office swilling booze the way he is."

She could feel the hand that held hers tightening and untightening as he talked, and her fingers slipping a little in his as they moved. They had come in a wide half-circle along the path; now the street with its long row of lights was beneath them again. They began slowly to descend the path toward the lights.

"The way it looks to me," Eddie said, "the first thing to do is to make good connections. That's the thing that counts in a conservative town like this. If you're in with the right people you get along, and if you're not you haven't got a chance." He repeated it a little bitterly. "That's the way it is in a town like this."

She bent her head, listening to him talk. This was a new wisdom, hard and repellent and strong, but she listened to it because she did not know and he did. Yet she felt a queer kind of pity for him, a pang somewhere inside her. He knew so much that she did not; all evening her own insufficiency had lain on her like a burden. Yet now there was this queer ache for him inside her. She saw that he was vulnerable, like herself, that he too was pushing his way uncertainly toward an indefinable goal.

They came back to the car again. He held the door for her as she got in.

"Are you sure you don't want to go somewhere else?" he said to her.

She shook her head. It was late, past twelve. They drove back toward Jeffersonville. She sat leaning her head back, feeling the black soft air blowing her hair against her face. They did not talk much while they drove.

Then they were back on Cobb Street again. The car slowed down and stopped before the house. Eddie put his arm around her and slowly drew her to him and kissed her again.

"Darling, did you have a good time?" he asked her, smiling.

She looked up at him. He seemed like a stranger to her again now, not as he had been when they had been walking together in the park.

"Yes," she said. "It was wonderful. Truly."

But she was looking toward the door. He kept his arm about her.

"You mustn't be in a hurry," he said.

"It's getting late."

She smiled at him placatively. But she wanted it to end now. All at once she was very tired; she felt as if she were carrying the whole evening about with her, everything that they had said and done.

He took both her hands for a minute. "All right," he said. "But we're going to do this again."

"Yes. If you want to."

He went to the door with her. Her mother had left a light on for her in the fitting room. She saw him glancing curiously at the shrouded dress form, the sewing machine, the fashion plates on the walls, all dim and ghostly in the faint light.

"Is your mother a dressmaker?" he asked.

"Yes, she is."

But she was less uneasy about it now, having him see how she lived. That was something that he would understand. They said

[32]

good night; when she had heard him go off down the steps and drive away, she went back slowly to her room. There was something confused and disappointed inside her, but she would not confess it, even to herself. She willed it to be otherwise; she willed herself to believe that it was all as she wanted it to be.

Chapter Three

IT was the middle of the afternoon before they got up from the table. They had been sitting there talking, with the best cloth on and the dessert plates from Anne Gunning's wedding china still before them, for a long while after they had finished with dinner. The hot late August air moved the curtains slowly against the screens and then lazily back again into the room, but sitting there at the table none of them could feel a breeze.

"Why don't you two young people go out to the porch, where it's cooler?" Anne Gunning said. "You'll hardly want to be sitting here in this hot room all afternoon."

She spoke in her brusque, frank way, looking at Eddie as she got up quickly from the table. She had been watching him all during dinner, Ella thought; and she thought too that there was something relentless behind that clear, civil gaze: her mother's likes and dislikes did not seem to be like those of other people, formed by prejudice or egotism, but were founded on some inalterable principle within herself. She had formed one of those dislikes against Eddie now; her civility to him had something withdrawn, a little ironical, in it. It was nothing that he had done; all through the dinner he had been alert and attentive to her, almost deferential. Only some centered certainty in him seemed to clash with an opposing certainty inside her. It made Ella uneasy, on the defensive; it was a deep strain on her, sitting there with that atmosphere of antagonism about her.

Her mother insisted that they leave her to clear up, and she brought Eddie back through the narrow hallway to the back porch. It was a still August afternoon, rather overcast; the air felt soft and thick with heat. She stood without looking at him.

"Shall we sit down?" she asked.

He glanced at her. She had on the same black jersey dress that she had been wearing the night she had first gone out with him. Her thin arms had been tanned slightly during the summer by the sun; they hung at her sides in that peculiarly lifeless way that he had learned to know meant some inner tension in her. He reached out and put his right hand on her wrist.

"Darling, what's the matter?" he asked her. "You've been all over the place ever since I came. Afraid I wouldn't like something?"

"I suppose so."

She moved to the railing dividing their side of the porch from the Wessens'. Eddie watched her.

"Your mother's very nice," he said after a moment. "Very remarkable."

"Is she?"

She colored faintly, not knowing what else to say to him. He was quick at catching other people's opinions of him; he would not have missed her mother's antagonism. She was nervous, wondering if there was not a slight irony, too, in his praise.

The Wessens' back door opened then and Lillie came out. Ella glanced over, almost relieved for a moment at the interruption.

"Oh," Lillie said, calmly. She stood on the porch, looking at Eddie. "I didn't know you were out here, Elly."

"Yes. We—" Ella knew that Lillie had heard them on the porch and had come out to have a look at Eddie. "This is Eddie Bernet," she said. She introduced them quickly.

"Oh, yes," Eddie said. His manner changed; he put on his civil air again. "I've heard Rita Dillard speak of you. It's nice to know you, Miss Wessen."

"I've heard a good deal about you, too," Lillie said. "From a certain young lady."

She and Eddie both smiled. Ella, standing apart, noticed again the odd way that Eddie had of adapting himself to other people; it was as if he were a magician, pulling moods out of a hat as they were required.

"I understand you're over at the telephone company now," he said to Lillie. "Do you like it there?"

They began to talk about the telephone company, and then about the Finn Company, and the people they both knew who worked there. Ella stood beside the railing, listening to them. They did not try to bring her into the conversation. The hot August breeze blew jadedly and intermittently against her; there was no sun.

After a while Eddie glanced down at his wrist watch.

"I don't want to break up the party," he said to Ella, "but if we're going swimming this afternoon we'll have to be getting off."

She turned around. "What time is it?"

"It's almost four."

"I'll go and get my things," she said.

She went into the house. Her mother was in the kitchen, just taking off her apron. Ella stopped and looked at her.

"Mama—?" she said questioningly.

Anne Gunning understood that she was asking her opinion of Eddie. She hung her apron up carefully behind the door.

"Oh, he's a fine young man!" she said, in her firm, straightforward voice. She added after a moment, turning and glancing keenly at Ella, "Only a little too fine for you, I should think."

Ella flushed up. "What do you mean?" she asked.

She looked at her mother almost hostilely. But Anne Gunning was in earnest; she spoke energetically, her own face coloring slightly over the cheekbones.

"I mean that a girl who takes up with a man who thinks more of himself than he does of her is making a poor bargain of it, all around," she said. "And I can thank my own experience for teaching me that—"

It was one of the few times that she had ever referred, even indirectly, to the difficulties of her own marriage before Ella. There was an uncomfortable silence between them for a moment. Neither of them knew how to go on from there.

"But I'm not going to marry him!" Ella murmured tensely, after a little. "Just because he's asked me to go out with him a few times—"

"Yes, I've heard that before!" Anne Gunning said.

But they could not continue talking about it there in the kitchen, with Eddie just outside the door. Ella went on into the bedroom to get her swimming things; when she came out on the porch a few minutes later, her mother was there talking to Eddie and Lillie. Eddie was telling her how much he had enjoyed the dinner; they were both very civil as they said good-by.

He and Ella went down the steps and around the side of the house to the street. His car was parked before the house. They drove east through a neighborhood of small houses, crooked brick sidewalks, and green, solid-looking elms. The streets had a hot summer Sunday-afternoon quiet.

Eddie said after a little: "Your friend Lillie Wessen seems to know what's what where business is concerned."

"Yes," she said.

But she was a little bitter that he should begin talking about Lillie, now that they were alone. He seemed to take her so much for granted; he was one person for other people, and another for her. When she had been watching him during those first weeks at the office, before she had come to know him well, she had imagined a different kind of relationship between them. She had thought then that he would see the things in her that no one else saw, because there were the same sort of things in him. But it was only rarely, as on the night when they had walked together in Sherwood Park, that this seemed to happen. She had a rather desperate feeling often that it was her fault that this was so; she thought that he must consider her too uninteresting, too inexperienced, so that she was under a constant feeling of inadequacy with him.

They drove out past the eastern edge of the city, where they were going swimming in a big new public pool.

"We'll have to look out for Inez and Tommy," Eddie said, as they left the car. "They said they were coming out here this afternoon."

She rather disliked having their afternoon broken into again by others. But there was nothing for her to do against it. They separated at the bathhouse and went in to put on their suits. When she came out again and looked around for Eddie, he had already joined a group on the other side of the pool. She went around slowly, seeing Inez standing beside a short dark young man whom she recognized as Tommy Shoup; with them were Tottie Dunlop, a pretty, leggy blonde from the office, and a tall young man with bright red hair.

"Hello — *hello!*" he said, seeing her come up. "What's this?"

"This is Ella," Eddie said. He put his arm around her shoulders. "Say hello to a lot of nice people, Ella."

She smiled round at them all.

"I hear Eddie's been having dinner over at your house," the red-haired young man, whose name was Morrissey, said to her. He had a quick, strong, wiry body, like an animal's, she thought, very self-assured and easy; his lips parted in a slight smile as he stared at her. "That looks serious."

"You don't know Eddie," Tottie said. She was a little jealous of Ella; there was a slight antagonism in her manner toward her. "He knows how to get free meals from all his girls," she said. "Don't you, Eddie?" She ran her forefinger quickly down the middle of his back.

"Do I not," Eddie said, turning around and smiling.

"I'll have to learn his technique," Morrissey said. He continued to look at Ella.

"We were just going to have a sand battle," Tottie went on quickly, to Eddie. "You and Ella can be reinforcements."

She picked up a handful of sand and flung it at him.

"Oh, we haven't even been in the water," Ella objected, looking at Eddie, half in appeal.

"That's right," he said. "Wait till I race Ella over to the island and back."

He waded out with her till the water was up to their knees. She stood looking across the pool, which under the dull blue-gray sky was also dull and gray, toward the small artificial island in the center.

"Come on," Eddie said. "I'll give you a start."

She hesitated for a moment, then waded out a few steps farther and struck out. She had never learned to swim well, and in a few moments she heard Eddie splashing past her. She kept on toward the island; when she reached it Eddie seized her hands and pulled her up.

"You lost by a mile," he said.

"I know I did."

She sat with her shoulders slightly bowed together, trying to get her breath. The water ran off her face and trickled down her arms and legs.

"The trouble with you is, you try to keep your head out of water all the time," Eddie advised her. "You have to learn to breathe without raising your head."

He sat down beside her. She liked the look of him in his bathing trunks: his smooth slender body, well-muscled, pleasantly like that of a young Greek athlete. But she felt depressed by his calm assumption of superiority; he seemed to do everything so much better than she could. She sat looking down at the water.

He reached over after a moment and pulled off her bathing cap.

"What's that for?" she asked, turning.

"I like you better without it, darling."

She smiled rather doubtfully, watching him fold the rubber cap between his fingers. After a while she asked him suddenly: "Do we have to go back to the others?"

"Why shouldn't we?" He frowned a little against the light. "Don't you want to?"

She shook her head.

"Here they come now." He tipped his head back, indicating the direction with his eyes. "What's the matter with them? They've got all their eyes and noses, haven't they?"

She wished that she had not said anything. She watched him reach out a hand and pull Tottie Dunlop from the water.

"Whoo-ee!" she gasped. "Did you see me beat them all?"

Frank Morrissey pulled himself up beside Ella.

"You only started half an hour before we did," he said to Tottie.

He looked over at Ella. "Baby, are you a rotten swimmer!" he told her. "Looks like you need somebody to give you a few lessons."

"You can let Eddie take care of that," Tottie said to him. "He's an expert."

She was joking about it, but her tone was a little sharp. Morrissey glanced around at her.

"Listen to who's talking," he said. "Maybe you need a lesson or two yourself."

He gave her a sudden push and she slipped off into the water. Tommy Shoup reached over and gave her a hand up as she splashed quickly in.

"Oh, you idiot!" she cried, to Morrissey, when she had gotten her breath. "What are you trying to do — drown me?"

"I thought you were such a good swimmer."

"All right. I'm a good swimmer. They can drown too, you know."

She was not really angry about it, Ella saw. She enjoyed being the center of attraction; she was as full of exhibitionistic, undirected energy as a five-year-old child. Now she pulled Tommy Shoup to his feet and insisted that they all begin a game of tag — "in the water or out; everything's fair," she said. "Frank — Eddie — come on now."

The others began sliding quickly into the water. Ella stopped to put on her bathing cap, which Eddie had tossed over to her, but as she raised her arms to draw it over her head Morrissey suddenly pushed her into the water. The next moment he had slipped in after her, and as she thrashed about blindly she felt him seize her, holding her firmly, his hands going over her quickly, as if he were some sort of aquatic animal, at home in its element. She caught a glimpse of his thin, ruddy face intent on hers; she could not bear it; for a moment she was furious as an animal herself, and she broke away from him, setting out strongly toward the shore. She heard the others calling after her, but she did not stop; only when she had stumbled up on the sand she realized that Eddie had followed her, and had reached the edge of the pool as soon as she had. He took her wrist and pulled her around so that she was facing him.

"What on earth's the matter with you?" he asked.

He stood staring at her, surprised and displeased. Her heart went down.

"Eddie, do we have to stay here?" she asked him. "I want to go."

He raised his brows angrily. "Oh, my God!" he said. "Just because you took a ducking? You don't see Tottie acting like this, do you? She took as much as you did without crying about it."

She saw that he had not noticed anything more than that Morrissey had pushed her into the water and jumped in after her, and she did not want to tell him differently. She drew herself free of him, almost crying; suddenly the whole unsatisfactory afternoon seemed to be falling to pieces before her eyes.

"You don't have to come with me if you don't want to," she said.

"That's likely," he said. She began to walk on again toward the bathhouse and he followed her. "What's the matter? Isn't that crowd good enough for you?" he went on. "You've been frozen up like an icicle ever since we came out here. I must say, you put on a hell of a routine—"

She did not answer him, walking on with her throat tightening with sobs. The late sun had broken through the thin clouds, and as she walked on toward it her eyes, jerking open and shut against the tears, showed her the sky and the beach and the gaudy bathhouse splotched with reddish-black patches of color. Her hair, dripping wet, clung to her face and neck; she felt that she looked ignominious and ridiculous.

Eddie maintained a sulky, excited silence till they had almost reached the bathhouse. Then she saw him looking at her, and in a moment he took her arm.

"It's no use our going on like this," he said rather stiffly. "I suppose I don't care any more for the lot of them than you do. But, darling, there isn't anybody else, for us —"

She could not say anything because of the thickening in her throat, and she walked on in silence. He stopped after a moment and dropped her arm.

"Well, listen, do you want to make up or don't you?" he asked.

[41]

"Of course — of course I do," she managed to say.

She felt the tears beginning to flow out of her eyes, and she put up her damp hand to brush them away. Eddie stood looking at her, suddenly a little overcome.

"You're not going to *cry*," he said to her. "It's nothing to get so excited about—"

She stood with her head averted; she was afraid that if she tried to talk she would begin to cry again.

"Look, we'll go inside and get dressed, and then we'll drive out to Veronda's and have something to eat," he said. "Would you like that?"

He was trying to speak in his ordinary tone, but she saw that he had not completely forgiven her for making a scene before the others. He said that he would tell them they were leaving and then meet her afterwards outside, and she nodded and separated from him at the bathhouse door.

Inside she dressed, and then toweled her wet hair dry as well as she could. She did not want to go to Veronda's with Eddie, but she knew that there would be a definite breach between them if she did not go with him now, after their quarrel. She felt shaken and upset; she had not imagined that he would ever speak to her as he had spoken as they were leaving the pool. Yet at the same time she was afraid of losing him. She did not want him to stop caring about her. There was something holding her to him, some curious bond, stronger than the uncertain fluctuations of her emotions.

She combed her hair, which still hung rather damp and severe about her face, and left the bathhouse to join him again. He was standing outside, waiting for her.

"Here I am," she said, trying to smile at him in a natural way.

He looked at her, smiling also. "That's a big improvement for a short time," he said.

He too was a little constrained still. They began to walk along together in the direction of the parking lot.

It was still early when they arrived at Veronda's. The dining room was not crowded, and a waiter wearing a checked apron pinned around his waist showed them to a table at the edge of the small dance floor. Ella sat down, looking around her. She had never been out here before, but she had heard the other girls at the office talking about it. She had been a little disappointed, when she and Eddie had driven up, to see that it was only a rambling, rather shabby one-story frame building on a country road. And inside it was not much more attractive. The dining room was low-ceilinged and dark, with red-and-white checked cloths on the tables and a few dim still-lifes in gilt frames on the walls. A three-piece band was mechanically beating out the popular songs of the moment.

"It's a hole of a place, really," Eddie said, seeing her glancing around. "But you can get decent food here, and there's always a good crowd on Saturday and Sunday nights."

He spoke in a matter-of-fact way, his eyes not meeting hers, but moving around the room. She looked down at the menu which the waiter had laid before her on the table. She knew that things were still not right between her and Eddie, and she wished again that they had not come. The regular twanging thud of the bass fiddle in the low-ceilinged room, the strident melody of the clarinet, made her feel uneasy and excited. At the table next to theirs was a group of middle-aged Italians, eating spaghetti and shouting at each other over the music.

"They come out here for the Italian food," Eddie said, looking over at them when he had given the waiter their order. "Listen to them — my God, what a racket! Tharp always says that Italian is the most musical language in the world, but you'd never think it, to hear this sort of thing—"

"No, but it's — dramatic, somehow," Ella said, watching a stout, dark-haired woman who, one hand lifted forward in a free, menacing gesture, was repeating several times a word that sounded to her like *brutta, brutta, brutta.* Ella leaned forward to watch her more closely, almost forgetting where she was for a moment. "That's the kind of thing — I mean, it's like an opera; now, the tones of her voice, so deep and harsh, just the tones of her voice and the way she flung out her hand, showing you that she's angry and — scornful," she said, hesitating in her attempt to put her thoughts into words. She turned back to Eddie, fascinated and excited.

The waiter brought their order, and they began to eat.

"Are you going to study over at the Institute again this year?" Ella asked him after a few moments, putting down her fork.

"Yes, I imagine so. It's really worth the money; I've met quite a few people that way whose families are right in the top row in this town."

He spoke still in a rather cool, detached manner, but she tried to go on talking to him as if nothing was the matter between them.

"I should think you'd get a good deal of pleasure out of learning so much about music too," she said, frowning slightly in her effort to speak naturally. "I know I would."

"You may think you would," he said. "But you've got to remember, there's more than just a bit of work connected with singing too. A kid like you is apt to see just the glamour and forget about all the work that has to go along with it."

"I wouldn't mind the work," she said.

"That's what you think, darling."

"I know." She contradicted him positively, growing more serious and more natural. "Ever since I can remember, that's what I've wanted to do — learn to sing. I wouldn't mind how hard I had to work if I had the chance."

She sat facing him across the small table, her eyes narrowing slightly with resolution.

"Well, it's no kind of life for a girl, anyway," Eddie said. He was a little piqued by the definite way in which she had contradicted him. "Only the ones with plenty of pull and the best kind of voice get to the top, and even some of them have a tough time of it for years."

"It's all right when you're doing what you want to do."

"I suppose you can see yourself at the Metropolitan right now," he said, with faint sarcasm.

"Well, you've never heard me sing. How do you know my voice isn't good enough for me to get there some day?" she said, her voice taking on a deep contralto note, as it always did when she became excited.

"All right," Eddie said. He pushed back his chair and got up. "Come on, show me."

"What do you mean?" She looked up at him, startled, not understanding what he wanted her to do.

"I mean, come on and let me hear you sing now," he said. "The fellows in the orchestra won't mind; it's been done out here before. Just tell them what you want to sing."

"Eddie, I can't do that. I can't do that," she repeated, flushing nervously. "Please sit down. I can't get up in front of all these people."

"What do you think you'd be getting up in front of if you were a real singer?" he said. His dark, thin face looked stubborn. "Come on; get up. Or were you bluffing when you said it about the kind of voice you had, and how much you wanted to be a singer?"

"No, I wasn't bluffing." She got up suddenly, pushing back her chair. "All right, I'll do it. I'll show you if I meant it."

She followed him over to the orchestra. The whole room seemed suddenly to take on a curious sensory texture, as if the music were throbbing in the walls and the lights, the wail of the clarinet vibrating through her body rather than through space about her, the deep constant thrumming of the bass fiddle rocking beneath her feet in swelling and receding waves as she walked. She saw Eddie saying something to the pianist, a thin, tallow-haired man with a blotchy complexion, and he swung around slightly on the piano stool, playing the final notes of the number, and looked at her curiously.

"O. K. What do you want to sing?" he asked.

She stood with her hands at her sides, staring at him.

"Do you — do you know 'Ah, Sweet Mystery of Life'?" she asked.

The music gone, her voice came rather weakly into the silence.

"Listen, sister, you may not know it, but these people want to dance," the pianist said, looking at her skeptically, his left hand beginning to indicate dance rhythms on the piano. "They wouldn't even listen to Jeannette MacDonald singing that kind of stuff."

She glanced at Eddie in desperation.

[45]

"How about something like 'Star Dust'?" he suggested.

Now that he had gotten her into this, he seemed more encouraging, as if he wanted to help her through.

"I don't know all the words." She jerked back to the pianist, her chest rising. "I could sing 'Song of Love.'"

"Well, it'll do, I guess." He played a few chords, indicating a key. "That about right for you?" She nodded. "All right. We'll give you four bars and then hit it."

He swung around to speak to the other two members of the band. Eddie patted her shoulder encouragingly.

"Good luck," he said.

He went back to their table as the music began. Then she was standing alone, facing a blur of people, her throat constricted, hearing the slow waltz rhythm of the music beginning, and knowing that in a space of moments she had to sing. She brought out the first notes raggedly, a little behind the beat, then quickened in panic and over-ran her accompaniment, so that the pianist had to hurry the beat to catch up with her. She heard him mutter something to the others, and for a moment she thought that she was going to break down completely. Half-turning her head over her shoulder, she glanced back at the pianist with an expression of abject, nervous pleading on her face, as if begging him to help her somehow out of her predicament.

"Go on, *go on,*" he ground out under his breath, hardly opening his lips.

He played a little more emphatically to cover the wavering of her voice, watching her with a resigned air of contemptuous impatience. She felt a sudden rush of anger cutting through her.

She forced a deeper breath into her chest, tightened her hands, which hung at her sides, and, lifting her head, brought out the next phrase in full, deep tones. Struggling to gain control of herself, she felt the music, the simple Schubert-inspired melody, gradually begin to take hold of her; she breathed more easily, attacking the phrases with growing confidence. Her voice smoothed, rounded to its natural velvety resonance. She took a second chorus; as she finished, the pianist nodded his head, smiling at her rather grudgingly.

"You haven't got a bad voice, kid. But you need plenty more experience," he said to her. "Want to try another one?"

"No. No, thanks."

She slipped back toward the table, conscious of a thin scattering of applause. Eddie was coming to meet her. The orchestra struck up another number.

"You were marvelous, Ella. I didn't know you could sing like that," Eddie said, smiling, and taking her arm.

He seemed proud of her, but she could not be glad. She felt tense and weak.

"Eddie, can't we go? Can't we leave now?" she asked him.

"But you haven't finished your supper."

"I don't care. I don't want it. Can't we go?"

She felt nervously that everyone was looking at her.

"Well, yes, if you really want to," Eddie said.

He spoke considerately, as if he had forgotten his anger. He paid the check and they went outside.

"Look, I'm sorry I put you in a spot like that," he said, as they walked over to the place where he had parked the car. "I suppose it wasn't such a good idea. But, you know, you had nothing to be afraid of, the way you can sing."

She walked toward the car, seeing that it had grown dark now; the air was soft and hot, the darkness like a kind of deepening mist over everything. She felt used up and limp; the tears that had been near the surface ever since her quarrel with Eddie that afternoon began choking her again. It made it worse when he was nice to her, as he was being now.

They got into the car.

"Where do you want to go?" he asked.

She shook her head silently, biting her lips to keep the tears back.

"I think I'd better go home," she said after a moment.

"What's the matter?"

"I don't know. I feel — Oh, Eddie, listen, have I really got a good voice?" She bent forward, crying, trying to get control of herself. "I want it so much, and just now — I made a fool of myself up there;

I was scared, scared sick; and I always said, if I had a chance—"

He put his arm around her, and she turned her face against his shoulder, crying, the tears wetting his sleeve.

"Sure, Ell, I know," he said. His voice sounded different from the way it usually did, worried and sympathetic. "My God, I've been scared myself. You feel you're all alone, just you up there and everybody against you — I know how it is. I've been through it myself."

They sat like that for a little while without saying anything, his arm around her and her face on his shoulder. She stopped crying gradually. After a while she turned her head and found a handkerchief in her bag and dried her eyes.

"I don't know what's the matter with me," she said. "I don't know why I acted like that."

"It's all right," Eddie said. "I suppose it hasn't been a very pleasant day for you."

They could hear the music from inside the dining room when they were quiet, the regular throb of the rhythm beating out to them persistently through the darkness.

"You don't know how it is with me about singing," Ella said. She clenched her hand about her damp handkerchief as she leaned back in the car against his arm. "I wouldn't care about anything else if I could be a singer."

"Not even about me?"

"I didn't mean that. I only meant—"

"It's all right. I know what you meant."

He tightened his arm around her. They looked straight ahead.

"It's a damned shame that, with a voice like that, you've never had a chance to do anything about it," he said after a moment, in a rather thoughtful, bitter tone. "But that's the way it is. There are girls I know over at the Institute who sing like crows, but their families have money, so they have lessons with the best teachers there. And here you are—"

"Well, I've been thinking about it, and I've just about made up my mind that I'm going to begin studying this fall; I don't care how much we need the money," Ella said. She spoke in a tone of half-

[48]

frightened resolution. "But I couldn't afford to take lessons from Mr. Tharp; I couldn't afford any more than — well, two or two and a half a week at most," she figured worriedly. "Could I have lessons from somebody over there for that?"

Eddie was silent a moment. She felt his arm tightening about her as he looked straight ahead into the darkness.

"Look," he said suddenly, "I'll tell you what we'll do. I'll take you over to sing for Tharp, and if he likes your voice, it may be that he can do something for you — I mean about the money part of it. It would have to be this week, before the term begins."

She turned toward him quickly. "Oh, Eddie, do you think he would?" A shiver of excitement passed over her. "Do you think I'm good enough?"

"Of course you're good enough," he said almost angrily. "I've heard some of those girls over there; they've had the training, and you haven't, but there isn't one of them that can hold a candle to you."

She leaned forward, clasping her hands about her knees, her face paling with resolution.

"Oh, do you really mean that, Eddie? You know, I've always had ideas about my voice, that it might be good, really good — not now, of course, because there are so many things I don't know about, things I've got to learn — I'll work like fury; you don't know how I'll work." She twisted around, facing him again. "When will you take me over to sing for Tharp?"

"Well, I'll have to see about that. I'll have to make an appointment." He put his arm around her again, drew her toward him, and kissed her possessively. "Listen, Gunning, you and I are both going to get ahead," he said. "We're both going in the same direction — up — and nothing's going to stop the two of us."

She let herself be kissed, but she seemed not to be thinking of it; she drew away again at once and sat back, smiling faintly, with an excited air.

"You've got to tell me everything that I must do when I go to sing for Tharp," she said positively. "I don't want to act the way I did tonight. I want to know everything in advance."

"There's nothing to know," he said. "You simply sing for him the way you would for anybody else."

He became a little cooler again, as if he had noticed how much more enthusiasm she seemed to have for her ambitions than for his love-making. His tone brought her excitement down.

"You're awfully good to do this for me, Eddie," she said, looking at him more constrainedly and a little anxiously. "I don't know what I'd do if I didn't have you to help me."

"I imagine you'd get along."

"No, I wouldn't. I don't know how to go about things the way you do."

He was mollified, and they sat in the car, talking and sitting close to each other, till some other people came by. Then Eddie said that there was still time for them to make the last show at the Strand if they hurried, and they drove back into town again. Ella did not say anything more about the singing except to remind him just before she left him that night of his promise to take her to sing for Tharp.

Chapter Four

HE took her over to the Institute the following Saturday afternoon, at three. The door of Tharp's studio was closed when they came down the corridor, and he said to her, looking at his wrist watch: "It's still early. We'd better sit down here and wait."

He walked over to a bench that stood against the wall just opposite Tharp's door. Ella followed him. They sat down.

"I hope we won't have to wait long," she said, a little apprehensively.

She laid the music she had brought with her on her lap and looked across at the closed door opposite. The corridor was empty except for the two of them; registration for the new term did not begin till the following week, and there were only the office workers and a few other people in the building.

"Look, sweet, you're not getting nervous now, are you?" Eddie asked. He looked at her with a rather tense impatience in his own manner.

"No, of course not."

She tried to appear calm, knowing that Eddie, after that evening at Veronda's, had not been eager to keep his promise to take her to sing for Tharp, and that he had finally done so only because he thought she would believe he did not dare to if he did not. She smiled at him, and to cover her nervousness began asking him questions about the building. It intimidated her, rather, the old-fashioned, imposing structure, with its severe, gloomy red-brick façade. Tharp's studio was in the older part of the main building, and as she sat there she felt the walls arching coldly over her to the high ceiling overhead;

it seemed to her as if music could not live here, in this silent, somewhat forbidding atmosphere. The glow that had been in her died out
quickly; she sat waiting, feeling herself grow cold with waiting, with
the high cold arching about her of the silent walls.

It was a quarter past three before the door of Tharp's studio finally
opened. Ella saw him standing in the doorway, a tall, meticulously
dressed man of sixty-five, imposing, with a face of the English type,
fresh and cold, and a heavy gray mustache with pointed ends. His
companion was a small, quick, middle-aged man with a long seamed
face and eyes like gimlets: Hobie Herschel, the Dean of Faculty,
Eddie said to her in an undertone. The two men stood in the doorway
talking for several minutes while Eddie and Ella, who had both
risen, remained standing at the other side of the hall. When Herschel
went off at last down the corridor, Eddie advanced.

"Good afternoon, Mr. Tharp," he said.

"Oh — Bernet." Tharp seemed to see him for the first time. He
held out his hand. "How are you?"

"First-rate, Mr. Tharp. And you? Did you have a nice summer?"

Ella, who was standing a little behind Eddie, noticed the alert
politeness that had suddenly sprung into his manner; he stood watching Tharp's face as if to anticipate his moods.

"Yes, we spent most of it in our place in Maine," Tharp said. "A
wonderful climate for the summer months."

"I understand it is," Eddie said. He saw that Tharp was looking
at Ella, and, interrupting himself quickly, introduced her to him.
"This is Miss Gunning, Mr. Tharp."

"How do you do," said Ella, advancing a little.

"It's awfully nice of you to give us your time this way," Eddie
went on, earnestly and rapidly. "I've heard Miss Gunning sing this
summer, and from the little I know about it, I think she has a voice.
Naturally you occurred to me as the person who could definitely let
her know whether she has a real talent or not."

"Why, yes. Won't you come inside now, Miss Gunning?" Tharp

[52]

let her pass before him into his studio. "Bernet, are you going to play her accompaniments, is that it?" he said.

Ella turned around again, facing the two at the door.

"No, I thought — I was going to play my own," she said, looking nervously at Tharp.

She had never had an accompanist, and had not thought of bringing one.

"No, that won't do very well," Tharp said. He considered a moment. "I believe Elinor Tilton is in 218 now," he said to Eddie. "Would you mind running up there and asking her if she would come down to my studio for a quarter of an hour or so?"

Eddie went off promptly down the hall, and Tharp, turning, closed the door and crossed the room to the grand piano which stood in the center.

"You've had some instruction before, I understand, Miss Gunning — both piano and voice," he said, standing before the keyboard of the piano and facing Ella.

"Yes. That is, I've had a few vocal lessons — only a few."

Ella had gained a certain amount of experience in the months she had been working at the Finn Company, but Tharp's reputation, his urbane, rather cold manner, the designedly imposing tones of his bass voice, had their effect on her now. She looked uncertain, standing beside the piano and holding her music on one arm. She was wearing her black dress again because it was the one that Eddie liked best, and her figure in it looked thin without fragility, tense and with a raw, undeveloped grace.

Tharp told her to put her music down, and, when she had done this, struck a pair of chords on the piano and asked her to sing the major scale of the key he had indicated. She brought out three notes and stopped, her breath failing. For the first time she was consciously frightened, almost frantic, feeling that she wanted only to get it over with, to get away. She began again quickly.

"No, no!" Tharp said, interrupting her.

She stopped, looking at him in confusion.

[53]

"Collect yourself a little," he said. He stared at her, his face, with its agatelike eyes and heavy mustache, appearing to her a sort of mask which did not express at all the feelings that lay behind it. "There's no need for you to be in such a hurry. Take a good breath before you begin; you're starting out with less breath than you should have left when you finish. Now, again."

He played the chords once more. His words unnerved her even further; there seemed to be some sort of constriction in her chest, preventing her from taking a full breath. She struggled with herself, lowering her head, so that to Tharp she presented an odd appearance of sullen, almost animal-like discomposure. Her face seemed void of reflection, embodying no other expression than that of an instinctive distrust.

"There's no reason for you to be nervous," Tharp said, coming away from the piano and going to the window. "Take your time; breathe deeply once or twice before you begin."

He stood watching her impatiently, but beyond a slight movement of her mouth, which remained tightly shut, there was no evidence that she had heard him. She simply stood there beside the piano, her hands at her sides and her eyes almost expressionless with terror.

Tharp, after waiting several moments in silence, came toward her with a look of definite irritation on his face.

"My dear girl, there's nothing for you to be afraid of," he said. "You must have sung for other people before — your teacher, your friends; isn't that true?"

She nodded silently, unable to trust herself to speak.

"Well then, why these nerves?" he asked, with a kind of impatiently soothing manner. "You are not going to do anything different for me than you did for them, are you? You're only going to sing for me, here in a small room with no one else listening, just as you always sang for them."

His manner showed that he did not quite know whether to set her behavior down to an almost unbelievable stupidity or to a display of sensitivity far beyond that which he usually encountered in his pupils. She made an effort, raised her head, and forced an expression of understanding to her face.

There was a knock on the door, and a tall, slender young woman wearing a green dress came into the room.

"Eddie said you wanted me, Mr. Tharp," she said. She looked at Ella curiously.

"Yes," said Tharp. "This is Miss Gunning — Miss Tilton," he introduced them perfunctorily. "I want you to run over a few songs with Miss Gunning, Elinor, if you will."

"Yes, of course."

She sat down at the piano, drew the songs Ella had laid down upon it toward her, and glanced through them. An expression of surprised curiosity crossed her face.

"Now, Miss Gunning," Tharp said, "we'll forget the scales, if you like, and you can sing something that you've brought along here. There's no need to attempt anything difficult."

"Well, I'll — I think I'll sing this," Ella said. She picked out one of the sentimental songs, a relic of the "parlor music" of the turn of the century, which Mrs. Ledru had given her.

Tharp glanced at the title, frowned, and leafed quickly through the other songs, then flung them down with a gesture of irritation.

"Why, this is nothing but trash; good heavens, look at this — 'The Poet's Dream,' 'Summer Zephyrs,' 'Dear Little Cottage in the Lane,' " he said to Elinor Tilton, picking up the songs again to show to her and speaking in a tone of offended disbelief.

The young woman smiled slightly without speaking.

"Is this the sort of thing you've been studying?" Tharp went on, turning to Ella.

She nodded, color flaming into her face.

"Well—!" Tharp looked expressively at Miss Tilton, and after a moment, with an air of washing his hands of the whole matter, turned away to the window. "You had better sing one of them then, I suppose," he said.

Miss Tilton picked up the song that Ella had chosen and opened it. She glanced up at Ella.

"Are you ready, Miss Gunning?"

Ella came a step nearer to the piano. Her tension and fright had been overridden suddenly by a hard, defiant determination; she took up her position beside the piano, standing naturally, in an unprofessional and unaffected attitude, with her hands hanging at her sides, and nodded to Elinor Tilton to begin. She was in a state of nerves in which she had either to exert herself to the utmost or break down completely, and her long-accumulated determination kept her up now when everything else seemed to have failed her.

The song she had chosen was the least vapid of the group, a simple ballad which she knew instinctively was not badly suited to the emotional intensity of her voice. Almost from the moment she began, she had the sense of power and conviction that usually came to her when she sang. Her voice was surprisingly resonant and easily produced, the upper tones clear and effective, the lower register full and round, with less of the dark contralto timbre than the highly colored one of the true mezzo-soprano. After the first few phrases Tharp, who was standing at the window, turned and looked at her, noticing her naturally good carriage and position, and the evidently highly sensitive dramatic instinct that she possessed, and that let her draw the maximum emotional effect from the music which she was singing.

"Yes, very good; now let us have a few of those scales," he said in a rather cold but not uninterested voice, when she had finished.

While the accompanist indicated the modulations from key to key on the piano, Ella then sang a number of scales on progressively rising tones, Tharp listening to the changes in caliber of the voice from the lower and middle registers, where its richness and power were most evident, to the upper range, which was ringing and easily produced, but without the cello-like breadth and purity of the lower tones.

"You haven't had much training; that's quite evident," he said finally, after several minutes of this, "and what you have had has been of more harm than help to you, as far as I can see; but you have a voice, Miss Gunning — a rather unusual one, I must say. How old are you?"

"Seventeen."

Ella, slightly flushed, faced him with the sense of confidence that always came to her when she sang. His words of praise, qualified as they were, went through her thrillingly; they were the first definite confirmation she had ever had of her own conviction that she had the sort of voice that could lead her to a professional career.

"Well, yes — you're young still; you have plenty of time before you," Tharp said, looking at her, noticing that in spite of her slender figure she had good shoulders, a breadth of chest, a frame that would some day provide the physical strength that is part of the necessary equipment of a singer.

"I want to work, to study — I don't mind how hard," Ella said, speaking more boldly in the excitement of realizing that her singing had made an impression on Tharp. "I want to study here—"

She paused, brought up suddenly by the thought that now was the time to mention her financial difficulties to Tharp. But she did not want to do it before Elinor Tilton. Tharp seemed to see the reason for her embarrassment, and he told Miss Tilton that they would not need her any longer, and that she might go.

After she had left the room, he began asking Ella directly about her financial position, inquiring in a businesslike way how much she could afford to pay for her lessons. She explained about her mother's work and her own job at the Finn Company with feelings of mingled anxiety and embarrassment. The elation which her singing had brought quickly faded, and she sat replying to his questions in quick sentences, trying to act as unemotional as he. Her heart was pounding with the fear that he would tell her that he could not do anything for her. And all the while this seemed to have nothing to do with singing, with the fact that he had knowledge which would make her a better singer if he would agree to pass it on to her.

He told her finally that, as she could not enroll at the Institute as a full-time student, she was not eligible to compete for the scholarships that were given there each year, but that, with his recommendation, she would be able to finance her lessons through the Florence Fund, a sum of money that was available to deserving students under certain conditions. By the terms of these conditions, she would be required to pay as much as she was able for her lessons — in her case three dollars weekly was agreed on — and the difference between this amount and the cost of her lessons would then be made up by the Fund. He explained further that the grant was contingent on her continuing to do satisfactory work, and on her agreeing that, if she was ever financially able to in the future, she was to pay back the money that had been given her.

Ella did not know what her mother would say to her making an arrangement of this kind; it was the first time that she had ever been in a position where it was necessary or possible for her to make a decision about her own future. But it was the only way, she felt; it was her only chance to learn what she had to learn if she was to be a singer, and she could not afford not to take it up.

Tharp sent her off to the office to get the necessary forms for her to fill out. As she came out of his studio, she saw Eddie waiting outside.

"I have to go to the office; will you show me where it is?" she said, coming up to him quickly, her face serious and glowing with excitement.

"What happened? What did he say?" Eddie asked.

He stood looking at her with a manner divided between curiosity and a kind of prepared superiority.

"He says I've got a voice; oh, Eddie, it was awful at first, and I couldn't sing a note for him, and my songs — well, I wish you'd heard what he said about them," she began, her elation returning now that she was released from Tharp's presence. "Of course *I* know they're not good, but they're all I had, and I didn't have any idea that he'd think they were *that* bad — I don't know about things like that; it's just things like that that I've got to learn," she said determinedly.

"But he did like your voice?"

"Yes, he did; he said it was an unusual one." She smiled briefly and confidently: the flash of her true nature, superb and self-assured, striking through the husk of convention and training in which it was enveloped. "I know I'm going to get ahead now," she said; "this is only the beginning, and it shows what I can do if I get a chance. I'm going to work, I am. And some day, you just wait, I'll be singing in opera—"

"Then you're really going to study with Tharp?" Eddie interrupted her. "And what about the money?"

He was trying to act as if he was not impressed by her success, but there was a look of surprise, almost of envy, on his face. It was one thing for her to be an aspiring singer, who looked up to him because of his connection with the Institute, and quite another for her to come here and make more of an impression on Tharp in a few minutes than he had been able to in a year.

"That's why I have to go to the office now," she explained it to him. "Mr. Tharp says there's a fund that will help me pay for my lessons — I told him I couldn't pay more than three dollars a week — and I have to get the right forms for that and fill them out. I don't know what my mother will say about all this, because I have to promise to pay the money back later, if I'm ever able to, but I'm not going to let anything stop me now." She lifted her head with a kind of radiant but worried defiance. "I'm making my own money now, and I don't care what else I have to do without, as long as I can take lessons here."

She slipped her arm through Eddie's and began to walk along with him slowly toward the front of the building, not seeming to notice how unenthusiastic he appeared.

"Well, darling, of course if you think it's worth it, you're right in not passing up the chance," he said, in a judicial tone. "But if I were you, I'd think it over a bit before I signed anything; after all, they're not giving you anything, if you have to pay the money back. I can tell you one thing, they're mad to get pupils here, all the teachers are, and this is a lovely way to do it; Tharp's not losing a cent on the deal, and the Institute — well, it's a gamble for them, but they have the money anyway, that has to be used for this purpose, and however you look at it, they're still getting over half their money right away. It's not such a charitable proposition as you seem to think."

"I don't care whether it is or not; I can have my lessons if they let me have the money, and that's all I care about," Ella declared positively. She looked over at him, a little hurt by his tone. "I thought you'd be glad — and proud of me," she said.

"Darling, I *am*," he said. "I'm only trying to be practical about it."

She shook her head. "I don't feel like being practical; I'm too happy. Only" — she began talking about her audition again, too much excited by it to think of anything else — "I wish I'd had some better songs to bring along, so that I could have made a better impression right away—"

"Yes, I thought your numbers wouldn't do very well, but the time was so short I didn't like to tell you, because you wouldn't have been able to work anything else up anyway," he said.

But he looked at her rather gloomily; her self-confidence seemed to diminish him somehow, that radiance of hers which looked past him with blind, dazzled assurance into the future. She had left him behind; in half an hour, behind a closed door, she had stepped into a new world where he could not follow her. Even now, walking close beside him, her arm through his, she was not with him; she had left him alone.

An hour later, when he brought her back to Cobb Street, she was still in the state of bright excitement that brushed aside ordinary habits and considerations. She hardly looked after him as he drove off; she ran up the steps at once, just glancing about her at the quiet, sober little street, where the red-and-white fronts of the houses looked more unhopeful than usual in the rich late sunlight of the September afternoon. But today she did not mind; it was as if she had suddenly stopped living her real life here, as if what she did in this street, in this house, was no longer of any real importance to her.

She pushed open the screen door and went into the house. After the bright sunlight outside, the fitting room looked reddish-dark and dim. She could see her mother sitting at the sewing machine with some steel-blue silk material spread out on it and overflowing on to her lap. On the other side of the room Lillie was sitting on the yellow plush sofa, talking to Anne Gunning and smoking a cigarette. She looked up as Ella came in.

"Here she is now," she said, and, to Ella: "Your mother's just been telling me where you've been."

"Has she?"

Ella, still a little dazzled, looked about her; the practical tones of Lillie's voice fell coldly on her inner happiness. Before she could say anything more, the screen door bumped open behind her. It was Ray Wessen, come across to hear the news. He stood there looking at them for a moment, a tall, satiric, slightly stooped figure, looming almost too masculine in the little room with its atmosphere of lost, discouraged attempts at feminine adornment, before he said, in a disappointed tone: "You don't seem very excited over here. What happened, Ell? Did those bastards turn you down?"

"Nice language!" Lillie remarked coldly, not looking at him as she flicked ashes into a tray on the sofa arm.

Ella smiled. "Oh, Lillie, it doesn't matter! They *didn't* turn me down; just the opposite; Mr. Tharp said I had a voice, an unusual one, and I'm going to have lessons from him. The Institute has a fund that will pay part of my expenses."

She saw them all looking at her in the little dark room, their three faces suddenly as startled as if she had flung a bomb among them. Lillie was the first of them to speak.

"Wait a minute," she said, cautiously and unbelievingly, "let's get this straight. You mean this Mr. Tharp just heard you sing, and thought you were so good that he's going to see that you get your lessons for nothing?"

"Well, not for nothing, no." Ella's radiance diminished a little as the time came for explaining the arrangements she had arrived at with Tharp. "I have to pay about half, and the rest will come out of the fund."

"What difference does it make?" Ray said. He put his arm around Ella's shoulders and hugged her roughly. "I think it's swell, honey—"

Ella glanced up at him gratefully, then over at her mother. Anne

Gunning had said nothing; she still sat at the sewing machine, the steel-blue material flowing over her lap, her face with an expression on it that was not quite premonition and not quite pride.

"Well, I don't know what to say," she remarked, after a moment. "Of course, if your father were here—" Her thin face flushed up slowly as she spoke of him, though the Wessens had been familiar with her story for seventeen years. "He always said, if a person had music in him, it would come out some way, and heaven knows *he* couldn't do without it. If he'd taken half the pride in his legal work that he did in his voice, he'd have been one of the finest lawyers in the state; everybody said so; he had the mind—" She flushed up still more strongly, with sudden half-forgotten pride. "*I* always thought it was foolishness; I may have been wrong. And now there's the question of money — The cost of the lessons isn't all there is to it, you know; when you're thrown in with people who have a good deal more money than you have, it usually works out that you want to keep up with them somehow or other—"

"Your mother's right," Lillie put in, decidedly. "You'll only make yourself dissatisfied, starting out over there; if you want to take a few singing lessons, now that you're working, why don't you go back to Mrs. Ledru? You know, with your mother in business the way she is, you ought to patronize her customers whenever you can—"

Ella stared across at her, her face growing more serious and more passionate as she felt opposition rising against her.

"That would be *worse* than nothing; Mr. Tharp thinks so too," she said quickly. "I've already made up my mind; I'm going to take lessons from him." She went on, determined and persuasive, trying to get them to see her vision. "He thinks I'm good, and — you don't seem to realize what that means," she said. "He's heard all the best singers, known a lot of them, like Caruso and Geraldine Farrar, and if he says my voice is good, he knows what he's talking about. If I study with him, I'll have a chance to be a big singer some day—"

Lillie shook her head expressively.

"If that's the kind of thing you have in mind in wanting to take singing lessons, you'd be better off to drop the whole thing right now," she said. "There was a girl I worked with once who had a nice voice, and took lessons for years somewhere out in Auburn; she was crazy to sing over the radio, and her teacher finally got her an audition at one of the stations, but she never got on there. The man she sang for told her he knew dozens of girls with better voices than hers, and some of them had even gone over to Europe to study, but there was so much competition in that line of work that if you didn't have more talent *and* more influence than the others, you never had a chance of getting anywhere. She had a lovely voice too, I always thought, but she finally gave up the whole idea of being a singer because she realized she was only wasting her time. And that's just the kind of experience you'd have too," she added, judicially. "You have a good job now, and you ought to be thankful for that, and try to get ahead where you are, without wasting your time on any foolishness—"

"It's *not* foolishness," Ella said, beginning to tremble with bitterness and anger. "You don't understand — I'd rather give up anything than this chance. I've never wanted anything the way I want it, and I'm not going to give it up, I'm not going to, whatever anyone says!"

She picked up a piece of the steel-blue material from the sewing machine, and, hardly knowing what she was doing, began pulling it nervously between her fingers. Anne Gunning, her face closed, still lost in the inner struggle between premonition and pride, broke in quietly: "There's no need to be so upset. We'll talk it over; if it's what you want—"

"Of course it's what she wants," Ray said angrily. "Oh Lord, you people, can't you see—?"

He looked at them, unable to find the words for what he wanted to say, the whole spate of his bitterness against a world that had imprisoned him in his own futility and was reaching out now for Ella too. Lillie got up, staring across at him in unmoved opposition.

"Well, I won't argue with you," she said. "Only let me tell you"— she turned again to Anne Gunning — "if you give in to Elly about

[63]

this, you'll be sorry later. It's not going to do her any good to get mixed up in something like this—"

"That's your opinion," Ray sent after her, as she pushed open the screen door and walked outside. He looked across at Ella triumphantly. "She can't stop you," he said to her. "Nobody can. Do you know this, honey? — you're on your way right up there now—"

Chapter Five

ON the damp Saturday in November she and Inez had to stay late to finish the work; it was after one when she put the cover on her typewriter and began clearing up her desk. She had a lesson with Tharp at two, and was in a hurry to leave; when the door of the general office opened and Eddie came in, she looked up without stopping in what she was doing.

"Do you want Mr. Barstow?" she asked. "He's gone across the hall."

He cast a glance down the big room, saw that it was empty, and came up behind her.

"Darling, I don't want anybody but you," he said. "How about coming out somewhere with me tonight?"

He put both his arms about her, standing behind her, but she slipped away from him, turning to face him, shaking her hair back over her shoulders.

"Eddie, please!" she said quickly. "Suppose somebody came in now."

"Who on earth's going to see? They've all gone, haven't they?"

"No, Inez hasn't, for one."

She turned back to the desk again, continuing her tidying process. Eddie sat down on a corner of the desk. She felt him watching her as she worked, his eyes fixed on her in a rather moody gaze. But he only asked, after a little: "Are you going over for your lesson after lunch?"

"Yes. Only I won't have time for lunch today; Mr. Tharp's changed my time to two o'clock. I don't mind, only I'm afraid some

Saturday things will pile up here even worse than they did this morning, and I won't be able to get away—"

"Tell the whole crew to go to blazes," he suggested. "You work harder than any other girl in this office as it is."

She finished with the desk and turned again, looking at him.

"I'd run you over today, but I'm going to be late getting away myself," he said. "What about tonight, though? Will eight o'clock be all right with you?"

She hesitated. "Eddie, I don't want to say this, but I think I'd better not go anywhere tonight," she brought out quickly, after a moment. "You know how it is, with only week ends and evenings to practice; and so often in the evening there are other things I have to do, and we've been going out week ends quite a lot. I was planning on getting in some really good work today and tomorrow; and then, you know, the singing isn't all of it. Mr. Tharp's been talking to me about languages, and I thought I'd begin brushing up on my high-school French—"

She stopped, watching the changes in his expression a little nervously. It was the first time that she had ever refused one of his invitations.

"Of course, if that's the way you feel about it," he said, rather sulkily. He slid off the desk and stood up. "I'm sorry I bothered you."

He turned toward the door.

"Eddie, wait a minute," she called him back, a little desperately; she did not want him to be angry with her.

"Well?"

She came around the desk toward him.

"You know I *want* to go," she said, standing before him and looking at him with a pleading frown.

"Oh, yes, I know. You want to a hell of a lot."

"Well, all right, if you don't care to believe me," she said, growing angry in her turn.

He stood looking at her indecisively. "You don't give me much reason to believe you," he said, after a moment. "First you won't let me come near you—"

"I only said that somebody might come in."

"*That's* a good excuse."

They stood staring at each other resentfully.

"Eddie, please, don't let's quarrel," she said, in distress. "I don't want to — and my lesson'll be all off—"

"And that *would* be a tragedy, wouldn't it? That's all you think about these days — your lessons, your singing—"

"That's not fair of you to say that, Eddie. I think of you just as much as I ever did."

She felt a little guilty saying that, because she knew that it was not quite true. Her feelings toward him were all a confusion; there were times, when things were going badly at home or at the office, when she felt as if she could not bear it if she did not have him there, to turn to; but when she actually was with him it was never the way she wanted it to be. There seemed always to be an antagonism between them, as if he were pulling one way and she another; and usually it was she who had to give in.

"Do you really mean that, Ell?" he asked her, in a different voice.

"Of course I mean it."

He came closer and put his arms about her.

"You know, if you said you'd go out with me tonight, I might really believe you," he said in a lower voice.

"I can't! Well — all right," she reversed herself, with a rather helpless feeling of defeat.

"That's better." She saw his face clear. "I'll pick you up around eight, then."

She watched him go out of the office; after a moment she got her hat and coat and went out too. She felt that she was in a predicament, between his demands and the demands of her music, and she could not help resenting it a little that he had had his own way again about the evening. She walked out the door of the Finn Company building and down the steps to the sidewalk, her brows still drawn together in a slight frown. It was a raw, early November day; it had been raining a few hours before, and the streets and sidewalks were still wet. But she rather liked this kind of day, the city all bare and glistening under the heavy sky, the aqueous grayness of the air, through which the washed red gleam of brick buildings came in bright glimpses.

Her bus came, and she rode over to the Institute. It was still early enough when she got there for her to walk down to the drugstore at the next corner and have a sandwich, but she knew that she would sing better if she did not eat. Besides, she liked to sit in the corridor outside Tharp's door and watch the people going past. She had come to know a good many of them by sight during the weeks she had been studying there — the blond young pianist who had the studio next to Tharp's, and who stared at her resentfully each time he opened the door for another pupil; the stout, spectacled, middle-aged violinist who always nodded to her cheerfully when he went past; Madame Collier-Brown, who taught singing and wore impressive clothes that looked as if they came straight out of Queen Mary's wardrobe. It was like being in a strange new country, to sit there and listen to their conversation as they went by, a country in which almost everyone had some sort of accent — French, German, British, Italian, Polish: she could not identify them all — and in which music wandered and throbbed through every wall. She had never been happier in her life than she was when she sat there quietly on her bench, watching the people, hearing the quick bright runs and trills of a flute from somewhere upstairs, a soprano's persistent repetition of a difficult vocalise, a muffled piano dashing through stormy music full of left-hand arpeggios.

She sat on the bench outside Tharp's studio and watched Hobie Herschel come past in his usual brisk hurry, his little keen eyes missing nothing, noting her in their sharp, friendly fashion. He was leaving for the day; he wore his overcoat and carried his hat in his hand. His wife, who taught violin, came hurrying after him, pulling on her gloves. She was taller than he, as homely, and as brisk, with heavy red hair which she wore brushed back smoothly from her face; there was something refreshingly matter-of-fact about the two of them. Ella watched them go out the door, and then listened to a pair of girl students who were gossiping near her in a corner.

"Madame C.-B.'s furious about it."

"It won't do her any good. Letroye says she wouldn't use Kitty if she was the last soprano between here and New York."

"Her voice is too light. That's why Madame C.-B. wanted to do *Traviata* instead. Kitty could have managed Violetta."

"I don't believe Madame C.-B. really cares. It's all a smoke screen; she'll end up with Warner singing Cavaradossi, and that's what she's really wanted all the time. Letroye will have to take him, after she's made such a fuss about turning down Kitty."

They were talking about the opera that the Institute produced every spring, she knew. Tharp had asked her if she could manage to sing in the chorus, but they rehearsed in the afternoon; she did not see how she could possibly do it. She watched enviously as the two girls moved away down the corridor.

The door of Tharp's studio opened and he looked out.

"All right, Miss Gunning," he said to her.

She got up quickly and walked into the room. It was dark from the gray day outside, and the lights were on. Walking into the lighted room gave her a feeling as if she were stepping onto a lighted stage. She looked around with a feeling of excitement, nervousness, and confidence, thinking that some day it would be a real stage, with an audience out in the darkness beyond the lights.

Besides Tharp, there were two other people in the room: Elinor Tilton, sitting at the piano, and another girl of about twenty, in a dark-red wool dress, who she knew was named Alice Gorham; she was gathering her music together in preparation to leave. Tharp, standing beside a tall music cabinet with one arm leaning negligently upon it, was watching her with an indulgent expression on his face.

"Oh, I know that's the sort of thing you say to all your pupils," the girl was saying as Ella came in; she was evidently continuing a conversation that had been going on a few moments before. She looked up at Tharp, laughing; after a moment she turned around to Ella. "Doesn't he say severe things to you?" she demanded, looking at her with a kind of frank curiosity.

"Miss Gunning is quite different from you," Tharp said, before

Ella could speak. He put one hand into his trousers pocket, present-ing his broad chest, in a well-tailored English vest traversed by a heavy watch chain, in a consciously effective pose to the three girls. "She's very serious; she works very hard."

The girl glanced curiously at Ella again, then smilingly back to Tharp.

"I don't think it would make any difference to you if I did work hard," she said. "You'd still say the same kind of things to me."

Ella envied the intimate manner in which she spoke to him. During the half-dozen lessons she had had with him, she had always felt that he was keeping her at a distance, that his tone with her was different from that which he was using now with Alice Gorham, for example. But she told herself that she did not mind how he acted toward her as long as he was teaching her what she wanted to know. She stood looking around at the heavily furnished room with its collection of photographs of famous singers on the walls, thinking with confident impatience of the day when she would be like them, imagining herself photographed in operatic costume, like Galli-Curci or Louise Homer.

Alice Gorham went away, and Tharp, who had gone to the door with her, came back across the room to begin Ella's lesson. She stood near the piano, holding her hands clasped lightly together before her in the way that he had taught her to do, a serious and concen-trated expression on her face. Elinor Tilton gave her her key on the piano, and she began without hesitation to sing the simple vocalises on which Tharp had been having her work during the past few weeks. But he interrupted her almost at once.

"No, no, no! You are breathing as if you had just finished a foot race — an audible gasp before each intake. Don't you hear your-self?"

He looked at her testily and gloomily, walking about the room as he criticized her. His good humor seemed to have vanished with the closing of the door behind his earlier pupil. As Ella began again, he pulled his watch from his pocket and looked at it.

His words made her a little nervous, and her next attempt was worse than the first. As he turned to her in irritation, she fixed her eyes on him with a kind of determined hardihood.

"I can do better than that," she announced.

"Then why in heaven's name don't you?"

He waited, almost petulantly expectant. She took the notes the next time crudely but surely, her voice dwelling on the tones, which she rolled out largely, and with an air of conscious power. Tharp listened to her for a short while in silence, and then interrupted her once more with an outburst of definite displeasure.

"Would you like to know what you sound like?" he asked. "A second-rate prima donna in the last act of *Bohème*." He walked impatiently up and down the room. "You are singing a vocalise, not an aria; I've told you before," he said, waving one hand in an exasperated gesture.

She looked at him with some trepidation, but stood her ground.

"I can't help putting some feeling into it," she objected.

"Feeling — feeling! My dear girl, singing is an art, not an emotion. If it were an emotion, there'd be no need for you to come to me for lessons; you have enough of that, and to spare, yourself."

She stood seriously, trying to take his tirade good-humoredly, though his sarcasms stung her, especially as they were offered before Elinor Tilton. She thought that he did not seem to understand how hard it was for her to accustom herself to the way he wanted her to sing. There were a dozen technical details of breathing, posture, tone production, of which she had been completely ignorant a few weeks ago, and which she had to try to keep in her mind every moment of the time that she was singing; so that what usually happened was either that she concentrated on them and produced careful, uncertain, self-conscious tones, or else that she was carried away by the act of singing and forgot about them entirely. When she was at home, practicing alone, she usually succeeded in following his precepts, but during her lessons she grew more excited, with the result that she sang in the old way, which was more natural to her, and brought down his irritation on her once more.

Still there had been better days than this, days on which she had been able to see the light of approval in his cold, self-contained manner. This was simply one of the bad days, only she had not learned yet to take them philosophically; she went home every time that the lesson did not go well with the feeling that the earth was about to open and swallow up all her dreams of the future.

"Now you're as stiff as one of those absurd talking dolls," Tharp said to her, bitterly. "What *happens* to you? — good God! simply because of a word of criticism — Isn't that what you come here for?"

She stood helplessly, hardening herself in defense. He had said that she looked stiff, but now, in the lighted room, with the dark afternoon lying still and damp outside the windows, there was something almost a little dangerous, menacing, in her lifted head and lowered eyes, the lifeless fall of her arms with the narrow fingers slightly clenched.

"You look as if you'd like to kill someone — me, I suppose," Tharp added, as if a little startled.

"No — myself. Because I don't do it right," she said unexpectedly. She turned to him with sudden energy, her face flushing up. "I don't care what you say to me; you can say anything you like, as long as you keep showing me the way to do things—"

They did not understand each other in the least. He retreated a little before her passionate wish to learn, then the next moment looked offended at the idea which she had half-suggested to him, that she knew better than he what they were there for. She was too strong for him, but he was too experienced for her; they faced each other week after week with the prepared embattledness of two strange animals who know no more of each other than that they are hereditary antagonists — a cat and a dog in a disputed back garden. He grew to dislike her fervently because she examined with passion the set of convictions which he had assembled with calmness as his musical creed, and she would have given him back the emotion with double the force if she could have overcome her desperate feeling that he must be right in everything under dispute between them.

[72]

Christmastime came. They were having an employees' party at the Finn Company, and she was to sing carols in a quartet: it had got around the office about her lessons at the Institute, and Mr. Jergens, who was chairman of the entertainment committee, had come to ask her if she would sing. On the afternoon of the party she cleared off her desk early, before four o'clock, and went down the hall to change into the costume that she was to wear. When she opened the door of the women's lounge, Tottie Dunlop, who was singing soprano in the quartet, was already inside, examining her costume. She held up a page's short tunic, made of black cloth and trimmed with a narrow white collar.

"I wonder whose bright idea this was," she said critically. "I'm going to look like hell in this thing, don't you think?"

Ella shrugged. She had not been on good terms with Tottie since the afternoon at the pool; there was a strain of antagonism between them.

"We'd better hurry, anyway," she said; "it's almost four. I don't know what Mr. Jergens *will* say if we're not upstairs before the others come in."

She began to take her own tunic out of its box. Tottie glanced over at her with a slight, curious smile.

"Eddie's going to look nice in his costume, isn't he?" she suggested.

"Oh — I suppose so."

Ella slipped out of her dress; without looking at Tottie, she sat down on the couch and kicked off her shoes. Tottie stood watching her, arrested by her idea.

"Are you two engaged?" she brought it out suddenly. "People are saying—"

"No, we're not," Ella said quickly.

"Oh? Lots of people are saying—"

"It doesn't make any difference what they're saying."

Ella spoke a little violently; it made her angry that people could not let her and Eddie alone. She did not want to have to think what she would say if he asked her to marry him — a problem that, up to now, had not arisen; he had only said to her once that a man was a

[73]

fool to marry before he had his feet on the ground, unless he married a girl who could be useful to him in his career. Recently there had been times when she had suspected he might change his mind about this principle if she wanted him to, but she did not believe that that was what she *did* want; the feeling that things were never going to be between them as she had imagined they would in her first naïve anticipation was growing stronger in her every day.

She turned the conversation back to the Christmas party, and Tottie, though she still looked curious, did not continue on the subject of Eddie. A few minutes later, in identical costumes, but presenting a very different aspect — Ella slight and boyish-looking, Tottie more theatrical-appearing, and flaunting rather than masking her sex in the tight-fitting tunic and hose — they stood giving themselves a final hasty survey in the mirror.

"Now then, off to the wars," Tottie said. "They can't say we didn't try, can they?"

They went out into the corridor and back to the freight elevator, which they took to go up to the fourth floor. The elevator door opened there directly on a large, high-ceilinged storeroom that had been cleared for the party, and as they rose slowly they could hear the voices of the men who were completing the last-minute arrangements reverberating strangely in the empty room. Then their eyes rose above the level of the floor, and they saw the room, half-lit, in the gray light of the dark, snowy afternoon, by unshaded electric bulbs suspended from the ceiling. The rows of neatly ranged folding chairs, the Christmas tree in one corner, and the long, festively decorated wooden table on which were standing punch bowls and trays of sandwiches, seemed curiously impersonal and out of place in this setting.

As they stepped out of the elevator, a pale, dapper little man in shirt sleeves came hurriedly down the aisle between the rows of chairs to meet them.

"Now, girls — Tottie, Ella — you're all ready?" He looked them over quickly, running his right hand over his chin as he supported his elbow with his other hand. "Good — good! Now, remember,

[74]

you're to be behind the curtain till Mr. Finn finishes his address and I give you the signal. You'd better get over there now."

They walked up the aisle between the rows of chairs to the opposite end of the room, where there was a green curtain drawn diagonally across the angle of the wall, so that it cut off a small triangular space from the rest of the room. When they had reached the curtain it was pulled aside from within for them to enter, and they saw Eddie standing in the aperture.

"I suppose you lovely creatures know you're late," he said.

Ella, coming into the small windowless space behind the curtain, could barely make out the barrel-chested, thin-legged figure of Alfred Guandolo, the tenor of their quartet, leaning against the wall in the corner. The two men were both dressed, like the girls, in page's costume, Eddie very Elizabethan-looking, with his clean dark head and indolent manner, like a young favorite of the queen's.

"Maybe it wasn't worth it, was it?" Tottie said, stepping inside. "And we're not the last, anyway; where's Bertha?"

Ella pulled the curtain aside a little so that she could look out.

"Here she is now," she said.

A short, heavily built, dark-haired young woman, carrying a roll of music in her hand, came hurriedly up the aisle and approached the curtain. Ella held it aside for her.

"Hello, dears!" She was breathing in the quick gasps of a stout person after exercise. "Lord, I only just made it, didn't I? Mr. Jergens says the others are coming up now." She looked around at them curiously in the semidarkness. "Don't you all look nice!"

"Darling, we know it," Eddie said.

She gave him a little push, and he took advantage of it to shift his position so that he was standing beside Ella. With five of them now in the narrow space behind the curtain, there was scarcely room for them to change position without touching the curtain so that their movements would be visible to those outside.

"Stand still now," Bertha admonished them. "You know what Mr. Jergens said about moving the curtain."

"That's sensible of you, when you're the one who's pushing about,"

Eddie said. He moved still closer to Ella, and slipped his arm about her waist.

"Well, I *didn't* push you straight into Ella's arms!" Bertha said, smiling.

Tottie suggested, rather mocking: "You two might like to be alone, I suppose."

"And mightn't that just be an idea?" Eddie said, taking her up promptly.

He drew his other arm about Ella, turning her so that she was facing him. She stiffened slightly, and pulled away from him.

"Oh, Eddie, can't we stop that now!" she cried.

She spoke a little sharply; she felt that he wanted to display his proprietorship of her before the others. Bertha broke in, covering an awkward moment of silence: "Yes, Eddie — or do you want to send the poor girl out there to sing all hot and flustered?"

Ella stood hanging her head and looking aside as Eddie let her go and moved a step away. The others began to talk again. She glanced at Eddie after a moment and noticed with a certain defiant anxiety that he looked cool and strained.

While they had been talking, the room outside the curtain had begun to reverberate with the sound of footsteps and the clatter of chairs. Bertha pulled the curtain aside an inch or two, and reported that the others were arriving. They all grew more serious.

"Al, now, don't forget, we decided that in 'We Three Kings' you should sing the solo part in both verses," Bertha said to Guandolo, who nodded, standing in his corner where he had remained ever since the girls had arrived. He was a foreman in the factory, an earnest, hard-working Italian with a fine natural voice.

A few minutes passed, and the sounds from beyond the curtain died down to a subdued hum of conversation and the occasional scrape of a chair on the bare floor. Then there was a sudden burst of hand-clapping, which echoed loudly in the high-ceilinged room. Bertha, peeping out, whispered to them that Mr. E. J. Finn had come up to the front to make his welcoming speech. They listened, and heard the weak, womanish-sounding inflections of his voice as

he began to speak. At last there was the conscientious patter of applause that signaled the end of his talk.

"Now, you kids," Bertha said peremptorily.

She clutched her roll of music more tightly in one hand and with
the other lifted the curtain. She walked out and across the floor
toward the small upright piano standing at the opposite side of the
room. The four singers, following her, ranged themselves with the
disguised self-consciousness of amateur performers in a row facing
the audience, their faces coloring up almost simultaneously as they
stood confronting the interested smiles and stares of their fellow
workers.

Bertha began to play the introduction to "Good King Wenceslas."
The quartet was to sing a group of several well-known carols, each of
the singers being given an opportunity to do a part of one of them
as a solo. Ella's solo came in the fifth carol, "The First Nowell."
As the time for it approached, the embarrassment which she had
felt in coming out before the others in costume disappeared; she gave
herself up to the mood of the songs, her face taking on a grave and
concentrated expression.

Bertha played the introduction to her solo, and she sang:

The first Nowell the angels did say
Was to certain poor shepherds in fields as they lay . . .

The others joined in the chorus, and then she began to sing alone
again. Listening to herself, as she had learned to do since she had
begun studying with Tharp, she thought that her voice sounded
well in the big bare room. It was fuller, larger, than it had been a
few months ago, the upper tones managed with more assurance and
ease. She felt happy about it, having a chance to try what she could
do before an audience, and hearing the improvement that she had
made.

Her solo came to an end and, still in the mood of excitement and
confidence which it had produced, she sang her part in the remaining
carols. When they had finished, there was vigorous applause from
the audience. The four singers broke into smiles, and stood exchanging uncertain glances with each other. Then Eddie led the way back

across the front of the room to the curtain again. Bertha came in last.

"Listen to that," she said, as the applause continued. "Do you think we'd better give them an encore?"

But before they could come to a decision the applause had stopped. There was a momentary silence, and then they heard Mr. Finn's voice again, announcing that Saint Nick had arrived to distribute presents.

"Oh God, he missed his vocation," Eddie commented, in a bored, rude tone. "He ought to be teaching a kindergarten."

Ella, her excitement over the singing beginning to lessen, saw that he was not looking at her; he was still angry. She felt a little surge of irritation; it was stupid of him to act this way over nothing. She turned to Bertha.

"Who's playing Santa Claus?" she asked.

"Mr. Barstow. He does it every year." Bertha pulled the curtain aside a little to look out. "Come on now; I think we'd better go out and sit down with the others," she said. "He's up there now, and everybody's watching him."

Ella, slipping outside the curtain, saw Barstow, almost unrecognizable in his wig, beard, and red suit, standing beside the Christmas tree, calling out the names on the packages that lay beneath it. They were the usual inexpensive gifts given by each employee to another whose name he or she had drawn by lot. Under cover of this activity, the five performers quickly passed down the aisle and sat down wherever they could find a vacant seat. Ella, seeing an empty chair beside Inez Shoup at the end of a row toward the rear of the room, walked back and sat down. Inez looked over at her.

"You were marvelous, Ella," she whispered to her. "Everybody's been saying so—"

"Thanks."

Ella looked to see where Eddie was going to sit. There was a vacant chair just behind her, but he either did not see it or did not want to see it. Instead he passed in front of several people a few rows ahead in order to sit down beside Rita Dillard.

She turned her eyes resolutely to the front of the room, to Barstow, but it happened that Eddie and Rita were sitting in her line of vision as she looked in that direction, so that she could hardly avoid seeing what they were doing at the same time. They were whispering together, and Rita was smiling. She was wearing a pale-blue blouse and a darker wool suit, and Ella, seeing her looking so quietly well-dressed, suddenly felt that her own costume was tawdry and conspicuous. She sat restlessly, watching impatiently as Barstow distributed the presents beneath the tree.

Her own gift was one of the last to be given out. As she passed down the aisle with it from the front of the room, she looked purposely away from the place where Eddie and Rita were sitting. She wondered if Eddie was watching her, but when she reached her seat and glanced up at him, she saw that he was talking to Rita again.

Bertha went up to the piano again and began playing "For He's a Jolly Good Fellow." Everyone joined in the singing, which was directed at Mr. Finn. He made another brief speech, thanking them, and invited them to join him in refreshments.

The rows of chairs emptied quickly; everyone lined up around the long table.

"I think I'll go downstairs and change," Ella said to Inez, as they got up.

Inez looked at her with a curious smile. "Dear, you really must be upset," she said.

"Upset? About what?" Ella frowned, drawing her brows together.

"Now don't pretend you don't know," Inez said. "Eddie and Rita, of course." She smiled slightly once more. "What's happened? Have you and Eddie been quarreling?"

"No, of course not."

Ella looked down the long room, which was echoing now with loud talk and laughter. As the short December afternoon drew to a close, the lights and moving figures, the decorated table and the electrically lit Christmas tree, began to be reflected dimly in the long dusty windows. Inez went up to the table, but she did not follow her; she walked over to one of the windows and pressed her face close to the glass and looked outside. The snow had stopped falling, and the street below seemed bleak and remote, with the thin snow showing a cold bluish-white in the dusk. She felt lonely and moody, all her excitement gone in the feeling that things were wrong again between Eddie and her.

He was over at the table now, standing beside Rita, and after a little, seeing that he did not glance in her direction, she went over to the elevator and slipped down alone to the first floor. It seemed very quiet here, a little ghostly, after the talk and the lights and the excitement upstairs; the lost, depressing air of an office on a holiday clung to it everywhere. She went into the women's lounge and changed slowly out of her costume; when she came out again, a quarter of an hour later, and walked down the corridor to the general office, there still seemed to be no one about. But as she came inside the room, she saw suddenly that Eddie was standing in the half-light near the windows. He had changed back to street clothes too; standing there, he seemed to be waiting moodily for something or someone. She hesitated a moment, then came forward resolutely.

"I only came in to leave my costume," she said in a stiff, clear voice, determined not to be the first to speak of what had happened upstairs.

She laid the box down and turned around again toward the door. But he came forward suddenly, as if the sound of her voice had unleashed him from his position there by the window; he placed himself between her and the door.

"So that's all it is to you," he said. She could not see his expression clearly in the half-light of the room, but his voice sounded bitter; her heart went down. "And now you're going to walk out like that—"

She tried to be angry with him, but she could not manage it; she only felt tired, and upset, and sorry both for him and for herself.

"Oh, Eddie, *don't* begin with anything now," she said. "I'm sick of it—"

"*You're* sick of it? What do you think I am? I'm sick of everything; I'm sick of myself, and this damnable office, and that foul party upstairs—"

She stood in startled silence; she had never heard him talk just like this before.

"And you — damn it, does it hurt you to have people see that you care about me?" he said. "And now you're going to walk out like this—"

She roused to defend herself. "I didn't think you'd care whether I went or not. *You* were busy enough with Rita—"

"Naturally I was busy with Rita. Who else do I have to be busy with? You're too busy yourself to care who *I'm* being busy with—"

He looked so stubborn and unhappy, his face, always overexpressive, making itself felt even through the half-darkness, that she could not quarrel with him.

"Eddie, can't we *please* forget this?" she pleaded. "It's Christmas — or almost—"

"Everything's always 'almost' something," he said. But he quieted down; he looked soothed a little by her concern. "Let's get out of this place," he said. "I'll drive you home. Have you got your coat?"

"In a minute," she said.

When she came back with it, they went out together, down the echoing, deserted corridor, to the street that was chill and dim with the winter dusk. He started the car and they drove across town, through the streets where the lights were coming on and cars went sliding through the blackening slush that the fresh snow had already become. He drove fast, keeping moodily silent; the thought that their small misunderstanding had magnified itself to such importance for him made her forget that she too had been angry and upset.

"Eddie, what's the matter?" she appealed to him, after a little. "Is it just because of what happened at the party—?"

"That, and everything else. That, and people I don't like, and work I don't like, and someplace to live that I don't like." He glanced over at her. "Don't *you* ever get fed up?"

"You know I do. But, Eddie, it won't last — it *can't* last, for us. Some day —"

"It's always 'some day'; I want it *now,*" he said. "I'm twenty-four. How long does a person have to wait before he has anything at all just the way he wants it?" He was still driving fast, a little recklessly, along the street that showed itself, as the winter darkness came, a thin blue-white length stretching before them. "I suppose you know I was up for a promotion," he went on abruptly. "Well, I didn't get it; they gave it to that fool, Feltrep, because he's been there two years longer than I have."

She said, "No, I didn't know," feeling as she said it that something had happened inside her, a sudden realization that his mood had nothing to do, essentially, with her; she, her little snub at the party, had been something only incidental, added on.

He seemed to guess what she was thinking; he looked over at her.

"And then you —" he began.

"Oh, Eddie, you don't have to. I know it wasn't me."

"*What* wasn't you?"

"At the party. It wasn't about me that you really minded."

She sat somberly silent; she felt as if something had come to an end, without her wanting it to, almost without reason. The fact was simply there for her to take in, as if she had suddenly seen a picture of herself and Eddie, and had realized in an instant that it was all wrong and had been that way from the beginning.

"I don't know what you expect of me — of us," he said after a little, with his old bitterness coming back again. "Going off that way about Rita, for instance — you're damned lucky you haven't got anything more to complain about than that. I couldn't have had less to do with any other girl if I'd been married to you these past five months —"

"It's not about Rita."

She did not want to talk about it any more; but he would not let it go.

"If it isn't about Rita, then what is it?"

"I don't know; I don't care about that," she said, with intensity. "What I care about is that we're sick of each other; we are, really; nothing's turned out the way we wanted it, and now we're sick of it —"

He looked at her; she saw that he had not expected this.

"Don't be idiotic," he said sharply. "When I said I was sick of everything, of course I wasn't including you." He was silent for a little, looking at the road, not at her. "I supposed we were in love with each other," he said suddenly.

She shook her head. "I don't think we know what we are — not tonight, anyway."

"But you *were* pretty taken with me once, weren't you?" He was sulky now, angry at her evasion. "You used to follow me around the office with those green eyes of yours, before I'd hardly spoken two words to you — do you think I didn't notice?"

She felt the anger coming up again in her too. "It's nice of you to say that!"

"I'm not trying to be 'nice'; I don't feel 'nice.' I feel like murdering someone."

"So do I." Her greenish eyes glanced at him a little menacingly through the dark. "If you didn't want to take up with me, you didn't have to, you know," she said.

"And disappoint you by ignoring you? Darling, you have no idea what you looked like in those days, with those big green eyes, and all your lovely bones showing under your dresses that were always a little too large for you — like a stray kitten that hadn't been fed in a week. I'd as soon have thought of not giving it its saucer of milk, when it came asking for it so nicely—"

"Well, I've had my saucer of milk now," she said. She knew he had only said it out of pique; she held on to her temper coldly, as she might have done with a child that was being disagreeable. "So you needn't feel obliged to bother with me any more."

He glanced over at her. "You sound as if you'd be very happy if I didn't." She said nothing. "Would you?" he persisted. Still she said nothing. "Ella — damn, answer me! Would you?"

She only looked at him out of her pale, somber face. "Would *you?*" she turned the question back at him.

He slid the car violently around a corner.

[83]

"Well, if that's the attitude you take — yes!" he said. "I don't see why either of us should waste the other's time—"

They were only a short distance from Cobb Street. He drove concentratedly; the houses and trees flashed by, the black hatchings of the bare twigs blurring against the pale gray sky. At the door of her house he stopped the car and sat waiting.

"Well—" she said uncertainly. She pulled at the handle of the door, which he made no move to open for her. It swung open and she looked around at him. He did not say anything, and she stepped out of the car, into the thin December dark. "Merry Christmas," she said, tentatively.

"Oh, a very merry Christmas!" he said violently.

He put the car in gear and started it off up the street. Watching its lights diminish and disappear, she felt at once the desperation and the exultation of a lost traveler who, for the privilege of choosing his own direction, has just parted company with his solitary companion. It was only after she was inside the house that she remembered she had not given him the Christmas present she had bought for him, a scarf and glove set that was lying now in silver wrappings in her dresser drawer.

Chapter Six

THE taxi drew up before the house shortly after seven, and Anne Gunning, who was waiting in the fitting room in her best blue silk dress, dark hat, and plain spring coat, went outside quickly and over to the Wessens', to make sure that they had heard it. When Ella came out of the house a few moments later, carrying her music, a light coat thrown over the long white dress that her mother had made her for the recital, old Mrs. Wessen was already getting into the taxi, and the others were standing on the sidewalk, discussing how they should sit inside. Ella came down the steps, holding her dress carefully. The sidewalks were still wet from the heavy shower that had fallen an hour or two earlier, but as she glanced up she saw that the sky was almost clear. A vague greenish light fell from it on the darkening street. The air of the early May evening was fresh and damp.

"Elly! Come on now. We want you to get in next," Lillie called to her.

She was arranging everything, very brisk and smart in a new tailored suit, directing the driver where to go, deciding how they should sit in the cab. Ella bent her head, getting into the taxi. But it was all unimportant; she was tense, isolated from them and filled with life; the world beyond herself scarcely touched her. She saw her mother and old Mrs. Wessen, on either side of her, trying to arrange the folds of her dress, worrying that it would become soiled on the floor of the taxi.

"Mama, please let it alone; you'll make it worse," she said rapidly, turning her head.

"But doesn't she look nice? Like an angel — like a bride," old Mrs. Wessen said happily.

She clasped a tall old-fashioned ivory-handled umbrella on her lap, sitting very erect, conscious of her best black hat and garnet earrings.

"Only the groom is missing," Lillie said. She looked at Ella. "I've been intending to ask you — what's happened to Eddie Bernet lately?" she said. "I haven't seen him around for months."

"Well, I suppose we're both busier than we used to be," Ella said, quickly and coldly.

She did not want to talk about Eddie now; she did not want even to think about him. That was something that she had put behind her — the ugly friction, the humiliation of seeing him turn with such apparent satisfaction from her to Rita Dillard, the dead sense of failure, on her part or on his. It had been a failure, but she had accepted that; she had been amazed to discover that it was not even particularly important to her. Only she did not want to think about it, to have to examine it in her mind.

The cab ran on through the damp, lighted streets till she saw the dark buildings of the Institute before her. As the taxi stopped and they got out, Anne Gunning gripped her hand.

"Ella, you're all right? Sure?"

She saw her mother's plain, intense face in the half-dark, the direct, questioning eyes.

"I'm all right — *sure.*"

"We're going to be very proud of you," Anne Gunning said firmly.

Ella looked quickly away. It made her feel strange to see them all suddenly rather separate from her, and feeling the separation, a little strained and as if humble. She saw Ray Wessen, who had stopped behind to pay the driver, come up to join them.

"This is a big night for all of us, honey," he said to her. His face was serious, without cynicism. "Go in there and show them what you can do."

"Elly will do just as good as any of them," old Mrs. Wessen said proudly. "And she will look just as good too, just as good. There isn't any of them will have on a nicer dress."

She stroked the folds of Ella's dress with one red knotted hand quickly and carefully, drawing her fingers over the soft fresh material as if she liked the feel of it, but was afraid that she might soil or damage it in some way.

Ella watched them go in the door of the recital hall together, a tight-knit, slightly self-conscious group. Something touched her; she was ready to cry. But then it passed at once; at once she was again the intense, detached creature that she had become for the evening, living her own secret life, quite apart from the others.

She entered the main building by a side door, and walked quickly down the lighted halls to Tharp's studio. The door was open; she could see half a dozen young men and women in evening dress standing about inside. She knew two or three of them. Eddie was not there.

Elinor Tilton came over to her.

"Hello," she said. "Don't you look lovely."

She was wearing a black dress and silver slippers. Ella felt awkward and badly dressed beside her. Her own dress, made in a schoolgirlish fashion with a loose bodice and short puffed sleeves, was becoming to her, but in an odd, quaint way; the effect it gave was not the sort that had been striven after by the other girls. Still it did not really matter. She stood in the background, listening to the others talk.

After a little, Eddie came in. He seemed to know everyone; she noticed that he made a point of it to say something to each of them that made it appear as if he were particularly interested in them. At last he came over to her.

"You look very nice," he said. He was a little short, rather offhand. "I've never seen you in a long dress before."

She took in his thin figure in evening clothes, everything about him carefully well-turned-out.

"You look very nice too," she said to him. "The people at the office ought to see you now."

[87]

"Maybe they will. I've asked a few of them to come tonight — Rita and Tom Jergens and his wife, only the ones who like music—"

She knew without his saying it that he had come with Rita. Something in his tone, the confident satisfaction of his manner, seemed to scorch her with humiliation. So he had spoken of her once. But she would not let him see her bitterness.

Tharp came to the door, resplendent in evening clothes. He was genial and composed, the pillar of experience about whom the others clustered for advice and comfort. The time for the recital to begin was coming near. Ella watched him as he stood in the hall outside the door leading to the stage, giving last-minute instructions to the girl who was to sing first, a plump frightened blonde in a blue dress.

"Remember you're not going to a fire," he said sternly. "Take your time, take your time. Elinor" — he turned to Elinor Tilton, who was standing beside the blonde girl, holding her music, and ready to go out on the stage with her — "see that she doesn't hurry the tempo too much."

"All right, Mr. Tharp." Elinor was not in the least excited; this was an old story to her. Her matter-of-fact manner was soothing to the frightened girl. "Ready, Bess?"

They walked out on the stage, and Ella, standing at the doorway, heard the polite applause that greeted them, and saw Bess Rogers duck a nervous bow, while Elinor went straight to the piano and sat down. She flushed with elated excitement, watching them.

"Now, Miss Gunning," Tharp said to her, "you're next, you know."

She listened, nodding her head as he cautioned her again on the manner of attacking a high note at the climax of her first number. He looked at her without smiling, apparently a little surprised by her self-confidence. Then they stood silently listening to the music from the stage.

"Isn't Bess a darling?" Alice Gorham whispered to Tharp. "I do love the way she turns her head when she sings—"

He turned around, smiling, and talked to her for a minute or two in a low voice.

Bess finished her songs, and came off the stage smiling and relieved, going out again twice to respond to the applause.

"That went well enough," Tharp said, smiling at her as she came back for the last time. He put his arm around her paternally and patted her shoulder. "You'd do better if you weren't always so frightened."

"Well, I can't help it," she said, pouting happily.

Ella, growing serious as the moment came for her to sing, stood waiting for Tharp to give her the signal to go out on the stage.

"Nervous?" Elinor Tilton said to her, smiling.

She shook her head. "No, I don't think so."

"All right, Miss Gunning," Tharp said.

She cast a rapid glance down at her dress, straightened her shoulders, and walked quickly out upon the stage. She had rehearsed her songs there on the previous Saturday afternoon, but now it was as if she were stepping into a world of strange new dimensions and sensations, filled with brilliant light and space, and breathing with the subtle sounds of an attentive crowd of people — small rustlings of programs, whispers, expectant respirations. A feeling of intense personal power suddenly flowed through her whole body. Every atom in her seemed magnificently alive and responsive; the music she was to sing welled up in her as if it were the spontaneous expression of her own emotions, rather than a succession of notes which she had learned.

She hardly heard the patter of applause that greeted her as she came forward to take her place before the piano. Joining her hands lightly together before her, she stood for a moment breathing deeply, with a serious expression on her face. The audience seemed a mere blur of upturned faces to her. She turned to nod to Elinor, and then she heard the opening chord of the recitative introducing her first number, and gathered her breath to sing.

The audience saw a slender, dark-haired girl in a rather stiff white dress standing in singer's posture — head up, hands clasped, shoulders carried boldly so that the deep, firm breasts were defined clearly against the thin cloth of the dress — in the curve of the long concert grand piano. She was singing an air from an early English opera, Purcell's *Dido and Aeneas* — the lament of the dying queen, as brief and hauntingly simple as an old song out of Shakespearean tragedy:

> *When I am laid, am laid in earth,*
> *May my wrongs create no trouble,*
> *No trouble in thy breast . . .*

The grave, pure voice sent the quiet notes out over the little hall, darkened to a more moving appeal —

> *Remember me, remember me . . .*

then leapt effortlessly up to the final poignant cry —

> *Remember me, but ah! forget my fate.*

The music died away in the slow somber chords of the piano.

There was a startled, appreciative silence, then a sudden wave of applause. Ella, a little dazzled, coming from the stillness, the grave, archaic music, to the lights, the audience, the clapping hands, bent her head; she looked almost imploringly at Elinor Tilton, as if asking her to begin the next number at once. She was confused, her vibrant calm already beginning to desert her; she could feel her hands trembling as she clasped them together again before her.

She was to sing an aria from "The Messiah" next, "O Thou That Tellest Good Tidings to Zion." Tharp, taking advantage of the un-usual flexibility of her voice, had assigned her the somewhat florid air, but she sang it now as the student sings, conscientiously, with no real insight into the meaning of the music, concentrating on correctness, on remembering all that she had been taught in technique and interpretation. Still there was the voice, full, thrilling, springing from the throat as from a well of pure sound. When she had finished there was again enthusiastic applause. She found herself ducking a bow as hasty and unpremeditated as Bess Rogers's had been, then hurrying off the stage before Elinor. Tharp stopped her and turned her around.

"Where are you going? They haven't finished with you yet," he said.

She went out again on the stage. But then, in a moment, it seemed, before she could collect herself, it was over. A young man whom she did not know was going out with Elinor on the stage; she heard the notes of the piano once more.

She looked at Tharp, radiant, a little dazed, for his opinion. There was an unaccustomed genial light of approval in his agatelike eyes.

"You don't sing like that at your lessons, Miss Gunning," he remarked.

He was not used to novices who did better before the public than they did when they sang for him; usually nerves, self-consciousness, overambition, took their toll.

"The Purcell, of course," he went on, "was a little overdramatic; I've warned you before—"

He was speaking to her with only half his attention now, listening to the music from the stage beyond. She stood looking at him, half-stunned by the casualness with which he dismissed her, her exaltation fading. Bess Rogers came up to her.

"I thought you were wonderful," she said, sincerely. "You didn't look a bit nervous when you were out there. Weren't you frightened? I was just frightened to death."

She asked Ella if she knew Alice Gorham, and the three of them stood in a group together, listening to the music from the stage. The singer, Madsen Hess, had been studying with Tharp for years, Bess explained; he was singing a group of Brahms *Lieder* now in an earnest, throaty tenor. Ella stood listening to them gossip a little about him, and then about where they were going to spend the summer. They seemed to be much more interested in discussing the comparative advantages of Maine and Colorado than they were in the recital that was going on. Her feeling of triumph dwindled more and more; even now, in the very midst of the recital, they seemed to place so little importance on singing and so much on those parts of their life which she could not share. They did not really know or care whether she had done well a few minutes ago, out there on the stage, and perhaps the other people who had heard her were just as indifferent. She felt her confidence in herself crumbling. It must be that she was not good enough, she thought, or she would have made more of an impression on everyone.

Madsen Hess finished his songs and, smiling and mopping his face with a handkerchief, came back into the corridor and over to talk to Bess and Alice. He was a stout young man in his middle twenties, with tightly wavy brown hair and an embarrassed, genial manner.

"Let's go out front and listen to Alice and Maxine," he said to Bess, after the two girls had congratulated him. "You're on right after Bernet, aren't you, Alice?"

"Do you want to come along?" Bess asked Ella. She was a kindly, homely girl.

"Oh, yes — all right," Ella said.

She felt lost and cold with all these people whom she did not know; the evening was lapsing into a dreadful time of utter futility and defeat for her.

"You don't know Ella Gunning, do you, Madsen?" Bess said cheerfully, as they walked along together to a side door by which they could slip unobtrusively into the recital hall.

He acknowledged the introduction in his polite, embarrassed, formal manner. But she kept aloof. She was not interested in him; she was sunk in the misery of her own failure.

They entered the recital hall in the interval between Eddie's songs. Ella saw Lillie, who had noticed her come in, lean over and speak to the others to draw their attention to her. She smiled at them quickly and sat down.

Eddie had begun his second number, an aria from a Haydn oratorio. She sat listening, gradually drawing out of herself to watch him with a lingering and nervous intentness. She was so used to seeing him intimately, at close range, that looking at him now, separated from her by the gulf between audience and performer, she felt almost as if she were watching a stranger. She looked with a fascinated critical detachment at his thin figure, his smooth dark

[92]

hair, and his clear-featured face, wondering what there was about him that had attracted her to him. He was nice-looking, but she felt that that had not had much to do with it; it was something that she had made out from the beginning about his inner self, an instinctive desire on her part to ally herself with a nature that, like her own, was sensitive, ambitious, and awake to the sensuous appeal of life. She realized dimly for the first time that what had aroused her feeling for him was something that had very little to do with personal affection; it had been a blind groping for similarity in a narrow world in which everyone else had seemed quite dissimilar. Their personal relationship, apart from this underlying basis of similarity, had never been a satisfactory one, largely, she now saw, because the things that had drawn her to him were not at all the same things that had drawn him to her. He liked her determination, the hard ground of her ambition which made her instantly appreciative of the things he was trying to accomplish in life; but these qualities had been comparatively unimportant to him in the face of his wish to proceed with her into a relationship that had nothing to do with them.

She sat listening to him now, watching almost with irritation the way his chin dropped and tightened as he took a low note at the end of the aria. But he was not really important to her any more; there was only that dead sense of failure inside her when she looked at him, and a hard, blind feeling of resistance.

After him, Alice Gorham came out on the stage. Her pleasant, commonplace lyric soprano left Ella feeling dull and impatient. She could not endure this sort of mediocrity, merely conscientious and well-trained. Something in her felt violated; her world of music was made less purely perfect. She wanted to get up and leave the hall, but she could not; she must sit through the whole.

But her attention roused itself again when the last of the group, a tall, stunning blonde named Maxine Neel, who wore a flame-colored dress and had her hair drawn in a heavy knot behind her ears, came out on the stage. Ella had seen her several times before, in Tharp's studio, and knew her by reputation: she was soloist in one of the large churches, St. Jude's, and did a good deal of radio work besides, so that she was well known in the city. Her voice was a florid mezzo-soprano; she began with a pair of arias from Mendelssohn's "Elijah" and "St. Paul," the sort of thing that had established her reputation at St. Jude's, and followed them with Rossini's *Non più mesta,* which she sang with a good deal of confident brilliance. Ella, listening tensely, comparing her own amateurish stiffness on the stage with the other's professional, smiling ease, noticed however that her intonation was not always exact, and that she used her voice as if it had been a big, resonant instrument, without much regard for nuance or expression. Still it was impossible not to respond favorably to its confident roundness, and to her smiling, friendly, imposing figure. Her group of songs was greeted with a storm of applause, and she had to return to the stage several times before the audience was satisfied to let her go.

When she had disappeared for the last time, Ella followed Bess Rogers and Madsen Hess back to the corridor beyond the stage. Tharp was there, with the others: the audience had already begun to flow out here. A tall, elderly woman in a large hat, a black dress, and silver-fox furs, came up to her after speaking to Alice Gorham and introduced herself as Mrs. Tharp.

"I enjoyed your singing so much, Miss Gunning," she said. She had a very cordial smile. "We haven't met before, I believe; I always like to know all of Hobart's pupils, but I've been away so very much this year."

Ella made her some response. But she noticed that Mrs. Tharp's attention was already a little absent; she was smiling over Ella's shoulder at someone behind her whom she knew. Someone else came up and spoke to her, and she moved away. Ella, a little at a loss, stood looking around for her mother and the Wessens. She saw Eddie talking to Rita and Tom Jergens and his wife. When she turned back quickly from looking at them, Hobie Herschel was standing before her. She had not seen him come up.

"Gunning," he said to her. "Ella Gunning." His sharp eyes went right through her. "My God, where has Tharp been hiding you?"

He seemed excited. Seeing him standing there, regarding her as alertly as a terrier, she felt all at once something in her own dark, vital self rousing again after the prolonged misery of the evening.

"Hiding me?" she said. "But he hasn't — he didn't —"

She smiled, rather dazzled, in pure confusion.

"He didn't teach you to sing the Lament like that, either," Herschel said. He looked at her shrewdly. "Your Handel, now, was pure Tharp; you hadn't any more ideas of your own about it than you'd have had about a Chinese newspaper. Had you?" he asked her, point-blank.

She stood considering for a moment. "No," she said. "I suppose I hadn't."

"But the Purcell was a different story. I've been sitting in there all evening wondering if I really heard what I think I did. If you've got a quarter of an hour to spare, I'm going to find out."

He was so quick, so definite, as if he absolutely anticipated no opposition and would brook none if it came.

"But my mother — my friends —" she began.

"Where are they?" He glanced around, as if he expected to pounce on them just behind him. Ella saw them then, standing near the door with some of the Cobb Street neighbors who had come to hear her. "Go over and tell them to go on without you," he directed her.

He stood waiting impatiently till she returned.

"Now then," he said, "I want Carla to hear you; we'll go on down to her studio."

She was too confused to gather that Carla was his wife. Only when they had gone the length of a long, half-dark corridor in one of the new wings of the building and he had pushed open the door at the end, she realized that the woman inside was Mrs. Herschel. She was playing something with three men — violin, viola, cello — two of whom Ella knew by sight: the stout, middle-aged violinist who always spoke to her when he passed her in the hall, and a tiny mustached French cellist. The third, the violist, she had never seen before; as he glanced quickly up from his instrument at the moment that she and Herschel entered the room, she had an impression of a pair of alert, vital dark eyes and a firmly set mouth. The four went on playing as they came in, and Herschel motioned her to a chair, perching, himself, on the window sill. The room was quite different from Tharp's studio, bare and utilitarian, with only a piano, a music cabinet, and some straight chairs for furniture.

She sat in a corner watching the intent faces of the four performers, and listening to the music. She had never heard a string quartet before, and something in the bare simplicity of the music produced by the four instruments rather repelled her. She felt somehow as if she were being shown the beautiful, delicate skeleton of music, stripped of all its color and human warmth. But she was so strange here, set down silently in the room with these unknown people; she could not really attend to the music. Only she knew that it was disturbing to her — the bare, vibrant string-tones, the swift, unceasing flow of countermelodies.

It ended; Herschel sprang up from his perch on the window ledge. "I thought you were going to wait till I got back," he said. He lit a cigarette, peering through the smoke at the sheets of music on the rack before his wife's chair. "Very reactionary," he remarked. He grinned over at the violist. "Tell you what I think about it later, Max. It's damned good."

"I'm not interested," the violist said. He had a final-sounding, definite voice that would not waste words. Still he was pleased about it; he was smiling slightly. He was younger than the others, in his early thirties, with something hard and confident and alive in his rough-cast face, with its dark, vital eyes and calm mouth. "I'm through with it," he said. "You tell me what I do next, Hobie."

"What you do next," Herschel said, "is to listen to this young woman sing." He looked at Ella. "Do you know these people? — Huisman, Dessieux, Tallan—" He nodded round at the three men. "They're not going to eat you up; stand up here now and sing the Lament for them."

He sat down at the piano, opened the music which she had brought with her, and struck the chord that introduced the recitative. But she was still confused, unready. Her strongly marked brows fell unconsciously in a half-frown.

"Hobie, for heaven's sake," Carla Herschel protested, "give her a minute to get her breath." She had a long, plain face that looked as if it might have been formidable, but the expression on it was friendly and matter-of-fact. She got up and went over to the piano. "You haven't even told us her name," she said.

"What difference does it make what her name is?" Herschel said impatiently. "It's Ella Gunning, if you have to know." He looked up at Ella again. "Are you one of those young women with nerves?" he asked her.

She stood there, half-frowning still. She did not understand why he had brought her here, what he expected of her. She was intimidated, too, by her audience; there was something detached and good-humored and skeptical in their waiting silence. And there was Herschel sitting at the piano, waiting too, dropping ashes from his cigarette onto the keys.

"Listen, Ella Gunning, are you going to let me down?" he asked abruptly. *"Somebody* sang that Lament out there like a risen angel—"

He touched the chord gently on the piano again. She raised her eyes, lifted her shoulders in a deep breath; all at once, scarcely knowing herself a moment before that she would do it, she sang the opening phrase of the recitative:

Thy hand, Belinda, darkness shades me . . .

The first notes were taken almost in half-voice, but once she had begun it was all clear again. She sang as she had sung earlier at the recital, the grave notes lifting, returning, rising to the poignant —

Remember me . . .

dying to the gentle close. When she had finished there was silence for a moment; then Herschel turned around sharply from the piano.

"Well?" he said.

He looked triumphant. Carla Herschel said, "My God, yes, Hobie, it's a voice," and the silent little cellist said something quickly in French. Ella felt oddly as if, for the moment, she had stopped existing for them as a person; they spoke of her voice as they might have spoken of an instrument, as if she had actually no more connection with it than a violinist with his Stradivarius. Herschel was saying, "And *that's* what Tharp's trying to put through his mill — turn out a good, solid church soloist when he's finished—" He swung back to Ella. "What the devil made you go to that old woman?" he demanded. "If you had the sense God gave you about that voice of yours—"

She stared at him. It had never occurred to her that there was anything about Tharp's method of training her voice that was open to criticism. Something in her roused, as if vindicated; she glanced from one to the other of them, questioningly. They were all interested and excited; only Max Tallan, the violist, kept apart, watching her, seeming in some way set in opposition to her. When she looked at him, she had the feeling of running against something that rang as sharply as steel to the impact.

Herschel drew the story from her of how she had come to study with Tharp. When she told him that she was working at the Finn Company, he said, "Well, we'll have to do something about that," as definitely as if it were already settled, whether she wanted it to be or not. She felt as if her life had suddenly been swept away from all its old moorings. And gradually the exultation came up in her. This was what she wanted. In the bare, narrow room, with these unknown people, she was in her own element; she was discovering a part of herself.

They wanted her to sing again, and she did the Handel for them, and Schubert's *Du bist die Ruh'*, and then Herschel rummaged through the music cabinet and came out with an old volume of Schumann's *Dichterliebe*. She read through some of the songs with him, *Im wunderschönen Monat Mai*, and the one following, *Aus meinen Thränen spriessen*, standing beside the piano in her stiff white dress, singing the lovely, simple melody —

> *Im wunderschönen Monat Mai,*
> *Als alle Knospen sprangen,*
> *Da ist in meinem Herzen*
> *Die Liebe aufgegangen. . . .*

[98]

She read German without difficulty, because she had been familiar with the sound of it from childhood through her association with the Wessens, but she did not understand all she read; she looked inquiringly at Herschel before she began the song. He translated roughly for her, in his dry, matter-of-fact voice: "In the lovely month of May, as all the buds burst forth, love came up in my heart: in the lovely month of May, as all the birds sang, then I confessed to her my yearning and longing."

They went over the song several times together, till the bare walls of the room seemed full of it. The windows were open; the spring night air came in soft and chill and bitter.

"Oh, I could sing that all night," she exclaimed, as they came to the yearning, unsatisfied ending once more. She repeated the last phrase softly, without the piano —

> *Da hab' ich ihr gestanden*
> *Mein Sehnen und Verlangen.*

Her eyes fell on Tallan; he was looking at her intently. She felt that there was something inescapable about those alert, deep-set eyes. And she was half-frightened, yet full of exultation. Something was happening between them; some connection had established itself. She was scarcely concerned about it; it was all a part of the music that rose and dipped and returned inside her, the music that was in the walls, and in the bitter spring odors of the night air, and in the faces of the people about her. Nothing of her ordinary self, of her ordinary life, seemed valid here. It was as she wanted it to be, something she had been looking for as long as she could remember. Only she was half-frightened when she felt his eyes upon her. She did not want anything but the music; she did not want to be involved.

Later the Herschels drove her home. It was past midnight; the streets were quiet. She felt already as if she had known them for a long time; she had told them the circumstances of her life as she had never told them to anyone else. They had even guessed, somehow, about Eddie.

"You're not going to marry that Sunday baritone, are you?" Herschel had asked her, in the car.

She shook her head. "Oh, no. He — we — " She colored up in the dark, not knowing quite how to put it for him. "He's not even interested in me any more," she said at last, bluntly.

"Good! I suppose there's not much use telling you not to start that business with anyone else, but remember, you're going to have to work, and work like the devil, if you want to put that voice where it deserves to be. You've got a job cut out for yourself without taking on any complications."

"There won't be any complications," she said definitely.

She was sure of that now; there was nothing that she wanted now but the music. She sat watching the dark streets roll past, and the whole silent spring night was music to her, nothing but the music shouting inside her, aching and bursting to be released.

Chapter Seven

SHE heard nothing more from Herschel till the following week, when he telephoned one evening to ask her to stop in and see him at his office at the Institute the next day, after she had finished work. She went over, not knowing at all what to expect. When she arrived, it was almost six; the corridors were empty as she walked along them to his office. The door to that was open, and there was a light on that showed the crowded, uncomfortable, untidy room — the upright piano in the corner, piled high with music, newspapers, manuscript scores; the narrow walls covered with snapshots and inscribed photographs of a bewildering variety of famous and not-so-famous opera singers, musical comedy actresses, instrumentalists, and conductors; the heavy bookcases; the desk with its litter of ash trays and papers. He jumped up from behind it as he saw her standing in the doorway, and came around to her quickly.

"Hullo!" he said. "Here you are." He looked her up and down. He was no taller than she, and his keen little eyes, gazing straight into hers, gave her the feeling that she was being summed up, measured against a previous impression. "Sit down," he said. "I want to talk to you. Can you find a chair?"

It was not the easiest thing to do; the only empty one was the one behind his desk, where he had been sitting the moment before.

"What's wrong with that?" he asked, seeing her looking at it. She sat down. He swept a pile of music off the chair before the piano and took that himself, glancing around for an ash tray, finding none immediately at hand, and ending by letting the ashes of his cigarette drop to the carpet. "All right; let's get down to business," he said. "How much do you make a week, Miss Gunning?"

She looked at him, a little startled. But it did not occur to her to feel embarrassed about discussing her financial situation with him, as she had been with Tharp.

"Fifteen dollars a week," she said.

"Fifteen a week? Good! I want you to quit your job."

He slapped his pockets for cigarettes, found them, and lit one from the glowing stub in his mouth before he glanced up at her; it did not seem to have entered his head that he had said anything unusual.

"But I couldn't—" she began, protestingly.

"Why couldn't you? I can't guarantee you a regular fifteen a week — Lautenheim, chap that has this little Lutheran church, can't afford more than ten a Sunday for his soloist — but people in this town haven't given up getting married and buried yet, thank God, and the better-heeled ones don't object to handing out ten or fifteen dollars to have things done up properly with 'I Love You Truly' or 'Oh, Promise Me.' We can steer you into quite a clientele here; you ought to make out at least as well as you do over at that office of yours."

She could not quite take it in; she only stared at him, half-frowning, afraid that she might somehow have misunderstood him.

"Then we'll see about your getting a full scholarship here in September," Herschel went on. He did not seem to notice or care that she had not spoken; he went his own headlong, energetic way, as if quite regardless of her. "There shouldn't be any trouble, with that voice of yours. It's about time you began to learn something about music besides how to open your mouth and sing. You'll have your courses in theory, piano, languages — And I'll see what I can do about Tharp. He hasn't any business handling a voice like yours; oh, he's sound enough, but as unimaginative as a bishop. He won't do any harm to the Madsen Hesses, but he'll take a good deal out of you if you stay on with him long enough. I'd like to see you working with Madame Collier-Brown—"

She sat there in the brightly lighted, crowded little office, with the early dusk gathering outside the windows, and listened to him rearranging her life in his impetuous, dictatorial way. And the excitement she had felt on the night of the recital came up in her again. It seemed to her as if there were some irresistible destiny in her life, which in spite of everything would find a way to its end.

Herschel wrote down for her the address of Mr. Lautenheim, the minister of a Lutheran church in an old, predominantly German section of the city, and told her that he had made an appointment for her to sing for him the following evening, at eight. His present soloist was going to be married in a few weeks and leave the city, and he was looking around for someone to fill her place.

"I don't think you'll have any trouble convincing him that you're the one for the job," Herschel told her. "Those Germans know a good voice when they hear one; they aren't taken in by a lot of fake musical sophistication, the sort Maxine Neel gives her fashionable crowd over there at St. Jude's. And you'll have a choir behind you that'll be teaching *you* something if you're not on your toes. A good many of them belong to some *Gesangverein* or other, and some of them have sung in the Spring Festival chorus for years—"

She was excited about it; she came and stood beside him as he wrote down the address for her. She wanted to thank him; still there was something in her that rather superbly took it for granted that, having recognized her, he should want to do these things for her. He seemed to sense that; there was a wry admiration in his glance as he said good-by.

"Carla said I'd caught a Tartar," he told her abruptly. " 'Sensitive, emotional, but with the devil's own determination.' She told me you wouldn't let go once you'd taken hold of something."

"I want to sing; that's all that matters," she said. She stood facing him, looking, in her plain dark coat and felt hat, like any one of a thousand other young business girls whom he might pass on the street, going home from their day's work. But there was something in her eyes, some tense confidence and determination. "I don't care how hard it is; I want to do it—"

She went home to tell her mother and the Wessens what had happened. They had all been impressed by the interest that Herschel had taken in her on the night of the recital, but they were not in the least prepared for her sudden announcement that he wanted her to leave the Finn Company for what seemed to them the wholly precarious living she could make through her singing.

"Yes, it *sounds* fine," Lillie said skeptically, "but how do you know how permanent that's going to be over there at the church, for one thing? And it seems to me that it's a pretty risky business to rely at all on anything as chancy as those other engagements. You've got a good job now, that a hundred other girls in this town would jump at the chance to get tomorrow, and I think you ought to hold on to it. If you can get the church job too, so much to the good; I don't see any reason why you can't hold them both down, if you want to."

They were all sitting in the Gunnings' little parlor: Lillie and old Mrs. Wessen had come over just after dinner to hear what had happened, and a few minutes later Ray had dropped in too. He sat looking at Ella with a slight frown on his face, listening to the others talk. Anne Gunning, too, was rather quiet; she had not committed herself one way or the other. But there was a new expression in her eyes when she looked at Ella. It was an expression at once of pride and of fear, as if she realized that Ella was going beyond them now, making a life of her own without need of them.

Her silence, and Lillie's outright objections, ended by driving Ray to flare up and lose his temper with them.

"My God, anybody else would be proud of the kid," he said. "She can make those people over there at the Institute sit up and take notice, but all she gets from her own family and friends is a lot of drivel about whether the job is steady or not. You people don't seem to realize, Elly's going someplace; she's got big things in front of her—"

"She won't have anything at all in front of her if she doesn't eat," Anne Gunning said brusquely. "I don't want to think of these things any more than you do, Ray, but you must realize, people don't always live up to their promises. Suppose things don't work out the way Dr. Herschel says they will. Will it help Ella's career then for her to be out of a job?" She turned to Ella. "Why couldn't you do as Lillie says," she asked, "and try to keep both jobs, at least during the summer, till you see how things work out? Then, in September, if you get the scholarship and are making enough with your singing, you can give up your job at the office—"

That was how it was decided, that she would stay on at the office till the end of the summer, till there was some certainty that matters would really turn out as Herschel had planned them. She could not blame her mother for her caution; she knew that things had been going badly for her that year in the shop. Some of her old customers had died, or moved out of town, and there were no new ones; it would have meant disaster to them just now if Ella's salary had been cut off too. And she knew that Herschel would understand the situation. There would not be a great deal of point in her leaving the office till September, at any rate, since she would not be studying at the Institute during the summer.

She went over to see Mr. Lautenheim the following evening. He lived in a big, old-fashioned house beside his plain brick church, and was waiting for her with his choir director when she arrived. The choir director, a German named Hassler, almost seventy, with the slow, deliberate martinet-manner of an old-fashioned music master, looked her up and down, shook his head, and sat down at the piano to play her accompaniments. She felt cold and nervous; Mr. Lautenheim too had an unsympathetic, formally polite manner, and the room in which she stood was of an almost institutional bareness and severity, with a virtuous odor of floor wax and furniture polish about it, and long lace curtains shutting it away entirely from the spring night outside. She had brought some of her own music with her, but Hassler laid it aside on top of the piano without so much as glancing at it, and handed her an old, broad-leaved, black-bound *Choralbuch* instead.

"I can tell more about your voice if you sing one or two of these first," he said bluntly. "Then you can show off with your fancy pieces."

She looked down at the page he had opened for her, reading the simple German words of the old chorale —

> *Gott, der Vater, wohn uns bei*
> *Und lass uns nicht verderben. . . .*

She had heard Mrs. Wessen sing it a hundred times, without knowing what it was — an old German litany, which Martin Luther had adapted. She put the book down, and nodded to Hassler to begin.

She loved the bare, strong melody, with its grave pauses and naïve, triumphant conclusion —

> *Amen, Amen, das sei wahr!*
> *So singen wir Hallelujah!*

The whole room seemed to fall into place as she sang: the cold walls might have been those of a sixteenth-century church; the strongly marked faces of Hassler and Lautenheim sprang straight back to the old German towns from which they drew their blood. When she had finished, Hassler sat still for a moment; then he shot around on his revolving stool and looked at her.

"They didn't teach you to sing *that* at your Institute of Music," he said, as if accusing her.

She shook her head. "No, I've known it a long time, as long as I can remember."

"But you're not German?"

She shook her head again. "A German friend of my mother's taught it to me."

He only grunted, still looking at her suspiciously. After a moment he began glancing through the music that she had brought, and asked her to sing the aria from "The Messiah" that she had given at the recital. He had an odd, old-fashioned way of playing, with back and elbows held stiff, and a good deal of dry precision in his fingerwork, in the outmoded German style. But she was more at home, singing the aria here, than she had been in the concert hall at the Institute. It seemed to belong here, and it went well.

She looked from one to the other of the two men when she had finished. The minister sat with his finger tips precisely joined, but there was an expression of satisfaction on his face.

"What do you think, Mr. Hassler?" he asked.

The choir director turned around to him.

"I like the voice," he said grudgingly. "Fit for the service of God — Not like the last one those fine musicians at the Institute sent round to you—" He stood up and looked threateningly at Ella. "A coloratura, she called herself; nothing but shrieks and twitters came out of her when she opened her mouth—"

Ella understood that she had been accepted. Mr. Lautenheim asked her to sit down, and they explained to her about the rehearsals, the music she would have to sing. Later Mrs. Lautenheim brought in coffee and homemade apple strudel. The two men unbent a little then, and the atmosphere in the room became more comfortable. They told her about the choir, and about the Bach cantata that they had given at Easter. They were both very proud of the music that was given in the church. She began to feel that she would enjoy working with them.

The next afternoon, Saturday, after she had had her lesson with Tharp, she stopped in at Herschel's office to tell him about her success. She was pleased with herself, and elated; he looked at her with his little wry smile.

"You're on top of the heap already, are you?" he asked.

"No, but it's *something*. You don't know what it's like, having people think you're such a *fool*, to waste your money and your time on singing. Now they're not quite so sure of themselves."

She had enjoyed her triumph that morning at the office, when she had told the others what had happened. Since her break with Eddie, the other girls, who had been somewhat jealous of her, had not lost the opportunity to parade the fact of his interest in Rita Dillard before her. They could not believe that it had been as much her doing as his, that she no longer went out with him, and she had fallen a point in their esteem. But even Eddie had been impressed that morning. And it had soothed her pride to feel that.

It had not been very pleasant for her in the office during the past few months.

While she was talking to Herschel, his wife put her head in at the door to ask him something about some grades.

"Why don't you come out to the house this evening?" she said to Ella, with the same abruptness with which her husband always plunged into a subject. "We're having some chamber music; three or four of the other boys and girls are stopping in."

"I'd like to," Ella said.

"Good! Around eight. Do you know the address? Hobie'll give it to you."

She vanished from the doorway.

"Out of your line, I suppose you think," Herschel commented, to Ella. She had the feeling that he liked her, and that at the same time he was quite apart from her, as if she had been some sort of spectacle that he was watching. "My God, I'd like to turn out a singer just once who knew something besides *Tristan* and *Traviata*," he said. He wrote down the address for her. "You come tonight and keep your ears open," he said. "There's no law that I know of against a singer's listening to chamber music."

But it was not for the reason that he had suspected that she had seemed to hesitate over accepting the invitation. If there was to be chamber music, she thought it was possible that the same group would be there that she had met on the night of the recital, in Carla Herschel's studio. She thought it was possible that Max Tallan would be there, and there was something in her that did not want to see him again. The feeling she had had on that night, that some relationship had established itself between them, though they had scarcely spoken a word directly to each other, was still strong inside her, like a burden put on her that she was impatient of carrying. She did not know what she had to do with him, with his good-humored, rather ironic manner and direct, inescapable eyes. From what she had heard on the night of the recital, she had gathered that he taught composition at the Institute, and that he was a composer himself; it was his quartet that they had been playing when

[108]

she had come into the studio with Herschel. And the music, too, had been incomprehensible to her; nothing in her had gone out to meet it. She had stayed apart from it, repelled and a little angry, as one is over a too difficult problem that one is expected to solve. Her life seemed very clear and simple and shining before her just now; she did not want anything to break into it with confusion or doubt.

The Herschels lived only a short distance from the Institute, in an ugly, comfortable Victorian house set far back on a long lawn behind an ornamental iron fence. When she came up the walk, a few minutes after eight, the windows were open to the cool rainy May night; she could hear the voices inside. She recognized Herschel's, which sounded pleased and excited.

"My God, this calls for a celebration," he was saying.

She rang the bell, and Carla Herschel came.

"Come on in," she said. "We're having big doings. Max has got a Stephenson—"

Ella had no idea what she was talking about. She followed her into the living room. There were eight or ten people: Huisman and Dessieux and Max Tallan, and some younger people whom she did not know. Tallan was taking his viola out of its case; he went over, struck an A on the piano, and began to tune his instrument. He was the only one who did not seem excited.

"You ought to go to Paris, Max," Herschel said. He was very definite about it. "That's the place for you; you'd be in touch with all the new ideas. Get you out of your rut—"

Tallan shook his head. "No Paris," he said. He was equally definite, smiling his slight, good-humored smile.

"Why not? What's the matter with Paris?"

"Too complicated, Hobie. I think I'll go to Vienna."

"To Vienna? What the hell's in Vienna now?"

Tallan, smiling still, did not answer.

"Well, you can always get a good glass of beer there," Huisman said. He laughed, calling over to Carla Herschel. "What about that, Carla?" he asked.

Everybody looked at her and Ella, standing there in the doorway.

"*After* the music," Carla said firmly. "As a matter of fact, there isn't a drop in the house. One of you people will have to go out and get some."

She went across to the piano and began looking through some music that was scattered over it. Ella remained standing in the doorway. She had seen Max Tallan glance over when Huisman had spoken to Carla Herschel. He was still looking at her now, standing there beside the piano with his viola under his chin while with his left hand he deftly manipulated the pegs, touching the bow gently to the strings as he brought them into tune. There was an expression of recognition, of communication, in his eyes. She felt herself imprisoned somehow by that steady dark gaze. She turned away and went over to Herschel.

"So you came," he said, with a quick nod of greeting. "You know all these people, don't you?"

She looked with her rather savagely shy glance at the other young people, one or two of whom she had seen in the halls at the Institute.

"They ought to know *her,* if they don't," Huisman said. He came up and put his arm about her shoulders. "The rest of you may turn out to be nice, solid musicians some day, if you practice your lessons and say your prayers," he told them, "but here's a young lady who's going to make herself very famous—"

She felt uncomfortable, standing there beside him. The other young people were a clique, a group in themselves, and though they were very polite she knew that they did not want her here. She guessed that they were familiar in the house as protégés of the Herschels, and that they did not want anyone else to supersede them. And they were a little jealous because Huisman had set her above them now. She liked Huisman, his blundering cheerfulness and good humor, but she wished that he had not spoken so about her.

Carla Herschel called to him from the piano.

"Hugo, stop dallying with Ella and come over here; we need your vote. Hobie wants to hear Max's quartet, and Max says we promised to play the 'Trout' Quintet—"

"Come on, Max, don't be so modest," Huisman said.

"I'm not modest. I'm sick of the damned thing."

"You're sick of everything as soon as you finish it, and before you finish it nobody can see a note of it. You'll never have any public if you go on like that."

"All right, I'll never have any public. Come on and sit down and play the 'Trout.'"

Huisman picked up his violin.

"We'll send him out for the beer after a while, and let John play viola," he said to Herschel; "then we can have the quartet and he won't have to listen to it."

"It's a deal," Tallan said.

Ella watched them settle themselves in a group about the piano, where Herschel had seated himself. A tall boy in spectacles and a girl with short-cropped dark hair made room for her on the sofa, and she sat down beside them. She glanced around the room. It reminded her, in its general untidiness, of Herschel's office; there was a big Steinway grand in the middle, with music strewn all across the top, and the rest of the furniture was simply pushed back against the walls in a haphazard way, as if nobody had ever thought to arrange it either fashionably or conveniently. Still it was a very nice room, comfortable and with a kind of cheerfulness about it. It was a room in which it was hard for anyone to feel formal or shy.

The others subsided at once into perfect silence as soon as the five began to play. Ella sat listening, but not really listening inside; she was too excited to settle down to the music. It was not what she wanted just now, the lovely, formally organized composition. The wet spring night air, blowing the curtains at the windows, made her desperate to go out to it. She felt that something was happening to her, that there was some fierce battle to be fought inside her, and she did not know what it was. Only she knew that she could hardly endure to sit there quietly, seeing Max Tallan's eyes leave his music and without hesitation find her out across the room. She felt mistrustful and defiant, pinned there in her place by the music, where he could not fail to find her.

[111]

The intricate, happy variations of the last movement came to an end. The listeners sat in pleased silence; the Herschels' brusqueness discouraged compliments.

"Next time don't rush us through those variations at such a rate, Hobie," Carla said. "What's your hurry? We've got all night."

Herschel turned around. "I thought it was just about right. What about you, Max?"

"Ask Hugo. I never interfere in family quarrels," Tallan said. He stood up and laid his viola and bow on the piano. "How about that beer, Carla?" he asked. "How much do you want?"

"Oh — enough for the crowd. The delicatessen down on the corner of Chestnut will be open. You might pick up something for sandwiches too. Get Hobie to give you the money."

"Never mind; I'll get it myself." He turned around and looked over at Ella. "How about coming along with me?" he asked her.

She was taken completely by surprise; for a moment she only stared at him. There was something matter-of-fact and civil about the way he stood there waiting for her. She knew before she answered that she would go. It would have been a little awkward, refusing. Still she knew that that was not the reason that she was going. She wanted to get outside, but that was not the reason either. She did not know, really, why she was going, but she knew that it was not for either of those reasons.

She got up and went out into the hall with him. She found her coat, and he went to the door and opened it. It had stopped raining; only the heavy drops were still falling slowly from the trees.

"Do you mind if we walk?" he asked.

"No."

She stepped out before him and he closed the door.

"It's a fine night," he said.

He looked down at her, not quite smiling. She felt as if he were waiting for something, watching her intently as if for some response. And she kept stubbornly aloof. She began to talk to him about what she had heard inside, taking a sort of satisfaction in hearing her own composed voice, rather proud of herself for appearing so collected.

"What were they talking about inside when we came in?" she asked. "Are you going to Europe?".

"Yes. I've got a Stephenson Fellowship for next year."

She felt a sudden envy, thinking what it would be like, to have the chance of going to Europe.

"I'd like to go some day," she said. "I'd like to study there."

"Well, that's not necessary any more. You can get good teachers right here in the United States today."

She glanced over at him. "But you're going."

"Yes. It's one of the conditions of the fellowship." He looked around at the dark street they were walking along. The sky overhead was perfectly black, and the houses were blurred masses under it with lights pricking through, and the smell of the wet spring night fresh and chill all around. "If I had my way, I'd stay right here and get in a real year's work — no new people, no traveling around — Where do people get the idea nowadays that a man can't write music in his own back yard? My God, look at this street now; look at this town. I'm not going to find anything in Paris or Rome that's going to say something better to me than they do right now."

She did not understand it; the sky was only the sky she had known all her life, and the streets had no magic of strangeness for her.

"Have you been there, to Europe?" she asked him.

"Ten or twelve years ago, in the early twenties. After I got out of college, I had the Paris bug, like a lot of others. My grandpop wrote me a letter after I'd been over there a couple of years. 'For the love of God, Max,' he said, 'a lot of people like your father and me had sense enough to come over to this country and give you the chance to be born in it and live in it; now don't you be a big enough damned fool to go right back in that mess we started from.' Or words to that effect, in German; he didn't come over till it was too late for him ever to feel very comfortable with English. I thought he had a good idea; I haven't changed my mind about it since."

[113]

She looked over at him, at his dark, rugged, clearly defined features, the mouth firmly set, but with a curious suggestion of the classic ogee-curve in its lines.

"You don't look as if you were German," she said suddenly. "Or as if you were a composer, either."

He laughed. "Austrian. And only on my mother's side. I look like my dad; he was Cornish. And it comes natural to write music, even if you don't look the part, when you've got a bandmaster for a father, and a grandfather who played the bass fiddle under Mahler. The kids in my family played musical instruments the way a carpenter's kids play with tools; my grandpop never did think of music as anything but a good honest trade."

She was half-offended to hear him speak so; music for her existed in a region quite removed from the everyday realities of life.

"It *isn't* a trade," she protested. "How could it be?"

"No, it isn't, but it'd be a good thing if there were more people who thought about it that way — as a decent, ordinary way to make a living — instead of as something apart — The best art's always been founded on that sort of humility; the builders of the great cathedrals, Shakespeare, Michelangelo, Mozart — none of them had an idea of doing anything more than a damned good piece of work—"

She walked on with her head bent a little, almost in antagonism. She did not believe what he was saying; she did not believe that it would ever be that way with her about music. She listened while he told her about his grandfather, who had brought him up after his father had died, when he was ten; he had played the double bass at the Vienna State Opera and later at the Metropolitan till he was past seventy, and had taught for almost ten years after that.

"Did you live in New York then, while you were growing up?" she asked him.

"Yes."

She glanced over at him again. "And don't you want to go back?"

"Why should I? I like this town. I was born here; we all lived here, till my father died."

She could not understand it, his rejection of everything that she wanted so much for herself. He seemed to bound her dream-world with a hard ring of reality.

They had turned down Chestnut Street, where the trolleys ran; the tracks gleamed wet under the black sky. The old brick houses, set flush with the sidewalks, ran down the hill. She saw their yellow doors and clean, severe stoops.

"Look at this, now," Tallan said. He stopped a moment, glancing around him. "A thousand people go by here every day and never realize that they're looking at something wonderful and beautiful. Nobody's ever told them it is, so they don't believe it. They can go all over the world and they'll never smell anything just like this air tonight, with the lilacs in it from that old bush there across the street, and the rain, and the wet bricks. The only trouble is, they don't know it. They don't know that if you want to write music it's got to come out of something like this, and not out of someplace with a French name, that you haven't got in your blood—" He caught himself up, smiling. "I don't usually talk this much," he said. "Why didn't you stop me? Come on; we'll get that beer."

The delicatessen was on the corner, a little dark place with a few cheeses and some sausages in the window. There was nobody inside but an old woman in a black dress and sweater, who talked to them with a German accent. They got the beer, and two big loaves of rye bread, and several different kinds of sausage.

"How about some cheese?" Tallan asked.

"No cheese," the woman said.

"What's that in the window?"

She grew excited, and went into a long explanation, half in English and half in German: the cheeses in the window were not real cheeses, but were only for display.

"All right," Tallan said. "You win. No cheese."

He looked over at Ella with his slight smile that was more in the eyes than on the lips. There was something good-humored and definite about him that she liked. But always there was that feeling of something hard and inescapable that she was not ready to understand. When she felt his eyes on her, it was always somehow as if there were nobody there but the two of them, as if there were no one in the world for him to look at but only her. It was no use not being alone with him, because they were alone every time she saw him looking at her like that.

They left the delicatessen and walked back up the street the way they had come. They were not talking now. He was carrying the beer and the sausage, and she had the two loaves of bread. After a while he said to her, "I hear Hobie's got big ideas about that voice of yours."

"Has he?" She felt a little self-conscious and wary, talking to him about herself.

"I don't blame him. You've got the real thing. You know that yourself, I suppose."

"I don't know anything — yes, I do," she contradicted herself suddenly, almost defiantly. "I've always known; I've known as long as I can remember."

"Well," he said, "it's quite a life. I hope you know what you're getting into."

"I know I'm getting into what I want."

She walked on a little faster; she was in a hurry to get back to the house. There was something about him that made her feel uncertain, unsatisfied; it was as if she had been walking straight ahead in a narrow path, and suddenly he was showing her a whole new world outside that path. She had never felt like this before; she could not bear to have her certainty invaded. She would not talk to him any more about herself.

When they got back to the Herschels', they were playing the last movement of his quartet. She sat down to listen, determined in herself that she would not like it. She recognized the themes now, the strong, brilliant one that rushed up in ascending scales to its sudden climax, and then gave way to the introspective polyphonic weavings that had confused and displeased her the first time she had heard them. Tallan had gone back to the kitchen with the things they had brought from the delicatessen. She could not put the two together, somehow, the man she had just been walking with and the man who had written this music.

Afterwards Carla went back and made sandwiches, and they all sat around eating them and drinking the beer that she and Tallan had brought. Huisman asked her to sing, but she refused. She did not believe that any of the younger people cared to hear her, and she did not want to sing before Tallan now.

"Nerves," Huisman scoffed. "You're too young to have them, my dear."

He was growing very paternal and affectionate with her; when they broke up, he offered to take her home in his car.

"She can go with me," Tallan said. He looked at Ella. "You won't have to walk," he said. "There really is a car out there."

She told him that she would go with Huisman; he had said that he was driving out in her direction. Afterwards, in the car with Huisman, she was sorry; he talked all the while, with a good deal of heavy-handed joking, telling her stories about things that had happened when he had been playing in orchestras under Mengelberg and Stokowski. She was not interested now; she wanted him to be silent. She could not have believed, a short while before, that she could fail to be interested in what he was saying, but it was so. There was something inside her that needed resolving; she wanted to be alone, to get back alone to her old single certainty about herself, that had nothing to do with anyone outside her.

Chapter Eight

THE summer came on: the term at the Institute was drawing to a close. On the day of her last lesson with Tharp, Herschel had left a message for her to see him in his office. She went down the corridor to his door. It was open, as usual, and he was sitting behind his desk, which had all its drawers open and the contents half spilled out.

"Look at this mess," he said, when he glanced up and saw her standing in the doorway. He jumped up, slammed a couple of drawers, and looked for his cigarettes. "Where did anybody ever get the idea of giving me this damned job, anyway?" he said. "I'm a musician, not an executive."

She was not upset by his ill humor. He was always excited, or angry, or in a hurry over something; it was simply the tempo at which he lived.

"Mr. Tharp said you wanted to see me," she suggested.

"Did I? Oh, yes — sure — it's about the summer opera. I thought I had hell's own drag with De Meyer and could get you in the chorus, but it didn't go; he can't afford to take up time with anyone who's quite as much of an amateur as you are. Pity you've never done anything in Italian; that, and your general greenness, were a little too much for him to take together—"

She was so disappointed that she lost her reserve; an almost challenging flush came up in her face.

"Why didn't you find out before?" she asked. "I could have learned enough; I *am* good at languages."

He glanced at her wryly. "It's not the worst thing in the world that ever happened to you," he said. "We'll see about it next year;

that's time enough. In the meantime, you ought to be hearing all the opera you can. Some of our girls here do it by ushering; you can go out and see Bernie Healy, at the Woods, about it. I'll give you a note—"

He rummaged around in his desk, found a sheet of paper, and scribbled a few words on it.

"That ought to do it," he said. "It's not the best company in the world, but it's not the worst, either, by a damned sight; they know what they're doing out there. Most of them have sung abroad, or with the New York or Chicago companies; they're not the big names, but they're no well-meaning amateurs, either."

She was still a little angry at having missed her chance. She stared down at the piece of paper he had given her as if she were going to crush it in her hand the next moment and toss it away.

"What's the matter?" he asked, watching her. "Don't you want to do it?"

"Of course I want to do it. Only I want to be *in* it more. *I* know I could do it—"

He shrugged. "That's lesson number one, then, that you've got to learn: it's never enough to *be* able to do something; you have to have the proper credentials to make other people *believe* that you can. Look at Max Tallan: there isn't a composer in America today who has more to say and knows better how to say it, but he's got about as much talent for building himself up a reputation where it counts as Johann Sebastian Bach had. He'll be lucky these days if he ends up as well as Bach — with twenty kids, a decent job all his life, and somebody to discover what a great composer he was a hundred years after he's in his grave."

She did not want to talk about Max Tallan. She stood there frowning at the paper in her hand.

"I *hate* wasting time; that's what it is," she said. "I'm eighteen; if I can't sing in the chorus now, how long will it be before they'll give me even the small parts—?"

"Oh, you'll go ahead like a house afire, once you get started; don't worry about that!" Herschel said. "The big thing is to be ready for it when it comes. Don't think you can't learn a lot this summer, just by keeping your eyes and ears open. They've got Jenny Grove out there for the mezzo parts; you couldn't have a better model to watch. She's a natural actress and a natural voice, so it doesn't matter if she hasn't an idea in her head how she gets her effects. If you can learn to do what she does with your head instead of only with your instinct, you'll be the leading mezzo at the Metropolitan before you can look around — which is where she'd be today if she had a little more musical intelligence and enough ambition to get down to work."

He told her as he sent her away that he and his wife were having a few people to dinner at the Carlsburg Garden the following Saturday evening, and that they wanted her to come. She had again that sense of a kind of danger to something in herself in being a whole evening in company with Max Tallan, who was certain to be there — a danger to her dream, perhaps, which Tharp's coldness, Herschel's bluntness, and the doubtful criticism which it faced at home, left intact, but which he had somehow the power to touch. Each time that she had seen him, since that evening at the Herschels', she had been conscious of his encroachment on her life, even when they spoke only a few words to each other. Still there was no excuse for her to stay away, no rehearsal for her church work that she could plead. She thanked Herschel and said that she would come.

The Carlsburg Garden was not far from Ludlow Woods, where the summer opera company had its theater. It was not a pretentious place: older people went there who remembered the good food and good beer that it had served in pre-Prohibition days, and that it now was able to serve again; and it was a favorite with the opera people during the summer, because they all knew Otto Carlsburg, the proprietor. When Ella arrived on Saturday evening, she found the lights already on in the garden behind the restaurant, and Herschel and his wife sitting at a big round table in one corner, with Huisman and Dessieux and their wives, and three or four of the younger people whom she had met at the Herschels'. She noticed at once that Max Tallan was not there.

"I'm late," she said. She went straight up to the table and spoke rapidly and brusquely; she was shy, as usual, of entering a large group, and protected herself with her aloof air. "I'm sorry; there was a jam on McKinley Street bridge—"

"It doesn't matter," Carla Herschel said. "We still have to wait for Max; he's even later. Isn't there a chair somewhere?"

Ella sat down. But Herschel was pointing out to her a handsome young woman in her late twenties, who had just come in with two older women and a man in a brown sports jacket, and was sitting down at a table on the other side of the garden.

"That's Jenny Grove," he said. "Come on over with me. I want you to meet her."

She got up silently and followed him across the garden. It had happened so suddenly that she did not have time to be excited. When they came up to the other table, she saw at once that everyone knew Herschel, and he introduced her to them quickly. They were all singers from the opera company except one of the older women, who was the wife of the man in the brown sports jacket.

"I wanted Ella to meet you, Jenny," Herschel said. "I couldn't say this to many prime donne, but you're a nice girl, so you won't want to scratch her eyes out when I tell you that in a couple of years she's going to do everything you do even better than you do it now—"

Jenny Grove looked up at Ella. She was extraordinarily handsome, Ella thought, in spite of her clothes — a printed chiffon dress, rather mussed and very short, a pair of high-heeled mauve satin sandals, a good deal of jewelry, and a blue velvet coat that was flung carelessly over the back of her chair. Her jet-black hair, blue eyes, and beautiful deep-breasted figure made her look as if she were either Irish or Spanish — actually she was a combination of both, Herschel remarked later. Ella liked her at once, though she was not at all her idea of what an opera singer ought to be: she was comfortable, friendly, commonplace; only the speaking voice was full and lovely and mellow.

"If Hobie says so, you really must be good," she said. "Hobie's the one who always knows."

"Don't flatter me," Herschel said. "If you thought so much of my opinion, you'd follow my advice once in a while. You'd work, you would — damn you, anyway, with a voice like yours, not to get everything there is to get out of it—"

She only laughed; she was perfectly good-humored before his tirade.

"I *do* work, Hobie; didn't they tell you I'm doing *Fidelio* this season? We're opening with it tomorrow; Jake has been putting me through an awful time—"

"It doesn't lie right for you; you're a fool to do it," Herschel said bluntly. "If De Meyer wants to do *Fidelio*, let him find the right voice for it, and not ruin yours because you're too good-natured to say no to anybody."

She shook her head, smiling still. "It won't hurt me. I really have the range, you know."

"You'll find out if you have it after a few years more of that kind of business."

The others wanted them to sit down, but Herschel said they had come over only for a moment; they had to get back to their own table.

"We've been waiting for Max," he said.

Jenny Grove laughed. "I haven't seen him since last year; he promised to write me an opera with a mezzo role that wasn't an old mother, a villainess, or a lady's maid. Has he done it?"

Herschel shrugged. "Max doesn't write for voice; he's too intellectual. He's done a damned fine string quartet, if that's any good to you."

He went off, taking Ella with him.

"I can't talk to her; it makes me see red every time I look at her," he said, walking back with her to their own table. "She's got the voice, all right, only she won't work with it; let her be a horrible example to you. And, my God, where does she find all that junk she puts on? She looks as if she'd robbed every five-and-dime store in town."

They went up to their own table. Max Tallan was there, sitting beside Carla Herschel.

"Hello, you bum," Herschel said. "So you finally got here." He pulled out a chair for Ella and then sat down himself. "We've been over talking to Jenny," he said. "She wants to know what about that opera."

"What about what opera?" Tallan said. He looked across the table at Ella.

"The one you promised to write for her," Herschel said. "With the mezzo role that wasn't an old mother, a villainess, or a lady's maid."

"Most mezzos look like an old mother, a villainess, or a lady's maid. What's the complaint? That's just good casting."

"You go over and tell that to Jenny."

"Thanks. You tell her. I want to live a little longer."

"And what about Ella, a couple of years from now?" Herschel went on. The waiter had begun to bring the meal, now that everyone had arrived; there was a good deal of talk and commotion at the table. "She's going to be pretty bitter about it when you leave her with nothing to sing but Fidès and Azucena," he said. "Or do you think she looks like an old mother too?"

"She looks like a naiad," Hugo Huisman put in. "Is that what I mean, Hobie? A *Wassernymphe*—"

"That's close enough," Herschel said. "Can't you write an opera with a good part in it for a *Wassernymphe*, Max?"

He was in a good mood tonight; the year at the Institute was over, and he did not have it on his mind any more. Ella sat there without saying anything, but she could feel the color coming up in her face. She wished that Herschel had not brought her into his conversation with Tallan.

"I'll do better than that," Tallan said. "I'll write a part for her in the new symphony."

"I don't believe it," Herschel said skeptically. "You wouldn't stand for a voice meddling in with your precious wood winds."

"Wait and see," Tallan said. He looked at Ella. "Will you sing it, if I do?" he asked her directly.

She colored up still more, glancing quickly at Herschel, as if to discover from him whether she was to take Tallan's words seriously.

"But could I?" she asked, as much of him as of Tallan.

Herschel did not meet her glance. He was staring, a little oddly, at Tallan.

"Damn it, I think you really mean it," he said.

"Why shouldn't I mean it?" Tallan was still looking at Ella; he had not taken his eyes off her face. "Is it a deal?" he asked her.

She was a little dazzled; there was a flame of pure excitement in her eyes.

"Yes," she said. "I'd love to."

"Where's your artistic conscience?" Herschel joked her about it. "I thought you didn't like the stuff he writes."

He seemed a little uncomfortable, as if he were putting on his bluntly jesting air to cover over some sudden disturbing perception. Ella turned to him quickly, her brows drawing together in slight resentment.

"Oh, I never said that!" she accused him.

"No, but you've got a very expressive face," Herschel said dryly. "My God, you're like all the rest; you'd perjure your immortal soul for three bars to sing."

Tallan looked at him with his direct, pleasant gaze.

"Take it easy, Hobie," he said. "You're beginning to sound a little bitter yourself."

"Hobie thinks you and Ella would make a poor combination. Musically speaking," Huisman said, grinning. They had all got hold of something by this time.

Ella could feel her cheeks burning; she was furious with all of them, impartially. As Herschel had said, she had an expressive face, and there was something so somberly, almost dangerously, unconciliatory about it now that Huisman gave it up and began to talk about the weather. She had an idea that they had all been having a joke with her, Tallan included, and she sat looking down at her plate while she ate, not talking to anyone. They began to discuss their plans for the summer: the Herschels were going to their cottage on the Little Buckeye River, just outside the city, and the Huismans were going to Michigan. Tallan was sailing for Europe in a week or two, and Dessieux and his wife talked about traveling east with him; they were going over to France to visit their people there for the first time in five years.

"You come along with us, Max," Madame Dessieux said to him. "I have a little *cousine* who will be just right for you — eighteen years — and she can cook!"

They were not going to let him off. Apparently it was seldom that they had the chance of catching him out like this, and they intended to make the most of it. But he said nothing; he would not rise to their joking. When Huisman, who had induced Madame Dessieux to go out on the little dance floor with him, said to him, "You'd better brush up on your waltzing too, Max, if you're going to Vienna; why don't you ask one of these nice young ladies to dance with you?" — he looked over at Ella at once.

"All right. What about that?" he asked her.

She found herself getting up automatically. The next moment she was out on the dance floor and his arm was around her waist, holding her lightly and firmly as he stood looking down at her.

"Do you know how to waltz German-style?" he asked her.

She nodded silently; she had had her first dancing lessons waltzing with Ray Wessen, round and round the little parlor on Cobb Street to the notes of old Mrs. Wessen's treasured music box. But she could not trust herself to say that to Tallan. At the first touch of his hand something had happened to her; a wave of darkness swept over her; some sudden knowledge of him seemed to press on her in great quickening waves. It was as if everything else had melted away — the people, the tables, the music, the lights that hung quietly

[125]

overhead against the still night sky — and had left her standing there alone with him. She shivered slightly.

"Are you cold?" he asked.

"No. I—"

She could not answer him. She put her hand in his and they moved to the dance, suddenly sweeping off together across the floor. She could feel the living pressure of his arm about her, drawing her into the close orbit of his being, as if he were adding her identity to his, making a single entity of their separate lives, their separate wills. And it was like a madness to her; she refused in herself, like a wild thing, to be absorbed. She wanted to be free of him, to assert her own identity, free and single and independent. Yet all the while she swept in responsive movement to each movement of his body; her white dress whirled and fluttered, her feet traced automatically the wide circles of the waltz. Neither of them spoke; it was as if they kept up a silent, stubborn duel between them.

The music ended, and they went back to the table. The tall boy with spectacles, whose name was Robert Font, asked her to dance. She turned to him from Tallan without speaking. He had long thin hands that clutched her a little desperately, a long thin body that moved conscientiously as they danced. She felt as if she had turned from life to a kind of death. It was intolerable to her, his bony, desperate hands and flat, eager voice telling her what fun he was having; she moved woodenly, holding herself separate from him.

He wanted her to dance again; he followed her back to the table, persistent and hopeful.

"No," she said. "No, I feel—"

"Oh," he said solicitously, "is anything the matter? It does make you a little dizzy, doesn't it?"

She sat down and he stood over her; she could not rid herself of his earnest attention.

"*Is* there anything the matter, Ella?" Carla Herschel asked.

Tallan, who was sitting opposite, pushed his chair back suddenly and got up.

"It's all right," he said. "I'll take her home."

He did not wait for her consent; he came around the table and stood beside her.

"Oh, couldn't I take her home?" Robert Font asked. "You don't want to leave the party yet, Mr. Tallan."

"No," Tallan repeated. "It's all right."

He stood waiting. She was conscious of Carla Herschel's eyes on her, watching shrewdly. She got up quickly.

"I'm sorry," she said to her. "I've had a wonderful time."

"We'll take that for granted." Carla smiled at them, nodding her head. "Now go along, you two. Robert" — she turned to Robert Font — "if you *must* dance, you may dance with me."

She pushed back her chair and got up, drawing him away across the floor. Ella looked at Tallan.

"We'll go out this way," he said to her, briefly.

She walked beside him to the garden door. Outside, the street was dark and quiet, with the music of the band coming with an odd, sad, remote gaiety, as if from another world.

"Are you all right?" he asked her.

"Yes. I didn't have to come away."

All at once she wanted to go back to the others; she felt as if she were walking toward something dangerous and irrevocable, going to meet it out of a compulsion stronger than her own will. She stopped suddenly on the sidewalk.

"*Could* we go back?" she said to him.

He looked at her attentively. "Is that what you want to do?"

She shook her head in indecision, regarding him out of darkened, almost tragic eyes.

"Oh, I don't know what I want to do!" she exclaimed.

She followed him across to his car; he opened the door. But when he had got in beside her, behind the wheel, he took the matter up again.

"I thought that was just what you did know," he said to her. "Isn't that what you told me that night at the Herschels'?"

"What do you mean?" she asked. She was a little startled, but still somber.

"You said you wanted to be a great singer; you said you were getting into exactly what you wanted."

She saw the dark streets passing beside her, and she felt as if she had never seen them before, as if they existed in some reality quite outside the reality of this moment.

"Yes," she said to him. "That's true. But that — hasn't anything to do with this."

He glanced over at her quickly. She saw his face in the dark, the rough-cast features, the decisive mouth.

"Hasn't it?" he asked.

She felt defiant. "No," she said. "It hasn't."

She would not give in to his nearness; she turned her head and looked out the window, at the passing streets, at the sudden lights. She could feel her body tense against the cushions of the car.

"It won't be enough for you," he said after a little, in his quick, final-sounding voice. "You ought to know that now — that you can't live on crowds and applause and exhibitions. You can't make a whole life out of that."

She turned to him suddenly.

"Why shouldn't I make a life out of it? Other people do. And I've never wanted anything else — never! You can ask anyone who knows me. It's something I've *got* to do—"

She broke out with it vehemently; for the first time she lost her reserve with him and spoke freely, with the old crude passionate ring that Tharp knew, and Eddie, and Anne Gunning. Tallan looked at her quickly. They were in a dark, tree-shaded street, with houses set behind iron fences and high clipped hedges. He brought the car to a stop. And she felt him turn to her, his hands bringing her close, his mouth set on hers in a kiss that was set on her like a seal, deep and hard, setting a seal on all of her life. She moved her head aside doggedly, but it came again; she felt as if she were dying beneath it, a part of her dying forever, something of herself that she would never have back again.

She heard him breathing quickly over her, and then she was free of it; they were separate again, two strangers sitting side by side in a

[128]

car on a quiet, tree-lined street. Neither of them spoke. Someone was passing in the dark, coming nearer, the sound of footsteps coming nearer but remaining always in that reality outside the dimensions of their reality. She shivered a little and drew herself away, into the corner of the seat.

"I don't want to stay here," she said to him. "I want you to drive me home."

She did not try to understand how she felt; it hurt her to think, as it might have hurt a creature to breathe that had to learn how to live in a strange new element. He started the car in silence, and they drove off down the street. After a little he said her name, but she turned on him at once, almost furiously.

"I don't want to talk to you," she cried. "I don't want to!"

His face changed. He drove faster, concentrating his attention on the driving, as if he had to do something with intensity. When they got out to Jeffersonville, she had to tell him how to go to reach her home, and she spoke in a hard, clear tone, as if she were speaking to an enemy.

"You turn down the first street to the right."

"Is this it?"

"Yes. The house is halfway down the block."

He stopped the car before the house, and got out to open the door for her. But she did not wait for him; she was already standing on the walk when he came around.

"I'll see you inside," he said.

"No. You needn't bother. They're still up."

There were lights on in the house. She turned from him suddenly and ran up the steps. The house door was unlocked, and she went inside without turning to say good night.

Her mother was in the fitting room, still working. She glanced up inquiringly as Ella came in.

"You're home early," she said. Her clear, observant brown eyes, behind the spectacles that she wore when she was sewing, looked quietly at Ella. "Is anything wrong?"

"No. I — was tired; I wanted to come home."

She looked around the homely little room, with its sewing machine, its old yellow sofa, its outmoded fashion plates on the walls, with a sense of sudden, overwhelming relief, like a child waking out of a strange dream to recognize the familiar walls of its own room. Anne Gunning continued to regard her quietly.

"Did somebody bring you?" she asked. "I heard a car stop."

"Yes. It was Max Tallan."

She said the name, but it was something out of that other reality; it had no validity in this room. Anne Gunning laid her sewing down and stood up; she put thimble and thread into her workbox.

"He's a good deal older than you, isn't he?" she said, thoughtfully and brusquely. "If he's teaching over there at the Institute—"

Ella had turned to the door of the parlor, but she whirled quickly about at her mother's words.

"What difference does it make to me how old he is?" she cried angrily. "I haven't anything to do with him."

"Haven't you?" Anne Gunning said. She looked at her with a faintly ironical gaze. "Do you think I don't know what it is?" she asked, after a moment. "Do you think it never happened to me?"

Ella stared at her, half-furious, half-frightened. The thought that there had ever been anything between her mother and her father but the vague history of hatred and suffering that she knew had preceded their separation had never occurred to her. And she *would not* admit to herself that she had entered into a world where such things as had happened to her mother might happen to her; she *would not* have the shining simplicity of the path before her darkened and confused. She went into her own room and shut the door; she would not hear another word from anyone that night.

The next day, Sunday, she went about very clear and bright, as simple as a child absorbed in its own intense occupations. In the morning she sang at the Bay Street Church, pleased with the sound of her voice lifting in pure, throbbing sound above the congregation, pleased with the bare walls of the church, with Hassler's gray head bent over the organ, and Mr. Lautenheim's stern, prosaic sermon. She went home to dinner, and afterwards, in the little parlor, she sang for her mother and the Wessens, some of the old German ballads that Mrs. Wessen had taught her when she was a child.

"There's nobody sings them like you, Elly," old Mrs. Wessen said.

She had tears in her eyes, sitting there in a corner of the room; and Ella felt the artist's triumphant happiness in having reached her audience. She loved them all; she wanted to pour out all the riches of her voice for them to have. Ray Wessen came over and put his arm about her shoulders.

"Honey, you're going to do big things one of these days," he said. "Don't let any of them stop you — any of them."

She loved his rough partisanship, the reluctant, almost embarrassed appreciation of them all. And then, later, there was her first evening at the opera, the excitement of the theater in the Woods, the audience drifting in, in summer frocks and white linen, the orchestra settling in its place, and then the music, the curtains parting and the voices beginning. She sat in an empty seat at the back of the theater, watching Jenny Grove, in Fidelio's boyish costume, listening to her voice in the magnificent, somber music. It was not, as Herschel had said, a part for her; the sultry intensity of her voice and acting was out of place in this large, classic frame; but there were moments when the voice overcame obstacles and thrilled through the audience like a blade. And, on the stage, she was almost startlingly beautiful. All the faint tawdriness, the overemphasis of make-up, that marred her appearance in street clothes, fell into its proper place behind the footlights, and left her as full of vibrance and life as a Goya. Ella watched her with a bright, clear admiration: she was all that she wanted for herself, the shining mirror of her future.

She went home, and slept; and in the morning, when she awoke, she awoke with the *Abscheulicher* in her head; she sang the splendid imprecation while she dressed. She went to the office through the early summer-morning streets, pleased with herself, pleased with everything in her world.

"What are you so happy about?" Eddie asked, meeting her in the hall.

She smiled at him without answering, pleased to be free of him, pleased that it was Rita's desk and not hers that he stopped by with his importunities.

And then, when she went home that evening, it all fell away in an instant; the whole bright fiction of her immunity, which she had been cherishing so desperately since Saturday night, collapsed and left her facing her new world of reality again. There was a box on the parlor table when she came in, a florist's square box that Anne Gunning had set there for her to see, while she talked to a customer in the fitting room. She opened it, frozen in resistance. Inside there was a bunch of purple violets, and with them a card on which was written only a few bars of music and the signature — *Max*. The music was the melody of the Schumann song that she had sung in Carla Herschel's studio, that first early May night that she had met him — *Im wunderschönen Monat Mai*.

She brought the violets into the kitchen and set them in a bowl — an old-fashioned bowl, made in the form of a flower basket, that her mother had had since she had been a child. When Anne Gunning came in a moment later and looked questioningly at her, she said in a light, hard voice: "Oh, they're from Max Tallan; aren't they nice?" — as if she were simply pleased, a little surprised, and no more. But she looked at the flowers in their familiar bowl, and something twisted inside her; the words of the song that he had written on the card ran through her mind —

> *Im wunderschönen Monat Mai,*
> *Als alle Knospen sprangen,*
> *Da ist in meinem Herzen*
> *Die Liebe aufgegangen. . . .*

"Then in my heart love came up—" She went to her own room, but the words would not let her be —

> *Da hab' ich ihr gestanden*
> *Mein Sehnen und Verlangen. . . .*

"Then I confessed to her my yearning and longing—" She had never thought of *him*, in her angry egotism; she had never thought that something had happened inside him that had driven him past reason, past pride, to the humility of that little bunch of flowers and a few scribbled notes of music that had to serve for everything he could not say to her. She felt all at once, not as if she understood him, but as if she were living with him in the same flesh; what was tearing her inside now was what was tearing him, the same desperate urgency and need.

Then it went away: there was only a bunch of violets in a bowl, and a card with a few notes of music written on it. What did it matter, what did it have to do with her? The Wessens came over, and Lillie raised her eyebrows at the violets.

"Has Elly got a new beau? Things must be looking up; Eddie never sent flowers."

And she smiled and said: "Oh, I'm afraid it's only a joke. Max Tallan sent them; it was about something that happened the other night."

They knew all her new friends only by name and her description of them; they were as satisfied as if she had said that Huisman or Dessieux had sent the flowers to her. Only Anne Gunning looked at her with her clear, sober dark eyes. She could not face that gaze; she went into the bare little fitting room, where she liked to practice, and walked up and down before the long mirror, beginning to sing some vocalises. But she could not keep her attention on what she was doing. There was other music sounding inside her, the lovely, simple melody that was written on the card —

> *Da hab' ich ihr gestanden*
> *Mein Sehnen und Verlangen.* . . .

It would not leave her in peace, and she wanted so much to be left; she wanted to have back her own world, where there was only the hard clear line of her ambition traced before her.

It was Monday night: there was no opera at the Woods that evening. She had to get through the hours somehow. She did not know what she was waiting for, but she was as tense as a soldier before battle. In spite of everything that had been wrong about the way things had ever been before, she had been happy inside, under it all, under the disappointments and the humiliations and the fears, because she had always been sure of herself, really, inside herself

[133]

where it counted most. Now she was not sure of herself any more, and she was not happy. She felt that her whole world was wrong, and through some fault of his. He had laid some intolerable responsibility on her, and she would not have it; she *would not* have that feeling of torment and bewilderment that came on her when she looked at the flowers waiting mutely in their little bowl.

In the morning she went to the office, but she had to force her attention to the work. The presence of other people was a misery to her; she was strung tight, waiting for something, and there they were going about their work as if it was a day like any other. Only for a short time, when she went out to lunch and saw the blue summer day fresh and serene on the busy street, the tension relaxed in her a little. But it did not last; someone passed her, whistling a tune that for a few notes struck at her with the tormenting, familiar sound. And afterwards, when she went home, there were the violets still, in their bowl on the table. She wanted them to be gone, to wither quickly so that she could finally be rid of them.

She had her dinner, and dressed, and went out to the Woods. She was wearing a white crepe dress, very plain except for a broad scarlet ribbon belt that made her look rather gypsylike, with her slender, brown-skinned face and straight dark hair. The opera was *Il Barbiere.* A celebrated tenor, now many years past his prime, was singing Almaviva, and she had looked forward to hearing him. But when the audience was seated and she had settled down herself at the back of the theater, she found that she could not concentrate on what was going on before her on the stage any more than she had been able to concentrate on her work that morning. The vivacious, artificial music fell in badly with her mood. She looked at the aging Almaviva, pouring out his amorous longings in the serenade, and she saw only a stout, elderly Italian, grotesque in his role of young, ardent lover, who acted very badly, in the ancient operatic tradition, and whose voice was a mere marred relic of a golden instrument. And the play itself, the broad, furious comedy, distracted her. She was living deep in some darkness inside herself, and she could not follow seriously the actions of the painted, gesticulating figures

[134]

on the stage; it was like some clever puppet show, quite divorced from reality.

During the interval between the acts she got up to stand with the other ushers at the back of the theater, listening with half her attention to their gossip about the performers — about Rosina's gowns, and the feud between one of the regular company's leading tenors and the imported celebrity of tonight's production. She stood with them silently, watching the people going in and out, the tall, heavy-leaved trees beyond the open sides of the theater, that looked green and dense in the glare of the lights. Someone came up beside her as the warning bell rang for the next act. She turned around; it was Max Tallan. He was standing there looking at her, not smiling; his eyes had an odd expression in them, tense and determined.

"Can you come away from this for a little?" he said to her abruptly.

She looked around, half in desperation, at the darkening theater, the orchestra settled in its place, the conductor just appearing.

"Oh," she said, "I oughtn't—"

"Why not? They don't need you here now."

She had the feeling that everything was running downhill. It had begun to happen now, and nothing that she could do would stop it. She walked away with him along the gravel walk that led from the theater. She did not say anything to him, and he did not speak to her either till they had come far enough away from the theater to have lost the stage lights and come into the pure creamy half-light of the moon. They could hear the music all the while, the shrill cheerful strings, busy as crickets in the night, Rosina's birdlike roulades, the heavier tones of the men's voices, all mingling oddly with the quiet sounds of the branches clashing overhead in the evening wind, and the sudden mournful flutter of an owl call from somewhere off to the right.

"It's good here," he said after a little, irrelevantly.

"Yes."

She would not look at him; she walked obstinately beside him, her head slightly bent. He went on with her, then stopped and looked past her, down the path that turned just before them.

"Why did you come out here?" he asked her suddenly.

She glanced up at him almost angrily. "Why? Because you asked me to."

She had not really looked at him since he had come up to her, at the theater. And now, when she saw his face, rather set, like that of a person waiting for a blow to fall, something turned inside her, just as it had done the day before, when she had looked at his flowers in the little bowl. She *knew* what he was feeling, as if it had been herself, but she would not give in to it; she clung to her separateness as if it were a weapon.

"That's the only reason?" he asked her.

"Yes," she said stubbornly.

"And if it had been anyone else, you'd have come just the same?"

She turned to him again, rather passionately. "That's no business of yours." She paused for a moment. "I'm going back," she said.

She turned suddenly on the path. He put his hand on her arm, holding her.

"Not till you've heard what I have to say."

But she pulled away from him, facing him almost violently. "I've heard all you have to say; didn't you write it all down for me? I don't know you; I don't want to; I don't know anything about you—"

It was all coming out now, but he would not let her finish. He stood there before her in the path, not touching her, but keeping her there all the same.

"Why do you lie about it?" he asked her, in his quick, unyielding voice. "You know everything about me, just as I know everything about you; can you stand there and tell me that you don't? You've known from the first night, and so have I."

She knew it was true: the strangeness between them was all on the surface, the same sort of strangeness that she had had with herself when she had been a child, new to her own identity, and had had to discover all the things about Ella Gunning that had nothing to do, really, with what was inside her — what she looked like, where she lived, who the people were to whom she belonged. These were the things about him that were strange to her now, that she had to learn; but there was some deeper knowledge of him that she had not had to learn. They had recognized each other that first evening, in Carla Herschel's studio, only she did not want to admit it; she wanted to walk her own narrow, shining, uninterrupted path to her own fulfillment.

She stood there facing him on the gravel path, not answering him, only waiting, as if her sole escape from him now were in silence. She heard the music coming faintly and then more clearly, as the wind blew, from the theater off behind her.

"You can't say it isn't true," he said. He was as stubborn as she was. "*You* know it's so—"

She looked up at him quickly. "What if it is true? What difference does it make?" she asked him, almost defiantly. "You want to stop me; you've said so yourself. But you can't do it; you can't make me any different from the way I am—"

"You don't know a damned thing about the way you are. You've got music in you; you've got a voice — do you think I want to change anything about that? But you're not the sort that can make a whole life out of concert tours and operatic roles; you haven't got that kind of soul, and some day you're going to find that out. You've got to have some ground of real life to walk on; you're hard, inside, but you're not shallow or egocentric or commonly comfortable—"

"Whatever I am, *you* don't think very much of me," she said bitterly. "You don't want me to be a person; you want me to be something added on to yourself. You want to have *your* life the way you want it, but you don't want me to have mine—"

He came a step closer to her and put his hands on her arms just below the shoulders, not as if he wanted to make love to her, but as if he would have liked to shake her.

"Damn it, don't talk about something you don't know anything about," he said, in a low, furious tone. "*My* life — if you asked me you could have it, for a tame composer to write your show pieces for you, and follow you around from city to city, and stand in the wings waiting for you to finish with your public and give me the charity of a few minutes of your time. Is that what you want? Is it?"

She felt the hard grip of his hands on her arms, and then all at once he released her; he stood looking at her with a queer drained expression on his face.

"All right," he said. "Let it go. You gave it to me pretty plainly, I guess, but I couldn't take it; I had to try again——"

She stood there staring at him without moving. It was over now; she could go; but she felt no sense of relief. Something was tearing at her inside, some new emotion that she had never felt before. She looked at him, her face perfectly white in the moonlight. And all at once she took a step forward and he met her; his arms closed around her and she felt his mouth set on hers. The blood beat up in her, answering him. He bent his head again, kissing her eyes and throat.

But she was coming to herself; the music, the wild stage comedy, forced its way back into her consciousness. She drew apart, a little dazed. He held her still.

"Say it's true," he said. She was almost afraid of his eyes, with the dark blaze in them. But his voice was shaky. "Say you love me."

She shook her head almost angrily. "I do — I do love you. I don't want to, but I do——"

She felt as if she had nothing more to do with it; it had all been decided for her; something bigger than either of them had decided it.

"It'll be good," he said to her. "I promise you." She heard his voice, always so final-sounding, as if the things he said could never be changed and never be unsaid. "It won't be anything but good."

He kissed her again, and she lifted her face, meeting him; she wanted it to be as he said. Still it was not happiness that she felt inside her; it was a fierce, restless longing, something that he wakened in her, and assuaged, and wakened again. And she could not bring it into the real world around her. When she drew away from him and looked about her, it was as if she had to live in two worlds at once, the new one inside herself, and the old quiet one in which the trees waited silently and the white path ran on and the music sounded brightly from the theater. She could not bear to be divided

[138]

so; she had to stay wholly in the new world that he had created for her or destroy it. She went down with him to the little lake and stood looking out blindly over the dusky water on which the moon lay quietly, but she did not see it; she only felt how her hand lay in his and how his eyes went searching over her face.

"You're so damned young," he said. "Why do you have to be so young? I'm thirty-four; I'm almost twice your age—"

She turned to him rather somberly. "Why does that make any difference?"

"It does. You're not all grown-up; I feel as if I were talking to somebody who doesn't really exist yet."

"Oh, I *am* grown-up," she said bitterly. "I've been working for a year."

She felt as if his words diminished her somehow; they made her seem less than a complete person, a mere sketch of someone who was to come. He put his hand on her arm and turned her about to face him.

"Look," he said, "tell me this — would you marry me now, to-night, if I asked you?"

She drew her brows together. She felt as if something was holding them both fixed there, confronting each other, with that question between them.

"Oh, I don't *know!*" she said. "Tonight—"

"You don't know what you *will* do; that's the long and short of it," he said. "You're for me one moment and the next against me—" He stood there, his face not changing, looking at her out of his intent dark eyes. "If I didn't want you so much, I'd let you go now," he said. "And you *would* go, damn you; you'd go straight off to that crazy tinsel dream-world you've got in your head, and I'd never find you again. But I'm not going to let you do it; I'm going to keep you "

His determination seemed to close her about. She felt that if she could stay with him so, only the two of them there alone in the darkness, she could live in this new world that he had shown her. But there was the sound of the music always behind them, bright and insistent, intruding on them with its implications of other people, another life. And she wanted that other life still; she could not give it away freely when she was just stepping inside its splendid circle.

"When are you going away?" she asked him suddenly.

"Next week."

She could not tell whether she was relieved or miserable, to hear it.

"If I asked you to come over there with me and study, I suppose you'd do that," he said, in a hard, flat tone.

She gave him a dark glance. "I could kill you for saying that. Do I act as if I wanted to use you?"

"You act as if you wanted to be a great singer; it won't matter much to you what you have to step on to climb up. What about Hobie? Or the kid who got you your audition with Tharp? What did he ever get out of it?"

She stared at him, amazed. "Eddie? Why shouldn't he have brought me to sing for Tharp? He thought I had a voice; we were good friends—"

"And now that he can't do anything more for you, you're not such good friends — is that it?" he asked.

"That hasn't anything to do with it. He's — interested in another girl; he was jealous of my singing, just the way you are, and we broke up. I suppose *you* never had another girl in your life!" she cried.

She was so furious, standing there before him, that her eyes seemed lighted from within; she looked as taut as a cat about to spring.

"One minute I'm not grown-up enough for you, and the next you're saying I'm — I don't know what," she cried. "I'm not any of the things you think; I'm only learning to sing the best way I know how to, because I've got to, I've *got* to — do you understand? *I* never had a grandfather who played under Mahler; I never even heard of Mahler till a few months ago — but I *can* sing, and I'm going to — and I'm going to do it without any of the rotten ways you think I will. I went with Eddie because he was the only person I knew who understood what I wanted, and because he liked me, and I liked him — and when things didn't turn out right with us, I stopped going with him, and that's all there was to that. And I never told him I loved him," she finished, in a high, hard voice, "and I *didn't* love him, and I don't think I love you either—"

She said the last words with sudden childish defiance. All at once she turned around and walked away from him, along the path toward the theater. He followed her.

"All right," she heard him say after a moment. "I was wrong. I'm sorry."

She walked straight on, without turning her head. He took her by the arm and stopped her.

"I said I was sorry."

She looked at him, her face closed and dark, a kind of definite innocence emanating from it: the blank and savage innocence of a face in a primitive religious painting.

"Nobody ever said anything like that to me before," she said.

"It's only because I'm so damned much in love with you."

"*That's* a queer way to show it," she said bitterly.

But she walked on with him. They came near the theater.

"Will you let me take you home when this is over?" he asked her.

She glanced over at him. She was still angry.

"I don't know. What's the good?"

"I'll meet you here," he said.

And she gave in. She went back to sit with the other girls, at the rear of the theater. She saw them glancing at her curiously, but it did not matter. The music, other people — she could not believe that they really mattered. She was full of doubts and urgings; she felt as fiercely alive as the young leaves spreading themselves in the swift green vitality of the early summer. And she did not know whether it was what she wanted or what she did not want — that she would be with him again in a short time.

But when she met him again they were both very quiet, apart from each other. He drove her home through the dark summer streets, past the sleepy brightness of suburban squares, down the long tree-lined streets of quiet houses.

"Are you still angry with me?" he asked her once.

She shook her head. "Oh, I don't *know*."

And when he left her at her home, she kept herself still apart from him, so that they separated almost as if they had been strangers. But she could not sleep that night. She lay staring at the square of her open window, feeling the night air that flowed dark and cool into the room, till she was almost mad with the stillness, and the faint moonlight, and the sense of the broad night lying outside. Everything in her was clenched tight, uncertain, alive, rather savage with wanting.

The next day, after dinner, when she was dressing to go out to the Woods, she heard his voice all at once in the parlor, talking to her mother. He had come to drive her out to the Woods, and when she had quickly finished dressing and come into the parlor, she found him and Anne Gunning apparently in the midst of an oddly intimate conversation.

"*What* did you say to my mother?" she demanded, when they were in the car.

"I told her that I'm in love with you, and that I want to marry you."

"But you had no right—" she protested. She felt cold, almost a little frightened. It seemed somehow to make it final, for anyone else to know his feelings toward her.

"Why hadn't I? I didn't tell her that you were in love with me."

She was silent for a moment. "What did she say to you?" she asked presently, in a rather small voice.

Tallan smiled a little. "She said I was too old for you; then she said I oughtn't to be in such a hurry; then she said she liked me."

"Oh, she's on *your* side," Ella said, strangely and resentfully.

She did not know what she could say to her mother about Tallan. She could not explain her feelings to her; there was that odd reserve, almost shyness, between them. But she knew that something must be said. The next morning, at breakfast, Anne Gunning brought the subject up.

"I suppose you know all about the talk Mr. Tallan and I had last night," she said, in her dry, brisk way, as she sat down at the table with Ella.

Ella frowned nervously. "He told me a little — But he oughtn't to have said anything; it's not that serious—"

"It may not be with you, but it is with him," Anne Gunning said. She was silent for a moment. "If you don't love him, you ought to break off with him right now," she said abruptly. "It's cruel to him, and dangerous to yourself, to go on."

"Yes, that's easy to say!" Ella said bitterly. "But he *makes* me love him; I don't want to, but he does—"

"He couldn't *make* you love him if the love wasn't there on your side to begin with," her mother said. Her face had an odd, embarrassed, determined look on it. "What do you have against him?" she asked. "He's a good deal older than you; I don't like that. But there's not *that* much difference, and it seems to me that you ought to get along with him otherwise. He's a musician, and the sort of quick-thinking person you always took to—"

"He wants to make me over — that's what it is — and I won't be made over," Ella said defiantly. "He thinks being a singer is something cheap, and vulgar—"

"I'm sure he doesn't think that. He said some wonderful things about your voice to me. Only he said he didn't want you to have to go through the mill that a young, unknown girl always has to, to get to the top. He said you were in such a hurry, you'd spoil yourself and your voice; you'd never be able to do the really fine things he thinks you could do. I don't doubt, if you married him, he'd want you to be his wife *first*, but I don't think he has any idea of wanting you to give up your singing altogether—"

"It doesn't make any difference what kind of ideas he has, because I'm not going to marry him," Ella insisted.

She put back her chair and got up from the table. Her mother looked up at her.

"You're afraid of him because he has as much character as you have yourself; you know you won't get around him," she said, with a flash of insight. "It was different with Eddie; you could always have *your* way with him when it really mattered enough to you to fight for it. But it's better to marry a hard man who's in love with you than a soft one who's in love with himself; *I* could tell you that, if you'd pay any attention to it when I'd told you."

Ella did not answer her. She went out of the room stubbornly, found her hat and purse, and started off to work. She wanted to cry; they would not leave her alone, and all she wanted was to go on in her own way. She was so sure of herself now; she had such complete confidence in her destiny. If only they would leave her alone, she could be happy and simple; she could live her own life without any of them.

She dreaded the days that must pass still before Tallan left for Europe. He would want something from her, some definite promise. And when she was with him, she would not be able to refuse. She did not know what happened to her when she was with him; everything else went down the wind but the fact of their being there together. He brought her to the opera every night, and after the intermission, when she was not needed at the theater any longer, they walked together as they had on that first evening. She said that she wanted him not to come, but it did not matter what she said; they both knew that she could not hold to it, not to go with him when he came. And she resented it almost, this power that he, or her own emotions, had over her.

But on the last night before he was to leave, she could not bear to think of it, that a whole year would pass before she would see him again. It was a sultry night, very close and dark. She walked down with him to the little lake and stood looking out over the water, which seemed heavy and still, barely rising to disturb its even surface of blackness.

"I don't want you to go," she said. It was like a confession that had been extorted from her. "I don't want you to go—"

He put his arms about her and drew her to him. "Come with me," he urged.

But she shook her head heavily. She was afraid; she clung still to her own life.

[144]

"No," she said. "Maybe when you come back—"

"You'll forget all about me in a year's time," he said, rather roughly. "You'll have someone else by then."

She looked up at him indignantly. *"Why* must there be anyone? I can do without all of you; I've got enough to think about without that. I'm going to *work* this year—"

She began to walk moodily away from the water. She was not sure of herself; during the past week it seemed to her that she had scarcely thought of her singing. But she told herself that everything would change again when he had gone away.

He brought her home that night, and in the little fitting room, with its sewing machine and dress form watching silently in the dim light, he kissed her good-by.

"Promise me you'll be here when I come back," he said.

And she promised; she wanted him now; she could not bear the thought that they might never be together like this again. After he had gone she lay awake for a long time, miserable with wanting him, the tears welling up in her eyes. Still, at the same time, there was a sense of relief somewhere deep inside her, a feeling of freedom at having her own life to live again completely to herself.

The next day, when she came from work, there was a jeweler's box for her, with a curiously plain band of narrow gold inside, set with a small emerald, and a card that read: "Don't wear this if you don't want to, but keep it — Max." She slipped the ring on her finger. It was a little too large for her, and she stood looking down at it, pleased with it because it was so pretty, but at the same time angry with him because he had sent it. She felt that he wanted to bind her to something. Her mother came into the room as she was standing there frowning at it on her finger. She walked over slowly and looked at the ring.

"Are you engaged to him, then?" she asked, in her direct way.

Ella pulled the ring off her finger and put it back into the box.

"No, I'm not," she denied. "He — wants me to have it, but I won't wear it."

"You oughtn't to keep it at all if you don't look at it that you're going to marry him," Anne Gunning said bluntly. "That's what he means by it, isn't it?"

Ella was silent. A trace of a smile crossed her mother's lips.

"I never saw the like of you for stubbornness," she said. "What good does it do you to say you won't marry him, when you know all along that that's just what you're going to end by doing?"

Ella flushed suddenly. "Maybe I will — but I'm *not* engaged to him now. And you mustn't say it to anyone. Lillie's been asking questions; I don't want her, or anyone, to know."

"Lillie's got eyes in her head like the rest of us," Anne Gunning said. "If you don't want people to know that there's anything between you and a young man, you oughtn't to see him every day in the week."

"Well, he's gone now, and I won't see him any more for a year," Ella said. "So that's the end of it."

But she did not send back the ring. She wore it sometimes, romantically, on a chain around her neck, slipped inside her dress. She wanted him very much at times, and it seemed to bring him closer to her when she wore the ring.

Chapter Nine

THE scholarship examinations were held at the Institute shortly before the fall term began. Herschel had said that he was positive of her success, and he was right: when the names of the accepted candidates came out, hers was high on the list. It was definitely settled now that she would leave her job at the Finn Company. She gave her notice at once, and the news filtered through the office that same day. Late in the afternoon, Eddie came strolling over to her desk.

"I hear you're leaving," he said to her.

She looked up at him. "Yes, I am."

"That's a coincidence. I'm leaving myself at the end of the month; I'm going over to Ascue Brothers as a buyer there."

"Oh — really," she said. She flushed slightly; there had been a sense of rivalry between them ever since they had broken off with each other, and she knew he wanted to impress her now. Ascue Brothers was the finest furniture store in town; it was a big step up in the world for him, to be going there as a buyer. "Well, everyone said you would do it, didn't they?" she said, smiling at him. "I'm awfully glad, Eddie."

"It's a step in the right direction," he said judicially. "There's not much future here; it's a good place to learn the furniture business, and that's about all." He hesitated a moment. "What about you?" he went on. "Are you going to give full time to your music now?"

"Yes, I am," she said. "I've got a scholarship at the Institute, and I'll be making as much, with my church work and odd engagements, as I make here."

"Good for you. I've about decided to give up my lessons over there this year. There won't be much time for them, with this new job—"

They were both a little stiff and ill at ease with each other. After a few more words he left her and walked away. She looked after him for a moment, remembering all at once how close they had been to each other only a year ago. And she felt a sudden sense of relief: what if Tallan had been right, and in another year she would feel as little for him as she felt now for Eddie? A year could be a long time when so many things happened. She was a different person now from the Ella Gunning who had gone to the Institute with Eddie for the first time to sing for Tharp, and another year might make a difference as great in her from what she was now.

But it was only for a moment that she could believe that. She knew that she had never felt in the least about Eddie as she felt about Tallan; she had been free of him always, even during their best times. It was a completely different sort of relationship that existed now between her and Tallan.

They were not particularly sorry at the office to see her go. She had done her work efficiently, but she had stayed a little apart from the others because of her absorption in her music, so that she had made no close friends there. And, on her side, she felt that she was leaving behind a part of her life that had never been of any real importance to her. She put it all out of her mind very quickly. She was absorbed in the new life that was beginning for her at the Institute. During the preceding year, she had felt that she stood only on the outskirts there. Now her world would center in it. It was an exciting prospect to her.

Herschel had arranged matters so that she was to study with Madame Collier-Brown this year. She did not know how he had smoothed this over with Tharp; she rather thought he had not succeeded very well, for Tharp was distinctly cold when he saw her at the beginning of the term, but she did not care enough about it to be upset. She was too much excited over the idea of studying with Madame Collier-Brown, who was the Institute's most famous personage: she had sung at Covent Garden in the golden time of Melba, Calvé, the De

Reszkes, when she had been one of the best-known contraltos in England. Now, at sixty-five, she was a tall, imposing figure in extravagantly outmoded clothes, with a ravaged voice and a face that she persisted in making up in an almost theatrical fashion.

The first day that Ella went to sing for her, she was a little nervous of her abrupt, imperious manner and her odd appearance, her hennaed hair and darkened brows and wide, ugly, mobile, painted mouth. She sang several things for her, while Madame stood silently in a corner, watching her intently over the back of a chair that she was leaning on, and only speaking to discuss briefly with her what she should sing next. The accompanist, a serious, plump, dark young woman named Lucy Flory, also said nothing; she stared shortsightedly at her music between numbers, as if she was not in the least interested in what went on between teacher and pupil. At last, just as Ella was singing the final notes of an English ballad, "My Bonny, Bonny Boy," there was a knock at the door and Herschel came into the room. He looked quickly from Madame to Ella and back again.

"Well, how is it going?" he asked.

He was smoking his inevitable cigarette, and Madame snatched it from him without ceremony and flung it out the window.

"How often have I told you, I *won't* have smoking in here, Hobie," she said emphatically. She sailed across the big room to a chair and sat down. "Do you expect us to *sing* in an atmosphere like that? Flory, you may go," she interrupted herself to say to the accompanist.

The dark young woman got up and left in silence.

"Well—?" Herschel said again, impatiently. He sat down, perching himself on the arm of a chair. "What do you think of her, Maude?"

"What do I think of her?" Madame Collier-Brown had an extraordinary voice; it had a great deal of inflection — she could have read a grocery list so that it sounded either like a challenge to battle or a love sonnet, as it suited her — but its flexibility was all harsh notes and broken lights now; it was as marred and cracked as if she had spent her days shouting fish in a market, instead of in uttering the noble lines of Orpheus and Brangäne from the operatic stage. "What do I think of her?" she repeated. "I think she's a raw young woman who needs to work like a stoker for two or three years before she'll have begun to find out what she can do — and I think that what she can do may be to become as great a mezzo as any we've had in three decades. The voice is there — that's the great thing; I haven't heard a voice like that these many *weary* years. Whether she has everything else that's needed is something we'll have to find out together. I can't tell you in half an hour whether she'll work, whether she has the constitution and the temperament, whether she's intelligent—"

"Oh, she'll work, all right," Herschel said. He looked over at Ella, and she had again the odd feeling of being considered quite impersonally, as a voice, an instrument — her existence as an individual left entirely out of account, except as it affected her existence as a performer. "And she's quick enough," he said; "you're right about it, that you've got your hands on the real thing this time, Maude. Tharp had no more idea what to do with her than a nice respectable pigeon with a nightingale in his brood. I think she's picked up a good deal of that self-consciousness of hers from him, trying to fit herself into his idea of a proper young singer. If she'd stayed with him much longer, she'd have sung Carmen like a choirboy, when she got around to it."

"Yes; the voice is not at all 'white,' but he was doing his best to make it so, I think," Madame said critically.

Ella stood beside the piano, feeling helpless, rather exposed, as they went on discussing her. They seemed to leave her so much out of account; there was something wounding to her in their detachment. Still the excitement was beating its way up in her. After all, it did not matter to her how they discussed her, as long as it would help her in the end. And she felt that Madame's criticism of her was quite different from Tharp's cold displeasure when she had done something that had not satisfied him. It had never seemed to matter to him, really, beyond the moment's irritation, and she felt that she *did* matter now, quite strenuously, to the large, queer, painted woman across the room.

[150]

"Work and experience — experience and work: there's the whole history of what she needs," she said to Herschel. "The work we can take care of; the experience, here in America, is another matter. Oh, I'll grant you there's plenty of the wrong kind — radio, musical comedy: young artists puffing themselves up on the praise of ignorant people who pay them much too well for doing something that they ought to be ashamed to do at all. What they need is three years of obscurity in a small opera company, where they can learn everything and sing everything that's in their voice."

"De Meyer'll take her on next summer at the Woods; that's certain, at any rate," Herschel said. "And in the meantime, why don't you see what you can do with Zélie about putting on something with a nice part for Ella this year? She was talking about *La Gioconda* a couple of months ago; that would give her Laura to do—"

Madame shrugged her shoulders magnificently.

"Oh, Zélie and I — you know what we think of each other!" she said. "If I tell her to do *Gioconda*, she'll put on *Die Walküre* simply to show me that she's not letting *me* meddle in her affairs. And aren't you forgetting Tharp's protégée, besides — the one with the teeth and the hair, who looks as if she ought to be advertising either a dentifrice or a shampoo? She calls herself a mezzo, probably because she's never learned how to manage her upper register—"

"Maxine Neel?" Herschel grinned at the description. "My God, Maude, even Zélie can tell the difference between Maxine's voice and Ella's."

"She makes an impression on an audience," Madame insisted. "She has that horrible light-opera smile to perfection, and she scampers up and down the scale, blowing her *horn* of a voice at the top of her lungs — Zélie's very fond of making an impression; it's why Roger adores her so; her little affairs are always so *extremely* successful at attracting students."

"Well, we'll have to work on Michael, then," Herschel declared. "*He* can put his foot down—"

"When Michael 'puts his foot down' on anything, please inform me," Madame said, with a grand show of irony. "But I'll do what I can with him—"

Ella listened in silence to their discussion. She felt a little bewildered by the fact that it seemed all on the level of personalities rather than on that of artistic considerations. Zélie, she knew, was Madame Letroye, the head of the department of opera, and Roger was Roger Perren, the Director of the Institute. Who Michael was, she had not the least idea, but she learned later that he was Michael Teubel, the conductor of the Institute symphony orchestra.

The three of them, with Madame Letroye's assistant, Forrest Marchpane, formed the committee which sat for the opera tryouts, held in late October. In spite of Madame Collier-Brown's objections, it had been decided that the opera to be given that year was to be Massenet's *Werther,* in which the only considerable part for mezzo-soprano was that of Charlotte. Madame Collier-Brown was certain that Madame Letroye would not give this long and arduous role, the most important in the opera, to a singer as inexperienced as Ella, and as an alternative there was only the part of Kätchen, which offered no more opportunity than a bit of silent byplay and a single solo phrase in the first act. Herschel was furious, but Ella was beginning to learn that his influence at the Institute was not without its limits; both he and Madame Collier-Brown were at swords' points with the whole Tharp-Perren-Letroye clique.

On the day of the tryouts, which were held in the recital hall of the Institute, Ella sat with Madame Collier-Brown and several of her other pupils at the back of the auditorium, waiting to be called to sing. It was a wet, gray, quiet afternoon, and she had a slight cold; she felt angry and uncertain, knowing that she could not sing her best. Beside her a plump, short tenor named Bartolomeo Ghedini, with a round face and quick liquid brown eyes, sat leaning forward with his hands between his knees, watching intently everything that was going forward on the stage, and keeping up a running commentary on it in an undertone to Ella.

"Look, it's all politics — nothing but politics," he said, with a conviction that would have seemed childlike if it had not been so toughly cynical. "Want to make a bet? Nine parts to cast — three for Madame C.-B., three for Tharp, Mrs. Fenwick and Frasco split the rest between them. And they'll split the leading roles: if I take Werther, you haven't got a prayer. You'd better keep your fingers crossed for Minott or Madsen Hess—"

Ella did not want to believe him, but she had come to the audition with her illusions already a little damaged by the conversations she had heard between Herschel and Madame Collier-Brown. She looked at Madame Letroye, sitting in the third row with the three men of the committee: there was not much reassurance for her in her pale, clear-lined Frenchwoman's face, with its mass of studiedly careless curls above, and its almost cruelly well-defined lips and eyes. She talked or was silent with equal emphasis; when she sat listening to one of her three companions, her opinions seemed to remain as definite a force for them to take into account as if she had condescended to argue with them. She managed everything with quick, dry little nods, a snap of the fingers, a gesture of her ugly, graceful hands.

Paul Minott, a pupil of Frasco's, was on the stage now, singing one of Werther's arias from the second act of the opera. Ella knew him slightly; he was a tall young man, taut and muscular as a ballet dancer, the sort who is inevitably at the center of things, and who manages his position there with a kind of matter-of-fact arrogance. His voice was good, a robust tenor, not very well established in its upper register, but full and dramatic where it was under his control. Ghedini sat looking at him jealously as he sang.

"Oh, my God, what it wouldn't be worth to me to be three inches taller!" he said. "Look at Letroye; she's like all the rest of you damned women. Hess and I might as well give up right now."

But he looked fully confident when he went up to the stage to repeat the aria that Minott had sung. He had the ease and satisfaction of his Latin ancestry in a dramatic situation; on stage he was not a carelessly dressed, round little student but a melancholy, impassioned lover, who stepped out of character only when he unconsciously rose on his toes to reach for the high B that climaxed his aria. Ella thought that his voice was purer, more naturally handled, than Minott's, but it was rather light, a lyric rather than a dramatic instrument. He was quite satisfied with his own performance: "Oh boy — oh boy, did I knock them in the aisles!" he crowed to Ella, when he came back. "Your goose is cooked, Gunning; I've got Werther in the bag."

She was called next, to sing the Letter aria from the third act. She went up the steps to the stage, feeling nervous; she always disliked singing for people whom she felt to be unsympathetic to her. From the stage she saw the row of faces upturned to her: Madame Letroye's cool, appraising one, Perren's gray, unreadable mask, Teubel looking polite and bored and rufous as a fox, Marchpane young, dark, obsequious, precious. At the piano, Lucy Flory began to play, and she drew herself together, turning her attention to the music she was about to sing.

She had been working over the Letter aria with Madame Collier-Brown during the past month, but she was still in the stage with it in which her own emotional response to it and her mastery of the technical details of the performance had not yet merged in a single artistically satisfying whole. She had the young artist's difficulty in using her emotions; she had still to learn that feeling, in performance, must be remembered and rationalized oftener than actually experienced. As a result, she was hampered by anything that disturbed her, kept her from calling up the emotion she wanted to express, as all the circumstances of the tryout did today. So she sang rather coldly, driven still farther from her normal ease of expression by the necessity of striving against a slight hoarseness. When she came down from the stage, she walked back to Madame Collier-Brown and stood looking at her from under her brows, somber and furious.

"It wasn't right, at all," she said. "*Why* couldn't I have done it the way I did it yesterday, for you?"

Madame shrugged. "My dear, it doesn't matter; they wouldn't have you if you'd sung like an angel. *This* is what they're after —

[154]

and heaven forbid you should ever satisfy them with anything like it."

She was talking about Maxine Neel, who was standing now beside the piano on the stage, smiling at everyone, then composing herself dramatically to launch into her aria. Her voice clamored brightly for their attention; she ran the gamut from tenderness to terror without losing sight for a moment of the fact that she was a handsome, good-humored young woman whom everybody liked; and when she finished there was a huddle of heads among the committee.

"There *you* go, Gunning," Ghedini leaned over to whisper to her. "It's a damned shame — they call that a voice? She ought to try to sing just once for an Italian audience—"

Ella hardly listened. She was looking at the committee, feeling her disappointment like a sick emptiness inside her. She turned to Madame Collier-Brown.

"Do I have to stay any longer? They won't decide anything today, will they?"

Madame told her to go, and she went out of the hall, out to the gray soft fall day, with the rain clinging to the almost bare trees, and a feeling of melancholy and things ending over everything. She went home; as she entered the house, Anne Gunning, who was sewing in the fitting room, looked up at her inquiringly.

"How did it go?" she asked.

Ella shook her head, too miserable to explain what had happened. She felt her mother looking at her with a rather exasperated pity, and it drove her wild: she did not want to be pitied; she wanted to assert herself somehow, to wipe out the humiliation of her failure. She turned toward the door.

"There's a package for you on the parlor table," Anne Gunning remarked. Ella looked around, surprised. "From Vienna," her mother added, in her calm, incurious voice.

Ella felt a sudden quick nervous thrill — whether of pleasure or displeasure she did not know. She had had two letters from Tallan since he had left, both brief, and somehow seeming to take it for

[155]

granted that what there was between them did not need to be put into words on a sheet of paper. What she had wanted of them was either that they should bring back to her the overwhelming certainty of the feeling that she had had when she had been with him during the summer, or that they should leave her free of any feeling at all; and they had done neither. They had simply reasserted his hard, tacit claim to her, presenting her with the fact of it and nothing more. She had answered him in a pair of stiff little letters of her own, that had not acknowledged him in a single line. Now she wondered what it was that he had sent her. She went into the parlor almost with dread.

The package was large and flat, wrapped in brown paper. When she opened it, there was a sheaf of heavy manuscript paper inside, and a note that said only: "Ella — These are for you. If you sing them, you are me for a while." She looked through the pages, seeing the notes dashed on the paper in his quick black notation that was hard for her to read, interlined with words in his scrawled handwriting. It was a group of songs that he had sent her, a half-dozen short lyrics by Blake which he had set to music. She had never read Blake, and the words puzzled her, the harsh, strange "Mad Song," the curious, gently Elizabethan cynicism of the one entitled "How Sweet I Roamed." She brought the manuscript sheets to the piano and sat down, puzzling out the accompaniments in Tallan's hasty notation, and singing the melody in half-voice. Her mother came in.

"What have you got there?" she asked, coming over and standing near the piano.

Ella glanced up. "He's sent me some songs he wrote," she said.

She looked at the music again, frowning slightly.

"You don't look very pleased," Anne Gunning said, with her faint, sober smile. "I should think most girls'd be flattered to have someone writing them love songs."

"Well, they aren't love songs; I don't know what they *are*," Ella said, exasperated at her inability to understand them. "And I wish he'd write so a person could read what he's written—"

[156]

She began to play over the first of the songs again. Outside it had begun to rain; the room was gray and quiet, with only the strange, halting, bare harmonies coming slowly into it. Slowly under her fingers the songs began to take shape; she sang the words half-out, feeling something come alive in her, the exultation of her response to the strange music that seemed to melt away into the dusk as it rose and died under her voice and her fingers. She had never sung anything like this before; her voice lingered hesitantly on the curious intervals, the sudden falling away of the melody from a soft clear head tone to the dark resonance of the chest register. After an hour her mother came into the room again.

"They are queer things, and that's a fact," she said. "It's like something you don't hear in this world, to listen to you singing them."

"I *love* them," Ella said. She turned away from the piano, her face full of light. *"Aren't* they wonderful? Only I don't understand them, really, yet — I like this one best; listen to it—"

She began the music which he had set to the poem to the evening star, the simple, dreaming melody, almost a monotone, placed against the cool dim harmonies of the piano:

> . . . . . . *Let thy west wind sleep on*
> *The lake; speak silence with thy glimmering eyes,*
> *And wash the dusk with silver* . . .

She broke off.

"Isn't it lovely!" she cried. "Only I can't do the rest of it; the piano part's too hard. Do you think he meant I might show them to anyone? I want to bring them to Madame; then Flory could do these damnable piano parts."

"You might write and ask him," Anne Gunning suggested dryly.

"But that would take weeks, and I want to bring them right away, tomorrow. He said they were for me; if they are, why can't I do what I like with them?"

Ella looked at her, as radiant and impatient as a child in her excitement. Anne Gunning turned away.

"It seems to me, you're ready enough to take from him," she said, "for a girl who wants to give nothing."

[157]

"But if he sends them to me, what else can I do? I can't send them back—"

Ella came down to earth, and sat staring a little angrily at the piano before her. Why, she thought, had her mother to bring in the personal element, when she was so happy with the songs in themselves? She looked again at the two lines that Tallan had written to her: "Ella —These are for you. If you sing them, you are me for a while." *Why* couldn't she have the songs without obligation or entanglement, as if they had fallen to her out of the sky? She loved them so, even the strange, curiously bitter ones that she could not understand; she felt as if they must belong to her by some natural right, not merely as the gift of someone else.

She put the songs away, but all the while she knew that she could not resist them. The next day, when she went to the Institute for her lesson with Madame, she brought them with her. She laid them down on the piano with her other music as Madame began to talk to her.

"I suppose you want to know what happened about that foolish business yesterday," Madame said briskly. "There's nothing official yet, but you're to have Kätchen, and that young woman with the teeth will do Charlotte; that's settled, and there's nothing that we can do about it. Now *don't* go off into high tragedy over it; I've had Barto Ghedini in here all morning raving at the universe because he isn't to do Werther and Minott is, and I've had quite enough of that for one day. This is the sort of thing that happens to a young singer a dozen times, and you may as well get used to the idea now that to sing is to squabble, and to squabble without winning, as often as not—"

She was glancing through Ella's music as she talked. All at once she halted, coming to the manuscript score of Tallan's songs. She picked it up and looked at it.

"What is this?" she asked.

Ella flushed darkly. "Max Tallan sent them to me; I want to sing them; may I?" she asked, in a rush.

Madame opened her reading glasses, which were dangling from

a cord about her neck, and looked with an appearance of suspended belief at the music before her.

"Do you mean that Max *wrote* these and sent them to you?" she asked, after a little. "What on earth has he been doing with himself, reading Blake? I thought he never read anything more mystical than the *Express* sports page—"

She sounded a little vague, Ella thought, as if she was not quite thinking of what she was saying; she looked almost abstracted as she leafed through the pages.

"Dear me, Hobie must see this," she said presently. "He won't believe it. Flory, will you go, like a good girl, and see if he's in his office? They're really very fine, you know," she went on, to Ella, glancing up at her. "How on earth did you get them out of him?"

"But I didn't; he sent them to me; I didn't know anything about it—"

Ella wished all at once that she had not brought the songs; she felt suddenly that something that belonged intimately to her and to Tallan was being thrust into a hard careless public glare. She looked nervously at Madame's stout, imposing figure bent over the songs, and she wanted to snatch them away from her; she wanted to have them back for herself alone.

Lucy Flory came back into the room with Herschel.

"What's this Lucy's been telling me?" he asked, as soon as he was inside the door. His little keen eyes darted for a moment to Ella, then went on to Madame and the music she was still examining at the piano. "What is it, Maude? Is it really Max's?"

She turned around to him. "My dear, you have no idea — !" she said. "He's done some lovely little things here, perfect little gems — Max, of all people! You know, I can't listen to his music; those two interminable symphonies — I admit they're very fine, but they bore me; they brood over the universe, and I prefer composers who brood over something a little more personal. Now some of these are *extremely* personal; listen to this one, for example—"

She motioned to Lucy Flory, opened the music on the rack of the piano, and stood beside it. The young woman sat down and played

[159]

the first bars of "The Clod and the Pebble," the simple music, as quaint and innocent as a folk melody, to which Tallan had set the first lines of the poem:

> *"Love seeketh not itself to please,*
> *Nor for itself hath any care,*
> *But for another gives its ease,*
> *And builds a heaven in hell's despair."*

Madame sang it in her famous *pianissimo*, now the best of her effects left to her, so that it fell like stillness itself into the stillness of the room:

> *So sung a little clod of clay,*
> *Trodden with the cattle's feet . . .*

The piano grew brighter, more insistent; an odd, bright cynicism subtly wreathed itself about the melody:

> *But a pebble of the brook*
> *Warbled out these metres meet . . .*

The voice strengthened, brightened, asserted itself also, going boldly to meet the curious waterlike wreathings of the piano:

> *"Love seeketh only self to please,*
> *To bind another to its delight,*
> *Joys in another's loss of ease,*
> *And builds a hell in heaven's despite."*

The piano ran on for a few measures farther to an ambiguous, mocking close. Madame turned to Herschel.

"Isn't that lovely? It's diabolical, how simply he does it — the contrast, the cleverness of that ending — And you must see the others—"

She picked up the sheaf of manuscript paper from the piano and handed it across to him.

"But how did you get hold of them?" he asked her, as he took them. "Lucy says Ella brought them in—"

"She says he simply sent them to her, out of the blue; that's all I've been able to get out of her. Really, I had no idea Max could be so *galant*."

Madame shrugged her shoulders, as if it was no concern of hers how a young singer came by her songs; she was of a day when prime donne had whole operas written especially for them.

"Hm — well —" Herschel said noncommittally, looking through the music. He glanced up at Ella suddenly. "I'd like to look these over a bit — mind if I take them along with me?" he asked.

"I don't know; I only brought them to sing —" she stammered, miserably.

"Good! Why don't you sing them then? Try this one; it looks as if it might be your sort of thing."

He opened the music on the piano to the setting of "My Silks and Fine Array." Ella shook her head, almost in panic.

"But I can't —I hardly know it — not before Madame—"

She felt herself coloring up till the tears came into her eyes. She could not bear to sing the songs for them now.

"You had much better take them along with you, Hobie," Madame pronounced. "I'm afraid we've embarrassed this poor child — though why you should be embarrassed, my dear," she said, turning to Ella, "I'm sure I don't know. It's a great compliment to you—"

Ella wanted to protest against Herschel's going off with the songs, but Madame gave her no opportunity. She swept him superbly out of the room, and returned to take up the lesson where it had been left off.

"You can bring the songs to me sometime when you have them back from Hobie, and we'll go over them then," she said, closing the subject. "Now let us see what you have been doing since last time—"

But it was not so easy for Ella to dismiss what had happened. She could not concentrate on what she was doing; Madame was first indulgent, then ironical, and ended by giving her some rather sharp advice as they parted at the door of her studio: "My dear, if you want to be in love, you may be in love, with my blessing, but you must learn to keep all that sort of thing in its own proper little compartment, where it won't interfere with the more important business of your singing."

Ella did not answer her; she hung there for a moment, with a brooding, half-angry look on her face, and then started off down the hall toward the door. But before she had gone half a dozen steps, she swung around and started back; she was *not* going without her songs. She walked back down the hall to Herschel's office, knocked at the open door, and stood in the doorway, looking inside.

Herschel was sitting at the piano, smoking a cigarette, and peering through the smoke at Tallan's songs, which were propped up on the rack before him.

"Hullo," he said. "Come on in."

She came in, but only a foot or two inside the door.

"I came for the songs," she said, flushing deeply.

He glanced over at her. "What's the hurry?" he asked. "Does Maude want them again?"

"No. I — " She stood half-resolute, a little somber. "I don't think I ought to have brought them here at all," she said suddenly.

He was silent for a moment; then he got up from the piano, looking closely at the end of his cigarette in his hand, in an abstracted way.

"Why not? Did Max tell you not to show them?" he asked.

"No. But he didn't tell me that I *could* show them, either."

She hoped that he would not make her say any more. But he did not give her the songs; he stood looking out the window for a while with the same dry, abstracted expression on his face. All at once he turned around to her.

"Look, it's none of my business, of course," he said, "but just what kind of terms *are* you on with Max?"

She stood staring at him; the blood leaped again into her face. She felt that she could not answer him; she did not know at all what to say, and she resented his interference.

"Why do you want to know?" she asked. "It *isn't* your business—"

"I want to know because Max is a damned good friend of mine, and because you've got a damned fine voice, and it isn't going to do either one of you any good if you get yourselves into a hell of a mess together." He walked a few steps up and down the room. "What do you want with Max, anyway?" he went on after a moment, as abruptly as before. "You're good-looking enough, the Lord knows; you can get yourself a dozen kids your own age around here, and nobody's going to get serious if you play around with them a bit—"

"Is that what you think — that I want somebody to 'play around with'?" she asked.

He turned around, a little surprised; her voice had been almost dangerous in its intensity. After a moment, with a slight frown on his face, he sat down on the edge of his desk.

"Look," he said reasonably, "I don't *know* what you want; I don't pretend to understand women, even when they're only eighteen. But you've always struck me as an absolutely straight kid, so I'm going to be as straight with you. Max Tallan is a hell of a good guy, but he's a composer, and that's as much as saying that he's as big an egoist as they come, just as every other creative artist who's worth his salt is an egoist first, last, and always. If he gets mixed up seriously with a woman, it had better be with one who's going to think the sun rises and sets in him, and who's willing to work *for* him, and *with* him, or there's going to be trouble all around. You told me about six months ago that there weren't going to be any 'complications' in your career, but believe me, you're heading straight for a complication to end all complications if you keep this up with Max. That's all I wanted to say to you, and you can take it or leave it, as a piece of advice."

She stood there with her eyes fixed on him. She had got over her anger; she only felt that things were sickening inside her, crumbling, collapsing. Herschel's hard knowledge and determination, scarcely veiled by his slight embarrassment, pricked some young, arrogant illusion she had had of her own importance; she saw herself judged, weighed in the balance and found wanting.

"You think I'm not good enough for him," she said. "Isn't that it? You don't want to say it straight out, but it's so."

The embarrassment deepened on his face.

"I don't think anything of the sort. Look here, young woman, don't you go putting words in my mouth. I meant just what I said — you've got your career to think about, and Max has got his work;

and the two of them just won't mix. I'm thinking as much of your side of it as I am of his."

She shook her head. "I don't believe it." For a moment, despairingly, she was seeing herself, not in the golden aura of her imagined future, but as she actually was — a raw young singer, picked up out of an unlikely background to flounder for a footing in the world of music. "You think I want to use him, and you're warning me off — Well, you needn't bother," she said, rather fiercely. "*I* don't want anything from him; why don't you tell *him* to let *me* alone? And you can keep the songs, or send them back to him, whatever you like; I don't want to see them again."

She walked out of the room and quickly down the hall to the outer door. On her way to the bus she stopped, gulped down tears, and took a deep breath: the whole dark autumn world about her wavered crazily through the mist of her emotions. She felt sore and ashamed; she went home and, on impulse, wrote a stiff little note to Tallan, thanking him for the songs, "which I liked very much, but Dr. Herschel wanted to keep them for a while, and he will send them back to you when he is finished with them." It was a brutal thing to do, she knew. And after she had gone out and put the letter into the mailbox, she came home and cried for an hour in her own room. She was confused; she did not know what she felt, what it was that she ought to do.

The next day she met Herschel in the hall after one of her classes.

"Come on into my office," he said. "I want to give you back those songs."

She shook her head. "I don't want them. I told Max you'd send them back when you were finished with them."

He looked at her closely. "Is that the real thing?"

She nodded.

"Well, you are a cold little devil," he said, queerly.

"Isn't that what you wanted me to do?" she flashed at him. "Only I didn't do it for *you*," she added somberly.

She was rather distant with him for a few weeks. Then the worst of the ache of resentment and guilt inside her began to fade; she tried to put the whole matter of the songs deliberately out of her mind. She had not stopped to think, when she had written to Tallan, what effect her letter would have on her relationship with him. Now she did not want to know. Only sometimes a phrase of one of the songs came into her head, and there was an ache of wanting inside her, and a sense of guilt.

The rehearsals for *Werther* began. She had very little to do in it, but she was excited to be even on the outskirts. On the day that the first act was rehearsed on stage for the first time, she sat with Barto Ghedini in the concert hall, watching Madame Letroye and Marchpane working over the group of youngsters, all children of Institute faculty members, who appeared at the beginning of the opera as Charlotte's brothers and sisters. Ghedini, who had almost refused to take any part in the opera when he had found that he was not even to have the second tenor role of Schmidt, but had been assigned only the small part of Brühlmann, sat slumped in his chair, pretending to be uninterested in what was going on; but Ella was not so detached. The interruptions, the discussions, the casual manner in which the music and the action were gradually knitted together into a coherent whole, were as fascinating to her as a new game to a child. She sat leaning forward eagerly, watching everything, pleased with everything, imagining herself in the role of Charlotte when Maxine Neel came on the stage and sang her first simple phrase: *"Eh bien! père, es-tu content d'eux?"*

She and Ghedini, as the two silent lovers, Kätchen and Brühlmann, were called to the stage to be ready for their brief appearance. They stood together at one side, waiting while Madame Letroye worked with the six children, who had each a solo phrase as they went off with the bread and butter that Charlotte had cut for them. They had gotten into a fit of giggles, and when she spoke to them they stood still and looked at her with their faces growing pinker and pinker with the effort to restrain themselves; then, when they opened their mouths to sing, the giggles burst out again, as wild as ever. Paul Minott strolled over to Ella and Ghedini.

"Why doesn't she settle for midgets?" he said. "We'll never get anywhere with those kids."

He stood looking at them out of his unsmiling gray eyes, which were of a peculiar hard clear color, like the color of rock. Ella was not at ease with him; she resented the complete self-assurance of his manner, which made him seem a little arrogant in contrast with the confusion or nervousness of everyone else on the stage. She could see Barto Ghedini stiffening beside her; he had all the murderous Italian civility for a successful rival in his voice when he spoke.

"I don't know," he said. "What difference does it make? The way a thing like this is thrown together, a little more bungling one way or another isn't going to matter much."

"No," Minott said. "You're wrong there. Letroye's got the real thing. Did you see what she did last year with *Tosca?*"

"And Warner doing Cavaradossi? That son — he can't hit a high C if you give him a ladder."

"He was all right. He's out in Hollywood this year; they're testing him for some musical."

"That's where he belongs, all right."

They stood staring at each other, their antagonism dimly concealed behind their mutual self-assurance.

"You wouldn't touch anything like that yourself," Minott said, with an almost imperceptible smile.

"All right. I wouldn't."

Minott lifted his shoulders slightly, in a gesture so disbelieving that Madame Letroye's voice, calling from across the stage, seemed to arrive only just in time to prevent an open outbreak of hostilities.

"Paul! We're ready for you again. *Must* you people go wandering off—?"

Ghedini, his face dark, watched him go.

"Letroye's young man," he commented, with the satisfaction of the Latin in the fitting insult. "Last year Warner, this year Minott. I can't see myself in the part."

The interchange had put Ella a little on edge; she stood waiting nervously for her cue. Forrest Marchpane came over to instruct her and Ghedini on their entrance: "You're madly in love, and up in the clouds. It's all dumb show, of course, so it means that you simply mustn't look at anyone else; there simply isn't anyone *there* for you but the two of you—"

They twined arms, under his direction, and gazed with a slight awkwardness into each other's eyes.

"Really, Barto, you can do better than that!" Marchpane protested. "You *love* the girl—and isn't she delightful, though!" he said, staring at her suddenly. "Dear, I don't know you, do I?"

"Cut it out, Marchpane; you've got your own harem," Ghedini said. "And don't worry about us; we'll do all right without a blueprint from *you*."

Marchpane lifted his shoulders, and walked off across the stage.

"What I hate about that amateur is, he thinks he knows more than anybody but God and Gatti," Barto said. "Don't let him tell you what to do."

They went forward together as the tired piano played the brief orchestral passage during which the guests came into the Bailiff's garden. The Bailiff, a slender, earnest young basso, welcomed them; they sang their brief phrases, and then retreated upstage alone.

"You—what's your name?—Gunning—lean your head on his shoulder," Madame Letroye called after them. "And see that you wear low-heeled slippers on the night of the performance. Barto, you poor boy, why must you be so short?"

"I'm as tall as Caruso," Ghedini retorted.

"And what does that make me?—my God! I'm as tall as Galli-Curci," Madame shrugged. "When you can sing like Caruso, then you may be as short as he was, and no one will have a word to say about it."

She turned her attention to the others again, and a little later, when Ella and Ghedini went off stage after the other guests, their moment was over; there was nothing more now for them to do. They went down to sit in the hall again and watch the others, Ghedini keeping up a running commentary on what went on up on the stage. His convinced, innocently tough cynicism was disturbing to Ella, who preferred to enjoy her illusions.

"I don't see why you want to be a singer in the first place, if you think it's nothing but intrigue and jealousy," she protested.

He smiled his slight, cherubic smile.

"Baby, I love intrigue and jealousy," he said. "I'll do all right when my time comes." He glanced over at her. "You'd better get your eyes open, too," he said; "you're going around here like a babe in the woods. I hear Herschel sold you big to Madame C.-B., but Tharp has got his knife out for you, and if Madame C.-B. leaves next year, you're going to find yourself in a cold, cold world here—"

"If Madame leaves—?" She stared at him disbelievingly. "But why should she? I haven't heard her say anything—"

He shook his head. "My God, where have you been? She's been threatening to go back to New York on and off for the past year, whenever she has another battle with Perren or Letroye. She had a studio there for four or five years before she came here, you know, but she got fed up with it — said she wanted to live someplace where the nineteenth century wasn't quite prehistoric yet. She ought to go back to England, but she won't do that; she's got her own private little war with the government there because they made Melba a Dame of the British Empire and didn't make her one too. You wouldn't believe a woman could get so bitter about a thing like that."

He went on with his curious, cynical gossip, which came so strangely from his round child's face and round liquid eyes. He seemed to know everything about everyone — all the little underground quarrels and ambitions over which she had been walking in such blithe ignorance. She was at once appalled and fascinated; her life at the Institute seemed suddenly to have taken on a new dimension. And when she left to go home, when she went out alone into the late afternoon, with the chill red sunset already lying over the bare trees and the old houses, a depression came over her; she did not know how she was to cope with this new world in which nothing was simple and straightforward. She did not know why the music, the essential thing inside her that she wanted to make perfect and complete, should be involved in quarrels and jealousies and petty dislikes. It frightened and depressed her, and still, at the same time, there was a certain satisfaction in feeling that she was coming into the center of things. She could not help being a little pleased that she too was becoming involved.

There was a letter from Tallan waiting for her when she arrived home. She had not heard from him since she had written to him about the songs, and she did not want to open the letter; she was afraid of what it might say. She felt very guilty still about the songs whenever she thought of them. It had all turned out so badly with them that she liked to keep it out of her mind as much as she could. But the letter was there; she had to open it.

It was very brief, and not so bad after all as she had expected. She felt suddenly, as she read it, as if she could really see his eyes, the slight, calm, faintly ironic curve of his lips. It almost displeased her that he seemed to understand her so well, that he seemed to know without her telling him all the difficulties that she had gotten into over the songs. She felt somehow as if she could never make him angry enough for him to leave her; there was always that odd, intuitive understanding that flashed between them.

She put the letter aside; she would not answer it yet. And by the next day her remembrance of him had faded again; the past summer seemed lost and far away. She looked out at the dark, iron-colored sky that hung over the city, and she could not believe in that summer world. She liked the world that she had now; she did not want to change it for another.

Chapter Ten

ON the February afternoon, the rain almost gone, the clean bare limbs of the trees showing their wet curve and gleam against the gray sky outside, she sat in the concert hall, waiting for the opera rehearsal to begin. Ghedini came in and sat down beside her.

"Have you heard what's happened?" he asked her.

She shook her head. "No. What do you mean? Is it about the rehearsal?"

"About the rehearsal — hell, no! It's about Maxine. Are you trying to kid me, you lucky stiff?"

"But I *don't* know, Barto," she protested. She saw that he was looking at her enviously. "What's the matter? Has anything happened about Maxine?"

"She got a wire this morning; they want her to do the ingénue in the road company of *Summertime*. She's not going to turn it down, and that means somebody else will have to do Charlotte. Damn it, that's the kind of thing that never happens to *me*."

She felt the blood come into her face.

"Oh, Barto, do you mean they're going to let *me* do Charlotte?"

He shrugged. "Who else have they got? Now don't you go counting your chickens, baby, but I think it's in the bag for you; there's not another mezzo around here who knows the first thing about that part, and they haven't got all the time in the world. Tharp'll probably kick up a fuss and try to palm off that moron Logan on them, but Letroye knows too much about this business to take a chance on anybody like her. She's crazy if she doesn't see you're her best bet—"

"I know the part now — really I do," Ella said. She spoke intensely, as if he were the one whom she had to convince. "I could do it as well as Maxine tomorrow. *I* know I could—"

"You could do it better, baby; you've got the voice, and that walking calendar ad hasn't. But there's more than that to getting the part. I saw Letroye and Perren and Tharp and Madame C.-B. with their heads together this afternoon; it's what comes out of *that* huddle that's going to make the difference."

The others were coming into the hall. Paul Minott walked up to them with his hands in his pockets and his score under his arm.

"I hear we're getting a new Charlotte," he said. "Are you the lucky girl, Gunning?"

"She won't be so lucky," Ghedini said. "Not with you mooing in her ear — '*Ah! ce premier baiser, mon rêve et mon envie!'*" He sang the phrase from the third-act duet in an emotional voice.

Minott smiled his slight, fixed smile. "It's all in the day's work," he said. "I'm sorry about Maxine, though; we made a pretty good team."

He moved away toward the front of the hall.

"He's going to be a big help," Ghedini said.

Ella did not say anything; she was waiting tensely for Madame Letroye to appear. Marchpane walked in, looked around, and came up to them.

"Madame wants to see you," he said to Ella. "Will you come outside for a minute?"

She cast a quick glance at Ghedini and got up. Madame Letroye was standing just outside the door, talking to Madame Collier-Brown. She looked up as Ella came out with Marchpane.

"Here she is," she said. Her eyes went over Ella in rapid survey, shrewdly, missing nothing. "We're thinking of you for Charlotte," she said to her immediately, in a businesslike tone. "Maude tells me you're very quick; have you picked up anything at all of the part?"

Ella glanced from her to Madame Collier-Brown, who looked satisfied and superb, with a slight, encouraging smile on her wide, ugly, expressive mouth.

"I know it fairly well; I know almost all of it," she said quickly. "That is, not all the words—"

She was too much excited to express herself well, and looked imploringly at Madame Collier-Brown.

"The child *devours* music," Madame helped her out. "There's nothing for you to worry about, Zélie. Give me three weeks and I'll have her letter-perfect for you."

Madame Letroye shrugged. "Yes, that's very well — 'letter-perfect' — but it's not a question of memory. She and Paul have to carry those last two acts between them—"

"She will, she will. You must just give her the chance."

"At any rate, we can see what she can do." Madame Letroye turned to Ella. "Is there something you can sing for us today? We might run through the first act; there's not too much for you in that."

They all went into the concert hall together.

"We'll take the first act from your entrance," Madame Letroye said. "Use the score, please, and don't try to do more than sketch your business; we'll take care of that later, if the voice is there. Paul — Edgar—" she called. "We're doing the first act from Charlotte's entrance — and somebody for God's sake get rid of those children; we don't need any more distractions today."

Ella, clutching her score, took her place at the back of the stage, waiting for her entrance. She felt empty and shaky with excitement, and when she stepped forward to sing her first phrase, her voice scarcely traveled beyond the stage. She missed her next cue; her dialogue with the Bailiff and Werther was self-conscious and unsuccessful. She saw Madame Letroye watching her, her brows raised slightly.

"I know the duet at the end better," Ella said defensively. "Let me do *that*."

"By all means. Edgar—"

Madame Letroye nodded to the pianist, as Minott came over to make his entrance with Ella. The delicate "moonlight" music of the first-act duet began, and upon it there floated Ella's voice: "*Il faut*

[172]

nous séparer. Voici notre maison; c'est l'heure du sommeil." Then
Minott replied, the two voices continuing their dialogue of wakening
love in the quiet, almost empty hall. This was the music that she
liked best in the opera, and she knew she was doing it well; she
knew it was just as it should be, and that she would probably never
sing it better, no matter how many rehearsals she went through
before the night of the performance. They went on to the end of
the act, and then the piano stopped, and she looked around at the
others. Madame Letroye was smiling slightly; there was an air of
approval all around.

"What did I tell you, Zélie?" Madame Collier-Brown's voice
came up from the first row of the auditorium. "You have absolutely
nothing to worry about; she's swallowed it all."

"She's made a good beginning at it, at any rate," Madame Letroye
said. "Certainly she's usable—"

"Oh, usable!" Madame Collier-Brown said. "She'll *make* the
wretched thing for you — all that French treacle of sentimentality —
for anything it's worth—"

They wanted to see what she could do with the third act, the
scene beginning with the Letter aria. She had found herself now,
and though she was not so certain of the music here as she had
been of the first-act duet, she brought it through with warmth, her
voice full and splendid as it rose to the climax of her scene with
Werther.

"She'll do — she'll do," Madame Letroye admitted. "It's rough —
my God, yes; but the voice—"

"The voice is something you haven't heard the like of in twenty
years," Madame Collier-Brown said. "I told you, Zélie, on the day
of the tryouts, you were making a mistake; she simply wasn't in
voice that afternoon."

Madame Letroye broke the rehearsal off and sent the others away.
Afterwards she and Marchpane and Madame Collier-Brown had a
session with Ella that lasted till after six, in which she was criticized,
scolded, advised, made love to by Marchpane in the role of Werther,
and instructed in the best method of falling on her knees.

"She's not the type at all, physically, of course," Madame Letroye said; "she's made for all those boys' parts they give mezzos and contraltos to do — Octavian, Frédéric, Orsini, Orpheus—"

"What does it matter, when they hear her sing?" Madame Collier-Brown shrugged. "And she has the emotion; she won't be a stick for you up there on the stage—"

Ella was so tired by this time, with the excitement and the long afternoon, that she was ready to cry. Marchpane, reclining in a straight wooden chair on the stage, insisted to her: "Dear, you've got to be a little more reckless when you kiss me; this is one place where our Charlotte throws duty out the window—"

"For heaven's sake, Forrest, let the poor child alone," Madame Collier-Brown said. "She's tired to death, and you'll have plenty of time for all that before the performance. Do you think she *likes* to kiss that ugly phiz of yours?"

"Others have — others have, Maude," he said, jumping up. "Why should she be an exception?" He looked at Ella pensively. "She's rather stiff with me, you know; I don't think I'm her type."

"You're your own type," Madame Collier-Brown said, superbly rude. "Come along, Ella; you've had quite enough of *Werther* for one day."

She sent Ella home, but there was more excitement for her there. The Wessens came over to hear what had happened; even Lillie was impressed. Ella had to tell them in detail all that had happened, and describe for them the part she was to play.

"What did I tell you?" Ray Wessen said. "Give the kid a chance; she'll be singing at the Met before we can look around—"

Only Anne Gunning was rather quiet. When the Wessens had gone, Ella asked her, disappointed: "Aren't you glad it's happened this way? You didn't say so—"

Her mother was silent for a moment.

"It seems a queer sort of life for you," she said presently, a little oddly. "Young people have a way of thinking that they're nothing like their own parents and grandparents, but that's in the blood, and it usually comes out sooner or later. Your father, of course, was a man

[174]

that liked display, but you have a good deal in you of my side of the family too, and all of them had the reputation of keeping themselves *to* themselves, even with their own people. And you'll be wanted to spread yourself thin, over all sorts of people you don't and can't care about—"

"Why should I have to care about them?" Ella cried. "I want to sing; that's got nothing to do with other people."

But, obscurely, she knew that something in what her mother had said was true. There was something disagreeable to her, which she could not get over, in the way everyone connected with the business of developing her voice took it for granted that she was, in a way, public property, with no part of her life that belonged to herself alone.

But she put the thought away; she would not have anything marring the brightness of her triumph now. And she could not help enjoying the importance that her new role gave her, the feeling that Ghedini envied her, that Madame Letroye grudgingly admired her, that at rehearsals she was at the center of things always, instead of merely standing on the outer fringe. She was like a young queen who had just inherited her kingdom; she felt for the first time that she was acknowledged for what she was.

The rehearsals were an absorbing interest to her. She scarcely thought of anything but the opera; outside of her classes, and the necessary time spent in eating and sleeping, she *was* Charlotte; she had not a moment in which to be simply Ella Gunning. She spent hours coaching with Marchpane, and before two days had gone by had firmly established herself in his opinion as "a demon — a demon with ideas," he complained to Madame Letroye. " 'This is the way *I'd* like to do it,' she says to me; and sometimes, you know, the ideas aren't half bad. I keep trying to tell her that it's unbecoming for an opera singer to think, but she doesn't seem to believe me; that's another one of her ideas— "

She knew that both Marchpane and Madame Letroye resented the necessity that had compelled them to make use of her, but it did not disturb her; she felt a rather heady confidence in her own powers. She almost enjoyed the feeling of conquering in enemy territory, instead of on her own ground; when Ghedini relayed the current gossip of the corridors to her while she sat waiting for her cue, she scarcely minded it that the two of them seemed to be alone together against the others.

"Minott doesn't half like it, your putting him in the shade the way you're doing," he said to her one afternoon, as she came down to sit beside him in the first row of the auditorium. "Even Tharp had to admit you were doing all right when he dropped in here just now. He had a letter from Maxine; she's in Detroit. Said: 'I do hope Ella's not having any trouble with my part'—"

She smiled at his tone. "Don't be nasty, Barto," she said. "Maybe she does."

"Like hell. When did you ever see a singer who hoped anything for a better singer except that he or she'd break a leg?"

"It won't do *her* any good if I break a leg." She stopped talking a moment to listen to what was going on up on the stage. "How does she like the tour?" she asked then.

"You know Maxine. 'It was roses, roses, all the way'— That's how she tells it; it makes a good story, anyway."

"Don't you believe *anybody?*"

Ghedini looked at her out of his wise child's eyes.

"Baby, in this business everybody's his own press agent," he said. "It pays to take what you hear with a grain of salt."

She was called back to the stage to rehearse her final scene with Minott. Kneeling beside the chair in which, as Werther, he sat mortally wounded, she felt for a moment the utter incongruity of her pouring out passionate words of love to a stranger whom she disliked, and who disliked her in return; she was too new to the stage to be able to accept the situation as a matter of course. She had to *be* Charlotte when she sang to him, and she willed not to see him as Paul Minott; she sang to a romantic eighteenth-century hero whom she created out of her own imagination.

The costumes were ordered from a theatrical supply house in town. Madame Letroye's critical eye, which oversaw every detail of the performance, chose the simplest white gauze for her first-act

[176]

costume, and drew her dark hair back from her face, dressed it high to reveal the clear outlines of profile and neck. When she came out on the stage for inspection — Madame Letroye left nothing to the last moment and nothing to chance — Herschel was standing at the door of the concert hall, talking to her and to Marchpane. They all glanced around at her.

"Look at her," Madame said, between admiration and dissatisfaction, her Frenchwoman's eye taking in the effect of the erect, slender figure in its white draperies, the small, shapely head demure and a little mysterious beneath its silky crown of dark hair. "I don't know what she *does* look like, but it's not a good little German *Hausfrau*. She won't be quite real, up there in that half-light; certainly she won't look as if she could possibly have anything to do with bread and butter; she'll look like—"

"A naiad?" Herschel suggested. "That's Hugo's idea." He called out to Ella: "Come on down here; I've got something to say to you."

She came down the steps, moving quickly and soundlessly in her narrow white slippers.

"Am I all right?" she asked, looking, half-doubtful, half-radiant, from one to the other of them.

"Don't ask us," Herschel said. "You'll be conceited enough as it is, after that audience gets through telling you what it thinks." He grinned at her, his slight, hasty, half-cynical twitch of the lips. "Look, what I wanted to tell you is this," he said. "Maude's friend Royce Woolwine is going to be passing through town on the night of the opera, and he's promised to try to catch an act or two between trains—"

"Royce Woolwine?" She took her breath quickly. "He's the critic—?"

"The biggest and best. I told Maude she had a hell of a nerve, to throw you at him in your first performance, but she says she's not worried; she knows what you can do—"

"You're a lucky girl," Marchpane said. He looked at Madame Letroye. "Zélie, won't this put us on *our* toes?"

[177]

She shrugged. "Oh — Woolwine; he's Edwardian; nobody reads him any more unless they're a thousand years old themselves. It's a marvel he'll come to anything *I* do; he and I quarreled ourselves sick one evening in New York over Stanislavski, and he's never spoken to me since."

"All the same, I'll tell Paul," Marchpane said. He looked politely from Herschel to Madame Letroye. "I suppose, even if he does come to hear Charlotte, he can't quite avoid listening to Werther too—"

"My dear, you have no idea what critics can avoid listening to," Madame Letroye said incisively; "they can sit through a whole performance of *Tristan* and hear nothing at all but two false notes from the bassoon." She turned to Ella. "Now, Gunning, are you going to stand there dreaming all afternoon?" she asked. "What about that third-act costume?"

Ella smiled, turned, and left them; she walked quickly and lightly, feeling as though she were treading on air. When she went home that afternoon, through the late March sunshine, she felt that she wanted to stretch up her arms exultantly to the sky as the trees were doing, with their new buds bursting and twinkling in the spring wind. The little dark house was too small for her when she went inside; it seemed as if everything here — the fitting room with its yellow sofa and faded fashion plates, her mother sitting quietly at the sewing machine — had stayed bound in the wintry past, while outside the spring had already come.

There was a letter for her from Tallan on the table. He wrote that he expected to sail for New York late in June, and, though he did not say it directly, it seemed to her that he was telling her that something would then have to be settled between them. She felt his resolution like a wall of steel, even in his letters; he would never be satisfied with a fumbling, drifting relationship, something that would go on and on, till eventually it wore itself out in weariness and dissatisfaction. Something flamed up in her, a remembrance of the past summer. But he was thousands of miles away, and she had the immediate, present spring in her blood, the powerful surge toward the fulfillment of herself in her music.

The following morning she had no classes at the Institute. She stayed at home, working at her singing, then going out to the little yard behind the house, where Ray Wessen was beginning to prepare the ground for the vegetable garden. She wore an old sweater and a scarf tied over her head against the cold bright spring air; Ray was worried that she might catch cold.

"If anything kept you from singing in that opera next week, I think you'd start cutting throats — your own first of all," he said. "Anyway, ought a future prima donna to be grubbing around in the dirt like this?"

She smiled at him, her eyes blazing and remote. "I can't help it; I can't stay inside today. Doesn't the spring make you *wild?*"

He looked up at her shrewdly, squatting on his heels on the damp, turned earth. "No, honey, it doesn't; I'm about twenty years too old for that," he said. "But I remember when it used to. I didn't have any operas to let off my steam on; I used to want to light out for someplace new — a couple of times I did. But I always came back, somehow or other—"

"I'm not coming back from where I'm going," she said confidently.

"I'll bet you aren't, kid."

She stayed out with him till almost noon, then had lunch, dressed, and went over to the Institute. In the corridor she passed Minott, who smiled at her a little oddly, and stopped for a moment as if he was going to say something to her.

"What's the matter?" she asked him. "Something about the rehearsal?"

He shrugged his shoulders. "Oh — nothing," he said. "I'll see you there in a minute."

He went on down the corridor, and she went into the concert hall and looked around for Ghedini. He saw her, and came quickly across the front of the hall toward her. She knew at once, from his face, that something was the matter.

"Barto—?" she said. "What is it? What's wrong? I just met Paul—"

"Did he tell you?"

"Tell me what? No, he only looked queer—"

"I'll bet he did," Ghedini said. He looked at her grimly. "Do you know what it is? Maxine's back. The show folded; she walked in here this noontime, fresh off the train from Louisville—"

She stared at him unbelievingly. "But, Barto, even if she is—" She clung to her incredulity, desperately. "The opera's next week; they can't—"

"Can't they, just?" Ghedini asked. "What's going to stop them? Maxine knows the part."

"But I've got my costumes already — and Royce Woolwine's coming to hear me — Oh, they wouldn't, Barto! Madame C.-B. wouldn't let them—"

She refused to give in; she sat down in the seat nearest the door, clutching her score tightly in her hands, as if by clinging to it she was clinging too to her part in the opera.

"She hasn't heard about it yet, either," Ghedini said; "she wasn't around when Maxine came in. But I can tell you this much — Tharp and Perren and Letroye have been in a heavy huddle for over an hour now—"

He broke off suddenly and looked over at the door of the concert hall. Following his gaze, Ella saw Madame Letroye and Maxine Neel coming in together, Maxine tall, smiling, good-humored, in a soft gray coat and hat, Madame tense and confident as a cat, her eyes roving expectantly about the hall.

"Oh — Ella — there you are," she said. She pounced on Ella as coolly as if she had only wanted to talk to her about the weather; her eyes held her pinned in their composed, brilliant stare. "I want to talk to you," she said. "Maxine's back, as you see, and I'm afraid that poses rather a problem for us. We can't have two Charlottes; one of you will have to step down; and, naturally, as Maxine was our original choice — Of course, you'll have Kätchen back," she said, as if it were settled now, as if there were no more to be said about it.

Maxine stood smiling beside her.

"It's too bad," she said to Ella, quite comfortably and superbly;

she too acted as if it had never occurred to her that the matter could be arranged in any other way. "Madame says you've worked so hard — But there's always next year; I'm sure there'll be a splendid part for you next year."

"What's Madame C.-B. going to say about all this?" Ghedini asked distinctly.

He stood looking at the two of them out of his round, imperturbable eyes, his hands in the pockets of his shabby trousers, waiting with a prepared cynicism for their answer. Madame Letroye stared at him in annoyance.

"Barto, if this is any of your business, will you kindly let me know how?" she demanded.

"Sure it isn't any of my business. But I'll bet it's going to be Madame C.-B.'s when she hears about it."

Madame Letroye flicked him from head to foot with an unhurried glance.

"Chevalier Bayard," she said clearly. "How touching of you, Barto."

She turned about swiftly and crossed the hall to the steps leading to the stage, clapping her hands sharply as she did so.

"Now, boys and girls," she said. "Is everyone here? We're taking the first act from the beginning."

Ghedini looked down at Ella. She was still sitting there, clutching her score; her face had gone still and tense.

"I won't do it," she said. She sat huddled together as if someone had struck her. "I won't sing Kätchen, Barto. I'm going home."

She got up suddenly. Ghedini put a restraining hand on her arm.

"Now, wait a minute," he said. "This isn't going to get you anywhere. Sure it's a dirty trick, but there's nothing you can do about it. Your best bet is to sit tight and wait for Madame C.-B. to get here. This is a heavyweight battle, baby; you're not in the class—"

He made her sit down again; he kept talking to her in his mellow, cherubic tenor, that sounded so innocently incongruous with what he said. On the stage the rehearsal had begun; through Ghedini's

[181]

words she heard the music, the men's earnest voices, the weary piano, and then Maxine taking her first phrase: *"Eh bien! père, es-tu content d'eux?"* She looked up then, seeing, as though from another world, the familiar stage, the world where she belonged, only in her place now there was someone else. It was exactly as if she had had to realize that someone else had become Ella Gunning; she felt that she had lost her identity, that she was nothing.

"We'd better get up there," Ghedini said; "we'll be coming on next." He glanced down at her as he stood up. "Don't let those bastards see how you feel," he said. "Remember, we haven't had our innings yet."

She followed him blindly up the steps to the stage. The others glanced at her curiously; she felt how they kept themselves a little apart from her, ranging themselves prudently on the side of authority. Her entrance music began, and she stepped forward automatically with Ghedini, returning automatically to the little part that she had learned months ago. But there was a flurry at the door, an interruption: Madame Collier-Brown's voice cut with sudden impressiveness through the music.

"What is going on here? Zélie, have you completely lost your senses?"

Everything stopped: the pianist turned round, the singers stared, Madame Letroye wheeled and stepped decisively to the edge of the stage. Before her, confronting her directly, Madame Collier-Brown stood in one of her famous theatrical attitudes, her head flung back, her bosom lifted, as if she had just made an entrance in the first act of a Wagnerian music drama.

"I should think you knew well enough what's going on here, Maude," Madame Letroye said, in her dry, clear tones. "We're rehearsing *Werther,* of course — and you're interrupting us—"

She adjusted a bangle on her wrist; if Madame Collier-Brown intended to overplay her part in the little scene, she was just as determined to underplay hers. The older woman effectively raised her arched, darkened brows.

"Interrupting you? I'm under the impression that I'm saving

you — if what Michael tells me is true, and apparently it is, by what seems to be going on up there. Apparently" — she stared at Maxine, who stood in careful detachment, whispering something to Minott, as if what was happening had nothing at all to do with her — "you've turned out Ella Gunning for this — musical comedy belle of yours—"

"Don't be absurd, Maude," Madame Letroye said, composedly. "No one's been 'turned out'; you know yourself that Gunning was merely a replacement. Now that we find Maxine's available again, naturally we intend to use her."

"Why?" Madame Collier-Brown asked, with portentous bluntness.

"Why? Because she was the choice of the committee, of course; that decision was made months ago. Really, Maude, must you be so difficult—?"

"Difficult?" Madame Collier-Brown repeated it. "I'm fully prepared to be impossible!" She looked, quite unmoved, at Madame Letroye. "My dear Zélie, if *you've* lost your mind, it's no reason for me to sit by and let you make your mistakes at my expense. I've put a good deal of work into that child's preparation; as you know, I've asked Royce Woolwine to come and hear her—"

"You may have asked every music critic in New York; I can't see what difference you expect that to make to me. I don't alter my casts for personal reasons."

Madame Letroye made a sharp movement, as if she intended to return to her rehearsal, but Madame Collier-Brown impaled her with a glance.

"That's very interesting, Zélie — because if anyone can possibly explain on any *but* personal reasons why you intend to use this young woman instead of Ella—"

Madame Letroye lifted her shoulders. "Of course we are all entitled to our own opinions. But, please remember, my dear, this *is* my department, and I use my own judgment in making my decisions. If I listened to Hobart, I'd have only his pupils in my productions; if I listened to you, I'd have only yours." She turned around to face the stage again. "And now, if you'll excuse me, we have work to do here. Forrest—"

Marchpane came over quickly, and for a moment Madame Collier-Brown looked at their backs as they stood conferring together, ignoring her; a dangerous gleam of battle lightened in her eyes.

"I'm to understand that that's your last word, then?" she asked, in a deceptively civil tone. "You do intend to use Miss Neel?"

Madame Letroye turned half-around, impatiently. "I've told you, Maude—"

"Then I'm afraid you'll have to find yourself a new Sophie and a new Brühlmann as well," Madame Collier-Brown said briskly. "Margot — Barto — Ella — will you come down here?"

Ghedini looked at Ella, looked at Margot Cheyne, the startled, rosy little brunette who was singing Sophie, seized an elbow of each, and started down the steps.

"Come on, girls," he said. "Let's not keep the lady waiting."

Madame Letroye stepped to the edge of the stage again. For the first time her face darkened; she looked really angry.

"I don't know what you hope to gain by this, Maude—" she began.

"I don't 'hope to gain' anything," Madame Collier-Brown said grandly. "I merely refuse to allow pupils of mine to appear in a production of which I do not approve." She glanced at the three who had come down from the stage. "Come along, children," she said, and started toward the door.

"I think you'll find other people have something to say about this," Madame Letroye called after her, in a cold, hard voice.

Ella followed Ghedini and Madame Collier-Brown out of the concert hall.

"Now what?" Ghedini asked, when the door had closed behind them. He looked bright and pleased, full of satisfaction at the turn of events.

"I'm going in to see Roger before Zélie has a chance to speak *her* little piece to him," Madame Collier-Brown said briskly. "It's a pity he hasn't the rudiments of a backbone, but if I can get him in deep enough, he may have the grace to be ashamed to back down later."

She disappeared down the corridor in the direction of Perren's office. But almost before she was out of sight, Madame Letroye came out and followed her quickly down the hall. Ghedini gazed after her sadly.

"That's going to complicate matters," he said. "You know something? I wouldn't be in Perren's shoes now, with those two both on his neck at once."

"Oh, why did this have to happen?" Margot wailed. "My folks are coming all the way from Memphis to hear me."

She threw a half-unfriendly glance at Ella. She had seemed uncomfortable about leaving the stage, and now she looked as if she would have liked to dissociate herself from the other two. She went down the hall and sat down on a bench by herself, staring a little angrily straight before her. Ghedini looked after her, smiling.

" 'My folks are coming all the way from Memphis to hear me,' " he mocked softly. "She's got a right to be upset; this is the nearest she's ever going to get to singing in opera." He sat down too and pulled Ella down beside him. "You may as well relax," he said. "This will probably take all afternoon."

Ella sat beside him, unyielding and silent. She would not give in to the situation; she could not bear the thought that her right to the part into which she had put her whole life during the past weeks should be decided by this petty, rather horrid struggle between people who had, really, nothing to do with it or with her. She could not understand how Ghedini could relish it, the eager excitement with which he speculated on what was going on in Perren's office. There was quite a gathering in there now: Marchpane had gone in, and a few minutes afterward Tharp and Herschel; last of all, Teubel, the director of the Institute orchestra, had come strolling slight and elegant and bored along the corridor to disappear behind the heavy oak door.

"I'd say you didn't have a chance," Ghedini remarked; "too many in there on Letroye's side; but Madame C.-B. may pull a miracle out of the hat. Perren doesn't like the idea of losing her, and he knows she'll really pull up stakes one of these days, if she gets this kind of deal much oftener around here."

[185]

Ella did not say anything; she sat staring downward, fixed and unbelieving. She saw the other members of the cast standing about in little knots in the corridor, eying her in vague animosity from time to time. Maxine talked volubly to Minott and Madsen Hess; she had a confident, self-righteous air.

At last the door of Perren's office opened and the conferees came out, Madame Collier-Brown at the head of them, her face still flushed with battle. She sailed up to Ella.

"My dear, I've got you the first two acts, and that's the very best I could do with these idiots," she said. She glanced sharply at her colleagues as they filed past. "When I consider," she said audibly, "the sort of creatures who call themselves musicians in this day and age, I must say I regret I wasn't brought up in a profession where there might be a few honest people to keep me company—"

Herschel came up, smiling wryly, his hands in his pockets.

"Maude, you're a wonderful woman," he said. "You remember that Brahms anecdote? — 'If there's anybody here whom I've neglected to insult, I beg his pardon—' You should have used that for *your* parting shot."

Madame threw back her head. "And do you suppose *I* wasn't insulted? I don't know what else you call it, this whole outrageous business—"

"It's a damned shame, I'll say that," Herschel agreed. He threw her one of his quick, penetrating glances. "All the same, I hope it hasn't put you in the mood to do anything drastic. You know, you're going to run up against this kind of thing wherever you go—"

"Not if I simply settle myself quietly in a studio of my own, with a few pupils like this one" — she nodded at Ella — "who are worth the effort. I was a fool ever to have left that when I had it—"

"You didn't see it that way four years ago," Herschel said. He slipped his arm about her portly waist. "Be a good girl, Maude; don't go off any more deep ends this afternoon," he said. "You and I have made ourselves unpopular enough for one day."

"I'd have a very poor opinion of myself if I *weren't* unpopular in *this* company," she said, with her grand scornful emphasis.

But she let herself be persuaded, for the time being; she said no more to him about leaving. Still it was in her mind; when Ella came to her the next day for her lesson, she spoke to her about it again.

"Naturally," she added, "if I do go back to New York, you're coming with me. I don't intend to lose the most promising voice I've had in years because these idiots here are driving me away."

"But how—?" Ella stammered. She was dazzled by the prospect; her eyes shone with pure excitement.

"I suppose you mean, how would you live?" Madame asked. "My dear, I know half of musical New York; I could pull a few wires. You can sing in a church there as well as in a church here, and there's always that accursed radio. You don't need more than bread and butter while you're studying, and you'll never be at a loss for that as long as you can open your mouth and sing—"

But it was, for Ella, as if they were talking of something without reality. She had dreamed this so often that it was almost impossible for her to believe that it might really happen now.

The day of the opera came — a cold clear spring day, full of wind and sunshine. In the short dusk that closed over it she went, early, to the Institute. There lights were blazing in all the corridors and in a dozen studios. In one of these, which had been converted for the evening into a dressing room, she found Madame Collier-Brown, who looked her up and down, shook her lightly, and said imperatively: "Now — no tricks tonight. You'll do the very best you're capable of, or I'll never speak to you again. You don't *look* nervous—"

"I don't know; I don't know how I feel. Is Mr. Woolwine coming?"

"His train gets in at eight-thirty; he should be here in time for your first entrance. You mustn't let him worry you; it's only an opinion — and, frankly, it's more for his sake than yours that I want him to hear you. The poor man's depressed over the state of the modern operatic stage. You may give him some hope for the future."

Ella did not believe that she was serious about this, but it helped; she needed the bolstering of encouragement, however it came. Except for Madame Collier-Brown and Ghedini, who rapped at the door and then opened it to display himself almost unrecognizable in his eighteenth-century costume and wig, she felt that she was living in an atmosphere of chilly toleration; Maxine's popularity threw her own comparative lack of it into sharp relief. She felt cold, fighting against her tendency to withdraw into herself, emotionally, in unfavorable company, which she knew always affected her singing adversely.

The quick little Italian who came to make up the singers brought in his shabby case, sat her down before the mirror, and set to work, looking with satisfaction at the clear, definite planes of her face, the well-cut greenish eyes.

"*Molto bella*," he said. "For the stage, you see, it is the line that counts; the face must project itself — Without it there is red and black and white that I put on, and that is all — no character, a doll face. You make your own face, now, and I improve on it only—"

She looked at herself in the mirror when he had finished, the brilliant, shadowed eyes, the emphasized winglike curve of the lips. Then the hair drawn high in its demure, unfamiliar style, the white gown, the narrow slippers —

Madame Collier-Brown came in again.

"You're perfect," she declared. "And now forget how you look; forget it completely. If you're ever to *be* anything in opera, you must learn to think only of your singing, no matter whether you're wearing a suit of armor or a string of beads. I knew a baritone once who never looked at himself in a mirror after he was made up and in costume; he said he preferred to believe that he was singing in a business suit, which is something of an accomplishment when you're playing Amonasro in a leopardskin and a spiked crown."

Ella smiled, but a little absently. She was concentrated in herself now; everything outside seemed unreal, unimportant. She was in good voice, she knew; the simple vocalises which she sang on Madame's advice came clear and full into the room. In the hall the orchestra had already begun the prelude; the six children, scared into meekness by stage fright and Madame Letroye's hard, businesslike eye upon them, were waiting on stage with the basso who was singing the part of the Bailiff. Ella went out to stand in the wings as the curtain went up. She did not want to miss any of it; little shivers of excitement ran up and down her back.

"You'll catch cold in that draft," Madame Collier-Brown admonished her. "Come back here; Hobie wants to say something to you."

"Just good luck," Herschel said. He took her hand. "I'm going out front to join your claque now."

She thanked him, but she hardly saw him either; the only world she knew now was beyond, on the stage, under the lights. She saw Minott make his entrance; the action progressed inevitably toward the moment when she must appear.

This was that moment, then: one instant in the dim waiting silence, the next in that dream-world of the stage in which she was Charlotte. She was not nervous because she was not Ella Gunning now; even when she made her exit, and waited off stage for her cue to reappear, her reality remained there, with the music and the voices and the unfamiliar costumes. Then the "moonlight" music began. She entered arm-in-arm with Minott, and they sang the duet on the half-lit stage, her white gown glimmering as she moved, the voice lifting pure and tender through the dimness.

The act came to an end. Madame Collier-Brown came around, kissed her, fussed over her a bit, told her that Royce Woolwine had arrived late — "just in time for the duet; I left him looking pleased and skeptical and a little dazed. He thinks the duet was a happy accident; he thinks that you're very handsome, and that he's been prejudiced by that. I assured him that you'd look much less fetching in this Quakerish costume Zélie's put you into for the second act."

Ella was wound tight; she could not grow any more excited than she was. She changed her costume and smoothed her hair; the second act was about to begin. Then she was on the stage again, the married Charlotte now, sedate in a plain gown. The second act, the least rewarding, dramatically and vocally, in the opera for Charlotte, had been, till Maxine's return, the weak point in her interpretation, but she had spent all her energies on it for the past week; she had made out of her small opportunity something lovely and simple, as naïve in its sentimentality as an old German woodcut. There was a storm of applause for her when she came out to take her call at the end of the act; she had given Maxine, as Madame Collier-Brown told her a few moments later, something to despair of coming near in the remainder of the opera.

Madame had come out of the hall with a gentleman behind her, a tall, stout, ruddy, baldish gentleman whom she introduced as Royce Woolwine. He beamed pleasantly down at Ella.

"My dear, you've given me one of the most agreeable hours I've spent in a dozen years," he said. "To find a voice like yours in this modern musical wilderness—"

"Don't, don't flatter her," Madame interrupted. "She has a head on her shoulders; she knows when she's done well." She was in a good humor; she insisted that they both go down the hall with her to her studio, where they could talk. "If you have only an hour, we won't waste it on any more of this — production," she said to Woolwine. "Ella, you come too; I can see that he won't go anywhere without you."

The three of them walked along the corridors to her studio, at the other end of the building. Ella, still dazzled by the sudden transition from the stage to the reality of her own life, felt that what was happening had no more to do with her ordinary self than the part had had which she had just finished playing. She could not believe that it was really Ella Gunning who was walking here beside Royce Woolwine, listening to him praising her voice, her talent.

"You oughtn't to hide her here — or yourself either, Maude," he said, in his hearty, didactic voice, as Madame opened the door of her studio and switched on the lights. He stood blinking about at the splendid Victorian room, with its long draperies that seemed to shut out the present as they shut out the spring night outside. "I'm fond of this town myself; there's something Continental about it, a flavor — Middle European more than Middle Western — and the music is certainly excellent. But we have to face it: New York is the center—"

[190]

Madame shrugged. "I don't like New York; I swore once that I'd never go back there to live. But now—"

"We've missed you; I've missed you," Woolwine said. He sat down, stretching his legs comfortably out before him. "And this lovely young lady of yours — she should be at the Metropolitan in a few years, and your responsibility to her won't have ended then. You're the one to coach her in the great roles — Kundry, Ortrud, Amneris, Delilah — She must do them all—"

"Oh, she'll do them, whether I'm there for her or not," Madame said; "she won't stop for me or for anyone else. She has determination enough for half a dozen."

"All the better." He looked over at Ella. "You know, my dear, you're one of a great line — Alboni, Scalchi, Trebelli — even their names are almost forgotten today by all but a few old people like Maude and myself. I heard my first opera in 1876, at Covent Garden, when I was nine years old — Patti and Nicolini and Scalchi in the first English performance of *Aïda* — and I won't be satisfied that I've heard my last till I've heard you sing Amneris in that same opera—"

He and Madame wanted to talk about those golden years, before the turn of the century. They told her of a performance of *Le Nozze di Figaro* on the Queen's birthday in 1884, with a cast that included Albani, Sembrich, Lucca, and Edouard de Reszke; of Patti's last performance of *Traviata* at Covent Garden, when she wore a gown studded with hundreds of her own diamonds and valued at two hundred thousand pounds; of the first London production of *Otello,* with Tennyson, Swinburne, and Oscar Wilde in the audience. She felt the magic of the past like a subtle fragrance in the room, and like a fading blaze of light quickening the brilliant blaze of her own future. And she was full of a wild restlessness to step into that future. She could not stay still; she wandered about the room, running her hand softly over the long polished curve of the grand piano, pulling the curtains aside to look out at the darkness beyond. They had quite forgotten her now, absorbed in their recollections of the past, and after a little she slipped between the heavy drawn curtains, letting them fall to behind her, and flung up the window to breathe the cold still night air outside. It was all there before her, in the darkness, everything that she wanted, everything that she had ever dreamed of. She knew it would come now, and nothing would stop her; there was nothing in the world that she would let stand in her way.

When she came back into the room again, Madame Collier-Brown had let herself be persuaded to do what she had already decided that she wanted to do. She would not renew her contract at the Institute; she would return to New York, and Ella would join her there in the fall.

Chapter Eleven

NOW, as the spring ran on into summer, there was a curious brightness about her, a tense, brilliant satisfaction in herself. She seemed already to have left the house on Cobb Street; for one reason or another everyone there but Ray Wessen disapproved of her plans to go to New York, and in defense she had withdrawn herself from them. She was nineteen now; she could not understand it, that Lillie and her mother should believe she was too young to have her own life, away from them. Her mother would not insist, would not use her authority to prevent her from going, though that was what Lillie had urged her to do. But she had made her opposition clear; there was a wall of misunderstanding between her and Ella.

"And what about Max Tallan?" she asked her once, abruptly. "What are you going to do about him?"

"Do about him? Why must I do anything?" Ella cried. "I'll tell him I'm going away. *He* went away for his work; why can't I go away for mine?"

She did not want to think about Tallan; she did not want to think about anything but the singing. The summer opera season opened in June, and this year Herschel took her to see De Meyer, the musical director, who heard her sing and agreed at once to take her on in the chorus. He was a small, fair, wiry man, almost completely bald, though he was still in early middle age, with a direct, affable manner when he was not concerned with music; but Ella learned soon enough that he shed his affability when he was at work. The rather motley company under his direction was expected to give him performances that were beyond reproach vocally and dramatically, and everyone connected with it, from the principal singers down to the dressers, had to answer to him personally for any shortcomings. And because there were, inevitably, the shortcomings of a minor company, he lived in a state of constant irritation. His temper wore thin, and he made himself disagreeable to everyone. Still, they could not help respecting him, in the half-grudging way that people who go through life carelessly do toward those who insist on perfection.

When Ella sang for him, he was attentive and complimentary, but after he had sent her to the chorus master he seemed to forget her existence; she was doubtful if he would give her anything besides chorus work to do that season. She felt, on the whole, after the first week of rehearsals had gone by, disappointed and uncomfortable about all her new experiences. The chorus consisted almost entirely of veterans from the larger opera companies, all much older than she, who made a big, intimate, squabbling family group in which she felt out of place and isolated; and Giovannoli, the chorus master, a dry, odd little man with large intent eyes, was impatient with her because she had to learn all the music which the others could have sung in their sleep.

"The worst thing that can happen to a poor chorus master is to have someone throw him a prima donna," he said to her once when, beating time perfunctorily as the sopranos and altos ran through the cigarette girls' chorus from the first act of *Carmen*, he had to halt to instruct her to observe a *diminuendo* which the others took automatically. "You know the Habanera, I'll bet you, Miss Gunning? You know the Seguidilla? But you never sing *Dans l'air nous suivons des yeux* before. Now let me tell you one thing: Grove, she sings the Habanera, she sings the Seguidilla, but *you* sing *Dans l'air nous suivons des yeux!*"

The others laughed. There was nothing particularly ill-natured about the laughter, but it irritated her; she withdrew in her old way, with savage shyness, into herself. She felt that she would never learn to be one of them. The comfortable, uninterested domesticity — there was no other word for it — of their attitude toward their

[194]

work was baffling to her; it stripped all the glamour from what she had pictured to herself as one of the most glamorous of occupations.

She felt baffled, a little frightened, all during those first days. Nothing was as she had dreamed it: the dusty stage, the singers in cottons and slacks at rehearsal, looking quite as ordinary as anyone she passed on the street, the endless shop talk, which seemed always to dwell on personalities rather than on the music that was to be performed. It was almost as if she were back in her first days at the Finn Company again; everything seemed to go on in such a purely businesslike way, as if music were simply a commodity to be sold. She could not bear it, that the other members of the chorus should care so little whether they sang *Carmen* or *Don Giovanni*, that they looked on an opera as a matter of entrances and exits, of so many bars to be sung and such-and-such wigs and costumes to be worn. At the stage rehearsals, when they were not needed, they sat playing cards or knitting, perfectly uninterested in what was going on, and the principal singers were almost as unconcerned. Only in De Meyer there seemed to be the intelligence and conviction that drew the whole production together and made it into a coherent, living whole. And she saw how the others resented it when, to satisfy his conceptions, they had to take the trouble to modify some mannerism that they particularly liked, or to sing in a way that required them to use emotion and intelligence as well as voice.

Unlike most conductors, he had a way of speaking very softly when he was angry; the more furious he was, the more gently his voice emerged from his scarcely opened lips, so that the singers had to come all the way to the footlights to hear him tear them to pieces. One of the early stage rehearsals with orchestra that Ella took part in was a rehearsal of *Carmen*. Jenny Grove was singing the title role, and the Don José was a tall, ruddy, middle-aged tenor who had sung a great deal in the smaller Italian opera houses, and had changed his Anglo-Saxon name of William Patton in the old-fashioned style to Guglielmo Patone. He had a voice as big as his bulky frame, and he used both with an equal disregard for any but the grossest means of expression. Ella could feel the conductor's furious resistance and antagonism to him, the persistent, steel-like endeavor to impress his own musical concepts on an unreceptive, self-complacent mind. The atmosphere of the rehearsal became tense; the chorus, knowing that the lightning would fall on them if they brought themselves into prominence, scuttled on and off the stage like silent, guilty children, and sang their familiar music with serious, concentrated attention.

Patone, flushed and angry, strutted about the stage, being brought up constantly by De Meyer's insistent, scarcely audible interruptions. The conductor had succeeded in bringing everyone on the stage into opposition to him. Even Jenny Grove, who had the reputation of being one of the best-natured members of the company, was beginning to lose her temper as the rehearsal dragged on, while the sudden dry rapping of the conductor's stick interrupted more and more frequently the course of the first act; she sang her lines with a mounting impatience, without regard for anything but getting through with them. At last, when De Meyer had broken in for the sixth time on the Seguidilla, she jumped up from the wooden chair on which she had been sitting, walked straight across the stage to him, and objected angrily: "Look, Jake, I've sung that damned Seguidilla for you for three years without any complaints, and I'm doing it the same way this year—"

De Meyer regarded her with his odd, slight, rather cruel-looking smile.

"No, my dear, you are *not* doing it the same way this year," he contradicted her softly. "Do you want to know how you *are* doing it? Like a clumsy novice — an amateur without an idea in her head except that she must sing such-and-such notes to such-and-such beats of the nice conductor's stick—"

She shrugged sulkily. "Yes, that makes a good line for *you*," she said. She dug her hands into her pockets, standing there facing him, handsome and obstinate.

"My dear, it's more than a good line; it's the truth," he said. "Would you like to hear, really, how you sound?" He raised his voice slightly to call to the assistant conductor. "Rellstab — will you send Gunning over here?"

[196]

She came uncertainly, afraid that she had misunderstood. He looked at her with his calm, deceptively civil manner.

"You know the Seguidilla, I suppose?" he asked. She nodded. "Good. Would you mind singing it now for Miss Grove? Don't trouble yourself about the business; I only want you to sing the music—"

He said something to the orchestra. The next instant his stick was raised; she heard the first familiar measures of the Seguidilla. For a moment she was so frightened and angry that she could scarcely breathe. The callousness of the request, the disregard of the humiliating consequences to her of his desire to use her as a weapon of ridicule against Jenny, struck at her like a blow in the face. Then her blood came up quickly. So! he wanted a clumsy novice; very well, but that was not what he would get. She challenged him back, drawing herself together, attacking her first notes in a voice that was harsh and full, almost dangerous. And she sang on, quite unconscious of all the others standing silently by, of the empty seats stretching before her, the dismantled stage, fixed in herself in the dark, living vortex of consciousness that is the highest concentration of the artist. Twice, failing to follow the conductor's beat, she overran the accompaniment and felt, rather than heard, the smoothness with which he accommodated himself to the deviation. She went on with the mocking melody, carrying it to its conclusion.

Coming to herself again, out of the darkness of that concentration, she saw De Meyer's face looming before her, his slight, odd smile fixed intently on her.

"Not quite what I was expecting," he said briefly, nodding to dismiss her. He turned to Jenny, who still stood sulkily by. "Now, my dear, do you think you can do better than that?" he asked her, a little satirically.

She marched back to her place. And when she began to sing again it was a different matter from the perfunctory performance she had been giving; his stratagem, however he had miscalculated it as a means, had been successful in its effect. Ella, meanwhile, effaced herself again among the other members of the chorus. Jenny was popular in the company, and Ella felt that she had earned a certain resentment among the others by doing well instead of badly in competition with her. They disliked it that they had to acknowledge something in her, an intensity, a kind of fineness, that was not in Jenny. So she was separated from them even farther.

But after the long, wearisome rehearsal had come to an end, she had her reward. De Meyer called her out to speak to her; he stood looking at her with his blue, remote, impersonal gaze.

"We're doing *Zauberflöte* next month," he said. "Get Rellstab to coach you in the part of the third *Genie*. And he might run over the bridesmaid's solo in *Freischütz* with you while he's about it; if you're sharp enough about it, you can have them both."

She flushed with joy; her whole face lighted up.

"Yes," she said. "I'm sure I can do them both."

He looked at her for a moment more intently. She had the feeling that he was measuring her, calculating her for the limits of her usefulness, as a man might calculate the strength of a tool.

"We do *Mignon* in August," he said abruptly. "Get a score and look over Frédéric's part; if you can show me you can do it, you can have it."

She could scarcely believe it, that she should have Frédéric, not a "bit" part, but a real role, with the Gavotte to sing, and the duel scene with Wilhelm to do. She went at once to Rellstab, a middle-aged German, trained in Berlin and Vienna, who was one of the few members of the company with whose work De Meyer seldom found fault. When she told him that she was to learn the role of Frédéric, he looked at her with insulting intentness, his head thrown back slightly on his heavy neck.

"Little girls!" he said, speaking the words as if they were an epithet. "I suppose De Meyer knows what he's doing. They won't hear you beyond the third row unless you open up the voice twice as much as you did today. This is the next thing to open-air singing, you know, with all those open sides of the theater—"

"Today was different. I wasn't ready for it; *you* try to sing when you're pulled out like that, with no warning at all," Ella said, with

[198]

the hardiness that she had only when she was excited. But she was too happy to resent his bluntness. She carried home her scores in great exultation, and pored over them in triumph — her first *real* professional parts.

The fact that De Meyer was giving her solo parts to do flung her full tilt into the complicated jealousies of the principal members of the company. The contralto who had sung Frédéric the year before, a local singer well-established in Bard City society, was furious when she discovered that De Meyer was grooming someone else for the part — perhaps fortunately for Ella, since she was unpopular with the other members of the company, and the mere fact that she had taken a dislike to Ella made many of them range themselves automatically on Ella's side. Jenny Grove, in particular, who might have blamed her for the part she had played in the *Carmen* rehearsal, forgot all about that in the pleasure of discomfiting her enemy, and took Ella, in defiance, under her wing.

Ella's first impressions of her, the night she had met her in the Carlsburg Garden, had been correct: she was a simple, impulsive woman, whose really magnificent voice and temperament seemed to have no connection at all with her ordinary life. Off the stage, Ella, with her own quick intelligence and sensitive perceptions, could not help feeling a little impatient of her, and superior. But on stage it was a different matter. She saw Jenny, as Carmen, sauntering across the stage in her short red skirt and white blouse with the insolent grace of Mérimée's Carmen herself — *"faisant les yeux en coulisse, le poing sur la hanche, effrontée comme une vraie bohémienne qu'elle était"*; she saw the startling beauty of the ivory-pale skin and the jet-black hair, and heard the superb voice, which could be velvety and caressing, or angry and mocking, as the changing moods of her Carmen dictated.

And afterwards, when Ella spoke to her admiringly, she only laughed, sitting in her dressing room with a cigarette, too lazy to remove the make-up that was already spoiling her lovely complexion. She had no idea behind her roles; she simply became Carmen for three hours, and so she could manage successfully only those parts with which she could easily identify herself. So she was an enchanting Mignon, a splendid Amneris, and a disappointing Fidelio, all without knowing or caring herself that she did one part better than the other.

But she loved to sing; and, as she had done Frédéric many times herself, she sang the part for Ella as often as she liked, sometimes jumping up to go through her stage business as well. She made it a swaggering young dandy, with a free stride and a petulant arrogance of gesture; she would press Ricardi, the thin, middle-aged Italian tenor who looked, with his seamed dark face, more like a cab driver than an opera singer, into service, and the two of them would go through the duel scene together, she enjoying herself all the while, and ending by throwing her arms around Ricardi's neck and pulling him down beside her in the big chair in her dressing room.

"Isn't he nice? Isn't he too nice for a tenor?" she would ask, while he sat silent, rather embarrassed, under her effusiveness.

There was an odd, demanding innocence in her relations with the men of the company; they treated her as if she had not quite grown up, as if she were really the half-wild, capricious Mignon that she portrayed so well.

Before two weeks had gone by, Ella felt as if she had left behind all the rest of her life except the part of it that existed in and around the opera. She did not know whether she liked it or not, this corner of a world that smelt of the staleness of stored costumes, that sounded of broken, unfinished music, that looked often like the meaningless, disjointed scenes of a nightmare. Sometimes she hated it fiercely, as when she was thrust by the others into some prominence of ridicule; they loved to joke, and her intensity exposed her to them, rather. But always, in spite of everything, it was *her* world, which she meant to rule over some day herself. And it fascinated her; she did not want to spend a moment outside it. Nothing else mattered to her just now but that she should do well in any part that was assigned to her, and particularly that she should succeed in the role of Frédéric.

She had a short letter from Tallan. He was in New York now,

visiting his brother, and he wrote that he expected to arrive in Bard City within the week. She was a little frightened when she read this, as if some sort of doom were closing in upon her. But then she put it out of her mind. She was going to New York in the fall; there was no decision for her to make, as everything had already been decided.

He came to see her one morning without warning, as she was getting ready to leave for a rehearsal. She heard his voice, talking to her mother, while she was in her room; a few moments later Anne Gunning came in herself to tell her that he was there. Ella, who had been brushing her hair before the mirror, stood with the brush still in her hand, looking at her mother with a pale, determined, half-apprehensive face.

"What did you tell him? What did he say?" she asked her quickly.

Anne Gunning shook her head. "I told him nothing. That's for you to do. You'd better go out to him; he looks as if he'd come straight in here after you if you keep him waiting."

Ella laid the brush down, glanced at herself automatically in the mirror without seeing anything — she had forgotten her make-up, and her face looked pale and softer in outline without it — and went quickly out to the parlor. Tallan was standing at the window, waiting. He looked exactly the same: the alert, vital dark gaze, the firm mouth with its curious, rather sensuous curves. And when she saw him she was afraid; she felt what there was between them, as strong as ever in spite of the year that had passed since they had been together. She stood in the doorway, and he came across to her and reached his arms about her and kissed her as if he had come a long way only for that.

"You promised you'd be here when I came back," he said. "Do you remember?"

"Yes," she said. She remembered that last evening, the feeling of misery that had come over her at the thought that they might never be together again as they were then. And now he had come back, and in an instant, when she saw him, she knew that everything was just as it had been on that night; all the plans that she had made, which had left him, and her feelings toward him, out of account, suddenly became meaningless and incomplete. She drew away from him a little, to look at him, drawing her brows together in a slight, almost childishly happy frown. "And you—" she began, "you— came back, too; somehow I never thought it was true, that you would—"

She felt as if she were standing on moving ground, nothing about her stable and familiar and settled, as it had been half an hour before. And all the while, through her happiness, she was a little terrified, as a person is who knows that something is happening to him which he cannot control. She wanted to grasp at something, to stop everything just as it was, so that she could see it clearly and exert her own will over it.

But there was no time. She had her rehearsal to go to, and while he drove her out to the Woods she was too conscious of him to gather herself together. She was full of an unreasoning joy in him, as unreflecting as her joy in the bright, hot summer day and the green leaves of the trees as they rode along, and the shade cool and fresh still from the early morning. There was no time to think while she was with him, and afterwards, when he was gone and the rehearsal had begun, there was still no time to think about what had happened and what a difference it was going to make. They were rehearsing *Aïda*, and she watched Jenny Grove as Amneris with the old desire to sing as she did, to sing better than she had ever done or ever thought of doing, growing in her again, crowding against the happiness of her thoughts of Tallan.

In the afternoon Carla Herschel telephoned her from the cottage on the Little Buckeye River, twenty miles outside the city, where she and Herschel usually spent the greater part of the summer. She was having Tallan and several other people out for dinner, and wanted Ella to come too.

"Max says you're free tonight," she said. "Can you come? He'll bring you out—"

Ella hesitated. She remembered the conversation she had had

with Herschel, months before, over the songs that Tallan had sent her; she felt uncomfortable about going to his house when Tallan would be there. But in the end she said that she would come. If she was to see Tallan, she would not hide it from anyone. It was their affair, and not that of Herschel or of anyone else.

Tallan called for her shortly before six. She was a little nervous, insecure, as if she were going out with someone whom she hardly knew. She wore a blue-and-white striped silk dress, very slender and cool-looking, with a sailor collar. At the last moment, on an impulse, she took the ring that Tallan had given her and put it on the narrow gold chain on which she sometimes wore it, slipping the ring itself inside the V of her collar so that it could not be seen.

They drove out to the Herschels' cottage through the yellow end of the long midsummer afternoon. Then, as they reached the river, the dusk began to come; the willows, the tall white sycamores, the graceful old iron bridges, melted into the grayness; the night was coming over the quiet summer land. She did not want to talk; she wanted only to feel that he was there beside her, waiting for her. She knew that he was waiting, and it was a joy to her, and a kind of fear. She was afraid because he would force her to some decision; he would not be satisfied only to wait, there in the growing dusk beside her. And she felt that she could not decide. She only wanted to go on in the present moment, with the future as veiled and full of sudden looming possibility as the world under the falling grayness outside.

When they arrived at the cottage, Huisman and Dessieux were there with their wives. There was a good deal of talk and laughter all at once, and Ella, feeling a little out of it, found herself seated presently beside Huisman at the big table on the screened side porch where they were to have dinner.

"So Max brought you out," he said, smiling at her and nodding his head. "I told Carla she'd better ask you; do you know what I said? I said: 'If little Gunning isn't here, you watch—Max won't be here either—'"

He was only trying to make a joke with her, clumsily, in his blunt fashion, but she felt at once that she had not been wanted here for herself, that she had been asked only because it had seemed expedient to the Herschels to do so. Something cold and unyielding hardened inside her. She sat listening silently to the talk around her.

"What did you bring back with you, Max?" Herschel was asking. "You'd better make it good; after a whole year of not having to teach a lot of earnest amateurs to write two-part counterpoint, you ought to have something to show. Have you finished the new symphony?"

Tallan nodded. "Yes. I saw Argiris in New York before I came on out here; he has the score now. He's going to do some guest appearances with the New York Philharmonic next season, and thinks he'd like to bring it out there then—"

"Good enough!" Carla Herschel said, pleased. "Only don't count on getting Thornburgh to do it here, then; he wants the première or he doesn't want it at all. Second performances don't make the papers."

Herschel shrugged. "Argiris'll do a better job of it. That fellow's going to be one of the best conductors in the business in another few years; look what he did with your first symphony—"

"My God, yes; he's the only conductor I know who can play that second movement without falling asleep in the middle of it," Huisman joked. "I hope you've been a little livelier with this one, Max. Did you write a part in it for Ella, the way you promised?"

Tallan glanced at Ella. "Yes," he said. "I did."

She crimsoned quickly, feeling everyone's eyes on her; she hardly took in the meaning of his words. Opposite her, she saw Herschel looking noncommittally at his plate. There was a half-embarrassed silence for a moment. Then Huisman, as usual, plunged cheerfully into the breach.

"She'll have you composing operas yet, Max," he said. "Do you know she's even made an impression on De Meyer? We hear all sorts of stories about that: Marburg's nose is out of joint because Gunning is getting all her best parts—"

"It's only Frédéric, and that's not sure yet," Ella said. She looked half-angrily at Huisman.

"Well, it's nothing to get upset about, you know," he said. "And you'd better get used to a little flattery before you go to New York; that's all you're going to hear there — flattery to your face and nice big knocks behind your back—"

"New York?" Tallan said. "What about New York?"

He looked at Ella, who stared at him a little challengingly.

"I'm going there in September, to study," she said. "Madame C.-B.'s opening a studio there."

It was out now, the gage of battle flung down between them. But he seemed quite calm; only there was something in his eyes and the set of his mouth, rather frightening to her.

"I thought I wrote you about Maude's leaving," Herschel muttered quickly, into the silence. "Didn't I?"

Tallan did not answer. Carla Herschel began to talk about Argiris, whom she had first come to know years before, when they were both students in Paris. But a feeling of strain hung over the table; the conversation went on somewhat disjointedly. Dessieux, quiet and sensitive, shrank unhappily into himself, while his wife and Huisman tried without success to bring back the atmosphere of sharply jesting good nature that had always before this been part of their gatherings.

Ella avoided looking at Tallan, and when the meal was over she went out to the front porch and sat down with Mrs. Huisman and Madame Dessieux, listening silently while they talked over some Institute gossip. The men had stayed inside; Herschel had some new records, and they began to play them over. The music of a Mozart symphony came out into the night while the women talked on. Then the screen door opened; Tallan stood on the porch.

"Would you like to walk down to the river?" he said to Ella.

She got up without saying a word, her brows drawing together heavily. She felt that the two women were looking at her with curiosity and interest. With a sullen, almost defiant stride she walked off down the steps with Tallan.

Neither of them spoke till they were out of hearing of the two on the porch. They walked down the rough path leading to the river, stumbling a little in the dark. Halfway down the slope she stopped and turned around to him.

"Well, I know what you want to say," she remarked abruptly. "So there's no use in your saying anything. I'm going to New York, whatever happens; that's settled."

A pang almost of dread went through her as she saw his face, the rather ugly, unseeing look on it, as if he wanted to smash through something. But she would not yield; she stood there fixed and sullen in her determination.

"You'll do as you like," he said, unexpectedly noncommittal.

"Yes, I will. Why haven't I the right to do as I like, just as you had, when you went to Europe last year? I have my own life to live, as much as you have yours."

"And if I go to New York too?" he said.

She looked at him, startled, a little afraid. "Why should you do that — and how—?"

"Why shouldn't I? I'm in love with you — or have you forgotten that?"

She turned her eyes away. She could not bear the feeling it gave her when he looked at her, the feeling that, whatever happened, she was bound to him and he to her. She wanted to be free; she wanted to have her own way, completely and splendidly, with her own life.

"How could I forget it?" she half-cried. "You won't let me; you want me to decide things when I'm not ready — I want to go to New York; everything's going so well now, and I *can't* spoil it; I don't want to; I want what I have—"

He walked on without answering her down the path, and she followed him helplessly. Her angry defiance went down; she wanted to cry. She slipped on the steep path and he turned and put his hand out, steadying her.

"Are you all right?" he asked.

"Yes," she said.

They went down together to the narrow beach. The river slipped by before them, pure darkness under the overcast sky. She heard the lovely calm Mozart music coming faintly behind her on the damp wind, in sudden bursts of sound.

But they stood like enemies, separately, looking at the water. It hurt her; it was such an unending struggle in her, to maintain herself against him. She wanted to yield, to agree to whatever he asked of her, but she could not; something inside her insisted fiercely on its own fulfillment.

"Then what do you think I'm going to do?" he asked her suddenly, in a dangerous voice. "Go on like this? And for how long? Every year you'll want me less and less; you won't want a husband, you'll want a manager — somebody who'll arrange your tours and your contracts, and feed you to the public in the proper doses, and see that you're comfortable in hotels and on trains — I don't want you to give up singing, but I want you to give up that kind of life and that kind of success. I want to mean more to you than all that does—"

"And what about you — do I mean more to you than your work?" she flashed in return. The anger came up in her again; she *would not* be less important than he.

He looked at her with the same strained, dangerous expression that she had noticed before, as if he knew his own impotence in the situation and was being driven almost mad by it.

"Yes," he said. "You *do* mean more — but that's a different thing; it may be that it oughtn't—"

"*Why* is it different? You want to do your work, I want to do mine. Is it because I'm a woman, that *my* work can't mean as much to me as yours does to you?"

"No, it isn't — and that has nothing to do with it. It's because your work, your singing — at its best, it's secondary, creatively speaking; and what you're after is far from even that. You're after your own personal success, your own personal fame, and the devil with the music, as long as it gives you what you want. *You* don't care about the music; you care less and less about it with every little success that comes your way; what you care about is yourself—"

She stood staring at him with a blazing, furious face; she felt in that moment that she could have killed him. Each of his words

[207]

struck against her like a separate blow, damaging her pride in herself, wounding her with hard, cold truth. She reached up suddenly and jerked the thin chain from her neck. The clasp broke, stinging her neck as it came apart. She pulled the ring from the chain and held it out to him in the palm of her hand.

"You'd better have this now," she said, in an oddly ringing, vibrating voice. "*I* don't want it any more."

He looked down at the little gold circlet in her hand.

"It's no use to me," he said, as unyielding as she. "You do what you like with it."

"Shall I?" She stared at him for a moment longer, then turned all at once and flung the ring into the water, as far out as she could. "That's what I think of you," she said, "*and* your love. What do you care about me? You want your own way over me, and that's all—"

She turned and began walking quickly up the path toward the cottage again. She was deeply shaken, and full of shame and bitterness; the whole world seemed to have turned dark and ugly around her. And she wanted to get away from him, only to get away, where she would not have to see his eyes which seemed to her to reflect the same shame and bitterness that she felt inside herself.

But it was intolerable, too, to think of facing other people now. Near the top of the path she hesitated, seeing the lights of the cottage, and hearing the music from inside it, the sound of Huisman's laughter. But she heard Tallan coming up the path behind her, and she walked on quickly to the cottage. The two women on the porch looked at her curiously as she came up the steps.

"Where have you left Max?" Madame Dessieux asked, in her downright way. She chuckled slightly. "You haven't drowned him down there, I hope?"

"He's coming now," Ella said.

She could not stay out there with their curious eyes upon her. She went into the cottage and sat down in a chair in a corner of the room where the others were standing around the phonograph, arguing about the comparative merits of an English and a German recording of the Mozart symphony they had been listening to. They were too much interested in their talk to notice her. After a little, Tallan came into the room.

"Hullo," Huisman said, turning around, "here's Max again. How about letting us hear some of that new symphony now?"

"Come on, Max; how about that?" Herschel said.

He knew that something was wrong. His eyes flickered sharply from Tallan to Ella and back again.

"Not tonight," Tallan said.

He glanced at Ella, then went over and stood beside the phonograph, picking up one of the records that the others had been playing.

"Oh, for God's sake, Max, don't be coy," Herschel said. "If you think we're going to let you get away from here tonight without hearing some of that symphony, you're crazy."

Tallan put the record down. "All right, you asked for it," he said. "But you'd much better wait and look at the score yourself—"

He went over to the small upright piano that stood across the room, near the chair where Ella was sitting. He did not look at her as he sat down, but began to play at once, concentrating completely on the music. But at the first bars a little shudder went over her, almost a shock; she could hear him communicating with her through the music as plainly as if he had been speaking to her, even more plainly, for he was always reserved, almost a little hard and mocking, in his speech, as if he were wary of his own emotions. She sat listening, clenched in herself, as he played the first movement, which began heavily and earthily, as if the music were trammeled, somehow, rising a little each time only to sink back again sullenly in itself. But then it burst forth all at once in fierce affirmation, a life-cry, furious and insistent, tearing through the heavy hush of the earlier theme. She had heard so little of his music; only the songs that he had sent her had stayed familiarly in her memory. And it was all strange to her; it set a world about her that was *his* world, of his creation, sweeping away entirely all the outlines of her own. She could not bear it now, with the division between them; she wanted to stop her ears, to go out of the room.

[209]

He went on to play a part of the second movement, the Adagio. It frightened her, this brooding music: the dark melodies winding intricately together, sinking for a moment as if in peace, only to rise again, searching in all the spaces of music for some finality, some ultimate consummation. She did not understand it; it went through her like some dark knowledge that she had yet to learn.

He broke off, looking at the keys.

"Go on," Herschel said, almost angrily.

He shook his head. "No, that's enough for now."

He got up and lit a cigarette. Herschel stared across at him, his eyes narrowing.

"My God—" he said. "My God—" He got up too, suddenly. "Do you know what you've got there?" he asked excitedly.

Dessieux sat with a bright, quiet, blissful smile on his face. Even Huisman looked serious and elated.

"Well, it's the best thing he's ever done; he's crazy if he doesn't know that," he said. "But what about the rest of it? The part for voice—?"

"Not tonight," Tallan repeated.

He looked a little angry, as if he had withdrawn from them, angry that he had been led on to this exposure of his inmost feelings before them. Ella felt the self-composed exterior that he usually showed the world hardening on him again. And for a little she felt, as she had at the river, that she could have killed him: *why* had she to feel that she knew exactly what was happening inside him now, as if they were not two separate people, but only two parts of the same body? She willed to be separate from him; he had shown her to herself small, and then had forced her to acknowledge the world of his music, the marvelous world of it that she could not even fully understand. She listened coldly as the others talked excitedly about the symphony, and asked him about the sketches for a string sextet that he had brought back with him also.

"You oughtn't to have to waste your time on teaching," Herschel said impatiently, "but there it is — you've got to live, like the rest of us."

He and Carla wanted Tallan to stay on at the cottage for a day or two, so that they could talk more at length than they could that night, with all the others there.

"Hugo and Emma can take Ella back to town," Herschel said. "You can't say you've got anything else to do tomorrow."

Huisman, a little embarrassed, glanced over at Ella.

"Why, yes, we'll be glad to take her," he began.

"Oh, would you?" Ella said quickly. "Yes, that's settled then."

The Huismans had to leave early, and she went to get her things. When she came out on the porch to join them, Tallan stopped her at the door. The others had gone down the steps to the car. He stood looking at her attentively in the light that streamed out from inside the cottage.

"Don't be too angry with me," he said, rather strangely.

She looked straight at him, tensely. "What do you mean — 'don't be too angry with me'?" she repeated it. "What is 'too angry'?" She spoke a little mockingly, not like herself.

"Angry enough to want to see the last of me," he said.

The others were calling her. She turned half-away.

"I don't think it makes much difference whether I want to see the last of you or not," she said bitterly. "You have *your* ideas; what I want or think doesn't matter to you—"

She went on down the steps and got into the car. And when she was alone again, at home, she told herself that she was glad it had all happened as it had. She thought that she was pleased that they had quarreled, because it had settled something between them. Only inside her there was some fear, a sense of cold, opening emptiness that frightened her. She made herself very busy; it was a relief for her that there was so much for her to do, her church work still, the long hours of rehearsal and performance, the regular vocal practice that she would not neglect even for a single day.

On the Thursday following Tallan's return she went over the part of Frédéric with Rellstab for De Meyer. She was in splendid voice, and quite certain of herself, with the appearance of curious, brilliant confidence that had descended on her ever since her quarrel with

Tallan. De Meyer was critical, but impressed; she saw the satisfaction in his eyes.

"It's a voice with extraordinary possibilities," he commented to Rellstab, speaking quite as if she were not in the room. "Pity the experience isn't there, or we could do a good deal more with it this season. And by the time it *is* there, she won't be for us any longer; that's the damnable luck in a case like this—"

She was to go into the rehearsals of *Mignon* as Frédéric; that was decided. And she went home full of satisfaction in herself. Only there was a little dread still somewhere inside her; she was afraid that when she went home she would find that Tallan was there, or that he had called. She did not want him to interfere with her now.

But he was not there when she arrived home; neither had he telephoned. She was pleased; she could go her own way then, without him. The days went by, and gradually it was as if he had never come back, as if he were still thousands of miles away, in Europe.

The rehearsals for *Mignon* began. Jenny was singing the title part; Ricardi was Wilhelm Meister. That pleased her; she was at home, singing with them; she knew exactly how they sang their roles, down to the last bit of stage business that they used. The rehearsals went well; even Rellstab admitted it, she would do well in her part. She lived in the joy and the young arrogance of her fulfillment; she would not live in any other world.

Then, two days before the first performance of *Mignon*, there was a misfortune. They were doing *Traviata* that night, and she was singing in the chorus. The weather had turned cool and wet, more like autumn than late summer; there was a chilly rain, and, in spite of the heavy drawn curtains at the open sides of the theater, the stage was cold and drafty. She had to sing in thin, low-cut dresses, and when she went home that night her throat felt sore; she was afraid that she had caught a cold.

By the next morning she was sure of it, and, a little desperate, she telephoned Rellstab, who told her to stay in bed, and advised a favorite remedy of his own.

"You'll be all right by tomorrow; there's nothing delicate about you," he said rather brutally; he detested emotion, and he could hear that she was almost crying as she spoke to him over the telephone. "And if you're not, you won't be the first singer who ever sang with a cold. My God, what do you think you are — a coloratura soprano? That's a contralto part; you could sing it if you were as hoarse as a frog."

She hung up, somewhat reassured. Her mother, coming into her room a little later, found her lying with wide-open, intent eyes, as if she were trying by sheer force of will to make herself well. Anne Gunning sat down on the bed and, with one of her rare, shy gestures of tenderness, put the dark hair back from the face on the pillow.

"You mustn't want things so much; you mustn't tear yourself to pieces over one disappointment, Elly," she said. "Suppose you can't sing tomorrow night; the world won't come to an end, even your world—"

Ella looked at her with the same intent, concentrated eyes.

"No," she said. "But I'm going to sing. I'll be all right."

She would not believe that it could turn out in any other way. And the next morning, actually, when she woke up, she was better. She tried some simple vocalises, experimentally. It was something of an effort still for her to sing, but she knew that she would sing that night.

She was at the theater an hour before curtain time, and it was a deep thrill for her that, instead of having to dress and make up in the common dressing room used by the chorus, she had been assigned a dressing room of her own, where her first-act costume hung in readiness for her — the dark breeches and coat, the hat, the wig, the boots, down to the very riding whip that she was to carry. While she was making up, Rellstab came in.

"Well," he said, "how is it?"

"I'm all right," she said. "I'm fine." She rolled out the lines of her second-act entrance dramatically: *"C'est moi, j'ai tout brisé, n'importe! m'y voici!"*

He nodded his head grudgingly. "And you're in a mood, too, aren't you?" he said. "Very satisfied with yourself! Wait till after the performance for that."

[213]

He went out again, and a little later Jenny, in her brief ragged first-act costume, wandered in and sat down, shaking her curly black mane back from her neck and stretching out her bare legs before her rather ruefully.

"Chilly again tonight," she commented; "you *are* in luck, with all those clothes. They never seem to do the weather right for summer opera; but at least you'll be comfortable tonight. I told Jake once I was going to wear this costume whenever the temperature got above eighty-five, no matter whether I was singing Azucena or Ortrud, but I'd trade it for a nice hot velvet dress tonight —"

She was in perfect good humor, perfectly calm; her presence had a soothing effect on Ella's feverish high spirits. But when she had gone, the tension returned. The dresser who came to help her chattered a good deal: Senator Ballard's daughter and her husband, John Bondurant, were in the audience and had brought a group of friends; Marrani, who was singing Philine, was in a nasty mood after a quarrel with her husband — "she'll push you right off the stage if you don't watch out." Then Ricardi looked in to wish her luck. The overture began, and she sat waiting for her call, feeling suddenly cold and panic-stricken as the music unwound itself toward the moment of her entrance.

But, once she was on the stage, dusting herself with her riding whip, exclaiming petulantly to Philine, *"Oui, oui, riez! je suis un sot de crever mon cheval pour vous revoir plus tôt,"* her feeling of certainty in herself revived. She had a vivid sense of her own vocal powers, and she could not help knowing that she looked piquant and exciting in her masculine costume, really like a charming boy. For the short time that she was on the stage she held her own with the more experienced Marrani and Ricardi, and there was noticeable applause for her at the end of the act.

But it was in the second act, with the Gavotte to sing, and the ensuing duel scene with Wilhelm Meister, that her real opportunity came. And from the moment that she leaped into Philine's chamber, with the entrance lines that she had sung for Rellstab an hour or two before, she made the audience completely her own. Her voice, purer in tone than Jenny's, and of an unlabored velvety clarity, won her an ovation at the end of the Gavotte, and then there was the duel scene, which she and Ricardi took with a kind of mock-seriousness that made the most of her masked femininity. There was no question about it, Ricardi told her at the end of the act; she was the pet of the audience for that evening.

While he was talking to her, Carla Herschel came in to congratulate her.

"Hobie's been boasting to everyone all evening that he 'discovered' you," she said, in her brisk manner. "He's gone around now to say 'I told you so' to De Meyer. Max is here, but he wouldn't come back; he said you'd be happier if he didn't. Would you like it if we all went somewhere to eat after this is over, or is there really something wrong between the two of you?"

Before Ella could answer, there was another tap on the half-open door, and Michael Teubel came in with a middle-aged couple whom he introduced as the Bondurants.

"They wanted to meet you; they've been singing your praises all evening," he said. "You ought to be flattered, my dear."

"I am," she said, a little dazzled, feeling her hand taken in Bondurant's. He was a trifle shorter than his wife, with graying hair, and a critical, detached, faintly ironical manner that attracted her. The wife was something different again — direct, self-interested, handsome, an ordinary type. She spoke to Ella, assuming an immediate relationship with her, as if by privilege.

"What you've done with that little part is really splendid. Won't you come and sing a bit for us after the opera? — we're all so interested — at my house, just afterward?"

Ella could not endure it, really, her calm assumption that she could not possibly refuse. Yet she was pleased too, and a little fascinated; she knew at once that she would go. In the excitement of her roused state she wanted strange, splendid things to happen to her, sensation heaped on sensation, so that she might delay as long as possible the moment when she would have to go back to the routine of her everyday life again.

"Yes, I'll come; I'd love to," she said to the other woman.

And she felt how she spoke the words with a brightness that was almost arrogant; she was so sure of herself, so triumphant, when she must have been expected to be a little impressed, and diffident.

The Bondurants left with Teubel, and Carla Herschel said dryly, "Of course that's the end of *our* little plan for tonight, then."

Ella stared at her, half-surprised. "Shouldn't I have said I'd go?"

"Of course you should. Bondurant's on the symphony board; he's very much interested in music; there are all sorts of things that people like that can do for you."

"Oh, I don't want them to do anything for *me*," Ella protested, and Carla could not help smiling, forgetting her slight resentment: there was really something superb about the girl's self-assurance tonight, as if she were a generous young queen with her own regal gifts to bestow.

She had nothing to do in the last act, but she stayed in costume for the final curtain calls, then dressed quickly, and went out to the Bondurants. There were several others with them: a middle-aged couple named Dean, a young French pianist who taught at the Institute, and another young man who was studying singing in New York. They all crowded into the Bondurants' big car, where Ella sat crushed behind the bulky young singer's elbow and shoulder. He was describing a tennis match to the Deans, and the opera seemed to have been left far behind; already she was a little sorry that she had come.

The Bondurants lived far out, in a fashionable new suburb; it was a long drive. Mrs. Bondurant asked her a question or two about Madame Collier-Brown, but she answered her briefly; her part in the conversation lapsed. She resented them all, rather, except for Bondurant, with whom she had established one of her quick, subtle relationships. And when they arrived at the house, he took her promptly under his wing. He asked her if she wanted supper, or something to drink, and when she said she would not have anything till after she had sung, he called the pianist to accompany her, and imposed silence on the others, who were relaxed and a little noisy across the room. She saw how he imposed his own will on them, the fine, complete dominance that he had over them, who were all somewhat will-less, inchoate, an amorphous bundle of stolidities and nerves. They did not know how to oppose him; they sat with a kind of sullenness, having had enough already of music, that was for them nothing more than a social entertainment.

And because she knew that they did not want to hear her, that they were assenting to her presence there only as a whim of Bondurant's, she felt all the more determined to make them acknowledge her. With fine perception — for she knew very little about this sort of people — she sang for them some modern French songs that she had studied with Madame Collier-Brown, clever but musically banal, the kind of thing that they could understand at once and yet flatter themselves on understanding, since the music was new to them and in the modern idiom. But she loathed the whole proceeding; it was worse, infinitely worse, than singing at a fashionable wedding, when she was frankly a paid performer, under no necessity of entering into any social relationships with those for whom she sang. She was silent under their compliments, a little perverse.

The French pianist got up to rejoin the others, and Bondurant sat down at the piano himself, suggesting, with his dry, keen smile, that if she was not too tired to sing more, he would play for her himself.

"Will the rest of you go across to the library, please, if you want to chatter?" he called to the others, imperatively.

And they trooped out, like children, even the hard, self-confident wife, under the absolute direction of his will. He glanced up at Ella.

"Do you know any of the old music — Purcell, Handel, Gluck?" he asked. "*That* seems to me the real thing for a voice like yours; that pure, velvety quality isn't modern—"

She sang *Che farò senza Euridice* for him, and the Lament from *Dido and Aeneas,* though she was feeling the effects of the long evening's singing; and he brought out some Purcell airs for her to look over. She felt his attention focused upon her, the force of his will, quite unused to opposition, enclosing her calmly, almost impersonally. Yet there was something else, as well: the critical, half-smiling glance with which he took her in, as if she had been a painting that pleased him — her dark hair and slender face, the intensity of her body beneath the narrowly gold-and-black striped dress that she wore. She felt that he was calculating on something from her, and rather pleased with the prospect. So he was waiting, unhurried, calculating on the future.

The others drifted back, and she had something to eat, and a liqueur. She was in an odd state; something inside her was sick, really sick; and at the same time she felt elated and powerful. Nothing was quite real — neither these people whom she had never seen before tonight, nor the strange house, set down somewhere in the darkness on a strange road where she had never been before. For hours, ever since she had arrived at the theater that evening, she had been living in a blaze of excitement that flared out from her like a beacon, but that left her dark and mindless inside. She did not know anything about herself, or about what was happening to her; she simply accepted things as they came to her, with only the instinctive pleasure or revulsion of her nature for or against them.

And even after it was over, when Bondurant had put her in a cab and she was riding home through the early-morning silence of the suburban roads, she could not come back to her ordinary self again. She opened the window and let the cool black air flow over her and as if into her mind, into the flashing darkness there. Only when she saw the familiar streets of Jeffersonville appearing around her, something began to awaken in her. She knew that she had to go back to being Ella Gunning again; she knew that she had to go back to an ordinary life, in which ordinary judgments were valid and ordinary things would happen to her. And she did not want that just now; she did not want to have to think again.

The cab stopped before her door, and she got out and ran up the steps and into the house. There was a light on for her in the fitting room, and as she crossed it toward the door of the parlor she heard someone moving about at the back of the house. A moment later her mother came out to her.

"You haven't been waiting up?" Ella asked.

She stared at her mother, a little dazzled in the light, not really parted yet from the darkness outside.

"No," Anne Gunning said. "But I was worried; it was getting so late—"

"I went to the Bondurants', out in Fair Hill," Ella said. "I met them tonight; they wanted me to sing for them."

The expression on Anne Gunning's face changed slightly. "The Bondurants? What do you want with people like that? They're not *your* kind."

"How do you know whether they're my kind or not?" Ella cried. "*You* don't know them."

She would not have it, for her evening to be examined critically now; she was too triumphant, too confused. Her mother looked at her quietly.

"Well, it's a fine thing, at any rate, to be wandering around anywhere till this time of night, when you're half-sick as it is," she said. "You go to bed now; we can talk about this in the morning."

She went back to her room, and Ella went to her own room and quickly undressed. There was a deep division between them; each of them knew that she could not communicate with the other. In the morning it would not be any different.

Chapter Twelve

SHE had a restless night, and when she awoke in the morning her throat was worse again. It felt sore and strained; she could scarcely speak above a whisper. Their family doctor, whom Anne Gunning called, said that she had a bad case of laryngitis, swabbed her throat, and told her to get some rest.

"What have you been doing with yourself?" he joked with her. "You always were a bit thin for my taste, but now, if you weren't such a hard brown little thing, I'd say you looked as if you were going to blow away."

But it was no joking matter to her. She had two more performances of *Mignon* to sing that week, and she could not bear to give them up. Still, there was nothing else to do; she could scarcely talk, let alone sing, and Dr. Schonner said it was highly unlikely that she would be able to use her voice for any extended time even by Saturday, when the last performance took place. Her mother got in touch with Rellstab, and she had to accept the fact that Marburg would take over her part on Thursday night.

At any rate, she thought, it was better than it might have been. She had had the chance to prove what she could do in the part, and there were the notices in the papers, all very flattering; no one could take that away from her now. And in the middle of the afternoon there arrived a great sheaf of American Beauty roses for her from the Bondurants, with a little note of appreciation for her singing the night before. She had them in her bedroom, feeling like a princess. She would not let herself think, as she had felt without thinking the night before, that there had been something false and unpleasant about her going off with them after the opera, as if she had accepted the fact that she and her voice were public property, belonging to anyone who could sufficiently dazzle or flatter her.

After all the excitement of the previous night, she was glad enough to follow Dr. Schonner's orders and rest in bed that day, but by Thursday morning she was restless again. She could speak almost in her normal voice, and she thought that, as she had improved so much in twenty-four hours, she might be able to sing Frédéric again by Saturday night. She got up in the middle of the morning, dressed, and went out into the parlor to try some vocalises. But at the first note her voice broke; she drank some water, tried again, and this time it was even worse; she could not force her voice even into the beginning of a sustained musical sound. And all at once fear came over her. It was a warm August morning, still and bright with sunlight; as she stood there, in the silence of the empty room, she could hear the lazy summer-morning sounds remotely from the street outside — the falling-to of a screen door, footsteps passing unhurriedly, the distant voices of two women gossiping from one doorstep to another. And, as always in a moment of sudden panic, all those sounds came to her as if from a world that was infinitely removed from the one in which she was living; they seemed the essence of the serene, everyday existence from which she had suddenly been excluded.

Her mother was out; there was no one in the house but herself. She found her hat and bag and walked quickly up to Jefferson Street, where Dr. Schonner had his office. When she arrived, his morning office hours were almost over; the nurse showed her at once into the examining room. He looked around at her. He was a good-natured, heavy man, past middle age, rather slow in speech.

"What's the matter with you? Throat worse?" he asked. "You oughtn't to have come out, if it is."

"No, it's better, but I — can't sing," she said, standing before him with a cold, desperate face. "I've tried, and I can't—"

He had her sit down, while he looked again at her throat. When he had finished, he shook his head slightly.

[221]

"What is it?" she asked.

He sat back in his chair, considering. "Well, you *have* got a bad condition there," he said. "It may clear up, nothing to it, but since you're a singer, it might be a good idea if you saw a specialist. I can send you to Dr. Woodburn; he's the best throat man in town — only about forty, but sharp as a whip—"

"Yes," she said. "All right. I'll do whatever you say."

He telephoned and made an appointment for her for the following afternoon, and she went home to wait. When her mother came in from her marketing, she told her what had happened. Anne Gunning did not say anything; only after a little she asked: "Do you want me to go with you to that doctor's tomorrow?"

"No; why should you?" Ella said. "It isn't as if I felt sick, at all; I'm fine now, after yesterday."

But the next morning, after she was up and dressed, she went out to her mother, who was already working in the fitting room, and said to her: "Would you mind going down to the doctor's with me, after all? If you really have the time—"

"Of course I'll go," Anne Gunning said. Her eyes searched Ella's face. "How do you feel this morning?" she asked.

"Oh, I'm all right! It's only my voice—"

Ella could not tell her that, when she had gotten up that morning, she had tried once more, standing beside the bed, still in her pajamas, to sing, and that the result had been the same as the day before — her voice was dead; she could not produce a single sustained musical tone. She had fear around her now like a net, but she would not admit it. She made herself believe that everything would be right again as soon as she had seen Dr. Woodburn.

She and her mother went into town at one o'clock, to the Medical Building, where Dr. Woodburn had his office. A receptionist took her name, and showed them into the big waiting room, all cool summery chintzes and pale walls, where they sat for a time in strained silence. Ella could feel her heart going fast; she was more nervous than she had been when she had sung Frédéric. She wanted it to be over quickly.

Dr. Woodburn was a tall, fair-haired man of forty, with a civil, businesslike manner that rather put her at a distance. She sat down for the examination.

"Dr. Schonner says you're a singer," he remarked, referring to the card that the nurse had handed to him.

"Yes, I am."

"And you've been using your voice a good deal lately?"

"I hadn't thought of it. Yes — I suppose so. I do church work, and I've been singing in the operas at the Woods. And of course my vocal practice—"

He said nothing, but sat down to begin the examination. She felt the impersonality of his attitude: he was not interested in her in the least, really, as a person; he did not even pretend to be so. When he had finished, he went across the room and dictated something briefly to his nurse in a voice that Ella could not understand. She sat waiting tensely. He came back.

"I'm sorry to tell you, the outlook is not very favorable, Miss Gunning," he said to her, in his direct, rather English-sounding voice. "Dr. Schonner was quite right about the laryngitis, but there is evidence of severe strain besides. I'm afraid there is a very strong possibility that you will never sing again."

She stared at him; she could not believe that she had heard him correctly. Then the fear that had been lying in wait for her came over her in a sickening wave; she felt her belly go hollow, and heard the sounds in the room fade and roar in the distance; her hands were cold and sweating —

"She'd better have a glass of water, Miss Allan," Dr. Woodburn's voice said, far away.

She gulped the water quickly. She had to get hold of herself; she could not faint here, with those two pairs of impersonal eyes upon her.

"Are you better now?" the nurse asked.

"Yes, thanks. I'm all right." She set the glass down carefully on the table beside her and looked at the doctor. "There must be something that you can do," she said. She spoke in a flat voice, restraining herself.

He shook his head. "No. It's a matter of rest and time. That *may* do it; we can't be sure. Of course you won't try to sing, and it will be better if you use your voice as little as possible for at least six months — speak in a low tone, and don't put it to the strain of long conversations. The less you use it, in fact, the better; even a single bad strain could be damaging now. Then you might come back again, after those six months, and we'll see what's happened—"

He had said all that he had to say; there was nothing for her to do but go. She got up and walked out of the room. Her mother saw her, and came out of the waiting room to meet her.

"Well?" she asked anxiously.

Ella shook her head. She could not say anything here, with the receptionist there at her desk, another patient just coming in. They went out into the corridor. Outside the door Ella stopped.

"Mama, I can't — I won't—" she began, in a breaking voice. She stood there, her whole body tense, as if she were defying something or someone. "I won't, Mama—" she began again.

She could not say any more. The words would not come, the words to express all that she was feeling. She saw her mother looking at her, the expression of hard, quiet endurance that she knew so well coming into her eyes.

"What did that doctor say to you, now?" she asked. "Something bad about your voice?"

"That I might — that maybe I'll never be able to sing again. But, Mama, I won't—"

She did not know how to say it: that she would not bear it, she could not. The sobs quivered in her throat. Her mother took her arm.

"Now, don't," she said, "don't — It may not be as bad as that; he may be mistaken." She stood there, helpless, with that hard, simple, enduring look in her eyes. "We'll go home now, Elly," she said, after a moment.

[224]

She rang for the elevator, and when they were downstairs she asked the doorman to get a cab for them. It was a beautiful day, sunny and fresh; there was a little green park across the way, with its trees sparkling in the light, between the rows of tall city buildings. The cab pulled up, and they got in; Anne Gunning gave the directions to the driver. He turned round his head as he started the car.

"Cobb Street, lady — is that in Jeffersonville?"

"Yes, off Jefferson Street."

Ella turned her eyes away. She felt that she could not breathe with these strange faces about her, the strange, inquiring, impersonal eyes. She sat clenched tight in herself, waiting till they should get home. And when at last they went up the steps, she said to her mother: "Mama, don't tell anybody—"

Anne Gunning looked at her white, set face. "Now, I thought we might get in touch with some of your musical friends," she said quietly. "It may be that they'd know of somebody better than this Dr. Woodburn—"

"No, but not today. You won't tell anybody today?"

She had a sudden desperate hope that it was not true, that perhaps by the next morning her voice would have returned. When the Wessens came over that evening to find out what had happened at the doctor's, she would not say to them how bad it really was; she told them it was nothing, that she only needed a little rest. And for the time that they were there she almost believed it. There was her piano, with her music piled upon it, and the score of *Tannhäuser*, with which they were closing the opera season. And there was a letter from Madame Collier-Brown that had arrived only that week from New York, saying that she was expecting her there by the middle of September.

But when she was alone that night in her own room, trying to sleep, the huge, terrible weight of fear that she had been holding away from her descended on her again. For the first time it came to her, really, what it would mean to her if her voice did not return; her whole life as it was now, everything that she had hoped for as long as she could remember, and that she had worked for with such determination during the past two years, would simply come to an end. She got out of bed and stood there in the white darkness of the summer night, breathing fast, casting her eyes about the room as if she was trapped there and was looking for some way out. She wanted to try her voice again, but she was afraid; Dr. Woodburn had said, even one bad strain — She felt that something was breaking inside her; the sobs came up thick in her throat. She cried for a long time, till she had exhausted herself, huddled there alone on the edge of the bed.

In the morning when she got up she looked pale and fixed. She had not slept at all, except for an hour or two just after dawn. Her mother spoke to her again about going to see Herschel, or the people in the opera company, for advice.

"Yes, I'll go," she said.

She put on her hat and took the bus out to the Woods, where she knew there would be a rehearsal that morning. She went first to see Rellstab, and told him what had happened. He shrugged his thick shoulders.

"Woodburn — yes, he's very good," he said. "He wouldn't be mistaken about something like that. Well, how old are you — nineteen? You've been doing too much, forcing the voice — too much ambition — It's happened before—"

"But their voices — those others — did they come back?" she asked him, tensely.

He shrugged again. "Sometimes yes, sometimes no. What does Woodburn say — wait six months? Well, you're young still; you can spare the time—"

Jenny looked in just then, saw her there with Rellstab, and came in to ask her how she was. Then De Meyer stopped by. He was a little irritable, and brusque with her, when he found out what had happened. Though he was so slightly built, he seemed to have no physical limitations himself when it came to hard work, and he had not much patience with the limitations of others.

"If Woodburn says complete rest for six months, he knows what he's talking about, of course," he said. "But, my God, what have you been doing with yourself? We haven't given you that much to do here. They make voices like china these days — knock them about a bit, and they fall to pieces—"

He went on to begin the rehearsal, and the others followed him. The members of the chorus trooped by, on their way to take their places on the stage. She saw how it all went on without her; she was of no use to anyone here any longer. Jenny had been friendly and sympathetic; Ricardi had put his head in at the door to tell her how sorry he was about what had happened; but it did not really matter to them; it could not. She was nothing to them but a young singer whom they had known for a few months in the casual intimacy of the theater, as they had known dozens of others, and would know still other dozens in the years to come. She heard them talking and laughing over something quite different as they went off together; and then the bustle of the rehearsal began, the angry voice of the stage director, who was not satisfied with something that was being done.

She could not stay and listen; she wanted so much, so much to be a part of it all. She went home again on the bus, sitting alone, not seeing the busy streets and the summer sunlight. She felt as if she was dead and everyone else was alive; their cheerful, normal lives struck against her and bruised her. She wanted to shut herself away from them, to go far away from the sound of their cheerful, normal voices.

Herschel came to see her, but again it was as it had been with the others: she had been a voice to him, as she had been to them, and now that it was gone they faced each other like civil strangers, with no real interest in common. He was a little ill at ease, and rather angry, to cover it: he blamed De Meyer for having allowed her to sing on Tuesday night.

"Yes, and I may as well blame myself, too, while I'm about it, for getting you on out there in the first place," he said. "And, damn it, what about you too — what were you doing, singing out at the Bondurants' that night, after the opera, with a throat like that?"

She sat without answering him, knowing only that he too brought her no hope. And he went on, unhappy, almost embarrassed, to the practical side of the situation. New York, the Institute, her church work and her other engagements, were all out of the question now, and yet she had to live; she needed money.

"I may be able to do something for you at the Institute," he said to her. "Your piano's not up to your doing accompanying, is it? But you've had your secretarial training; they may be able to use you in the office—"

Anne Gunning, who was in the room, glanced quickly at Ella.

"There's no need for her to work at all, if it will do anything to hurt the chances that her voice will come back," she said firmly. "We got along somehow while she was growing up, without her working, and I suppose we can do it again."

Herschel's eyes darted across the room to her. He recognized the same determination that he had met so often in Ella.

"Yes, but — I imagine it would be better for her, to have something to do," he said. "It's always harder when there's nothing to do but wait. And, besides—"

"And, besides, *you* don't think my voice will ever come back, or be worth anything if it does," Ella broke in, almost fiercely, and then, remembering what Dr. Woodburn had said about raising her voice, she controlled herself with an effort and was silent again, looking at Herschel with a defiant expression on her face.

"I don't think anything of the kind," Herschel denied sharply. "That's not my business; I don't know anything about that — but I do know that it's not going to do you any good to sit around and brood about it."

"I'm not going to do that; I'll go back to the Finn Company first — but I'm going to sing again, I *will*, no matter what you or anyone else thinks—"

Her chest heaved suddenly with sobs; she got up and ran out of the room. And in her own room she stood in despair, hearing their voices as they continued to talk. They did not know what was happening to her; they could not know, or they would not be able to speak of it so calmly. She wanted to tell them, she wanted them to understand how it was with her, that she felt she could not go on living if she had to give up everything that she had built her whole existence around.

Herschel went away, and Anne Gunning came in to tell her he had suggested that she go to see Miss Christianson, at the Institute office, the following week.

"But you needn't go if you don't want," she said. "It's just as I told him — we can get along, and if it's going to help you to have a good rest—"

She stood in the doorway, looking at Ella. She was frightened for her when she saw the strained, passionate expression on her face. But she did not know how to reach her; as in the old days, with her husband, her clear, sober nature remained apart, unable to cope with emotions that she did not understand.

Ella shook her head. "No, I want to," she said. "Only I won't go *there*; I'd rather try somewhere else—"

She felt that it would be more than she could bear, to go back to the Institute now, with music all about her, and yet be able to have no part in it herself. Still she had made up her mind to the necessity of finding a job somewhere, and that evening she looked through the advertisements in the newspaper: there were two places that she might try. Her mother wanted her to wait a little, but she would not; in the strained state she was in, she felt that everyone was blaming her for doing nothing.

The next morning she answered both the advertisements, without success. One place had already been filled, and at the other the personnel manager lost interest when he learned that she had been studying music, and had only given it up, as she hoped, temporarily.

"I'm no use to anyone this way," she said to her mother and Lillie, when she came home. "They're like all the rest; they want me to be one thing or the other — a singer or a stenographer—"

"Well, you don't have to tell them that you're not interested in keeping the job permanently," Lillie advised. "After all, you *may* be, you don't know—"

Ella looked at her with a pale, unnatural face.

"Yes, I *do* know — and I know that if I can't sing, I don't want — and I can't go on—" she burst out with feverish vehemence, and with a cold, determined, almost vindictive expression passing suddenly over her face.

She went again to shut herself in her own room; she could not be with anyone now. All their attempts at sympathy or at practical advice seemed to her only an expression of their secret conviction that she would never sing again; she felt that they were her enemies, and that they were trying to force her to accept their point of view. And so that they would have no excuse to criticize her, she went into town again the next day, and the next, in the late summer heat, to look for a job. She took Lillie's advice, and did not say that there was a possibility of her leaving at the end of six months, and as a result she came home at last with a job in the business office of a chain of restaurants, where she would begin to work on the following Monday.

Then she was satisfied and vindicated, and something in her, that had been keeping her up, sending her out into the exterior world in which everyone was either indifferent or her enemy, dropped away; she was left in a blank, sudden quiet, facing the accomplished fact of her immediate future. She was caught in the cage now, with only the dim hope of a future release, and she could not bear it, she could not, she could not. There was the music inside her, stronger than ever, and she might never have it again; and there was all the splendid life that she had been building for herself sunk down into the gray ash of a prosaic existence. She rebelled against it with all her force; she wore herself out in a passion of resentment that was only the more bitter because she kept it all shut up inside her. She was making herself really ill; at night she did not sleep, but lay awake tormenting herself with remembrances of the opera, and of her last year at the Institute. Sometimes one of the songs that she had used to sing ran persistently through her head, over and over and over, even in her dreams. And in the morning she would be up again, with her pale, fixed face, going about the house silently, scarcely uttering a word.

[230]

Since all this had begun, she had heard nothing from Tallan, though she knew that he must be aware of what had happened. And, though she would not have admitted it even to herself, something in her was hurt and bitter because he had not given her any sign. It seemed to her that he was like the others — quite illogically, since she herself had sent him away. But she would not think of him; only when something forced a remembrance of him on her she felt bitter and somehow ashamed. She could not bear to remember at all the last time she had seen him, when she had flung away his ring into the river.

Then, on the Sunday before she was to begin at her new job, at almost ten o'clock in the evening, he came to the house to see her. Anne Gunning went to the door; he asked to see Ella, and she brought him into the parlor. Ella, looking round, saw him standing in the doorway. She colored up quickly, and a frowning, unwelcoming expression crossed her face. But inside she had again that feeling of bitterness and shame that she had had so often lately when she thought of him.

"I'm sorry to come so late," he said, seeming to speak rather to her mother than to her. "But I've just heard what's happened; I've been away, in New York, and only got back today."

He looked directly at Ella. She let her eyes fall on her left hand, which she was clenching and unclenching nervously in her lap.

"What difference does it make to you? I should think you'd be glad—" she said suddenly, surprising herself by the cold, almost vindictive voice in which she spoke. She could not believe that it was really she who had said those cutting, disagreeable words; it was as if there were a sort of demon in her, which drove her and drove her, till she had avenged her own unhappiness on everyone who came near her. She heard her mother's surprised voice remonstrating: "Now that's a nice thing—"

"Well then, it's not 'a nice thing' — but I didn't ask him to come — and why did you come?" she burst out, in a suffering, furious voice.

She felt that she would begin to sob with anger and humiliation if she stayed in the room a moment longer, and she jumped up, intending to go and shut herself away from everyone in her own room, as she had done so often during the past days. But he came over quickly and put his hand on her arm, stopping her.

"Look," he said, "I want to talk to you."

"No, I can't," she said. She felt the sobs rising higher and higher in her throat. "I don't want to."

"You don't know what you want. I've got my car outside; get your coat and we'll go for a drive."

Anne Gunning regarded him with her faint, ironical smile.

"Well, there's no need of that. I was just going to my room—"

Tallan glanced around at her. "Thanks, but I'm going to take her out. Would you mind getting her coat, Mrs. Gunning?"

Anne Gunning, with a slight shrug of her shoulders, went into the bedroom and came back a moment later with a light coat. Ella stood with her shoulders slightly drawn together, a little sullen now, unyielding. It only deepened her feeling of humiliation that her mother was so ready to fall in with his plans. So! she was finished now, defeated, and they thought they could have their own way with her. She looked at Tallan, hardening herself into control. No doubt he thought he was being very magnanimous. But she wanted none of his charity; she would let him see how little she cared for it.

She accepted, almost as a challenge, his invitation to come out with him; she threw her coat over her shoulders and went out into the cool darkness of the early September night. He started the car and they drove through the quiet, shabby little streets.

"Hobie says that you've been to Woodburn, and that he wasn't very encouraging," he said after a little.

She glanced at him defiantly. "Yes, but he doesn't know. No matter what anyone thinks, I'm going to sing again. So I don't need your sympathy—"

"You don't need anything, or anybody, to hear you tell it. You're pretty tough, aren't you? You're doing all right alone—"

"Maybe I'm not doing all right now, but I was — and I will again."

She felt him looking at her through the darkness.

"And what do you intend to do till that time comes?" he asked.

"I'm going to work; I've got a job."

He drove on for a little while in silence. They were driving out toward the city limits, taking the road that led along the Little Buckeye River.

"Did you ever think that you might marry me?" he asked her suddenly, in an abrupt, careful voice.

And all at once she realized how difficult it had been for him to say that, to come and see her now at all; she had another of those moments of sudden clarity in her relations with him when he seemed to her, not like a separate human being, but like a part of a whole of which she also was a part, and which she understood as she understood herself. She knew that he had come to her, not because he was sorry for her, or to take advantage of the opportunity her misfortune might give him, but because he could not help himself, because he felt that to stay away now, when there was the slightest chance that she might want him to come, was impossible. She sat silent, not answering his question, and feeling that she could not answer it, simply because all at once it seemed to her, as it had the previous summer when she had been with him, the natural, easy, and inevitable thing for her to do, to marry him and be with him always, no matter what changes came into her own plans because of it.

"You know," he began again, seeing that she was not going to speak, "last summer you said—"

But she interrupted him quickly, flushing crimson.

"It doesn't make any difference what I said last summer — and if I wouldn't then, there's much more reason now—"

"More reason now? But why?"

"Why? Because you think — and everyone else — that I'd marry you because my voice is gone, and I can't — myself—"

She could not go on. She broke off, and sat looking tensely down at her hands in her lap.

"Don't be a fool," he said. "If you marry me, I'll know why you do it, and it won't be for any reason like that. Do you think I don't know you any better than that?"

[233]

She felt a sudden passionate sense of warmth, almost of gratitude, toward him for saying that; it was so *good* to have him understand that that had nothing to do with the matter between them, that she would never marry him merely as a means of escape. But she would not acknowledge it. She stayed tensely in herself, watching the dark landscape slipping past her, the river, with its willows and sycamores threading blackly along beside it, disappearing and re-appearing.

"Where are we going?" she asked him abruptly. "Isn't this the road out to the Herschels'? I don't want to see them—"

"You won't; they're not there. I was with them in town this evening; that's where I heard what had happened to you."

"Ah!" she said bitterly. "And I suppose this is what Dr. Herschel was afraid you'd do — come and ask me to marry you; and of course he expects that I'll say yes—"

"What has Hobie got to do with it? It's none of his business."

"He thinks I want to use you; he thinks you oughtn't to marry me. Hasn't he ever told you so himself?"

She grasped at the remembrance of her quarrel with Herschel over Tallan's songs to harden her sense of how the situation must appear to others; she would not for a moment yield to the delusion, as she had done the summer before, that they were alone in a world of their own, only the two of them, with no one to consider but themselves. But it was a battle to do this. Whenever she was with him, there was the dark, silent feeling between them that she could neither escape nor deny. Always before this she had done battle with it for the sake of her independence, and now, for the sake of her pride, she would do the same.

He did not answer her question about Herschel. It was not important to him, or he did not want to bring others into something that he felt concerned only the two of them. The car ran on along the road. And all at once she could not bear it any longer, to sit there beside him as they passed through the darkness together.

"What's the use of this?" she cried. "Why don't you take me back?"

He turned his head and glanced at her. "Back to what?" he asked.

"You should have seen yourself when I walked in that room tonight. You looked like something caught in a trap."

"What did you expect me to look like?" she asked. A sudden, unbearable sense of all that she had gone through during the past weeks rose up in her; she could not hold it back any longer. "Nobody understands what it's like, nobody — none of you—" she cried.

He stopped the car. She felt him draw her to him, and for a time, as she wept, she simply gave herself up to the sense of his presence there beside her, to the immense opening consolation of being not alone, but with him. But then, as she gradually quieted herself, she drew away; she found a handkerchief and dried her eyes, casting a quick glance at him, as if she were half-ashamed. He smiled slightly.

"Better now?" he asked.

Her old anger flashed up in her again. "You say that as if I was a child — as if it wasn't important—"

He shook his head. "No. It's important all right. Only we're important too. What happens to us. Why can't you give that a chance too?"

She looked at him through the darkness. Somehow it seemed to her that she had never really looked at him before; she had only felt him as a traveler feels an obstacle in his path, as something to be gotten over. And now, in an instant, she seemed to see him in his completeness, not simply as a man who was in love with her, but as a complete human being, living through twenty-four hours of every day, living with all the years of his own past of which she knew, really, nothing whatever. And it frightened her suddenly, the knowledge that he wanted her to share that strangeness, the sum of himself, everything that he had been and would be.

She felt all at once that she had to get away from him. She pushed open the door of the car, got out, and began to walk moodily along the quiet road. He did not follow her, and she went on till she had rounded a bend in the road, where she could see, down through the trees, the curve of the river which followed the curve of the road. A mist was coming up: it was still and cool, with the first feel of autumn in the air. In the perfect stillness she could hear the steady creak of the crickets and the faint rustling sound that the turning leaves of the trees made overhead. Across the river a few scattered lights looked lonely. And she had a sudden sense of herself, quite alone here, as — like most city dwellers — she so seldom had been in her life; she felt the night big and silent and impersonal about her, living its own secret life in the river and the trees and the silent earth. She was afraid; she was alone, stripped of all her identity that was not valid to the night and the river and the earth. She was not Ella Gunning here, nor a singer; she was only a living creature that breathed and moved in the darkness as other living creatures breathed and moved. And she could not endure it, suddenly, to be alone; she had to go back, to be with him. She turned and walked quickly back along the road.

He was standing at a little distance from the car, smoking a cigarette while he waited for her. She came up more slowly.

"I was coming after you in a minute," he said. "I didn't know how far you might go—"

"I didn't go far," she said. There was an odd, half-wistful expression on her face. She was so tired, physically and spiritually, after the strain of the past weeks, that she felt as if it would be too hard, when she had come to him for companionship, if the conflict between them should begin again.

He looked at her attentively. "No," he said. "I thought you might have gone off for good."

She shook her head. "I only wanted to be alone for a little."

"And now you've come back to be with me?"

She did not answer. He approached her, as if tentatively. She did not raise her eyes; she stood with her head slightly lowered.

"If I thought it was really nothing between us, I'd go away — you know that," he said, in an odd, final voice. "But it isn't nothing; I knew that the first time I saw you, and you know it too. There aren't enough people in the world for us to be able to throw each other away and say we can find somebody else that'll do as well. There isn't anybody else; there's only the two of us—"

She knew it now; and now, when she was empty of everything but her own fear and disillusionment, she knew too that she must give in; she could not stay alone any longer. He drew her toward him, and she went to meet him; as he bent and kissed her, her whole life seemed to her to dissolve into a new darkness, as wide as the night, but a darkness in which she was not alone.

"I want to say it now," he said; "I want to say it to you now. I love you, Ella, I love you, I love you—"

She began to cry a little, still in his arms; she could not bear it that he should be at once so hard and so vulnerable. He drew apart, to look at her.

"My God," he said, "tell me I'm not wrong; tell me it's what you want too."

"Yes," she said. "Yes. I don't want to stay alone any more—"

She felt as if the weight of fear and suffering that had been smothering her during the past weeks had suddenly been swept away, and now she was light and dazed, feeling herself overtaken at last by the comfort of rest. And she did not want to think or act; she wanted only to taste that exquisite relief from tension, to feel that she need not struggle, nor plan, nor suffer any longer. Physically, she was so tired that she breathed heavily, like a child who is ready for sleep. She relaxed against him, giving herself up to her weariness, and he looked down at her, then drew her toward the car.

"I'll take you home now," he said. "You're worn out—"

But she held back. She was afraid for him to leave her now. She would begin to think again if he left her alone; she would go back to that world of fear and doubt in which she had been living.

"No," she said. "Not yet."

That was still the real world for her, and she felt it waiting to seize on her again as soon as he had gone. She walked slowly along the road, and he went beside her, holding her close against him. They passed the bend in the road where she had stood alone, but the night was different now, without menace, a part of her. She was a part of the night and the earth and the river, scarcely living in herself, without identity, but without fear. And she loved him for having

[237]

freed her from that fear; beyond the dark, tormenting sense of her oneness with him, her feeling for him blazed out for the first time unhampered, to the full limits of her nature. She had lost her old responsibilities in this night stillness, that stirred so keen and secret through the rising mist. What did it matter now if she sang again or not, what business was it of hers to see to it that she kept her life completely for herself, to do with exactly as she saw fit?

And then, after a little, a half-amazed expression came over her face. "But what is it that's happened to me — what is it—?" she asked herself.

But she did not want to think about that. Neither did she want to be swept on to a more serious love-making; there was something new and wondering, almost primeval, about her happiness now. She went with him along the road, through the mist that wreathed smokelike about the trees and clung low, in a milky cloud, along the earth.

"It's as if everything was new, somehow, coming out of the mist and the dark like that — as if it wasn't quite real, and solid, yet," she said. And she added after a moment, "And as if we were all new, too, and not very real. Do you feel that way?"

He nodded. "Yes. At any rate, about you — that you may dissolve, like the mist, and disappear any minute now — Hugo was right; you do look like a *Wassernymphe.*"

She was silent for a little, walking along slowly beside him in the aqueous darkness.

"Is that why you love me?" she asked him suddenly.

He shook his head. "No," he said. "I love you because I can't help myself." He glanced down at her interrogatively. "Do you understand that?" he asked.

She thought for a moment. "Yes," she said at last. "Only I thought it was that way with me, and not with you. What is it that makes us, do you think?"

"I don't know. I don't even want to know. I don't have to know why I want my eyes, or my hands. It's the same way with this: I know, and that's enough."

She was content to leave it at that. Whatever it was, they were together, and that was a sufficiency in itself. They turned again, rounding the curve in the road, with the river like a vague white rising cloud below, and came to the place where they had left the car. He looked at her, again interrogatively.

"Will you go with me to be married now?" he asked her suddenly.

She stared at him. "Oh — tonight — now?" she stammered. "But I don't know — Where would we go?"

She was taken too quickly out of her new, disconnected world into the world of reality once more, where plans were necessary, and contact with other people. And she remembered all at once, with a sense of shock, that in a few hours she was due to present herself at her new job; it would be Monday morning soon.

He opened the car door for her. "We might go almost anywhere," he said. "East, somewhere, or up to Michigan; it's good there at this time of the year — I still have a few weeks before the Institute opens."

But at the mention of the Institute she felt the outer world rolling in on her once more, and something stiffened inside her. She would not go off to a runaway marriage with him, with nobody knowing; she wanted it to be free and deliberate, before all the world.

"No," she said. She got into the car. "I'd rather wait a little, till we've told people."

He smiled slightly. "Why, they won't try to stop us," he said. "What is there so terrible about our wanting to be married?"

"But I'd rather they knew," she said stubbornly.

"Well — in a few days, then? A little later this week?"

"On Saturday," she agreed. And, seeing him with a slight, dissatisfied frown on his face as he came around and got into the car beside her, she said half-appealingly: "I don't want to wait, but don't you see, I can't—?"

He looked at her closely. "You know what it is, don't you?" he asked. "I'm afraid you'll change your mind—"

"No, I won't change my mind," she said. "You know that, really—"

And he bent and kissed her again. "Yes, I know it," he said, almost satisfied.

He drove her home through the dark roads, with the silent, brooding mist of the countryside gradually merging into the prosaic streets and buildings of the city, raw and spectral in the gray quiet fog. Something in her went down as they ran on through the familiar streets of Jeffersonville. Was this the reality, then, or was it that other world that she had just left behind her, in which she was alone with him and in which nothing else was of account? She would have to learn in some way how to reconcile the two, and she did not want this; she would have preferred to give up the old world entirely.

But it was there for her, whether she wanted it or not, when she went back — all the other people who had to have their part in what had happened between her and Tallan. Her mother was at once pleased and relieved and a little frightened that she was to marry Tallan; she knew too much of Ella's imperious need for self-fulfillment to believe that marriage could change her, and she feared, from her own experience, the close, dreadful conflict that a marriage could be. Still she relied on Tallan; he was older, better balanced, and she knew his feeling for Ella was something to build on. The Wessens, who did not know him, were impressed but distrustful; they felt as if they were losing her altogether. And she had to go through the business of arranging the details of the wedding with them; she could have cried with impatience at their insistence that everything be done in the proper manner. Often she regretted that she had not done as Tallan had wanted, and simply gone off with him to be married that night. What did it matter to her who was asked to the wedding, or what they ate afterwards, or what anyone wore? She let them have it all their own way; she was irritable and withdrawn with them, only wanting to be left alone.

There was the question of where they would live. She thought that it made no difference to her; it was only another external detail, like so many others. Tallan had an apartment near the Institute, and she said they might live there, if he liked. But when she saw it, something in her was frightened and displeased. It was *his* place;

she felt like an intruder in it, as if she could have no life of her own there. She decided suddenly that she did not want to live in an apartment at all; she wanted to have a house of her own, away from everyone and everything.

"A house of your own!" Anne Gunning said, when she heard that, with a slight, disbelieving smile. "You've cared little enough about this one all these years—"

But she insisted, and brought Tallan over. They would find a small place, and have a woman in by the day to do the heavy work. And, by luck, he knew of a place that might suit them. It belonged to one of the violinists in the Bard City symphony orchestra, who was ill and going to spend some time in Arizona. It was out rather far, past the city limits, on the edge of one of the little towns that clustered about the larger city, but Ella loved it as soon as she saw it: it was sturdy and gray, with an old-fashioned wrought-iron railing about the porch, and a big yard that ran back to open, rolling fields. They took a lease on it at once.

Saturday came, the day of the wedding. The house on Cobb Street was in a turmoil from early morning; the guests would come back there from the church, after the ceremony, for the wedding supper, and, though there would be only a small number of them, they would tax the facilities of the little house. Old Mrs. Wessen herself had made the wedding cake, after a recipe that had been used when she had been married fifty years before, in Germany.

When Ella arrived at the church with her mother and the Wessens, the others were already there. She saw the Herschels at once, and the Huismans, with Tallan's sister and her husband, and his older brother and his wife, who had come out from the East for the wedding. She felt lost and nervous, and, as usual when she was unsure of herself, she fell back on her old defiant shyness. She knew, at any rate, that she looked well; she wore a dark-green suit and a small hat that swept up on one side to show the clear line of her profile from forehead to throat. But she was ill at ease, ready to cry with vexation at the necessity of pledging her life away before these others. And she blamed Tallan, illogically, because it was his relatives and friends whose presence troubled her most. She had a moment of almost terrified alienation from him, when it seemed to her that he was as strange to her as all these others, that she might as soon join her life with the first stranger whom she met in the street as with him. But then she saw him looking at her, waiting, and something in her rose in passionate assurance: "My God, it's all right — it's all right," she thought. "If only there weren't all these people — if only they would leave us alone—"

She heard the minister repeating the familiar words of the marriage service. Behind her, old Mrs. Wessen was crying, and muttering something under her breath in German. The church seemed so quiet and unaccustomed, almost tragic, with its little cluster of people crowded round. Only the two of them, she and Max, seemed vivid, and rich with life. And they must be surrounded by all these everyday gray shapes of people, and bound in by these quiet gray walls, while the minister read the words to them that reminded them of the hard gray realities of life which they must face together — poverty, illness, even death. They were not *her* realities; she did not acknowledge them. She resented it, even, that they should be mentioned now; what had they to do with her? She could not wait to escape from these everyday walls, the contact with these everyday lives, into the deep, vital life that was prepared for her.

And afterwards, when they were all together in the house on Cobb Street, she kept apart from everyone still; she was silent, surrounded by an envelope of impervious, almost awkward silence, so that she made the others slightly uneasy. She knew that she was not making a good impression on Tallan's relatives, but she did not care about that. She resented it a little that they should be there, tangible representatives, as it were, of their claims on him, just as she resented it, too, that her mother and the Wessens should be there with their claims upon her. Yet she knew that under ordinary circumstances she might have liked them, particularly the brother, who was a tall, direct, heavy-set man, not at all like Max, but with something of the same hard, vulnerable assurance. He was a cellist, and the sister's husband was a musician too; they made a tight-knit family group, really united, she felt, in spite of the fact that they lived in different cities and usually saw each other only for a short time each year.

But she did not want them now; she resisted their efforts to draw her into their circle. She was afraid, really, that *they* did not want *her;* she heard the sister make some laughing remark to Max about a girl in New York, and immediately she came to the conclusion that it was she whom his family would have preferred him to marry. She was not jealous; she knew too well that he loved her, but she felt herself stiffen inside, hearing it. She did not want to know him in his past, or in his relations with others. She had put aside all that for her own part, and she wanted it to be the same with him.

The others were beginning to grow less constrained as the solid, excellent food and drink that Anne Gunning and old Mrs. Wessen had prepared passed among them; the little house was filled with talk. But it was all meaningless to her — Huisman's sudden, round laughter from the corner where he sat, circled by men, the lighter voices of the women, very animated and civil. Herschel came up to her.

"Ella Gunning in her latest role — Mrs. Max Tallan," he said. He looked at her keenly. "You'd better be good in this one," he said.

She frowned at him slightly. "Are you worried?"

"Not worried. But I'd like to be shown."

"Yes. You will be. But it's not *your* affair," she said, irritated, and as blunt as he.

He shook his head. "Listen, young woman, if Mozart and Brahms are my business, Max Tallan is my business too. He's got work to do, and you'd better see to it that you help him do it, instead of hindering him—"

"Why should I hinder him?" she said. "He'll do as he likes."

She could not let him see her feelings toward Max. She felt, as she had said, that it was none of his affair; it was no one's affair but their own. Carla Herschel, who had been standing near, turned about and spoke to her.

"Don't let Hobie bully you, Ella," she said. "You're the best thing that ever happened to Max; he's always shut himself up too much, away from other people, no matter how chummy he seems with them."

Her eyes met Ella's, and a kind of understanding flashed for a moment between them, the sudden instinctive freemasonry of women. But Ella turned away. She did not want that, either; she wanted to be connected with no one in the world but Max.

When it was time for them to leave, she went to the bedroom to put on her things, and her mother followed her. She stood just inside the door, watching, as Ella put on her hat before the mirror.

"I remember my own wedding day," she said abruptly. "Please God, you'll have a better life of it than I had."

Ella turned about. She felt, for the first time in her life, as if she and Anne Gunning were not mother and daughter, but two women facing each other, equals.

"Did you love him?" she asked, in an odd, inquiring voice.

"Love him?" A faint, curiously bitter smile crossed her mother's face. "I thought, those first months, that he was God. But he — I don't know why he ever married me, except that old saying is true, that opposites attract—"

She wanted to say something to Ella. She was afraid for her, the intensity with which she was going into marriage, as she went into everything else; and at the same time she seemed to stand apart from her, seeing so much in her at this moment that she had seen years ago in her own husband. They *would* have what they wanted from life; and she, who was so used to submitting, could never understand that, never, if she lived a thousand years.

Ella kissed her, and went out of the room to join the others again. The car was waiting before the house. They were going to drive up to Michigan for the ten days or so that Tallan had before the Institute reopened. Everyone crowded out to the steps to wish them good-by. It was a cool, clear night, with a few clouds, and a wind blowing strongly. She got into the car, waving in answer to the confusion of good-bys.

"Elly, hadn't you better put your coat on? — it's turning colder," she heard Lillie call.

[244]

Then the car started; the voices faded quickly behind it. She glanced over at Max.

"Now —" she said, breathing deeply, smiling at him.

He turned and looked at her. "Yes — now," he said.

Without taking his hands from the wheel, he bent his head and brushed her hair with his lips. They would drive north only a matter of some forty miles that night; the rest of the journey was for the following day.

Chapter Thirteen

THE little house outside of Bekesbourne was so far out of the way that they could live there quite undisturbed. Four days a week Tallan drove in to the Institute for his teaching there, coming back usually before the close of the afternoon, so that they had the whole long autumn evening free to themselves. And the necessity that Ella was under of conserving her voice gave them the excuse to keep a great deal to themselves; outside of Mrs. Garth, the woman who came in twice a week to do the cleaning, scarcely anyone stepped inside their doors from day's beginning to day's end.

She had the feeling that the Ella Gunning whom she had known all her life had vanished away on the day of her marriage, and that with her had disappeared the painful limitations and harassments that had always previously bounded her existence. In this new world in which she stood, the old validities of struggle and experience no longer held; she was one with Max and, through him, with everything about her, which passed now into her knowledge directly, and not, as formerly, through the medium of her own ego. So it followed that now, instead of seeing the world as good or bad as it affected her, she simply recognized that it existed, and that its existence in itself was good. For the first time since she could remember, she knew what it was to accept herself and her surroundings without striving or impatience; she had lapsed into a deep, active contentment, in which there was neither past nor future, but only the perfect satisfaction of the present.

So she saw nothing to criticize in the house, which was commonplace, almost ridiculously unimaginative, in its arrangements and furnishings; it was quite as she wanted it, when she took notice of it at all. On the evening that she and Tallan had returned from Michigan, Anne Gunning, who had come out to the house to see that everything was ready for them, had spoken to her about some changes in the living room, which was crowded to overflowing with furniture, so that the piano had to be pushed into a corner, almost hedged off by a grandfather clock and a whatnot shelf; but Ella had scarcely listened to her.

"No, it's nice," she said indifferently. "I don't want to change it."

She could not understand how anyone could spend her time thinking seriously about furniture; she would as soon have thought, just now, of trying to rearrange the position of the stars in the sky to suit her convenience. It was there as it was, and that was the end of it, since it was good, as everything else about her was good. And she saw that her mother, who was a little exasperated at first that she would not put her mind to the ideas that she was explaining to her, soon gave up and simply smiled and shrugged, pleased at the happiness that radiated through her indifference.

"Well then, I suppose it's all right, as long as the two of you are satisfied," she said. "But I'm afraid there'll be some queer house-keeping around here, if that's all the interest you're going to take in it."

She had had dinner ready for them when they arrived, and she stayed to clear up afterwards, but then she said that she would leave; she had the third person's slight ache and awkwardness in the presence of a happiness which she could not share. Tallan drove her back to Cobb Street. When they had gone, Ella went upstairs to the bedroom where they had left their suitcases and began to unpack. But she could not do much; for so many days now she had been used to having him with her, always there beside her like a part of her own self, that she felt his absence, even for this short time, as a cruel division. Without him the house seemed strange to her, a stranger's house, filled with a stranger's things. She went downstairs again and waited tensely for him, curled up on the sofa, hearing the fall night wind blowing up the stranger's leaves outside.

Then the car turned in. She opened the door, and he came in out of the sharp, windy night. She went to him, and put her head against the cold rough cloth of his coat.

"I missed you," she said. "I don't want you to go away."

He bent his head and kissed her. "No, and I don't want to go away, either," he said. "I cut your mother off; she wanted to talk—"

He took off his coat, and they went in together to the living room.

"Is it really all right here? Do you like it?" he asked.

She glanced around the room, which a few minutes before had seemed so strange to her.

"Oh yes, it's perfect," she said. She sat down with him on the sofa, curling herself up again as she had been, only now with his arms about her, so that she felt whole once more, relieved of her separate tenseness. "I'd like it if we could lock the door and stay here forever, just the two of us — and it would always be night outside, and the wind coming up," she murmured, her face half-buried on his shoulder.

She was tired from the trip, and completely content to remain there so with him. The clock ticked; the wind stirred in the darkness outside; occasionally there was the sudden brazen stroke of the clock, very strange and disconnected in the stillness, as it sounded the quarter-hours.

"It isn't ours yet, is it?" he asked her once, as she started slightly at an unfamiliar creaking and flapping at the side of the house, a shutter that had come unfastened in the wind. "It takes time to make a place belong to you; we're only set down here now."

"Yes," she said. "But it's nice to be set down, isn't it? I don't want old things, that belong to us; I want it all to be new, the way we are."

And she was quiet again, resting against him, while the night and the wind lapped round the house. Till gradually she recovered herself, the perfect sense of their unity, and was ready to meet him as he came seeking her more closely, always more closely. She went to meet him with the whole splendid passionate force of her nature,

[248]

at once bestowing her gifts and rejoicing in the fullness of his life that he gave her. There was nothing she wanted now that was not comprised in him; the circle of her existence seemed everywhere complete.

She suffered very much when, in a day or two, he had to begin his teaching at the Institute. But she adjusted herself quickly. After all, there was work now for her to do as well, the new responsibility of the house that had fallen on her. She loved the little living room, with its incongruous furniture, its Empire sofa upholstered in olive-green plush, its Oriental rugs and dark familiar Italian reproductions on the walls, and the small bright dining room, the kitchen, the two quiet bedrooms overhead; this was her domain, which she would have perfect for his coming.

And her domain, too, was the long yard behind the house that ran down to the fields, with a gate at the end to let her into their autumn solitude. She had seldom before in her life been much alone, never at all alone where there were no houses or streets or people to shut her away from the earth. As October came on, as the leaves began to turn, bronze, clear yellow, and red, and brown, and the sunlight fell more thinly through the air, with the sky blue and magnificent over it all, she felt that she had been translated, not merely inwardly, but outwardly as well, into a new world. She took fierce joy of it, sheer physical joy in the tingling air, and the sky that grew calm and still at sunset, with the red stain dying slowly in the west, and the twilight dropping clear and remote over the land, the distant trees, the far spire of a church. It seemed to her that she had never seen before the strange, active, superb death of the trees, the transition from the heavy green fullness of late summer to the burning colors of early autumn, which they scattered about them in perfect golden or scarlet showers at the wind's demand, stretching themselves then erect and unencumbered against the sky, showing themselves so exultant and delicately lovely in their sudden nakedness. She was almost envious of them; it was that kind of beauty, so proud and various and poignant, that she would have liked to bring to Max.

In the evenings they went down together to the fields, or sat on the sofa watching the fire that they had built in the small brick fireplace, with its ridiculously unimpressive copy of the Parthenon frieze above the mantel. They talked only at intervals, odd, disconnected conversations; it was extraordinary how little they had learned about each other as social, intellectual beings in the weeks that they had been living together. They were almost impatient of that sort of knowledge, which seemed to them pale and insignificant beside the immense riches of their immediate discoveries in each other. And, as long as they lived so, as long as they could remain in that perfect unity in which they wanted nothing, and could conceive of wanting nothing, that was not comprised in the other, it was sufficient; they needed nothing more. But the time came, inevitably, when they had to draw apart, when their lives had to overflow from that dark channel of their absorption in each other into the broader waters of their normal interests.

He, with his artist's compulsion to express his life in something beyond his own sensations, was the first to pass from the perfect state. One Sunday morning late in October, when she came, impatient, to look for him from her morning's preparations in the kitchen, she found him upstairs with sheets of manuscript paper spread out about him. He had brought out the sketches for the string sextet that he had begun while he was in Europe, and was looking them over, so completely absorbed in what he was doing that he did not even hear her at the door. A sudden pang almost of fear came to her; she felt that he had left her alone, that he was not even aware of her existence. She went across silently and looked over his shoulder.

"What is it?" she asked. "What are you doing?"

He glanced up at her. "I was thinking of doing something with this sextet," he said. "I've got some new ideas about the second movement. Last night, after you'd gone to sleep, the damnedest loveliest theme came into my head; I must have stayed awake half the night, thinking about what I could do with it in a set of variations—"

She looked down at the music jotted on the paper in his quick black almost illegible notation. She had not thought of music, nor wanted to think of it, since the day that she had agreed to marry him; it was as if she had found something else, which gave her all she had ever had from music, and infinitely more, so that she had been able to see it lapse out of her life without regret. And, somehow, she had imagined that it must be the same with him. She could not believe that he wanted something now that she could not give to him, something that had nothing to do with her, but that, for the moment at least, could be more important to him than she was herself. She was cold and afraid, as if a cloud had suddenly gone over her sun.

"I'll go down and wait till you've finished," she said, a little helplessly, going toward the door.

She wanted so much for him to call her back, to say that he did not want anything but to be with her. But he only nodded and went back to the music. She stood in the doorway for a moment, looking at his dark head, the hard, clear lines of his features and of his body, that seemed as much a part of herself now as her own body; she could not believe that they could be separate from her, and indifferent. She went downstairs and wandered through the empty rooms, looking for something to do; but there was nothing that she wanted to do. She wanted *him;* her whole being was motionless, at a dead center, without him.

And when he came down at last, with the keen, incisive exultation of a rising creativeness upon him, he did not notice that she was over still, unlike herself, watching him with doubtful eyes. Till gradually, as they had their dinner together, and the new kitten that they had taken from a neighbor amused them with its tiny, delicate lapping of a saucer of milk, the concentration went down in him and he came close to her again. She was back in her old place, and she lit up at once with the radiance of her happiness; she came and pressed herself close upon him as he kissed her, so that she might obliterate completely the sense of any separateness between them.

But the next afternoon, when he came from the Institute, after she had spent the whole day in waiting for the time when he would return, he went upstairs at once to take up the sextet again; she had to call him away from it for dinner. She tried valiantly to feel that this was as it should be. She was not upset that he left her to go to the Institute to teach; why should she resent it that he took the time to do other work, of infinitely more importance than that? So she made up her mind to enter into it.

"What are you doing?" she asked him, at the dinner table. "Would you show me tonight?"

He smiled, looking at her for a moment, half-curious. "There's not much to show," he said. "Do you really want to hear it? I didn't think you'd be interested."

"Why shouldn't I be interested?" she challenged him, suddenly a little irritated by his calmness. He was so sure of himself, and she — she had sat waiting for him all day, and now had to ask for his attention as a favor. Almost for the first time since her marriage, she found herself standing apart from him, in opposition, as she had done so often in their earlier times together.

She went into the living room with him after dinner, and sat silently on the sofa while he went to the piano and played for her parts of the sextet: the first movement, which he had almost completed abroad, and then the new theme around which he was building the second movement. It hurt her, this wonderfully moving music, which seemed to have come out of her own life, *their* life, of the past weeks; it brought her into sudden passionate consciousness of the world of music that she had put apart from her since her marriage. She wanted to take those strange, clear-dropping melodies into herself, and have them, and sing them, make them a physical part of herself. She had not known it would be like this; she wanted to tell him to stop. It hurt her too much to listen, and know that her voice was dead, that she could do nothing but sit there dumbly and take each note like a wound inside herself.

He glanced around at her after a time.

"You're quiet enough," he said to her, smiling. "Don't you like it?"

She started out of herself. "Yes — I do," she cried. "I love it — only—"

"Only what?" he asked.

She looked half-desperately at him; she did not know how to tell him what she felt.

"Only — I want you," she said imploringly, coming over to him as he sat before the piano and putting her arms about him, pressing herself almost fiercely against him. "And you go away from me—"

But he drew her down so that she rested upon him; he held her and soothed her against him.

"Do I go away from you?" he asked. "I don't think so; do you think I could have written that without you? I have to put it into music; that's all it is—"

"Is it? Is it?" she insisted.

But it soothed her, that he should say it to her. It seemed to give her some part in the music, to bring it closer to her in some way. And after a little she had him play it for her again. It was true, she thought, it was *her* music too; something of her as well as of him had gone into it.

Still she could not help being envious of him, that he had his world of music whole and full and good, while she had to satisfy herself, as it were, with the crumbs from his table. She had hardly thought of her voice all this while, to worry whether at the end of the six months, when she went back to Dr. Woodburn, he would find that she might begin to sing again; her fear had been eclipsed by the larger assurance of her happiness. But now it began to possess her again. She wanted to sing; she wanted to have her music, as he had his.

He was working very steadily, very concentratedly, on the sextet now. In the evenings he brought it down to the living room, so that he could use the piano, and, because it disturbed him to have anyone about when he was working, she went into the dining room, or sat upstairs in the bedroom, a book open before her, pretending to read. But there would come the sudden muffled sound of the piano from below, a dissonance strangely resolving, or a fragment of melody; he could not leave her in peace, with his music.

And gradually the anger came up in her. So! she thought, he

had lured her into living only through him, and now, when he was
satiated, he had left her, with a calm confidence that struck at her
like insolence; he had gone back to his own world of music, leaving
her with nothing but the empty routine of her household responsibilities to fill her life. And all her old defiance of him arose in her.
Very well; if that was what he wanted, she would show him that
she too could assert herself. If he left her with nothing but the
house on which to exert her energies, she would take the house, as
other women did, and make it the fetish of her life.

So, on Saturday, when he settled down in the living room, expecting to have several hours of uninterrupted work, she began with
dustcloth and sweeper, coming and going through the room.
He looked up after a few moments, frowning slightly, surprised.

"What's going on here?" he asked her.

She scarcely interrupted her work. "Well, you can see — I'm
cleaning," she said.

"Yes, I do see — but can't it wait for now? Mrs. Garth was here
yesterday, wasn't she?"

She straightened up from moving a chair and looked at him with
a matter-of-fact expression on her face.

"Mrs. Garth had the windows to do, and the scrubbing," she said.
"And I can't leave the house in this state over the week end. Why
don't you go upstairs with your work? Didn't you tell me that you
could do without a piano when you composed?"

He shrugged, gathered together his things, and went upstairs.
And something went down in her at the sight of his face, which
showed his impatience and irritation at this interruption of his creative activity. Still at the same time she felt a new fierce flow of energy
in herself, satisfaction that she had had the victory over him. She
went on briskly with her cleaning, shaking her dustcloth out triumphantly into the cold clear autumn air.

At lunchtime she was bright and mild with her victory, but he
was abstracted, hardly noticing; he was still absorbed in his work.
As soon as the meal was over, when she was intending to ask him
what they should do together that afternoon, he went off upstairs

and brought his work down to the living room again. She heard the piano, and the second-movement theme in its new variations, some harsh and strange, some so deeply moving and wonderful to her. And she had to remain apart from it all; she was outcast; neither he nor the music belonged to her.

She could not bear it, that he was so satisfied and absorbed; she wanted to make him suffer as she was suffering. She cleared away the lunch things, and then, with a closed, prepared look of determination, she went out to the living room again with her dustcloth, and began taking down and dusting each of the innumerable little objects that crowded the whatnot shelf beside the piano. He looked up at her in amazement and exasperation.

"*Now* what are you doing?" he said to her.

She marshaled herself against him. "What I was doing this morning — I haven't finished," she answered obstinately.

She took down another of the ridiculous and useless little objects that encumbered the shelf, and ran her dustcloth over it with care, as if it were something important and precious to her.

He sat watching her, a look of anger coming into his face, as if he understood now how deliberately she had come to break into his concentration.

"Why don't you put that damned thing away someplace, where it won't be cluttering around?" he said. "The Lord knows, there's enough junk in this room already—"

She turned round to him, her face stiff with opposition.

"Well, *I* like it," she said. "And I don't want it put away."

He swung around to the piano again, hunching his shoulders in indifference. "All right, keep it then," he said. "Only let it alone for now, for God's sake; can't you see that I'm trying to work?"

She felt a certain fierce joy coming up in her. This was what she wanted, the direct, immediate conflict between them, the chance to assert her own will in contradistinction to his, as by his work he had asserted his will in contradistinction to hers.

"Yes, I see," she said, in a vibrant voice. "And I see what you think, too — that the house is yours, that you'll do what you like in it, and

I can do the best I can with what you're willing to leave for me." And she went on, in that vibrant, level voice, which she would not raise in anger because it might do it harm: "Why don't you go upstairs and work, as I asked you this morning? Do you think I *like* doing this work? But it's there to be done, if you want to live decently—"

"We can live decently enough with a few grains of dust on that bric-a-brac, I suppose," he said.

She flinched slightly as she saw how his face had hardened, the cold darkness of his anger descending on it. He gathered his things together and went upstairs. And when he had gone, she stood there with a sudden almost terrified sense of what she had done: she had driven him away from her; she had erected a dark ugly barrier of anger and misunderstanding between them. She wanted to go up to him, but she was afraid; he would think she had come only to interrupt him again. The tears rose in her eyes as she stood there. Why had this had to happen, why had anything come to spoil the first perfect happiness of their life together?

She finished her work downstairs, and lingered about aimlessly, hoping that he would come down, as the quarter-hours struck away with their brazen inevitability from the grandfather clock. But the house was silent; he did not appear. At last she went upstairs to change her dress. The door of the spare room, where he was working, was closed, and she could not summon up her courage to knock. She thought that he might hear her moving about and come out to her, but she washed, and brushed her hair, and changed into a dark-blue dress that she knew he liked, and still the door remained closed against her. Rather desperate in the quiet house, with the autumn sun falling mellow and silent toward late afternoon, she went downstairs and put on some coffee, then called to him from the foot of the stairs: "Max, I'm making coffee; would you like some?"

He answered her through the door, his voice impersonal: "No, thanks, not now." And then there was silence once more; that was all that he would say to her. Her anger rose again suddenly; she said to herself that she had been a fool to want to make up with him. She had been ready to go to him, to confess that she had been wrong, anything so that there would not be this division between them; and he had let her stand there, calling him vainly, like a suppliant. She could not endure it, that she had humbled herself to him; she wanted to fling her defiance of him in his face.

But something in her was afraid; she was afraid of him, so much older and surer and stronger than she was herself. She pulled on a sweater and went out to walk in the fields. The tears came up in her eyes; she could scarcely see where she was going. And at last she came back and sat down on the wall at the end of the yard, her shoulders bent together forlornly, in the chill red of the autumn afternoon.

Then she saw him coming down the yard toward her, walking quickly, his light, rapid stride that she had always loved. Her heart moved inside her at the thought that he was coming to her. But she turned her head away obstinately. She would not have him think that she was glad to see him.

He came up and touched her shoulder. "Ella—" he said.

She drew away. "Have you come because you want your dinner?" she asked. And she was pleased because her voice was cold and bitter; she was pleased that she had that much control over herself.

"Ella, you know this is all wrong—" she heard his voice again.

She stood up suddenly, facing him. "Do I?" she said. She looked at him defiantly, her brows heavy. "And why is it wrong, then? Because it doesn't suit your convenience? Is that it?"

"No," he said, "that isn't it. It's wrong because it doesn't suit the way we feel about each other—"

She stared at him through the chill gathering dusk. She had loved him so much, so perfectly, and now she felt herself in equally perfect opposition to him. As if she were in a horrible nightmare, everything about him that she had loved — his hard, clear confidence, his sure comprehension of her, his dark, vital face and ready body — seemed twisted into something that aroused in her pure hatred and repulsion. She would not endure it, that he should come to her so calmly when

[257]

she was suffering so much through him. And her passion blazed out suddenly; she said to him in a shaking, furious voice: "How do you know the way I feel about you? You take it all for granted, and I — it isn't — Oh, go away, go away!" she cried, feeling that she could not possibly frame the words for what she wanted to say, and that if he stayed there looking at her a moment longer she would either strike him or burst into tears.

"No, I won't go away," he said, in a voice that was almost as strange as hers. She stared at him; for the first time she saw that, behind the calm expression that he wore, there was something else — anger, humiliation, suffering — she could not tell what. "You know that this way, there's nothing—" he began, still trying to keep that assumption of calm. "Only to ask me to give up my work — that's unreasonable—"

"Then I'm unreasonable," she cried, catching at the word. "I know you think that — and worse — only I *don't* ask you to give it up; I only want you to know that I'm there—"

She felt the sobs rising in her throat as she saw again that strange expression in his eyes, that look at once of anger and of an agonizing bondage, so like what she was feeling in herself. And she heard his words, almost as if they had been taken from her own mind: "Know you're there! My God, what else do I know? What do you think it's been like today? Only you ought to see—"

"What ought I to see? That you care more about your music than you do about me?" she took it up. But even as she said the words she felt that they were not true. Only she could not stop herself from uttering them; she could not break down the wall of bitterness that the day had built between them.

"You ought to see that I can't be without you, and that still I can have work to do," he said. "You *know* that it's like that — and then you put us through a hell like this anyway—"

She shook her head. *"Has* it been bad for you?" she cried. *"You* seemed perfectly happy—" The sobs came up in her again. "But I'm glad if it *was* bad," she managed to say, still in a bitter, defiant tone, "because it was for me — you can be satisfied that you've made me miserable—"

He came close to her, and with an odd, divided expression of tenderness and opposition on his face took her into his arms; like two figures under a tormenting compulsion they stood motionless in the chill gray of the coming evening. It was very still; a single crow went slanting across the sky, leaving behind it the faint raucous challenge of its distant call. And gradually she relaxed against him; she felt his warmth folding her about, penetrating and dissolving the cold shield of her bitterness. Only there was a deep grief inside her for the lost day. She felt that something in her had died, some of the intense golden bliss of their first time together.

They went out to dinner, to a place on a country road, where people came to eat and dance and be amused on a Saturday night. She sat like a quiet, disillusioned child in the midst of the lights and the noise and the brazen rhythm of the orchestra, pretending dutifully that she was pleased with where she was. Till gradually the sense of their unity, their complete, separate identity in themselves and against these others, began to beat up in them, and they turned to each other in pride and gladness. They were separate from these others; they did not need them or want them; they had no desire to be a part of their bright, jangling, noisy world. They got up and left the place, and outside, in the darkness as they walked to the car, she stopped suddenly and flung her arms about him.

"We won't quarrel any more — we won't, will we?" she asked him, clinging to him, glad and possessive, in the darkness.

And he stood kissing her till she was breathless, his hard, eager, unsatisfied kisses, that always seemed to her so immediate and alive.

They were completely reconciled; but the situation that had caused their quarrel was still there, unaltered by what had occurred. They were afraid even to discuss it with each other; it had touched them too deeply. Only he did not go off alone to work on the sextet quite so often, and when he did, she held herself calm, knowing that he would come back to her. Still it was a strain on both of them; they had not really adjusted themselves. He had his own piano, which had been stored when they leased the house, moved into the spare room upstairs, and everything else but a table and a chair moved out of it, so that he could work there in comfort, without disturbing her. And she knew that the work was going well; there was a confidence about him, a complete, inevitable security in what he was doing, that made him, when he came to her, even more wonderful to her than before.

In early December, when the sextet was completed, the old group with whom he had played chamber music so often before his marriage — the Herschels, Huisman, and Dessieux, with one of Herschel's protégés at the Institute, John Banton — came out to the house one evening to try the new work over together. As this was to be a rehearsal rather than a social evening, Huisman and Dessieux had not brought their wives, and Ella found herself, when they had all settled themselves at their instruments, an audience of one, curled in her usual place on the green plush sofa. Huisman called over to her, joking about Herschel, who, with his imperturbable, jack-of-all-trades versatility, was going to take the second cello part: "Why don't you come over and help him out, Ella? — you can play the high notes and he can play the low ones; maybe that way we'll get them all."

Herschel, crouched over his large instrument, peering at his music, glanced up briefly at Ella.

"You can leave Ella out of it," he said. "Her part in the program is to look decorative and provide us with inspiration." He added abruptly: "From the looks of this sextet, I'd say she'd done all right in that direction already, as far as Max is concerned."

She flushed slightly, feeling that he was pleased with her, and for a moment a sense of pride came up in her, an identification of herself with the music. But it was not enough; she wanted more. She wanted to be a part of the music as the six of them were a part of it. She heard the first dark energetic theme come to life under Dessieux's bow, with the whisper and shimmer of the other strings playing about it; she felt the music pass into her veins, thrilling her blood, and pulsing for release, and there was nothing she could do but sit there quietly, beyond it, while it went running splendidly on to its fulfillment.

The second movement, with its intricate problems of rhythm in the variations, held them for more than an hour as they went over and over the more difficult passages, and when they finally put it aside she went out to the kitchen to make coffee and sandwiches for them. Carla Herschel came back to help her. She smiled rather curiously at Ella, who, with an apron tied round her waist, moved efficiently about the large, old-fashioned kitchen, putting the coffee on and getting out the materials for the sandwiches.

"Don't you look domestic," she said. "What on earth has Max done to you — and, incidentally, what have you done to him? He's always been a rather slow worker, but he seems to have gotten off this sextet in double-quick time. And it's really a marvelous thing, you know. Hobie thinks it's more lyrical than anything he's ever done—"

"He says it came well," Ella said, briefly.

She disliked it when anyone told her something about Max that she did not know herself; it seemed to give them a kind of proprietorship over him, excluding her. Carla looked at her shrewdly.

"Well, and what about you?" she asked her suddenly. "Are you satisfied with this—?" She shrugged around at the kitchen. "I never was; Hobie always says he might as well have stayed a bachelor, for all the comforts of home he gets."

Ella turned round a little fiercely. "What else can I do but be satisfied?" she said. "You know how it is about my voice."

"Yes, but if it comes back—?" Carla began.

"If it comes back, I'm going to sing again," Ella interrupted her. "And it *will* come back; it *has* to—"

"I hope so. But in the meantime — I was wondering if you mightn't want to go back to some of your classes at the Institute. You could begin now with some piano and harmony lessons, at any rate—"

Ella flushed suddenly. "Yes, I never thought of that," she said. "We — Max and I—"

Carla laughed. "You and Max have had better things to think of than piano lessons and theory classes — is that it?" she said. "But

[261]

you can't live in that world forever, you know. I was watching you while we were playing the sextet; you looked like the little girl who wasn't asked to the party."

"Did I? Yes, it's bad when everyone else has the music and you haven't—"

"You'll have it again," Carla said. She put the cheese sandwiches she had been making on the tray and began on another loaf of bread. "You oughtn't to worry. Nine times out of ten, a condition like that will clear up with rest."

Ella shook her head. "I do worry. I can't help it. But it's got to come—"

They finished the sandwiches, piled some cups and saucers on the tray with the coffee, and brought it all out into the living room. When they came in, the others were talking about the symphony that Tallan had written when he was in Europe. Argiris would bring it out the following month in New York, and Herschel was talking about going on there for the première.

"What do you think, Carla?" he said to her. "We don't have to stay — just leave the day before the concert and come back the day after it—"

"It sounds fine to me," she said. She looked over at Tallan. "What about you, Max? You and Ella are going, of course?"

"Yes," Tallan said. "We'll have to stay a little longer than that, though; I want to be there at least for the final rehearsal."

"If you were the right kind of husband, Max, you wouldn't let anyone do it at all till Ella had her voice back and could sing the mezzo part herself," Huisman said. "After all, you wrote it for her, didn't you?" He nodded over at Ella. "You ought to hold him to that, Ella," he said. "It sounds to me like breach of contract."

"No," Ella said. "Argiris probably wouldn't let me do it anyway."

"He'd let you do it all right if Max got after him. Haven't you ever heard about composers' wives?"

Ella smiled, not looking up from pouring coffee. "No," she said. "What about composers' wives?"

[262   ]

"They're the best-hated performers in the business. Except for conductors' wives, that is. Because they have all the parts handed to them that other singers have to work like hell for—"

"It sounds wonderful," Ella said.

"Doesn't it?" Carla said. She was handing around the sandwiches. "Unfortunately, Max has principles—"

"With a wife in the picture? Don't you believe it," Huisman said. "A composer — any composer — will transpose the Queen of the Night's aria for low contralto if he can't get his wife in the act any other way."

They all laughed.

"How about that, Max?" Herschel asked.

Tallan smiled. "Ella's a mezzo," he said. "I wouldn't have to take it down quite as far as that."

Ella did not mind their joking about her. She liked the feeling it gave her of not being out of it entirely. They talked about her singing as if it could not happen that she would not have her voice again soon. She wanted to talk to Max about what Carla Herschel had suggested to her in the kitchen, about taking up some of her work at the Institute again. All at once she began to realize how much there was for her to learn in music, apart from the matter of learning how to use her voice. She wanted to know as much as the others, to be able to understand Max's music as they did.

They finished the sandwiches and coffee, and went back to the sextet again. The room was very quiet except for the music, and she felt as if it were something alive there; there was the living thread of it running through the still, waiting air, quickening it with its own splendor. And it seemed so inevitable, so complete in itself; she could not believe that it was really the result of Max's labor and knowledge, that it had come into being as a result of those hours he had spent shut away from her, alone with it. It made her reconciled to those hours. She would never be able to create this kind of splendor herself, but he had said that she was a part of it, and she could be proud of that. And soon there would be her voice again, and she could sing his music, and then she would be more a

[263]

part of it than ever. She had never felt so certain that her voice would come back as she felt now, listening to the music sound through the quiet room.

The others went away, and they closed the front door behind them and then looked at each other, pleased with the sudden quiet after many voices, and at the sense of being alone together again. She moved through the living room aimlessly and happily, straightening chairs, gathering the music together as they had left it. Tallan stood for a moment watching her.

"Leave that for tomorrow," he said. "I'll see to it then."

"Yes," she said. She came over and reached her arms about him, her eyes shining. "I love your music," she said. "Wasn't it wonderful tonight? Only I wanted to have it just for the two of us, without any of the others—"

He looked down at her intent, eager face. "Yes," he said. "Because that's what it is — only for the two of us. You know that now."

"I always knew it. Only you don't know what it's like — I want to be part of it *really*, I want to have it *really*, the way I have you. And tonight I'm sure I will have it—"

"To sing it?"

"Yes." She looked up at him. "I can't help being that way, Max. It's *me*."

"Why should you want to be any different?" he asked. "I don't want you to change; I never have. All I want is for us to keep our life together; I don't want that to be crowded out."

"No," she said. "It won't be." She was silent for a moment. "Carla asked me tonight if I wouldn't go back to the Institute now, to go on with my piano and theory," she said. "I think I'd like to."

He nodded. "Yes," he said. "That's an idea. I've been thinking, you're out here too much alone—"

Something in her stiffened slightly; she resented the way he spoke, as if she were looking only for something with which to amuse herself. But it was only for a moment. She could not divide herself from him now, when she was full of her joy in his music. And she was afraid of those divisions; she knew how terribly they could destroy her. So she lapsed into peace with him at once, forgetting that there had been the possibility of anything different.

She took up her work at the Institute again the following week. It was very difficult for her at first, to return to that life; it was as if her new world fell from her at the door and she was Ella Gunning again, with all of Ella Gunning's half-forgotten ambitions and desires. Barto Ghedini came and talked to her about the opera that Madame Letroye was doing that spring; it was *Manon*, and he was singing Des Grieux. With his innocent Latin cynicism, he had transferred his allegiance to Tharp, now that Madame Collier-Brown was gone, and had gotten himself into high good favor with the whole Tharp-Letroye-Perren faction.

"Baby, you haven't done badly for yourself either," he said to her, in admiring approval. "They tell me that Tallan's going to be one of the biggest names in his field before long; whether your voice comes back or not, you're going to miss out on a lot of the sweating that the rest of us have to do."

"I don't care about that; I want to sing," Ella said. She looked at Ghedini enviously. "You could have all my chances, if I only had my voice; I could make them myself then—"

It was very bitter to her, when she heard him declaiming *Ah! fuyez, douce image* in full, satisfied voice as he went off down the hall, that she could only go to the piano and struggle patiently with a Czerny exercise. She could not play well enough to take any esthetic or emotional satisfaction from it, and there were times when she felt that she was only aggravating her longing for music by trying to go on with it when she could not sing. But then the whole quick, eager force of her intellect came up to meet the challenge of a new problem. Under Tallan's influence she was beginning for the first time to realize that music was something more than pure sound and directed emotion. The whole architectural field of musical form, the intricate, almost mathematical problems of harmony and counterpoint, which had formerly seemed abstract and remote to her, took on a sudden fascination for her. It was as if she had been given a new land to explore, and she flung herself into it with her characteristic intensity.

She scarcely minded it then that Tallan had begun to spend a good deal of time on the initial sketches of a new orchestral work, to be scored for mezzo-soprano and chorus as well; she had her own occupation now apart from him, and when they were together she often catechized him as a student might a teacher. She wanted to know everything at once, with an impetuousness that was the more determined because she knew that beneath it there was still the desperation of her desire to sing. Sometimes, at the Institute, when she heard others singing, she felt that the constraint she lived under with her voice was almost unbearable. And she went back to the little house in Bekesbourne and looked around at the quiet, commonplace walls as if she wanted to break out of them, as if she could not sit silently within them a moment longer.

Then Tallan would come, and she would be cold and taut with him, withdrawn. At such times she felt she needed him so much that a mere careless inflection in his voice came to her like a betrayal, and she retired savagely into herself, refusing to give him the opportunity to wound her again. And he, who always began by being tolerant of her moods, eventually, as she persisted, grew angry in his turn; they were like two armed antagonists, each with the power of destroying every vestige of peace and happiness in the other.

And each time, when they had worn themselves out in this futile, self-lacerating battle, they came to each other again out of the agonizing darkness and humiliation of the quarrel with a new and frightening realization of their dependence on each other, so that when the next occasion for a disagreement arose, they were a little slower to take it up, a little more forbearing of the other, out of the feeling that nothing could be worse than this division between them. She knew that she was the one who was most often to blame for their having quarreled, and this made her the bitterer at the time of the actual conflict between them, and the more remorseful when it was over. Sometimes, when she was alone after one of these times, when they had made their peace with each other, she almost wished that she had never known him; it seemed to her that nothing, no happiness that they could ever have together, could be worth the misery that she had just been through, and the terrible insecurity of a life in which that same misery could arise again at any moment. And then he would come home, and in an instant everything was changed; she felt that she would have suffered anything only to see him come in the door and stand there looking at her with his slight, expectant, challenging smile.

At the end of January they went to New York for the première of his new symphony. They were to stay with his brother and his family, but at the last minute one of the children came down with the measles, and they went to a hotel instead. She was glad; she was still a little ill at ease with his relatives, not wanting to share him with them, nor to acknowledge their greater intimacy with his past.

The city excited her, but less than she had expected. She felt even a little irritated at the necessity of admitting new surroundings, new people, into her life just now; there seemed to be so little room left in the days she spent there for what was really the vital core of her existence — the exploration of her relationship with Max. Even Madame Collier-Brown, whom she went to see one afternoon at her studio, seemed like a stranger to her here. She could not believe that it had almost happened that she had taken her life here, with her, instead of sharing it with Max. Madame looked her up and down sharply, and summed her up by saying that she looked happy — "revoltingly happy," she said. "I suppose you've given up altogether thinking about your voice."

Ella shook her head, looking around at the familiar photographs on the walls, oddly strange to her in their new surroundings — Calvé, Lucca, the De Reszkes.

"No," she said. "Only there's nothing I can do yet; Dr. Woodburn said six months—"

"And when the six months are up, you'll still think it's more important to be Max's wife than to sing at the Metropolitan," Madame said. "I gave you a piece of advice once, which you didn't take; I told you to fall in love as much as you liked, so long as you didn't let it interfere with your work. A sensible singer marries her manager, her accompanist, her vocal coach, if she has to marry at all —

someone who makes his own bread and butter out of her career, and knows it—"

"Well, I can't help that," Ella said, flushing up. "I married Max because I love him."

"What rot. You could have loved a nice safe person just as well, if you'd set your mind to it; you're a very determined young woman. *I* was a determined young woman, and I saw the advantages of falling in love with dear old Collier; I never regretted it afterwards. He was perfectly happy adding up my receipts, and I was perfectly happy with someone to take out my bad temper on. Now I can imagine how much interest Max will ever take in your receipts, and he has enough bad temper of his own not to care for any more from you—"

Ella smiled. "Do you think so? I was beginning to think I was the bad-tempered one."

"That *is* rot. Of course you've been quarreling already — you two determined people?"

"Not — we don't, really—"

"You needn't admit it. I know Max; he doesn't *give* — and neither do you. You're going to run head-on into each other one of these days, and then you'll be glad enough to bring me that voice of yours again — if you have any voice that's left to bring—"

She made Ella stay, as if out of definite, malicious purpose, to hear a pupil of hers who was coming on the half-hour, a young soprano for whom a Metropolitan audition had recently been arranged. Ella sat listening to the familiar routine of the lesson, the voice progressing surely through the difficult vocalises, then the close, intent work on a pair of Mozart arias. She could scarcely bear it; she wanted to get away. When the girl had gone, Madame turned to her.

"My dear, you have twice the talent and intelligence of that block," she said. "I have to push everything into her — it's like stuffing a goose — and you see where I've put her, in spite of that. Don't be a fool; do exactly as Woodburn tells you with that voice of yours; try a little coaching with Ricardi if you can this spring, and next fall, Max or no Max, come here to me—"

Ella went back to the hotel, feeling miserable. In spite of everything, the fierce grip of her desire to sing *would* close in on her; she felt as if she could not breathe if she could not satisfy it. Tallan was there, in the hotel room, when she returned. He looked quickly at her downcast face.

"What's the matter?" he asked.

She sat down, unresponsive, on the edge of the bed.

"It isn't anything."

"No, there's something — Did you see Maude? She's been talking to you, I suppose."

She glanced up at him almost hostilely. "Why shouldn't she talk to me?" she asked. She was silent for a moment. "She says I'm a fool if I don't come here, to study, next fall," she added suddenly.

He stood watching her. "Do you want to come?" he asked.

"Oh, I don't know!" She got up again from the bed, restlessly. "I don't even know if I'll have a voice then."

"But if you have—?"

She could not endure it, the calm, rather dangerous pressure on her for a decision. She turned around to him quickly.

"How do I know? You said once, you'd come to New York too — And you have what *you* want," she accused him with sudden bitterness, quite without warning, "so you needn't think of me; you have Schroeder to sing in your symphony tonight—"

The instant she had said it, she was ashamed. She did not want to spoil it for him tonight; it was too mean, too petty, for her to resent his success because she could not share it. She stood looking at him, stricken by what she had done.

"No, I didn't mean that," she cried. "I don't know why I said it—"

She ran to him, to make up. But afterwards, when she was dressing for the concert, he brought the matter up again.

"Do you really mind it, that I let Argiris do the symphony without you?" he asked her. "You know I don't care anything about tonight, if it hurts you—"

"It doesn't, it doesn't!" she said. She loved him for worrying about it; she was always ashamed because she wanted to be reassured that he put his feeling for her above everything else, but it was an intense pleasure for her all the same when he showed her that this was so. "I only said that because Madame upset me; she doesn't understand about *us*," she said. And, seeing from his face that he believed her, she went back to brushing her hair before the mirror. "Did you know her husband — Mr. Collier?" she asked after a moment.

"No; he died years before I ever saw her. I met the second one a couple of times, before he left her; he was fifteen or twenty years younger than she was—"

"Oh! I didn't know," she said.

She looked at her own face in the mirror, seeing behind it Tallan's figure as he stood knotting his tie in careful concentration. And a feeling of triumphant happiness suddenly swept up in her; she was so sure of herself now, as if she had been vindicated. How should Madame be the one to tell her what she was to do with her life — a raddled, sharp, deserted old woman, living bitterly in the past? She would find her own way; she would do as she pleased, regardless of everyone but herself and Tallan. She turned round to him with her victorious, radiant face.

"I don't know why I was upset," she said. "You won't let it worry you, will you? I want everything to be perfect tonight."

Afterwards, as she sat beside him at the concert, listening to the music that always came to her with such a strange, unreal remembrance of the night at the Herschels' cottage when she had first heard it, the night when she had flung his ring into the river, she was proud with a humbling, self-abnegating pride before his achievement. It was very wonderful to her that he should have created this world of sound, so perfect and complete now that it was being brought to its full life by the hundred instruments on the stage before her. Only when Schroeder took up her part in the final movement, a pang went through her. That was for her, her part in this magnificent whole, and she resented the assurance with which the older woman appropriated it to herself. She saw Max glance over at her.

[270]

"No, it's all right, it's all right," she whispered quickly.

She did not want him to know; she was ashamed that she could think of herself now, when the music was rising to its splendid climax.

But afterwards, in the excitement and confusion backstage, she could not help being unhappy again that she was merely an outsider; it was the old wearying battle inside her, the necessity of being herself more than a passive part of it all. She resented it that Argiris, who was a short, abrupt man with a shock of dark hair brushed back from a high, square forehead, spoke to her without interest, as if she were only another empty-headed young woman, and that she was appropriated by a group of gossiping wives instead of being allowed a place in the circle of musicians around Tallan. The symphony had not been an entire success; it was too deeply serious, too lacking in the sharp and often superficial brilliance that audience and critics alike had come to expect in new music, to have won immediate appreciation. She heard fragments of the argument going on around Tallan, and then Argiris's voice, sharp with scorn: "Neoclassic — neoromantic — make up your mind, Hoffner; you can't pin a tail on both ends of your critical donkey. I know this much: it's music you'll be hearing when most of the stuff that's being written today is as dead as yesterday's newspaper—"

She was interested, at once attracted and repelled by his manner of speaking, so jarring and certain of itself, and by his whole appearance, which was completely insignificant, almost ridiculous, except for the head, with its stern, dictatorial expression and uneasy eyes. Afterwards she and Tallan and the Herschels went back with him to his hotel apartment, where they sat talking till it was nearly dawn. She saw in him the excitement, the inability to come down from the heights of emotional tension, that she had always felt herself after a successful performance. He wanted to talk, and walked up and down the living room of his suite, his face, with the marvelous plasticity of a trained pantomimist, completely expressive of his changing emotions.

Once he turned and looked directly at Ella, half-closing his eyes, as if he were examining something in which he had a sudden passing interest.

"So," he said almost insultingly, over his shoulder to Tallan, "I see you've picked yourself up a pretty wife since I saw you last."

Tallan looked at him, half-smiling. "Take it easy, Mitya," he said. "You may do the same thing yourself one of these days."

Argiris shrugged. "Young, too," he said. "You had to do it up well, while you were doing it. No, I'm not so stupid—" He began walking up and down the room again. "I suppose she likes your *lovely* music."

"You needn't be so patronizing about it," Carla Herschel said. "Ella has a voice; she's having a bad time with it just now, or she'd give you something to listen to that would put Schroeder in the shade."

"Yes, I know all about the voices of composers' wives," Argiris said. "I'm even learning — you wouldn't believe it, but it's true — to be polite to them: 'A little more training, my dear — only develop your talent—' "

"Well, you needn't be polite to me," Ella interrupted him, with defiant bluntness. "When I sing for you, you can tell me exactly what you think."

He shrugged again, without looking at her. "Let us say — we will hope the circumstances never arise."

She was furious with him for dismissing her so, and equally furious that Max stayed apart, as if he were rather amused by the whole occurrence. When they returned to their own hotel, she wanted to charge him with it, but she was too tired; after the excitement of the evening, something had gone down in her like a stone. She felt as if somewhere a door had closed on her, shutting her forever into the world of silence in which she had been living since the previous August. Long after Max had fallen asleep she lay awake, clenched in herself, watching the winter dawn slowly brighten in the room. She felt that she had no place here; she wanted to go back to the little house in Bekesbourne, where she would not have to stand alone, on the outside, watching others take up and use the life that she wanted so much for herself.

When they arrived in Bard City there was snow in the air. A heavy fall began as they were driving home from the station, and by evening, under a pale clear sky from which the clouds had withdrawn, the ground was thick and glittering with its bluish-white covering. In the stillness, the clear bitter cold that had descended after the storm, the house seemed set down remotely in a world of white death. All night she lay close beside Max for warmth and life, and in the morning, when he left to go to the Institute, she felt as if she could not endure the unnatural silence in which the still world outside held the house. She put on a coat and scarf and plunged out into the white even expanse of the back yard, finding a certain sullen sense of victory in the sight of her own footsteps marring the unbroken surface with heavy tracks.

She went down through the gate into the fields beyond. It was early, not yet eight o'clock. There was a pure bright light in the east, where the sun was rising, and a faint rosiness behind the black trees, but the earth was heavy and cold, still in its white dawn-shadow. She dragged on aimlessly through the snow. There was a kind of terror to her in its frozen immobility; it was as if everything in the world had suddenly become fixed in an icy quiet, a white death-quiet that surrounded her wherever she looked. It was only a few weeks now till she would go back to Dr. Woodburn to find if she might try her voice again, and she was afraid. She was afraid that there would never be anything for her but this utter stillness; she would be shut into it forever, without hope of escape. Once she stopped, standing for a few moments, breathing the sharp air deeply after the exertion of walking through the heavy snow. An odd panic came over her. She had to try her voice now, here, at once; she had to be reassured. But she was afraid; she did not dare. She went on down the slope as if she were running from something. But there was nowhere to go; wherever she looked, there was the same flat glittering featureless expanse of snow, the fences obscured by it, the shrubs obliterated, even the trees burdened and still.

She turned and walked back helplessly the way she had come. There was the house, standing empty and silent under its weight of

[273]

snow; but she did not want to go inside. She brushed the snow from the wall at the end of the yard and sat down, facing away from the house, looking down the long empty field. The snow was brighter now, lit with the cold pure morning flush of the sky. As she watched, she saw a few sparrows light delicately on the snow crust a few yards away; their busy cries came to her with a faint impudent remoteness through the cold surrounding silence. She sat so still that they could afford to ignore her; they brought their small separate existences for a minute or two within the circle of hers, then rose suddenly and rushed indifferently away, as disconnected with her as if they had been a flight of birds in a Japanese print.

Then the silence closed again. She got up and went into the house. Max would not be back till late afternoon; she had the whole empty day still stretching before her. She went up to his workroom and looked in at the scattered sheets of manuscript paper lying about. That was the world of his creation, only waiting for his labor to bring it into life. She looked at it, half-wistful, rather desperate. And all at once, like a shock of victory, it came to her that she too had the power to create; if not through music, there was her own flesh; she might have a child, she might bring her own life and Max's again into the world. Her eyes kindled suddenly with amazement and victory; she had never seen motherhood in this light before. She might have her life to live after all, richly, richly; she need not be left empty and waiting, afraid of the future.

She crossed the room and threw up the window. The keen air came in, sharp and full of vigorous life.

"My God, yes," she thought, "yes — and it's all there waiting — How is it I never wanted it before?"

She felt suddenly active, and triumphant with life. What she might not have in one way, she would have in another; there was no force that could shut her away from her fulfillment. All day she moved about, secure and powerful in her own riches; she felt as if she had discovered a new land.

Chapter Fourteen

SHE went to see Dr. Woodburn on a gray February morning, with Carla Herschel; she did not want either Tallan or her mother to be there if it was bad news that she had to hear. If it was to be bad news, nothing that they could say would make it better, and she had a fear of letting them see how bitter her disappointment would be, as if it implied a kind of disloyalty to Tallan. She had said to herself that she would build her life in another way if she was not to have her voice, but now that the moment had come, she wanted to have them both; she could not bear to be denied either one or the other. Carla saw how tense she was as they sat in the waiting room.

"But Woodburn's not infallible, you know," she said; "he's not God. And six months — it's nonsense, really, when you look at it. It might just as well be five months, or seven, or a year, before you'll be ready to sing again."

She knew that, but it did not help her. When she went into the examining room, she felt as if she could not sit there quietly as the doctor asked her questions about her throat, and then went methodically through his examination; she wanted him to tell her at once. And she hated him so, his cold, civil manner that did not take into account in the least what happened to her as a human being. There was something terrible to her in the idea that he should be the one to pronounce a decision on her voice, as if she depended somehow on his mercy.

He asked her at last to try to sing a few notes in her middle regis-

[275]

ter, without forcing or straining. She stood up with a feeling almost of panic.

"But can I? Will it be all right?" she asked.

"There's no reason, as far as I can see, why it shouldn't be. There's no evidence of strain now; your throat is in very good condition."

She stood staring at him, her brows drawn together, trying to control herself. She felt exactly as she had years before, when she had come to have her audition with Tharp — that she could not produce a sound, nor even draw a whole breath into her lungs.

"What is it?" he asked, watching her.

"Nothing — I —"

But at the sound of her own voice, the tension broke inside her. She raised her shoulders, drew in a full breath, and gently, easily, the sound throbbed from her throat, the fragment of a scale, rising, note from note, and clear, round, unbroken as a bell.

She broke off, looking at him, amazed and frightened and triumphant.

"But it's all right — is it?"

"I should think so. You might go home and try this — only a few minutes a day, of course, now at first — and come back to me in a week. I needn't remind you, I suppose, that if you overdo it you may find yourself back where you started from very quickly."

She wanted not to cry, but the relief was so great; she drew two or three long, shuddering breaths, trying to get control of herself.

"I'm very glad," Dr. Woodburn said, correctly. "De Meyer has spoken to me very highly about your voice. It would have been a pity—"

She had to get away from his meticulous, lifeless courtesy. She cut him off, and went out quickly to Carla, in the waiting room. The older woman looked at her keenly.

"I don't have to ask," she said. "It's good news, isn't it?"

She was very much pleased; she let Ella telephone Tallan and Anne Gunning, and then took her home with her for lunch.

"You'll have to have someone to talk to, or you'll sail clear off the planet with excitement," she said. "Then we'll go over and see Ricardi; he'll keep you in line, see that you don't overdo—"

Ella went with her, but she felt that it was not what she wanted. She would rather have been alone; she did not need even Max at that moment. What she wanted was to stand in a silent room and feel again the slow, perfect throb of her voice in her throat, to hear the sound part from her lips and fall pure and lovely into the waiting stillness. That was her newly rediscovered paradise, and she wanted to be alone in it so that she might find out again all the marvelous, half-forgotten bliss that it contained.

She went with Carla to see Ricardi, who had a studio now at the Institute. It was irksome to her that he would let her sing only a few sustained tones in half-voice, beginning in the middle range and going upward by semitones, then, starting again with the same tone, progressing downward in the same manner, as if she had been a beginner just learning how to use her voice. But she submitted, in spite of her own certainty that her voice was there, strong and perfect as ever, for her use. She could wait, now that she knew that; she could take the way back step by step into the full bliss of her satisfaction.

In the meantime, she flung herself with redoubled energy into her theoretical studies. The new term at the Institute had begun, and she had a full schedule, so that she had scarcely the time any more to look after the house. The responsibility of it began to intrude on her other occupations; she suggested suddenly to Tallan one evening that they sublet it, and take an apartment in town.

"But why?" he asked. "I thought you liked it here."

"I *do* like it," she said. "But there's so much to do — and just the time we spend, going back and forth—"

She was half-impatient that she should have to explain it to him. They were sitting together on the sofa in the living room, late in the evening; she was tired, resting herself against him, but full of the superb new radiance that had come to her now. He looked down at her.

"Well, we might have Mrs. Garth come in every day; that ought to help," he said. "How about that? Would it do?"

"I don't know." She rather wanted to leave the house; she felt as if it were an encumbrance, in some obscure way, holding her to a kind of life that she had already left behind. "Why should we stay here at all?" she went on. "It isn't as if we had anything here to leave."

"Let's get sentimental for a minute," he said, a little oddly. "I thought we had a damned lot of things—"

"Oh, I didn't mean *that*," she said. Again a faint wave of impatience ran through her nerves. Why must he put it on that basis, as if there were something integral to the first perfect weeks of their marriage in the walls of a house that was not even their own? "We could have what we have here anywhere at all," she said. "What difference does it make where we live, as long as we're together?"

"If it doesn't make any difference, why should we leave?"

"I mean, it doesn't make any difference about the way we'll be with each other." She sat up suddenly, drawing away from him so that she could look at him, her face flushing slightly with the warmth of her insistence. "But there are other reasons—"

"More important reasons — is that what you want to say?"

"I didn't say they were more important." She felt a little anger rising in her; it seemed to her that he was deliberately choosing to misunderstand her. And it irked her that he seemed always so sure of himself, doing as he liked, deciding as he liked, while she had to come to him explaining and defending, waiting on his consent to do as she wanted to do. "But they *are* important, to me," she went on. "Only you don't care about that; you want things your own way, and that's the end of it, as far as you're concerned—"

"That's a fine simple statement," he said. She saw the dangerous look that she always dreaded coming into his face, as if he were holding something in leash against her, the whole force of his will that was rousing against her. "But it's a little too simple to be true. Or maybe it is true for you, after all. I thought we both wanted the same thing; it's beginning to look as if that was where I made my mistake."

She roused herself also, refusing to yield. "I've told you, it has nothing to do with *us*," she said. "I only want us to have more time — and you're deliberately trying to twist it to mean something altogether different—"

"I don't have to twist very hard," he said dryly. "I'd like to know one thing, anyway — just how much does what we've had together mean to you, now that you've got your voice back?"

" 'Now that I've got my voice back' — yes, I thought we'd come to that, sooner or later," she seized on it quickly. She felt the tears coming into her eyes. How could he say that, how could he imagine even for a moment that she had not been sincere in everything that had passed between them since their marriage? "And it would have been better if you'd come out and said it in the first place," she went on, holding herself in, speaking in a calm, bitter voice, "instead of pretending it was the house you were thinking about—"

"You still haven't answered me," he said. "How much *did* it mean?"

There was something so level and intent in his voice, as if he were fastening his will on her with it, forcing her to admit to him that there was nothing, really, of any significance to her beside her feeling for him. She stiffened herself in challenge. She had her own will, that could go its own way, separate from his; she would fight him with it, as he fought her with his.

"And would you believe me, if I told you?" she asked. "You've made up your mind about it, and that's all that matters—"

"I haven't made up my mind about anything; I want you to tell me," he said. "But, my God, don't lie about it—"

Her eyes lightened furiously. "Yes, that's all it needs, for you to tell me what you really think of me," she cried, "that I've lied to you, and tricked you—" She got up quickly from the sofa. "And I'm glad I know now, I'm glad! And you can make up your own mind whether it's true or not; you've shown me how good you can be at that—"

She turned and ran out of the room and up the stairs. He did not come after her, and she sat crouched in a chair beside the bed for a time, the tears coming freely now that she was away from him, and a feeling of absolute despair rising in her heart. She could not have believed that he could have doubted her so; and at the thought that even in the moments when they had been closest to each other there might have been a suspicion in his mind of her sincerity, she felt a wave of unbearable shame and fury flooding over her.

But then, in the dark and quiet of the empty room, the storm went down in her; something still and hard descended on her spirit. She arose, switched on the light, and got ready for bed, moving automatically, as if everything had gone out of her, leaving a mere physical shell that performed the routine actions of her existence. When she was in bed, and had turned out the lights again, she heard his footsteps coming up the stairs, but still she remained in that same clear, empty world, in which nothing mattered to her any more. She heard him come into the room and cross over to her.

"Ella—" he said.

She did not answer; she lay cold and quiet. Only when he touched her she drew away slightly, as if she had come into contact with something that stung her.

"Ella, for God's sake—" she heard him again.

But she kept herself aloof. And, after a little, she felt his anger coming up again; he turned away abruptly, and she knew what he was feeling, the despair and humiliation that he had come to her and she had rejected him. Something like triumph arose in her, that she could make him feel the same humiliation and despair that she felt herself. But chiefly it was a weariness to her, a terrible cold weariness. What was the use of it all — what was the use of either the suffering or the triumph? She felt that she was lying in an empty darkness, as passive and solitary as if she had died.

For several days she went about in that inner state of terrible, careless stillness; she could not get back to her normal world again. She saw how he suffered, in a blackness of rage and humiliation, but it did not touch her; she saw it as if it were something that was happening on another planet. Till one evening he came to her to say that he had spent the afternoon looking at apartments in town; there were two that he wanted her to see, and they might take either of them, if she liked. She stared at him; all at once, as if a barrier had been withdrawn, she saw his face that she loved so, with the mouth set and humbled against his submission, and the eyes black, almost cruel-looking in his misery. Something struck against her, a great wave of emotion, full of shame and love.

"No," she stammered, "no, I don't want to go. No, I'm sorry—"

It seemed suddenly incomprehensible to her that she should have allowed anything so unimportant as the question of where they should live to jeopardize their feeling for each other. And she saw, with a strange, joyful, frightened sense of responsibility, that she had become not only an important, but an essential part of his life; she understood suddenly that it was not that he did not want her to have her full satisfaction from her music, that he was not as glad as she that her voice had come back, but that he was afraid of losing her to it, as he had almost lost her before their marriage. Always before this she had felt that it was she who depended on him, that he had a life apart from her and almost independent of her; and the realization that this was not so was one of the most wonderful and at the same time one of the most painful experiences of her life with him. She felt as if she wanted to give him the heart out of her breast; there was such compassion for him in all her veins, and such infinite love. And she could only repeat helplessly, "I don't want to go — oh, I don't want to go, Max—"

The division between them was healed, and they were full of a passionate gratitude to each other, as if each, after being completely to blame, had been divinely forgiven by the other. And it was better even than it had been before. She felt that she could never quarrel with him again, that she could never forget this moment when he had come to her in his need. Again she was full of splendid, active life; the whole world seemed to spread itself marvelously only for the two of them to exist.

She was with child, and that too pleased her very much. She knew that he wanted children, and she wanted to give them to him, out of a queer, exulting, oddly impersonal creativeness, as he was giving her the magnificent music on which he was at work now. About the actual consequences of motherhood, the love and responsibility that she must have toward the child she was to bear, she scarcely thought; she was too much absorbed now in the bliss of the present.

And it surprised her a little that everyone should take her news so seriously. She did not want her mother to lecture her on what she must do to take care of herself, or the Herschels to concern themselves, or Madame Collier-Brown to write to her tragically from New York, as if she had ruined herself finally by her imprudence. She showed Tallan the letter, in amusement.

"She couldn't be more upset if we weren't married; sometimes I think she wouldn't be so much," she said.

He looked up at her. "She thinks children and careers don't mix," he said.

But she shook her head victoriously. "Oh, that's stupid! What did people do in the old days? Clara Schumann had seven, and she didn't give up *her* career."

She was perfectly happy. Her voice was growing stronger every day, and she discovered to her delight that she had a new comprehension of the music that she sang: her months of study, and Tallan's influence, were having their effect. And she was gradually learning to understand his music. She loved it when he played for her parts of his new work, which took its vocal text from Isaiah, and which seemed as magnificent to her as the new world of fulfillment in which she lived. In particular there was a solo that she sang till she felt its radiance about her like a shower of bliss: "For ye shall go out with joy, and be led forth with peace: the mountains and the hills shall break forth before you into singing, and all the trees of the field shall clap their hands." She took it to herself; this was *her* music, as much from her own life as from his.

In May, when he had nearly completed it, except for the orchestration, Argiris came to town to conduct one of the final concerts of the Bard City symphony orchestra's season. He wanted to hear the new score that Tallan was working on, and they met at the Herschels' one evening for dinner. Afterwards Tallan went to the piano.

"Ella, you'll sing the mezzo part — will you?" he said to her.

She glanced at Argiris. She had not forgotten what he had said about her singing when they had been in New York.

"No," she said, a little obstinately. "It'll be better if I don't."

[282   ]

Argiris, in a good mood, looked at her benevolently.

"My dear, I'm going to listen to the music and use my imagination," he said. "You can't possibly sound less like my idea of a fine mezzo than Max at that piano is going to sound like a full orchestra and chorus — so please consider yourself forgiven in advance."

"You can keep that forgiveness, Mitya; you're the one who's going to need it," Tallan said. "At least, as far as Ella is concerned—"

He began to play the opening phrases of the rhapsody, and she sat listening tensely. It was the first time since she had lost her voice that she had sung for anyone outside the circle of her friends. But then, as the music progressed, she lost her feeling of constraint and fear. She was not afraid of Argiris; what had he to do with this splendid world that Max had created? It was his world, and hers; and she went to the piano and looked down at him, waiting for the moment of her entrance, smiling at him in confidence and pride.

She did not look at Argiris as she sang; she was involved in the music, concentrated upon it. But when she came to the end of her first long solo, she glanced over at him. He was an odd, solitary person, given to sarcastic repressions and fixed dislikes, but she saw now that his face was pale with excitement and happiness. As Tallan stopped playing he jumped up and came over to the piano.

"No, no — go on, go on!" he insisted.

He went across the room and stood at the window, with his back to the room, as if he did not want anyone to see his face as the music went on. At the end, when he turned around, he had recovered his usual abrupt, suspicious manner, but it was not quite convincing; there was an almost childlike look of happiness in his eyes behind his glittering spectacles.

"Now that—" he began, "that—" He shook his head; he did not want to put it into words. "When is that going to be ready for me, now?" he asked roughly, coming over and picking up the score from the piano. "You ought to have plenty of time for it this summer; I want to do it in the fall, no later, you understand?"

Tallan smiled slightly. "Is that an order?"

[283]

"All right. It's an order. What do you want to do with yourself — go off on a vacation, like a fat bourgeois?"

"Don't get so excited. You'll have it as fast as I can get it down on paper."

"And this young woman—" Argiris went on, turning suddenly to Ella. "I beg your pardon, Max; I should have given you credit for a little musical judgment, even where women are concerned. I want her to do the solo part, of course."

Ella looked at him; a thrill of triumph and regret went over her.

"Oh, I'd love to!" she said. "But I'm afraid I won't be able to — not in the fall—"

He stared at her, throwing back his head. "You won't be able to? And why not?"

She flushed up, smiling slightly. "I'm going to have a baby," she said; "that's why not."

His stare deepened in astonishment and disapproval.

"A baby — with a voice like that? My God, what kind of business is that? There are plenty of other women with nothing better to do than to have babies—"

"Not Max's baby," she said. "Or, at least, there had better not be—"

Tallan glanced over at her, smiling quickly. "Look," he said to Argiris, "what's the rush about this? You can do it just as well later on in the season."

"No, I can't do it just as well later on in the season. I've got just the place for it — one of the broadcasting companies is throwing everything I want at me next fall for three special concerts, to celebrate their anniversary, or some such foolishness; I don't pay any attention to that. They want something new for the first, to make a big noise, you know. I've been on and off with Morvin about that new suite of his for three months now, but it's turned out to be even lighter-weight than the rest of his trash, and Kalinsky's symphony — my God, it's nothing but a theory set to music; I might as well try to play a textbook of modern harmony. No, I'm going to do *this*, and that's the end of it; and you — you *husband* — you ought to be grateful for the big splash I'll make for you, instead of bellowing to me about your beloved—"

"Oh, shut up, Mitya," Carla Herschel said. "Just because you haven't any human feelings yourself is no reason you should begrudge them to everyone else."

"Human feelings? — babies, fatherhood, dangling about after an attractive female — those are feelings any healthy animal knows all about," Argiris said rudely. "Max has a brain and a genius to make music with; and it's to the extent he makes use of those that he's *human*."

Tallan looked at him with an odd light in his eyes.

"If I didn't feel sorry for you, Mitya, I'd break your neck," he said. "Suppose we forget all about this deal; it's not going to work out for either of us."

"Yes, it is, it is," Ella broke in. She looked angrily at Argiris. "You needn't think I care whether I sing it or not," she said, "or — that's not it — I *do* care, but not if it's better—"

She was too indignant to say clearly what she meant, but they all understood her. Herschel stepped in to try to make peace.

"For the Lord's sake," he said, "let's stop insulting each other and get together on this. Mitya, if you haven't stopped getting upset over the facts of life by this time, you'd better go off and retire to a monastery. People *do* fall in love, they *do* get married, and they *do* have children, and nothing that you can do about it is going to stop them — even if they are musicians. Personally" — he grinned briefly — "I don't even think it's such a bad idea—"

Argiris shrugged. "Max may have as many children as he likes, with my blessing — as long as he doesn't expect me to wait till after they're born to play his music," he said, with sarcastic politeness. "That's all I'm concerned about."

"Well, you needn't be," Ella said. "Because whether I sing it or not doesn't make any difference; it's only the music that counts."

He gave her a grudging glance, as if half-appeased by her directness.

"Well, it's all right, then," he said. And, with a sudden awkwardness, he even excused himself by paying her an abrupt compliment: "You know, if you didn't have that magnificent voice, I wouldn't have been half so angry, so it's your fault in the end—"

He would not stay any longer after that; he went off with Tallan's piano score of the new work, promising to return it in the morning.

"Now he's sorry he made such a fuss," Carla said, "and he knows we know it, so he'll be twice as unpleasant the next time we see him, to erase the good impression." She looked at Tallan. "You've got to let him do the rhapsody, though, really, Max; Ella doesn't mind—"

"Yes, he'll get Schroeder for it," Herschel said. "Ella's got thirty years ahead of her to sing your music."

Ella joined with the others in urging him, but she could not help feeling the disappointment sharply. It was too bad, when she had set her heart on singing it, and when Argiris was willing to use her, to have to step aside for someone else. For the first time she felt the burden of her condition; she fought against it, but still it was there, a curious, hampered, rather ugly feeling, as if she were caught. But she would not let Tallan see it. When he spoke to her afterwards about the new work, she repeated what she had said before, that it was only the music that mattered, and that he must let Argiris do it in the fall.

She was very grateful that she was caught up almost at once in another immediately satisfying musical activity. Ricardi had been coaching her in the role of the Princess of Eboli, in Verdi's *Don Carlos*; he knew that De Meyer wanted to do this comparatively unfamiliar opera at the beginning of the approaching season, and it was not in Jenny Grove's repertoire, so that there would be little difficulty, he thought, in getting the part for Ella if she knew it. He had got in touch with De Meyer about it, and she was full of excitement over it. The role of the handsome, vengeful princess was almost as important as that of the leading soprano, and contained some of the most effective moments in the opera — the *Canzone del velo* in the first act, the second-act scene with Don Carlos and Rodrigo, and the superbly dramatic aria in the third act, *O don fatale*.

Now, with De Meyer's arrival in town, the preparations for the opera season were suddenly in full swing. She went one morning with Ricardi to sing for him, so that he could decide definitely whether to let her do the promised role of Eboli. But here again there were difficulties. When Tallan came out from the Institute to take her home, she was so silent that he thought at first that she was not to have the part.

"You look as if you'd had bad news," he said. "What's the matter with De Meyer — has he gone crazy?"

"No, he hasn't — and it's not bad news. I could do Frédéric too, and Siebel, late in the season; but I won't possibly be able to do boys' parts in late August—"

He was silent for a moment. "Are you sorry?" he asked her suddenly.

"About the baby?"

"Yes."

She shook her head. "No, I'm not sorry. Only I'm sorry about the parts."

"There'll be other parts. You'll be so damned sick of Frédéric ten years from now, you won't care if you never sing it again."

"Ten years from now I won't be singing Frédéric; I'll be singing Mignon."

"All right. You'll be sick of Mignon then."

He smiled at her slightly. She saw that he was all right again because he had believed her when she had said she was not sorry about the baby. She smiled too.

"I don't believe it," she said. And after a moment, thoughtfully, "I'll bet I could do Mignon as well as Jenny right now, if De Meyer'd give me the chance."

"Don't be in such a hurry. You've got Eboli, haven't you?"

"Yes, I've got Eboli. Only De Meyer doesn't much like the idea of taking a chance with me, even in June. Ricardi had to tell him some wonderful stories about singing Rudolfo with a Mimi who had twins on stage on her deathbed just after the final curtain—"

She felt better at once, now that she was with him; what did it matter if she missed singing a dozen parts that summer? But there was something in her that still rebelled, that wanted to be free to go straight forward on the shining path of her own success. There were so many worlds for her to conquer; it was too bad to have to see time slipping by again while she did nothing but wait.

She was very pleased, full of a bright intense life, when she was back in the world of opera again. Even the sense that she was in the midst of jealousies and animosities there was rather stimulating to her than depressing; she had her own weapons, her voice, her youth, her quick intelligence, with which to hold the place that she had won for herself. Barto Ghedini, who was singing in the chorus that summer, and had already managed to get in touch with all the undercurrents of gossip going about in the company, kept her informed on the subject of what went on behind her back. Jenny Grove, as she knew, had accepted her success with her usual good nature, but Leitha, the soprano who sang Elizabeth of Valois to her Eboli, "had her knife out for her," in Barto's frank phrase.

"She's made some lovely statements about 'local amateurs,'" he said. "Baby, it's been a good many years since anybody could call *her* an amateur at anything, and she knows it. It's not only your voice she's worried about; it's what a nice figure she's going to make, trying to convince an audience that Don Carlos isn't either blind or crazy to turn you down for her."

She was having lunch with him and the Ricardis at the Carlsburg Garden. There were a good many people, many of them from the opera company; she felt superb and excited, being in the midst of rehearsals again, and at the center of things now, instead of merely on the outskirts.

"But I've never done anything to her, Barto," she protested. "She oughtn't to dislike me. And she has a fine voice herself—"

"Only a little too piercing when she lets it out," Ricardi said wryly. "My God, have you ever sung a love duet with a woman with a voice like that? When she reaches for that high B flat in the last act at the top of her lungs — 'Va, va, di più non tardar!' — I'd be only too glad to take her at her word and run like a rabbit."

They all laughed.

"But — speak of the devil — " Mrs. Ricardi, who was facing the entrance, said with sudden significance.

They glanced around to see Leitha, accompanied by Heidemann, the baritone who was singing Rodrigo, come into the Garden. She was a tall woman, with the hard, powerful slenderness of the thin German type, and a fair, slightly freckled face, over which her heavy hair, worn high on her head, slipped loosely. She saw the group with Ella, said something to Heidemann, and came over slowly, with him following behind her.

"May we sit with you? No — you have finished, I see," she said, in her precise English. Her speaking voice, like that of many sopranos, was unpleasant, too high-pitched and carrying, and particularly enunciated, so that it seemed insincere. "You ran away in such a hurry after the rehearsal," she went on, to Ella, fixing her with her clear, small, heavy-lidded blue eyes, with an almost insulting lack of expression. "I wanted to tell you how nicely you did in the first-act trio. It didn't go at all at first, did it? — it's a tricky little thing — but you're coming on with it—"

Her tone of patronage irritated Ella, but she only said civilly, "Yes, I think it should go well now." She sat waiting for the other to move away. After a moment, as she did not, she asked her, "Would you like to sit down, after all?"

"No, no, since you've finished — We'll find a smaller table." But she remained standing there, her eyes fixed on Ella with their odd, surveying expressionlessness, as if she were examining something that amused her internally. "And how is your husband?" she asked suddenly, bending her head down a little, as if she wanted to be sure to hear Ella's answer.

Ella flushed slightly; she hardly knew why; only the other's curious attention made her feel as if she were somehow ridiculous.

"Max? He's very well."

"Isn't that splendid? It's been so long since I've seen him." She looked at Ella with the same absent, internal smile. "And isn't it nice for you that they're all such good friends," she went on, in her high-pitched, definite voice, "he and the Herschels and Jake de Meyer?

I do think that's nice," she repeated, as if she relished saying the words.

The heavy baritone behind her sniggered vaguely. "Käthi, Käthi — " he said. He was a little uncomfortable, but enjoying himself. The woman turned on him slowly, as if she were surprised.

"Yes? What?" she asked. "What did I say? It *is* nice; it is — isn't it?"

He did not answer her. Ricardi, whose face had also become completely without expression, except for the eyebrows, which were slightly raised, said politely, in his place: "Yes, it's nice, Käthi — and it's nice too that Ella has got the best damned voice in this company; that's even nicer, if you want to know what I think. No offense to present company, of course," he added, looking around so blandly that Ghedini began to laugh.

"Hell, I'm going to get out of here before somebody notices I'm around and starts on *me*," he said. He got up, glancing at Ella. "Coming?" he asked.

"Yes, I think so."

She stood up, nodded curtly to Heidemann and the woman, and started toward the door, with the Ricardis following.

"Saved by the bell," Ghedini said. "She looked as if she was really getting ready to start swinging this time. What is this between the two of you — about round six?"

Ella frowned passionately. "I don't *want* to quarrel with her, Barto," she said. "It's stupid, and so *small*, somehow — but she won't let me alone, and there's something nasty about the way she looks at me—"

"There's something nasty about her, period," Ghedini said. "But why should you worry? *You're* the one with the voice and the looks. Let her do the worrying; she's got the reason to."

She tried to put it out of her mind, but it was irksome to her, to have her pleasure in her singing marred without cause. All during the rehearsals she was conscious of the net of animosity which the woman flung about her, and of the baritone Heidemann watching beside her, as pleased as a malicious, overgrown boy at her embroilment. Still all the while she knew that she was the victrix; there was nothing that they could do against her voice, her splendid youth. Something hardened in her, triumphant. She took herself under control, and it became almost a kind of pleasure to her to feel herself winning, always winning, against the other.

And then, when she went home, something went down in her again; she was half-ashamed. She felt how degrading it was, after all, this endless, petty, jealous struggling. She saw Tallan's life, so free of this sort of ugly competition; she saw how, at the expense of reward and recognition, he refused to allow himself to be drawn into it, doing his work simply, satisfied with that, with the inevitable recognition that came to him from people who were willing to look beyond cliques and fashions for absolute merit. But there was something so hard and sure in him, something that she felt she would never have in herself. She had to assert herself directly against her competitors, to feel the satisfaction of acknowledged victory. She wanted very much to be like him, but she did not know how to accomplish it.

So she went back to the Woods and let herself be drawn again into the old internecine battle, holding herself against the stage director, whom she had always disliked, against Leitha, against Heidemann, against everyone and everything that wanted to keep her from her proper place. And on the opening night she had her reward. In spite of all of them, she was the splendid success that she had fought to be, as if, in the midst of the imperfections and shortcomings about her, she stood in a perfect circle of radiant immunity. The audience was excited, as even the most imperceptive and negligent group will be before something which forces itself on it as a rare and wonderful phenomenon. And she stood in her velvet gown and glittering paste diamonds like the princess she portrayed, receiving their homage, full of thrilling excitement, as if her veins were flowing with a golden warmth.

It was a very wonderful time for her. She went home with Max, but she was as clear and abstracted with him as a child who is living in its own splendid world of fantasy; it was impossible for him to reach her. She was very tender with him, but her radiant docility came to him out of the overflowing riches of her own satisfaction, and not out of the impelling force of her feeling for him. She saw that he was not satisfied, and the old wearying sense of division between them began to come up in her again. But she would not have it. She pretended that she did not notice, that everything was as it should be between them.

The week went on. She was happy, and she wanted to be friends with everyone; it almost seemed unreasonable to her that Leitha was not as pleased with her success as she was herself. Still the struggle had to continue, the constant alertness against the other woman, who perpetually took advantage of her superior experience to confuse or extinguish her. By the evening of the final performance she felt that it had settled down to a duel of wills, in which her hard youth and quickness, her splendid vocal resources, were matched against the other's slow, enveloping, destructive maneuvering. During the first act, as she sang the trio with her and Heidemann, she felt that she was being at once eclipsed and ignored; she had to pit her voice against theirs as if in a contest of sound, and they kept to the footlights, securely in league with each other, dominating the scene together while she remained alone against them. And, inevitably, the music suffered. The trio went badly and awkwardly; she could see De Meyer's angry, decisive beat as he tried to pull them together.

At the interval he came around to her dressing room.

"I've talked to Leitha," he said, "and now I'm going to talk to you. This sort of thing I will not have in the company; I don't care who is at the bottom of it. And I don't care either what kind of bitches you and Leitha want to act toward each other off the stage; on the stage you'll keep your head and follow direction."

She looked at him, stunned and furious.

"But what did *I* do?" she cried. "I can't help it if she dislikes me; I've never given her any reason—"

He cut her short. "I'm not interested in reasons; I'm interested in results," he said, in his malevolent, hardly audible voice. He

[292]

turned toward the door. "And I've had enough experience with singers to know that the *perfect innocent* doesn't exist among them," he added cynically, as he went out.

She was not calm enough to realize that he was almost as angry about the incident as she was herself, and was only taking out his displeasure indiscriminately on everyone involved in it. She went into the second act ready to cry with indignation at the injustice of it, but once on the stage she got hold of herself. Only she was glad that the music she had to sing now was full of bitter emotion, so that she need not pretend to be calm. Heidemann, singing with her after her duet with Ricardi, was prudent and correct in his manner, and the scene passed off well enough to her exit.

She had an interval between this exit and her appearance on the stage in the third act, and Tallan, who was in the audience, came around to her dressing room to be with her. She did not want to complain to him about what had happened, but after a time it all came out — her grievance against Leitha and Heidemann, and De Meyer's interference. He stood looking a little angry.

"Yes, everybody could see that something was wrong," he said. "I'll talk to De Meyer if you like, but I don't think there's any real need. He was excited; he knows as well as anybody where the fault is."

"No, I don't want you to talk to him," she said. She was thinking of Leitha's hints that Tallan had used his influence with De Meyer to get her into the company; she would not give color to the accusation by allowing Tallan to interfere. "Only it's so unfair, for him to come to me," she cried. "I didn't do nearly so well just now as I should have, because of it—"

"You shouldn't let it upset you so much; it's not that important," he said.

She turned round to him, rousing slightly. It seemed to her that he stood apart from her, in criticism, as if he were not involved.

"It may not be important to you, but it is to me," she said warmly. "And I should think it *did* matter, for her to make a public fool of me—"

"She made a public fool of herself," he answered. "If she has to drag you into it, can't you ignore her, or keep from worrying your immortal soul about it, at any rate? She can't hurt you half as much as she hurts herself."

It was too much, to have him look at it with such detachment, when she wanted someone to agree with her completely, to feed her grievance with sympathy. She began to answer him rather bitterly, but Ricardi came to the door just then, weary and sweating under his wig and Spanish beard.

"Act Two — *finito!*" he said. "And a good thing, too; this is a fine performance we're giving tonight." He dropped into a chair and glanced over at Tallan. "What does it sound like on the receiving end?" he asked.

"The second act went all right, as far as I heard it. I came around when Ella went off."

Ricardi shrugged. "It was better than the first act, I'll agree. But you wait — we're not through yet. You wait and see what Leitha does to that quartet, and her scene with Ella—"

"Max says it's unimportant," Ella said, frowning quickly. "Well, I don't — and I can't—"

She broke off, not wanting Ricardi to see that she was angry with Tallan. Ricardi glanced at her, and kept somewhat awkwardly silent.

"I didn't say it was unimportant," Tallan made it clear. "I said it wasn't important enough for you to be as upset as this about it." He looked at Ricardi. "You talk to her, Joe," he said; "she'll believe you if you tell her this isn't the end of the world for her."

Ricardi looked embarrassed. "Well, she knows that," he said. "But, see, Max, anything can be the end of the world when you're in the middle of a performance. You hold her hand and don't argue with her; believe me, as a man who's been married to a singer for seventeen years, that's the best way to handle the situation."

He got up and said, with his usual blunt tact, that he would be getting along to his own dressing room. When he had gone, Tallan looked at Ella.

"Is that what you want, then — somebody to agree with you, no matter what it is, and keep you in a good humor?" he asked, in a rather flat tone. "Maybe I'm not up on my responsibilities as a prima donna's husband—"

She turned to him passionately. "Well, I'm not a prima donna — and I don't ask you to agree with me if it's not what you want to do; only I should think you would, now — But I ought to have known; you don't *care* what happens to me as a singer—"

"I care enough to tell you honestly that you're only harming yourself if you let Leitha get to you with this," he said. "That's what she wants—"

"And what you want is that I shouldn't sing at all, so that I won't mix you up in nasty situations like this," she cried. "But you needn't worry; I don't need your help; I can take care of myself."

She felt as if the whole world were against her. But then a hard self-confidence came up in her, protecting her. She needed nobody; she could win over all of them, alone. There was another tap on the half-opened door. Forrest Marchpane came in with some people whom she had never met, and she was very cordial to them, as if she were perfectly in control of herself. They gossiped with her about the situation between her and Leitha.

"Darling, what did De Meyer *say* to the woman after that first act?" Marchpane asked. "There's a rumor that he threatened her with worse than the Inquisition if she doesn't behave — Certainly Heidemann looks as if somebody had cracked the whip over him; he was meek as a lamb all the while you were on stage with him in the second act."

She shook her head. "I don't know what De Meyer said to them," she said. It fed her sense of self-justification that they were all so much interested in the matter, as if that raised it in importance. "But he was sharp enough with me," she said, in an expectant, brilliant, accusing voice.

"With you?" one of the women repeated it. "But why on earth with you?" She looked around at the others, as if for confirmation. "Can't he *see* that you're only the innocent victim?"

"Innocent, but not quite a victim," Marchpane said. "Not with a voice like that. You can actually see Leitha turning green under her rouge when she listens to it — like a sick sunset—"

"And how she's gotten herself up — isn't it marvelous?" the woman took it up enthusiastically. "She's so afraid nobody will notice her that she's positively done herself up like a Christmas tree — one of those big, bare, straggling ones with its branches all at awkward angles—"

"Do you think so?" one of her companions, a young man whom they all called Stukie, asked. "*We* were going on the scarecrow theory — a very superior scarecrow, of course, dressed in only the best hand-me-downs—"

Marchpane giggled. "Oh, *have* you heard what John Bondurant said to her?" he asked. "Oh, it's too wonderful — you *must* hear it. She condescended to admit to him that Ella 'might do very well some day in secondary parts,' and he said to her, in that lovely dry way of his, 'My dear, it's all very well to have high standards, but until we discover a method of inducing seraphim to join our opera companies, hadn't we better be satisfied to let Mrs. Tallan sing the *leading* roles, and simply admit that she's the best we have?' I *don't* know what color Leitha turned at that; she has such an enormous range — dear me, of color, of course, I mean to say!"

He and the others stayed till it was time for Ella to get ready for her third-act entrance. She sat listening to their flattery and gossip, pretending to herself and to them that she was enjoying it, and glancing occasionally, with a pleased, brilliant smile, at Tallan, who was taking no part in the conversation. When they left, he got up to go too, and wished her luck in a noncommittal tone. She suddenly flushed all over, looking at him.

"Don't pretend that it makes any difference to you whether it goes well or not," she said, in a cold, shaking voice. "You've done all you could to see that it doesn't; you can't have thought you were helping anything just now by being rude to my friends—"

She despised Marchpane, really, and the crowd he ran with, but because they had been sympathizing with her she would maintain them obstinately against Tallan. She sat waiting, her eyes expanded, expecting him to retaliate, but he only said, in the same reserved tone, "I'm sorry; you know I don't like those people," and went out of the room at once.

And, as usual when there had been a disagreement between them, her heart went down as soon as he had gone. She had not wanted to quarrel with him; Marchpane and his whole crew were not worth his little finger to her. She was ashamed suddenly, the shame ran like fire through all her veins, that she had sat there looking so pleased with their flattery and malice, joining herself with them against him. But she had no time now for her own feelings. The third act had already begun, and in a short time she would have to go on stage.

She dreaded singing with Leitha again; she was intensely nervous, not knowing what to expect, when she made her entrance. But then she took hold of herself. There was an atmosphere of tension on the stage, but the quartet in which she sang with Leitha, Heidemann, and the basso who was doing Philip II progressed smoothly, with an outward semblance of co-operation. Only she was conscious of Leitha's eyes on her in a single relationship of pure hatred, her intense blue eyes fastening on her in the final naked admission of enmity and fear.

The quartet ended, and she was left alone on the stage with the other woman. It was the climactic moment of her role, when she threw herself on her knees before the Queen, to confess her betrayal of her. And she felt for an instant, with the music, the fictitious remorse of Eboli flooding over her, as if she had actually done the woman before her some deep, unforgivable wrong. She looked up at the tall angular figure drawn stiff with hatred, the long face faded beneath its rouge, the small blue eyes fastened on her in the bitter humiliation of conscious inferiority.

"My God, she knows she's beaten; everyone knows it," flashed through her mind, as she listened to the worn, rather strident voice responding to her own. "And if I were in her place, wouldn't I feel just as she does—?"

She was ashamed of it all, the whole ugly struggle; she at least could have afforded to be more generous. And she had joined so eagerly with Marchpane and the others in ridiculing the woman, as if she herself would gain by the other's humiliation.

The music went on to Leitha's exit. Ella, left alone on the stage to sing the great aria with which the scene would end, felt the attention of the house close upon her, the strange, half-splendid, half-terrifying feeling of being at the fixed center of the concentrated attention of hundreds of people. And she knew that Leitha was watching her also from off stage, drawn to listen in weariness and jealousy, hoping for some accident that would mar the performance and erase something of the humiliation of her defeat. But there was no accident, and in Ella's nerves, as she bowed and bowed again to the ovation that greeted the end of the aria, there ran a kind of sickness, as if she were somehow merged inextricably in the other's hatred, forced to feel, in pity and repulsion, the disease of jealousy that had fastened in the other's veins.

She went back to her dressing room. Tallan came around again. He looked warm with admiration, but rather tentative and withdrawn.

"It goes better every time," he said.

"Does it?" she asked.

She wanted to talk to him about what had happened between them earlier, but she did not know how to begin. It was always so difficult for her to say that she had been in the wrong. She wanted him to realize how she felt without her telling him.

But he answered her as if he did not notice.

"Yes," he said. "I passed De Meyer as I came in; he said he'd never heard that aria sung better anywhere." .

She colored slightly with pleasure. "Then he's not angry with me any more?" she said.

"What do you think?"

She was silent. "I know it went well, but I don't feel good about it," she said abruptly, after a moment.

"What's the matter?"

"I don't know. I was thinking, if I were Leitha—"

"You won't ever be like that," he said.

"Won't I?" She wanted to be reassured; she looked at him half-pleadingly. "I don't mean the voice; I know mine will go some day too, when I'm old enough. But I don't want to be like her—"

He glanced at her attentively. "What makes you think you might be?"

She was a little confused, not knowing how to say it. "She hasn't anything but this, and she won't give it up till they've pushed her out," she said at last.

"No. It's not easy when you begin to slip. She used to have a pretty big name ten years ago, in Europe."

"I don't want to be like her," Ella repeated.

She shivered a little. He came over and put his arm around her shoulders.

"I can't kiss you properly with all that stuff on your face," he said.

She looked up at him. She was very grateful to him, that he came to heal the breach between them.

"We'll be home soon," she said. And then: "You won't ever let me be like that, will you?" she repeated.

"There's not a chance."

She believed in him implicitly, that he could keep her safe from that ugliness and misery. But it was a new feeling for her, that she must have him to stand between her and something in the world that she had wanted so long for herself. It frightened her a little, this new uncertainty, the sense that he had been right all along in maintaining that she would sooner or later reach a blankness and a bitterness in her merely public life. She was content that for her immediate future she would leave all that behind her, that she would go back once more into the warmer, more personal world of her relationship with him.

Chapter Fifteen

THEY had some quiet months, which they spent very much alone at home, or with the Herschels at their cottage on the Little Buckeye. Tallan finished the orchestration of the rhapsody and sent it on to Argiris; after that, not ready to settle down to another major work, he wrote, at intervals, half a dozen songs for Ella. Because he was not teaching, he had more time to spend with her than he had had since the first days of their marriage, and she felt as if they had returned to the close, intense bliss of those early weeks. She was very happy; it seemed to her, as it had then, that she wanted nothing that she could not find in him.

But in September, when he went back to his work at the Institute, the old restlessness came up in her again. She remembered Madame Collier-Brown's plans for her, that she should come to New York this fall: all that had been forgotten almost as soon as it had been brought up, because of the child, but now she thought of it again, just because it was so impossible for her to do anything about it. She fretted a great deal against the quiet routine of her days. And it irritated her so because everyone about her, Max, her mother, Mrs. Garth, treated her with special consideration for her health, as if she were a semi-invalid. She would not admit it, that she was tired, or strained, or feeling badly; she wanted to be as she always was. She heard Mrs. Garth gossiping about it to Anne Gunning one afternoon: "She won't *give in* to it, Mrs. Gunning," she said; "to hear her talk, there isn't any more to having a baby than walking down to the corner grocery and buying yourself a pound of tea. It almost makes you feel like she didn't want the child—"

She was furious; she wanted the woman out of her house at once. When Tallan came home she told him about it, beginning to sob with anger in spite of herself.

"I *do* want the baby — you know I do," she said to him. "What has it got to do with my wanting it or not, whether I go around acting as if I was made of glass? I'm as careful as I need to be."

Afterwards she was ashamed that she had let herself get so upset about it. She knew she had done so only because, in her heart, she felt guilty over her own impatience with her condition, as if it in some way reflected on her feeling for the child. She had her days when she felt so happy, so rich, that she could not conceive of anything that could add to her fulfillment; and then, against her will, the restlessness would begin burning up in her again.

Then she went to her music; she seemed to separate herself from Max and the child as if they were mere physical encumbrances upon her, having nothing to do, essentially, with her. She did not know what she wanted — not to be free of him and the child, but to find some balance, perhaps, in her life between the extremes of living wholly in him and living wholly in herself. The scales were weighted now on one side and now on the other, and the alternation from one fulfillment to the other was so agonizing to her. She wanted to find some perfect equilibrium on which she could rest.

The future was oddly blank to her. She lived in the present; she could not think of what her life would be after the child was born. That was the limit of her imagination now, the birth of the child. She thought sometimes that they might go to New York. Tallan, with his growing reputation, might establish himself there without much difficulty, and she might go on with her own career. But she did not really care about living in New York — not in any real way, inside herself.

Tallan's new work would be performed there that fall at the radio concert, as Argiris had planned. She wanted him to be there, though he and Anne Gunning had persuaded her against going with him; she would have her mother to stay in the house with her while he was gone. But on the Tuesday before the concert, something happened to change all their plans. Early in the evening, when they had just finished dinner, the telephone rang. It was Argiris, calling from New York. Ella, in the living room, heard Tallan's voice, sounding first surprised and upset, and finally rather angry. He hung up at last and came back into the living room.

"What's the matter?" she asked him. "Is it something about the concert?"

"Yes," he said. He did not sit down again, but stood with his hands in his pockets, looking down at the rug. "Schroeder's in the hospital with acute appendicitis; there's no chance of her singing on Saturday night," he said abruptly. "It's a hell of a mess; Mitya thinks he may be able to get Paulsen, if she can do anything with it in four days—"

She stared at him, startled and disturbed. "But she's never even seen the music, has she?" she protested. "And Madame C.-B. says she's so *slow*; you know, she studied with her in New York — Does Argiris really want to use her?"

Tallan shrugged. "What Mitya wants and what he's going to get are two different things," he said, definitely. "I told him to ditch the whole damned thing if he wanted to. Let him play Tschaikowsky instead; everybody'll be a lot happier."

She sat up straighter, surprised by his tone. "But that's — stupid, to say that," she said vigorously. "There must be some way; why couldn't I go to New York and sing it myself, if it's all right with Argiris?"

Tallan looked over at her. "It's all right with him," he said; "as a matter of fact, that's what he really called about, to see if you couldn't manage to do it. But it's not all right with me."

She was growing excited about it; there was a rising flush on her face.

"But why not?" she asked. "It's a month before the baby is due; I can go on to New York for rehearsals tomorrow, and come back just as soon as the concert is over. It'll only be a matter of a few days—"

"It'll be a matter of your taking chances that you oughtn't to have to take," Tallan said. "Mitya's idea of a rehearsal isn't any tea party;

[302]

he doesn't care about a damned thing, once he's started, but getting exactly what he wants to get out of his performers. You'd have to work like hell all the while you were there."

"Oh, I don't care about that," she said impatiently. "I'm perfectly all right; I can take care of myself. And you know what a long, devilish thing you've made that mezzo part; *I* wouldn't want to sing it on a few days' notice, and if it goes wrong, the whole thing's ruined—"

"Then let it be ruined," Tallan said. "The music'll still be there, no matter how bad the performance is, but if anything happened to you—"

"Nothing is going to happen to me," she insisted. "My goodness! the month before I was born, Mama came to Bard City from Indiana, and then spent days walking around town, looking for a place to live; and she had to see to all the moving—"

He shook his head. "She did that because she had to, not because she wanted to," he said. "Look, I couldn't even go with you; with Forster out this week, and his classes to take over, I can't possibly get away before Friday afternoon—"

"I can take Mama; she'll go if I ask her," Ella said victoriously.

She was very pleased and excited about it; it was a change for her, something wonderful and unexpected, coming just when she wanted it most. And she loved the thought that she would sing his music after all. Though he held back still, not wanting to agree that she should go, she would not be deflected from her idea. She called Anne Gunning, got her reluctant consent to go with her to New York, and confronted him with it radiantly.

"You see, *she* thinks it's all right for me to go," she said, disregarding the fact that she had had to persuade her mother against her better judgment.

And he agreed at last to call Argiris in New York, and tell him that she would take over the part.

She was to leave the following day. He drove her to the station with her mother. He was rather silent, unconvinced still of the wisdom of what she was doing. As they stood waiting at the track gates, he said to her suddenly: "You know, you can still change your mind about this—"

But she shook her head. Even in her pain at leaving him there was something else, a thrill of triumph over the fact that she could be separate and independent of him, going her own way, as she pleased. She was very tender with him, not wanting him to see. But there was something disagreeable about their parting, a kind of dead, corrosive flatness, as if the real connection between them had lapsed.

Her mother noticed it, and spoke to her about it when they were settled on the train.

"I'm wondering if I did the right thing, to go off with you this way," she said. "Max doesn't like it—"

"But why?" Ella said. She was a little defensive about it. "Why shouldn't I go? There's no reason not to—"

"No reason, except your responsibility to him, and to the baby," Anne Gunning said dryly.

"My responsibility — no, that isn't sensible, to say that," Ella said, growing warm. "It can't hurt the baby, and it's just *for* Max that I'm doing this, for his music—"

"Well, I wonder," her mother commented, unconvinced.

Ella was a little angry, but she did not want to let her mother see it. She turned the conversation, and they did not come back to the subject again. But later, when she was lying in her berth, trying to sleep, she felt all at once that her mother had been right, and that she should not have come. She remembered those moments in the station when she had said good-by to Max, and the feeling of pleasure she had had at the thought that she could act separately from him, followed at once by the sense that something blighting and disagreeable had fallen over their relationship.

Then, in the morning, it all passed away again. They arrived in New York, and she was caught up at once in the excitement of the city, beautiful to her on a bright autumn day. They went to their hotel, and she telephoned Argiris, who asked her to come on immediately for rehearsal.

[304]

"He might give you time to get your breath," Anne Gunning said disapprovingly, when Ella told her.

She insisted on going with Ella to the rehearsal; she had no intention of letting her go about alone. Ella knew what an ordeal it was for her; she cared very little about music, and went among Ella's musical friends and associates with the air of a sensible woman cast among rather cultivated savages. She would sit in a corner somewhere all afternoon, neat and indomitable in her navy-blue hat and silk dress, her long, practical face with a faint, ironic smile somewhere behind the eyes. She had been to New York years before, on her honeymoon, and she would have preferred now, with half-bitter sentiment, to go about revisiting the remembered places where she had spent the happiest moments of her life. But there was no opportunity for that, if she was to stay with Ella.

So she sat through that day and the following one, a detached, patient observer in the rehearsal room. She had taken an instant dislike to Argiris, who returned the feeling with interest; he complained to Ella that she looked at him as if he were a not completely responsible person, whose whims the performers were hardly justified in humoring.

"It's nothing to her, how badly you sing, as long as you take good care of yourself," he said. "And you—" he accused her — "you that have the privilege of seeing great music created under your eyes, you want to slide through it any way at all; you're satisfied with yourself if you sing all the notes. Well, I tell you, that may do for Max, but *I'm* not in love with you. When you sing for me, you sing the music, not the notes."

She had had enough experience to know that his strenuous rudeness was merely the nervousness of his intense effort to produce a perfect performance, but it upset her all the same. She was being strung tight, to the same pitch of nerves that he had reached himself. When Tallan arrived on Saturday, he found her full of a quick, rather irritable vivacity. She said she felt very well, and plunged at once into a discussion of her disagreement with Argiris over the tempo at which he took her first long solo: "It's much too slow," she said. "We always took it faster, and I try to tell him, but he won't listen—"

She did not want to talk or think about anything but the music. She was so tired, after the concentrated hours of rehearsal, that she knew she could never get back to performance pitch again if she once let herself go. And she was irritated when she saw Max and her mother conferring together about her; she felt that for the moment she had more in common with Argiris than with either of them. The supreme thing to her now was the music. Nothing could be more important than that it should go perfectly that night.

The hour of the broadcast came. She was a little frightened, just before she was to sing, by a sudden faintness that came on her without warning, as if the world were melting and swaying about her, but it passed away at once. Only her mother saw her close her eyes and bend her brows together tightly in the effort at control.

"What is it?" she asked quickly.

"It's nothing — it isn't anything, Mama." Ella opened her eyes and smiled. "I felt a little faint; I'm always queer before I sing."

"I'm not surprised at *that*, the way you go at it," Anne Gunning said, in disapproval. "But I'm taking you back to the hotel the minute this is over, all the same."

It was time for her to take her place with the others. She gave her mother a tense, brilliant smile, hardly listening to what she said, and stood up. And the old superb confidence came up in her as the performance began, the feeling of her own complete and magnificent response to the music, as if she had been created only for it and it only for her. She saw Argiris's face, imploring or frowning, at moments blissfully happy; she heard the great swell of sound as the voices of the chorus burst out triumphantly behind her, and the paean of the brasses, the strings soaring above, or murmuring in accompaniment as her voice poured out its own victorious beauty.

But so soon it was over: the splendid world of sound that she and Max and Argiris and each of the others had contributed to create dissolved, and let her fall back into the ordinary validities of life once more. She had the satisfaction of knowing that they had achieved, among them, a major success; the excitement in the studio was electric, very real. Anne Gunning came up to her. Even for her, there had been something wonderful in the room.

"Do you see now?" Ella asked, looking into her face. "Wasn't it worth it—?"

She wanted to stay and share in Max's triumph; she had come very close to him in the music, and her pride in him came up warm and glad. But Anne Gunning would not hear of her staying.

"You've had enough and too much for one day already," she said. "I'm going to see to it that you get right to bed."

Tallan came up too, and insisted that she go back to the hotel. He wanted to come with her, but she would not take him away from the others.

"But don't be late—will you?" she asked, looking up at him. "We've hardly had a chance to see each other—"

She felt very near to him, with a kind of triumphant happiness, as if the cloud there had been between them when she had left Bard City had completely disappeared. And she got into a cab with her mother with his music running full and magnificent in her head. It was a splendid fall night, fresh and soft, as if before rain; she felt that she could not possibly shut herself up in a hotel room and go to sleep. After a little she turned to her mother suddenly in the cab.

"I want to go back," she said to her, pleading and eager. "I won't sleep — it's no use — I want to go back, only for a little—"

She felt the accumulated fatigue of the past few days lying in wait for her, beneath her excitement; something almost like dread made her urgent to cling to these last moments of her pleasure. But her mother was unyielding.

"No, I never heard of such foolishness," she said plainly. "You're ready to drop now; you're going straight to bed, as I promised Max."

But she would not take her mother's answer; she argued with her a little bitterly as the cab drew up before the hotel.

"What can it matter? — a half-hour more," she protested.

"It matters that you ought never to have begun this in the first place," her mother said. "And you know as well as I do, if you turn up there again, Max will only bring you straight back here himself."

The doorman came up to open the door of the cab for her and help her out. It made her furious, the caution with which she was surrounded, when she had the free, splendid music running still in her veins. She went on quickly into the hotel, leaving Anne Gunning outside to pay for the cab.

"No, I'm all right, thank you," she said almost angrily, to the doorman.

There were four steps leading down from the entryway into the lobby. She stepped past the doorman with an angry, hasty movement — but suddenly, with the movement, she felt that the faintness which had come over her before the concert was returning; the floor was moving under her, and she did not know whether to step up or down on it. And at the same instant she realized that she was falling.

"But what's happening? — It can't be—" the thought flashed through her mind, in terror. She tried to reach the railing beside her, but instead she fell heavily down the steps, throwing her hands out before her as she fell.

For several moments she lay without moving. The pain and shock prevented her from thinking clearly, almost from breathing, and she had a confused animal instinct to keep perfectly still, as if she could hide herself so from whatever danger was attacking her. But it came tearing at her again; she could not rid herself of it so easily. There were people around her now, frightened voices. She recognized her mother's, saying rapidly and sternly: "Somebody call the hotel doctor; let her lie there a moment—"

She did not believe that this was really happening to her, something that she could not control, with all her will. Oddly, it was not at all for herself that she was afraid; she felt herself hard and serviceable for life even now, in the midst of her pain. But there was the child, defenseless, dependent upon her, and she could not help it; she felt that she had given over its fate, herself, to the strangers who came now to care for her.

And how she hated them, that they held her child's life in their hands, and yet were so businesslike and unhurried in all that they did. They brought her to a hospital room and spoke quietly at the foot of her bed while she slipped past them into a black nightmare-world of confusion and pain. She did not know what was happening any more, or why it had to happen; she had lost the thread of the real world outside her, and at last it was blotted out altogether.

She was very ill, but there was never any serious danger to her own life. When she came back to herself, her mother was with her; she had to tell her that she had lost the child. She felt that she had known all along that it would happen so. She lay without moving. Outside her window was gray daylight. It had begun to rain; she could see the fine, mistlike drops falling gently against the pane.

"Was it a boy or a girl?" she asked.

"A girl," Anne Gunning said.

And she turned her head quickly on the pillow when she heard, strangled with pity and shame. It seemed infinitely worse to her, that it should have been a daughter whom she had failed. She wanted to hear how the child had looked, as if somehow in that way she could bring her alive, at least in her own mind. But Anne Gunning would not tell her.

"You're best not knowing," she said. "It's best to forget it. You'll have other children, and you won't feel you've lost this one if there's nothing for you to remember about it."

She did not believe it. She did not believe that she would ever forget the child that she had so wantonly, as it seemed to her, deprived of life. Anne Gunning, seeing her lie there unmoving, her eyes closed, thought at last that she had fallen asleep again, and went out quietly, leaving her alone. But she was not sleeping. She had only closed her eyes because she wanted to shut into darkness everything that existed outside herself; she wanted to shut herself up with her own bitterness. All through the months that she had carried the child, it had never seemed quite a reality to her; but now it was here before her, separate and piteous and accusing, and the love came up hot and agonizing in her. She wanted it; she could not bear to think that she had failed in giving it life. The tears came up under her closed eyelids and flowed down her cheeks, gathering

[309]

slowly and falling without ceasing, till her very blood seemed salt and drowned in their bitterness. So she lay there for a long while, inert as if she herself had died, only the tears moving slowly down her face.

The nurse came, with her matter-of-fact presence, and she hardened herself into control against her. She came back out of the drowned infinite world of her grief into a world as hard and sharp and cold as glass, from which everything had been washed clear but the outlines, that it seemed to her she had never seen before. It was a world in which there were facts, but no emotions or sympathies, a world that ran on as automatically as some perfect machine, grinding out its logical and immutable conclusions.

In this world she saw that one paid for one's happiness or fulfillment as over the counter of a shop — so much pain, so much struggle, and the commodity was received; only it was necessary that the payment be made in full, down to the last penny of the purchase price. She had paid for her voice, and so she had been given its rewards; all the hours of unremitting work, the plans, the suffering, that she had given to perfect it had been weighed in the balance and found sufficient. But for the child the measure had been short; the purchase price in sacrifice had not been paid in full. And as she lay there it seemed to her that there must always be this dilemma, always this necessity of choice, of expending the limited resources of her life on one or the other side. Always there would be one side on which she would fall short of the purchase price. It was like a madness to her, the sense that she was shut up inescapably in this gray, pitiless world of mechanical necessity. And she could not fight against it; she had to submit, to fling one or the other side of her nature to this gray, devouring Moloch.

Tallan came into the room, and when she saw him it seemed to her with a weary, inevitable logic that here too was something for which she must expend herself. She had accepted his love as if it had come to her as a splendid gift, but was there not a price on it as well, a price that she had already begun to pay? She remembered the misery of their quarrels, the feeling that she had always to bear the burden of a responsibility to him that would never leave her perfectly free. And unless she went on paying in this way for his love, it would be withdrawn from her; she had to hold the balance of the scales with her own suffering and sacrifice, or all the riches at the other end would fall and drain away. She lay looking at him silently, thinking of this, with a kind of gray horror of irony in her eyes.

He spoke to her about the child.

"Yes," she said. "It was my fault. I know it."

"Don't say that," he said. "If anybody's to blame, I'm the one. I agreed to your coming, simply because I didn't want my music bungled—"

She saw that he had been tormenting himself with that thought ever since the night of the concert. But the knowledge remained outside her, and apart from her; she only looked at him with the same expression of helpless irony in her eyes, wondering how it was that he, who was so much older and wiser than she, had not yet discovered that simple, terrible law of life which had come to her during the hours just past. If it was really true, that he had been influenced by his desire to have his music performed well to agree to her coming to New York to sing it, then he must have expected that he would pay for that performance in misfortune to the child.

The one thing that upset these logical calculations in her mind was the fact that she could not believe that he really had cared enough about the performance to risk any danger to her or the child on its account. She felt instinctively that he was suffering without cause, suffering simply because he loved her, and so wanted to take on himself the burden that was weighing so heavily upon her. And she felt too that this suffering had nothing to do with the system of bargains made and value received that she saw all about her, but was something outside it and beyond it.

Physically, she grew better quickly. In spite of her depression, the uneasy and excited state of her mind, life flowed back quickly into her young, resilient body. She was permitted to have visitors, and at once Madame Collier-Brown came to see her. She had heard the broadcast of the rhapsody; she was full of enthusiasm over it.

"I suppose you know what an impression you made," she said. "Oh, Max's music, of course — it was splendid; but *you're* the one who created the real effect. I've had dozens of people speak to me about you; and I tell them all you were my particular prize pupil, and will be again soon—"

She paused, looking at Ella with a brusque, inquiring expression, as if challenging her to contradict her. Ella was silent.

"You realize, of course, that all you need is to be *launched*," Madame went on, in a tone as argumentative as her glance, "that, and work, work, and more work, so that you put yourself at the very top of your field, instead of being satisfied to rest where that natural voice of yours will put you. And now that you've had your fling at domestic bliss, maybe you'll be willing to admit that I was right, and that everything you want and need is here in New York. Only get your strength back quickly, and then see what splendid things we can do together—"

She talked on and on, persuasive and domineering by turns, till the nurse came to tell her that she must go. She got up with one of her theatric movements.

"My dear, I've been here for heaven knows how long, and I haven't said a word to you about your misfortune," she said. "You mustn't think I'm a heartless woman; I simply dislike misfortunes. I've had so few of them in my own life, I suppose I've never quite become convinced that other people ought to have them either. But of course I'm sorry about what's happened—"

She went away, and Ella lay thinking of her with the cold, bitter clarity that had characterized her view of everything about her during the past few days.

"That's nothing but selfishness, too — and she wants to work with me because it's to her advantage; she'll be sure of good value there for the price she pays," she thought. "She said she hadn't had many misfortunes; she means there's no need for me to have many, either; there's no need for me to go through all this again to have another child, or to have the misery of trying to make my life and Max's run together. I can simply let all of that go, and have the music instead—"

The odd and terrible thing to her was that this idea, the idea of pursuing her own success through music, which she had been following for so long, did not seem important to her any longer. Now that she had established the fact, to herself and to everyone else, that she could have that success, it had lost its magic attraction for her. She had no interest in piling success on success, year after year, till the time came at last when her voice would leave her. And at the same time there was the feeling inside her, as strong as ever, that she could not live without music, and that to try to make a life in which it was not of daily and hourly importance to her would be like cutting herself off from the air she breathed.

Another night passed; another morning rose. Tallan came into her room to say good-by. Now that she was out of danger, he had no valid reason for staying in New York any longer; he had to get back to the Institute, to his work there.

Since she had lost the child, there had been a barrier between them. When he sat with her, they talked of things that did not matter, and rather avoided meeting each other's eyes. She felt that this was her doing, but she could not help it; she did not even want to help it. In their past relationship, it had always been he who had carried her along with him, and she did not want it to be so now. In all her misery and depression, she felt almost irritably that now she had to stand alone, that she had to come to her own decisions about her life, whether or not they agreed with his. There was a kind of hostility in her attitude toward him, as if she were holding him off, waiting to see what would come of it.

Today, when he came, he brought her some flowers, chrysanthemums, very wonderful and fresh, with their great, thick curled flowers. The pleasure came up in her a little when she saw them. She put her face to them.

"Aren't they nice?" she said. "And as cool as snow—"

He waited, watching her, while the nurse went to fetch a vase for them. And at once she forgot her pleasure; a vague restlessness came up in her instead as she saw him standing there at the window, watching her with an expression on his face that she could not read — patience, or determination. She became a little nervous, and talked quickly to the nurse as she came back and arranged the flowers in the vase.

The nurse went out and left them alone again. They were awkward with each other; they did not know where to begin.

"Madame C.-B. was here yesterday," she said to him suddenly, breaking the silence. "Did you know?"

"Yes," he said.

"She says the rhapsody was a great success."

"I suppose you could say that."

She smoothed the sheet with her hand. "You don't care about it, do you?" she asked him, again suddenly.

He shook his head. "I care about you, I care about the music. That's all I care about."

She felt a sudden intense shock of feeling, as if of happiness, as she heard him say that, but she did not stop to analyze it; she went on obstinately in the old dreary path of reasoning that she had been following for the past few days.

"You can't care about them both," she said to him, in an irritable, positive tone.

"Why can't I?" he asked.

She wanted to explain to him the conclusions she had come to, the logical system of bargaining to which she had reduced all of life. But she could not begin; all at once it seemed clear to her that what she had taken for the whole truth was only a partial agreement of fact and theory. She saw him looking at her with the expression in his eyes that she had not been able to read a few minutes before, and suddenly she knew that, whether she "paid for" it or not, whether she gave him a return or did not give it to him, he was bound to her by his feeling for her, and that all the misery of the past few days had only made that feeling firmer and stronger than before.

"And what about my feeling for him?" the thought passed rapidly through her mind. "Isn't it because I was thinking only of myself — of how much satisfaction both things, my life with him and my life in music, would give me — that it seemed to me that I couldn't have them both? He wants to live *for* the music, and *through* it, and *for* me and *through* me, not the other way around, where the music and I are only necessary to him because we satisfy his need to be important and loved—"

She did not think all this logically, in so many words; only the conviction, like a lightning flash, passed through her mind, and left her possessed of an inescapable knowledge of the reality in the darkness through which she had been groping. She looked at him, wondering how it was that she had never seen this before; and the feeling of doubt and irritation that had never left her during the past few days melted away, just as the doubt and irritation of a child given a problem too difficult for it to solve disappear when the simple and natural solution is pointed out to it.

She did not want him to go away; in the first eagerness of her new perception, she wanted to make him feel that now at last she understood what he had wanted of their lives. And she was angry with herself because she did not know how to put any of this into words. She looked at him, wanting him to understand her. But he only saw that she was looking at him for the first time since she had come here, to the hospital, with the old expression of life and eagerness in her face.

"What is it?" he asked, gazing at her attentively.

"It's nothing — No, it is, but I don't know—"

She wanted him to come over to the bed. He understood, and came and sat beside her.

"Are you going soon?" she asked him, quickly and irrelevantly.

He glanced at his watch. "Yes, in a minute now," he said. "I'll have to."

"I don't want you to go," she said suddenly. "I want you to tell me—"

But she could not say what it was that she wanted him to tell her, and she knew that if she could have, he would not have been able to answer her. It was not so easy as that, to learn how to apply that sudden conviction to her life. She had a moment's prevision of the struggle it would be, the endless need to balance between the demands of her music and the demands that he would make on her, the inevitable assertion of her old habits of thinking when she would be back on the normal level of everyday life again. But she did not want to think of that now; she could not think of it. She only cared that she had withdrawn the barrier between them, and that he was happy, as she was.

He kissed her, and stood up to go.

"It won't be long," he said to her. "You'll come home soon — will you?"

"Yes," she said. "I'm better today, already."

He was at the door, but she called him back. He came over and kissed her again.

"Let the damned train go," he said.

"No, you mustn't. We've got all our lives—"

She watched him go out the door. When he had gone, she lay back, seeing the calm autumn sunlight falling on the flowers that he had brought her. She was at peace, very quiet, feeling him still with her. In the silent room, her body stretched motionless under the covers, she was like a young warrior resting after her first long battle, resting and recovering herself in hope and confidence for the more difficult struggle still before her.